Chapter 1

Anna Cole ran through the copse of trees, ignoring the thorny scratches that raked across her face. A damp earthiness mixed with pine needles filled the night air as she plowed on, running as fast as her feet and lungs would let her. The recent rainfall was making every footstep treacherous, as she made her way down the steep bank of the valley. She was closing in on him; she could feel it. Instinct and sheer determination were pushing her onwards. He was headed towards the row of terrace houses, where the back gardens nestled against the purple bruise of the Wenalt Hill landscape.

The suspect, Bevan, was on the move, desperately trying to outwit, and out-run them, knowing that they had found the girl and that they were moving in on him. Four-year-old Layla, had been discovered in the loft of a house near her home. Snatched from her back garden and plunged into a living nightmare. Her soft, blonde hair was matted and unkempt, so unlike the perfect image in the photograph that had become synonymous with the case. The photograph that had haunted Anna's dreams.

She powered on, gulping in the damp night air as she made her way down the hillside. With every thump of her feet on the uneven, grassy ground, Anna thought not of the girl, but of the parents and the little brother, too shocked and horrified to do anything, but sit mumbling her name over and over. *Layla, Layla, Layla.* As if it was magical mantra he could use to conjure her back from the depths of horror. Now it ran through Anna's head like trance music on loop, helping power her onwards.

A flash of something caught Anna's eye, making her change direction. From her vantage point on the hillside she could see

1

him vault over a hedge, straight into the back gardens of the terrace houses. By the time she would reach the houses he could be anywhere. She prayed Aled and Lewis where positioned in the street ready to release the dogs on him, should he make it that far. The hillside was boggy and slick in places, causing Anna to stumble, fall forwards, and almost career into a tree before righting herself. She was closer to the houses now. Minutes away from the gap in the hedging where she had seen him enter.

She skidded to a halt as she reached the back of the houses and forced her way through copper beech hedging, feeling her jacket snag on the dense brittle branches. She entered the garden and listened – the only sound the yap of dogs in the distance. The house looked shut up for the night, curtains drawn against the dark, rained-washed skies.

She stilled herself, tried to steady her breathing and crept along the perimeter hoping the darkness would allow her the advantage of surprise. The shed door had a single sliding lock, and it had been pulled back, even though the door was held fast. He was on the other side, listening as the bark of the dogs came closer.

She braced herself ready to kick the door in, when suddenly, he was there, almost upon her, the flash of a metal rod in his hand, glinting in the moonlight. Anna noticed his eyes, wide and unblinking in their terror, before she felt the heavy thump of his weight punch into her chest, knocking the wind straight out of her. At the precise moment he stabbed her, she thought of her mother's last days, how the past months had been torturous, how she needed something to change. To find a way to start again. She fell backwards, landing onto the hedging that she had clambered through moments earlier. He moved fast, but the dogs were coming. Their yapping roar telling Anna that he was surrounded.

* * *

Anna checked the wound site and saw the square of white dressing had become stained. It was weeping again. She pulled down her t-shirt quickly, before Jon appeared fussing over her and making valid arguments about why she should consider a career change. He didn't understand that it was just another day at the office. These were the risks she had to take to know that children like Layla, weren't in danger from bastards like Bevan. She had taken a puncture wound from a screwdriver, nothing major, but her right breast would carry a scarred reminder of the Hawthorne case for evermore. The wound didn't require anything beyond stitches and paracetamol, not even an over-night stay in hospital, but that hadn't stopped Jon from using it against her. Reminding her at every wince and dressing change that she didn't need to do this for a living. That there were other ways to live.

She put her head back into the pillow, thinking about how she'd tell him that she had made her decision. She was leaving Cardiff.

* * *

He watched the bridesmaid float along like an apparition, her pale pink chiffon dress skimming the mossy damp ground. She had taken off her shoes and carried them in her right hand, holding them by the long slender heels that made him think of wine glass stems.

The ground underfoot was cool and springy soft, save for the odd twig that cracked beneath their weight. He could sense the river nearby as the earth began to meander downwards. The wildlife unseen, but there all the same.

'God my feet are killing me,' she laughed, leaning in closer to him, making him catch his breath and forcing him to steady himself.

'We're nearly there,' he said sounding assured. She wobbled, her bare feet unsure on the uneven ground, feeling the effects of too much wine. He felt her hair as soft as a rabbit pelt, as it brushed against his arm when he held her close.

'I wish I'd gone for a pee,' she blurted, 'but I'm gasping for some blow. There's only so much the drink can do,' she giggled, as if what she had said was funny and that he would understand.

'Aye, sure we'll skin up when we find the spot. Nearly there.'

They reached the clearing; the river glistening back to the moon as its glow seeped through the foliage overhead.

'I feel like I've walked for miles and I can still hear the music,' she said as she took his jacket from her shoulders and spread it out on the damp ground. 'There, now I can sit without ruining my dress.'

The creaking and rustle of the trees swayed gently in the night as a low thump, thump of the distant music drifted towards them.

'Aw, I hope I don't miss any good songs,' she said leaning back against a tree before jerking forward again, 'I'll go behind that bush over there,' she said, 'while you skin up – and no peeping.' She smiled at him, her body swaying as she clambered up from the ground, seemingly more unsteady as the night air filled her lungs, heightening the alcohol in her blood stream.

Getting her here had been the easy bit. He could hardly believe his luck when he recognised her. He knew the next part would be more difficult, but he was ready, and well prepared. He swallowed hard and felt the stirrings of his erection in anticipation. She was hunkered down with her thong around her ankles. He always thought them a sorry excuse for knickers.

'What the fuck! I told you not to look,' she bawled.

It happened almost as he had thought it would. Swift and sure. She cried out, a sharp animal like cry as she realised what was to come. He knew the blunt blow of the heavy branch would easily take her down. The thump of the impact reverberated through his body like a rhythm. He hadn't counted on her falling forwards on to a fallen bough, that was an added bonus. How simple it all seemed. How perfectly attuned he was to the rise and fall of her chest, her heart racing to keep up with the blood loss.

He felt the life drain out of her, as she gurgled and choked on her own blood, writhing beneath his body in her vain attempt to struggle free. His fingers, reached for that soft place between her collarbones, and he pushed down on her windpipe, her eyelids fluttering in desperation. She shuddered one last gurgle, before relaxing into death, and as the life in her ebbed away, so too did his urge. He could feel his penis shrivel and retreat back within. There was no need to violate her in that way. Her death was enough.

The cleanup was strategic. He knew how to leave no trace. He retrieved his holdall bag which had been hidden in the hallow of an old felled tree. He changed into his trainers, two sizes bigger than his work shoes, to keep them on their toes, should they find a footprint. Carefully he swept away his path with a long piece of fir tree, using it like a broom to erase their trail. The fairy tale of Hansel and Gretel came to his mind. He never liked the simpering kids, dropping their breadcrumbs in the hope of finding their way home.

As he scaled the fence surrounding the hotel, avoiding the car park and the rear surveillance cameras, he allowed himself a moment of satisfaction. Job done, he thought, exactly as he planned it.

Chapter 2

Declan Wells had watched with the analytical eye of the forensic psychologist as all those around him fell into stereotypical roles. His wife, Izzy, was sobbing; huge gut-wrenching sobs that rendered her pretty, previously made up face, ugly and twisted. He knew she would be horrified to see how dreadful she looked, how her carefully applied mascara was a smudge of bruise grey on her bronzed cheekbone. The designer fascinator was set at a jaunty angle to the side of her head making her look comically macabre. She grasped at people as if they could tell her something to make it all right, to annihilate the news she had been given. Her glossy brown hair, so carefully dressed that morning, was coming undone. A loose curl slipped down her face, adding to her disheveled appearance. Yet, he had no desire to comfort her, knowing his attempts would be rebuffed.

Lara, still in her ivory wedding gown, all ruffles of silk and shimmering crystals, was wrapped in her groom Rory's arms like he could protect her from this mess of a wedding. He could barely conceal his dislike of his new son-in-law but he had promised Izzy that once they married he would back off. It wasn't so long ago that Lara would have ran to him and expected his arms to hold her tight while he whispered *it's okay, daddy will make it okay.*

A few of the younger guests were crying, cousins on his wife's side, one or two of them sobbing in that teenage way of having no regard for anyone else. The men were standing around looking perplexed awaiting instructions on how to react. They had sobered up by the rush of news. The hotel staff had been instructed to keep everyone in the ballroom, making everyone feel under threat or suspicion. Those with victim type personalities, thought

Declan, would feel they were being unfairly judged, and those with a sense of flight, would feel trapped and at risk. Twenty-four years of experience working in the police service, first the Royal Ulster Constabulary and then later the Police Service of Northern Ireland, before a dissident republican car bomb interrupted his service, taught Declan that people nearly always reverted to types when faced with tragedy.

* * *

There would be the wailers who cried out asking, why, and demanding an unseeing God to intervene. Others would run, like headless chickens, with no purpose beyond movement, unable to stay still for fear that the catastrophe would touch them, like some floating black cloud of evil which could be avoided by perpetual motion.

Then there was the catatonic; the person who would appear to be incapable of movement, who would stay absolutely frozen still. Struck dumb by shock and unable to process what had occurred. Declan wondered where the disassociated catatonic was in this calamity, before realising, the catatonic was himself.

Being wheelchair bound had given Declan a precise, static view of the aftermath. He had learnt early on that disability renders one incapable of quick, purposeless movement. If he decided to move, it required a little forethought, a moments' preparation of unleashing the brake of his chair, angling his upper body to make the necessary movements to put the chair in motion. Therefore, he rarely moved without intent, whereas all around him, people were in motion, seemingly agitated but going nowhere and achieving nothing beyond making their anxiety heard and seen.

From his chair, he had a front row seat to the drama of life. People talked down to him, literally and figuratively, or even worse over his head. But while they reacted to him differently, he too found that his view of others was altered. The chair itself created a sort of barrier and he found himself considering aspects of them and himself that before the bomb he would not have given two thoughts to. He looked around the ballroom, festooned with flowers and disco lights still casting a blue light over everyone. The music had been silenced but the room reverberated with the hum of talk, questions no one could answer. He felt that old resentment stir inside, that sense of uselessness. He wanted to be out doing something purposeful. Discovering for himself, what had happened. To see with his own eyes and to know that it was true. Had they really said his daughter Esme was dead, murdered in her bridesmaid dress? Fate had struck with the worse blow of all. His injuries, his mangled body, crushed, tossed and mottled with shrapnel hadn't been enough. He was being asked to pay more.

Chapter 3

Our lives are made up of stories, Anna thought. Some we are told and others we tell ourselves. Her mother once told her that each day makes up a lifetime of experiences, bleeding into each other like the colours merging on a damp sheet of paper as the brush strokes complete the scene. For Anna, the story of her arrival was where she began. Not her birth, no, for that was unknown, another life of untold possibilities.

Sometimes you have to go back to the beginning to know where the ending will take you.

She had presented the secondment to Jon and to her dad as a way of helping her to figure out what she wanted from life and perhaps an opportunity to look into her biological family. Jon didn't get the whole 'I need to find myself crap'. To be fair, Anna would have been the same with him, but she couldn't help feeling a need to fill in the blanks. Maybe if she could paint in some of the background of her birth family, then she could concentrate on the foreground of her life. She knew she sounded full of herself, that old 'on the couch' mentality of needing to know oneself, but there had to be some truth in it.

'It's always your job,' Jon had said a few weeks ago, when she told him about the post.

'It wins hands down every time.' Anna could hear the hurt in his voice.

'Come on, it's only six months, a chance to learn how new policing techniques work in a different environment. Think about the breadth of experience it offers.' Even she could hear how hollow her words sounded.

'After everything that's happened with your mum, that bloody Hawthorne case, this is the last thing you need,' he took her face in his hands, feeling sure of himself now. 'You can't go Anna. Maybe you should take some time off before you throw yourself back in.'

He had no right trying make her feel weak and vulnerable and his words only served to make her more steadfast in her decision.

'I've already accepted. I'm going.'

He had walked out after that and didn't return until she had fallen asleep. Anna had left early in the morning for her run and the next time they spoke, it was as if they hadn't disagreed and that her moving to Belfast was part of their grand plan after all.

* * *

Saying goodbye in a crowded airport was not ideal, but hands down it beat the alternative. At least here, surrounded by people, Anna could contain her emotions. Jon would know better than to expect tears. She didn't do crying. Didn't do I love you or overt displays of affection. He'd be better off getting a dog, she'd told him, more than once.

Leaving had been easier than she thought. One suitcase full of work clothes, underwear, a few tops and a couple of pairs of jeans, a rucksack containing her art stuff and she was gone. It was surprising how little any one person needed. The books, the vinyl albums, jewellery – none of it mattered to her. Not really.

'You'll ring me, won't you?' he asked, pulling her into his arms, his mouth pressed down on to the top of her head. Anna knew she was being selfish. Childish even, but for once she didn't care about how he felt. She bent down to release the handle of the pull-along suitcase and without another word, headed off towards security clearance for flights to Belfast, turning only once to catch a last glance of his face.

* * *

When she was planning the move, she hadn't given much thought to the house. It was somewhere to stay, a base to lay her head. Now, as she climbed out of the taxi, she was pleased to see it was decent. The semi-detached Victorian red-brick house was edged with a neat lawn and a driveway. It all looked quietly expensive and smug. It was a 'mixed' area according to the documentation. Protestants and Catholics living in middle-class harmony. The political turbulence was generally kept in the working-class areas, although the relocation specialist in HR had warned her to be vigilant against dissident extremists who operated under the radar. She was to consider herself a so-called legitimate target.

Anna had worked her way methodically through the paper work, the figures and the dry reports explaining the statistical breakdown of incidents. The terrorist attacks, the riots of the summer past, the flag protests, the shooting of two policemen in September, the maiming of a prison warden – all in a days' work it seemed for this part of the world. But experience had taught her that all the research in the world couldn't compete with practical, on-the-ground experience. Talking to people. Hearing their take on their situation. That was how you got a feel of a place, and Belfast would be no different.

* * *

In the quiet of the strange house she felt even more lost than usual. Thirty-one-years-old, with an increasing sense of purposeless, she had a strong desire to try to make sense of her life. She didn't want her job to define her – she risked becoming too institutionalised and cynical, but she didn't want to start a family either. She could hear her mother saying *you can't have it all ways girl. Be grateful for what you have.*

Maybe she was expecting too much from life. Maybe this is as good as it gets – chasing bad guys and sleeping with the good ones. Lately she had felt depleted, wrung out and too tired to rise above it. Belfast was supposed to be her saviour. In the small kitchen, she rummaged around, opening and closing cupboards. She'd have to shop for the essentials and stock up for the week ahead. She glanced out the window, across the patch of lawn at the back, and saw a grey and white cat dart into the undergrowth of shrubs.

Looking for distraction, she switched on the television and caught the evening news.

Police in Belfast have stepped up security and carried out searches and vehicle checkpoints following an attack that saw a 130lb proxy car bomb partially explode in the main shopping district of the city.

So much for the peace process, she mused. It seemed that nothing much had changed. In spite of her briefing and what she knew of Northern Ireland's dissidents, she hadn't expected bombs to be going off outside shopping centres. The broadcaster moved on to the second item of news, the murder of a young girl at a wedding. Anna sat up. Bombs and punishment beatings were the usual for Northern Ireland, but a young woman being murdered wasn't so commonplace. That type of murder was lower than the average for the rest of the UK.

Police have issued a further appeal for any information on the brutal murder of seventeen—year-old Esme Wells. Miss Wells was acting as a bridesmaid at her sister's wedding and was last seen in the vicinity of Malone House Manor on the outskirts of South Belfast, the venue of the wedding. A press conference will be held tomorrow marking one week from the time of the murder.

No doubt, she'd learn all about it tomorrow, when she officially took up her new post in the Serious Crimes Department. The SCD was responsible for investigations into organised crime, serious crime, terrorism and murder. Anna had been told she would be working alongside in-house specialists, crime analysts, and others to manage intelligence and carry out investigations. She hoped she wouldn't be kept outside of the proper work.

She was here to contribute, not job-shadow and she had made sure her Super in Cardiff had spelt this out to his Belfast counterpart.

Her colleagues in Cardiff thought she was mad. '*Belfast?*' Bethan had asked, her eyes wide with incredulity. 'What on earth do you want to work in Belfast for? Is there not enough action for you on St Mary Street on a Saturday night?' Anna had smiled and said as little as possible. The opportunity had come up and the timing was right. She didn't need to explain herself.

Besides, Northern Ireland was where she had been born. Where her story had begun.

* * *

It had been a while since he had been with a woman. He didn't feel the same need these days. The flirting, the dating, it all seemed so superfluous.

He thought back to the last one he'd brought home. He had met her in Aether and Echo, one of his favourite haunts in Lower Garfield Street. She had been hanging over him all night, whispering in his ear and making it clear she fancied him. Her friends eventually moved on to another club, probably Thompsons, and left them finishing off their drinks before he called for a taxi.

She was half way to being unconscious when he fucked her, but he didn't mind. Afterwards he enjoyed lying back and stroking her hair while she slept. It spread out across the pillow in a halo of glorious abundance, dark at the top of her head and faded to a pale golden brown towards the ends, reminding him of autumn.

She slept deeply, with her mouth slightly open, oblivious to his study of her. He listened to her murmuring in her sleep and watched as she burrowed down into the duvet. It was while she slept, that he reached over to the bedside cupboard and retrieved a pair of scissors to snip a section of her hair. He was certain that because it was so thick and long, she wouldn't notice.

He had only needed one good snip, that was all he required for the doll. He knew Maude, his old aunt, would love it. It had been a good find. He could tell from the matte finish of the face that it was made of bisque. It had a translucent quality, pale and cold looking. He liked how it seemed to represent a dead girl rather than a living one. The doll's hair was painted on, fair curls painted in fat whorls. He could improve on it by using real hair. It would be a painstaking job, but he knew he could thread small sections of the hair together in tight little bunches and glue them into place on the doll's head.

It was a few days later, while working with the doll that he first thought of his plan. The cold bisque face stared up at him like a dead girl, creating an image in his mind. An image that he couldn't shake. It taunted him, begging him, making him hungry for it.

He didn't need to go clubbing and looking for pick-ups after that. There was no going back, after he had thought of what he could do.

Chapter 4

Declan watched as Izzy shuddered, her head over the toilet as she threw up again. He could see her grief was physical. Raw, uncompromising and resolute. She had been sick from the morning after the wedding. He couldn't bring himself to call it the day of the murder. He wanted to refer to the day as Lara's wedding rather than Esme's death. He was stupid and pig headed. It didn't change a thing – no matter what he called the bloody day.

He could imagine no end to this. How could they find their way back from the horror of losing a child in such a brutal way? There would be no finding a 'new normality' that God-awful phase that had been bandied about after his legs had been blown off. He reached from the chair to hand Izzy a towel to wipe her face. She had been sick during her pregnancies. Hyper emesis the doctors had said – grave sickness was the translation from Latin. Now her body appeared as if it was being held hostage by the same sickness only now it was bearing witness to death instead of new life.

She ran the cold water and splashed her face. 'Thanks,' she said. 'I can't seem to keep anything down.'

'It's shock,' he said, stating the obvious. 'Your body is reacting to the stress and trauma.'

Declan manoeuvred himself out of the downstairs bathroom, the door had been made wider to accommodate his chair. Lots of little changes and alterations to help make his disability more palatable. He could think of nothing to help lessen the grief he felt now. Nothing beyond catching the bastard and seeing him brought to justice.

'Do you know, I can't for the life of me remember who told me about Esme,' Izzy said following Declan into the living room. She sat looking out over their garden.

'My brain has blanked out the messenger completely. I keep asking how it could happen to Esme, to us?' she bent over clutching at herself as if there was a physical pain surging through her body.

He was at a loss as to know how to help her. He instinctively wanted to hold her and offer some sort of comfort but they were past that kind of affection.

Turning her head towards him she said, 'Isn't it ridiculous that only a week ago we were up to our eyes in all the wedding planning. Chair covers, buttonhole flowers, bloody twinkling fairy lights.' She grasped at her head as if she could dislodge the horror. She made a sound, like a strangled sob.

'It's as if I'm drowning. Declan, I can't take this,' her tone was almost pleading, as if she needed Declan to fix it all, to make this nightmare dissipate.

'I know Izzy. Life has a way of doing that – everything turns on an axis and we go from one extreme to the other.' He had seen it before. The grandmother raped and murdered in her bed. Someone's son shot in the back of the head for dealing drugs in the wrong area. A Filipino girl, traveling miles from home, to start a new life only to find the nannying agency is really a sex ring. Bearing witness to someone else's nightmare was different from living in your own. The bomb should have been his lot. He often thought over the years, that surely nothing worse could ever happen. Though sometimes in the dead of the night fear, that it might, nagged at him.

'To think of all the time taken up by the wedding preparations. I was cross at Lara for insisting on burlap wrapped jam jars with tea lights instead of the crystal candleholders. All the while Esme had kept to the background, consumed with her life at school and going out with her friends.'

She put her face in her hands, 'Jesus, I can't even remember when I last spent time with Esme, one on one. What with work and the wedding, life ran away from me. How had any of it seemed important?' She was walking around the room now, without purpose. Her grief scared Declan. He needed her to hold it together.

She turned abruptly, 'You don't think a guest did it, do you? It can't be someone we know.'

'God, I hope not.' They both fell silent, contemplating the unthinkable. He couldn't bring himself to tell Izzy that in most murder cases the killer knows the victim.

'They'll catch whoever did this, won't they?' again she was pleading with him.

'I'll make fucking sure they do.' His clenched fists were lodged down the sides of his chair. Every muscle in his body was tight, as if ready to spring in to action.

'Did they tell you what she was like? How she was when they found her?' her voice was hoarse, worn out from crying.

'Only that she hadn't been dead long.' Declan had no wish to tell Izzy that in all likelihood their daughter's body had been flaccid, not yet rigid from death. That her features may have been frozen in place, her mouth open in a silent scream for help. That her pink bridesmaid dress had been bloodied and dirty, possibly tore and that a huddle of forensics people in white bodysuits would be scraping at her fingernails, collecting samples of secretions, while the photographers would be documenting the scene, click by click. Like all young girls, she was constantly photographed in life, by her friends and by herself, searching for the perfect selfie or profile shot to post on Facebook and Instagram. Now in death she would also be documented.

He knew that where she had been found was little more than a ditch running alongside the river Lagan that the hotel backed on to. A scenic spot by day, which would now take on all the trappings of the macabre, for kids to visit and taunt each other with tales of the girl, their daughter, found murdered in the undergrowth at her sister's wedding.

Chapter 5

"For Fuck's Sake is there never a friggin printer in this place working?'

Anna turned to the barked-out comment and shrugged. 'Don't ask me. First day and all that.'

'Cole? Isn't that right?' he asked.

'Yeah, Anna Cole.'

'I'm Richard McKay, Detective Superintendent, your new boss,' he reached out to shake her hand. His grip strong and dry with surprisingly soft skin.

'Right you'll be hitting the ground running. Busy time for us as you can see,' he said indicating with the document in his hand towards the heads down in the quiet bustle of the office, signifying work being done. 'The daughter of Declan Wells, a former police psychologist, has been killed.'

Anna said, 'Yeah, I heard.'

'So you'll understand that we don't have time for preliminaries and a welcome party,' he sighed. 'Terrible case all together, but we need to make sure we are on the ball and that nothing gets missed.'

'I'm not looking for hand holding, just let me know what you want me to do,' Anna replied.

He nodded, 'Settle yourself in and if you need anything ask Holly over there, she'll tell you who to go to for all that HR shit.'

Anna looked over to the girl with hair dyed a blue-black colour cut in a razor-sharp bob, giving her a hard look, as if she was trying to be intimidating. She wore stylised make up, a cat's eye flick of dense ebony eyeliner, precise and clean and a ruby red matt lipstick. It was a uniform of sorts. Anna wished she could have enough interest in herself to devise a style, but she had never been good with make-up, preferring to rely on a quick smudge of mascara and a sweep of coral blusher to warm her pale complexion.

'Don't mind him,' Holly said, without taking her eyes off her computer screen. 'He's a gobshite.'

Anna looked perplexed, unsure of the colloquialism.

'Full of shit? Comprehendy vous?'

'Yeah, I get it.' Anna said staring at her.

'We're all under a lot of stress. Murder of Declan Wells' daughter has everyone on edge.'

'I'm sure. One of your own always hurts the most,' Anna offered.

'Nah she isn't one of us,' Holly said finally taking her eyes of the screen giving Anna a once over look. 'Not that we think that way these days,' Holly added.

'I thought Declan Wells worked with the force?'

'Yeah, he used to – forensics section, psychologist. He's a doctor, not a real cop. Never got his hands dirty on the job.'

Anna absorbed the conversation realising she had considered the murder of Dr Wells' daughter to be more personal to the force. She found it unsettling when 'one of your own' didn't include your work colleague.

* * *

The briefing packs were passed out during the 10.30 a.m. meeting. Anna flicked through the pages, taking in the format, the highlighted information and the subheadings. The bare bones of the investigation to date reduced to six pages of print.

Richard McKay took to the floor and waited for the hush to fall before starting to speak. 'Right as you all probably know the funeral is today. There will be a significant representation from the force. We are there to pay our respects first and foremost, but of course keep an ear open and your eyes peeled. You never know what could be said at these things or who's rubber necking.' He looked around allowing his gaze to fall on Anna, taking a second to place her.

'Anna Cole is here with us on secondment. I'm sure you will all go out of your way to ensure she is welcomed, and show her how we do things over here. Anna if you want to accompany me to the funeral today we can get to know each other on the way to the church.'

'Sure, sounds good.'

Anna noticed Holly smirk and raise her groomed eyebrow. His easy authority and intense dark eyes were bound to make him desirable even if his manner was lacking.

Suddenly she felt intensely homesick for the security and familiarity of her own incident room in Cardiff. Here she was the new girl and an outsider to boot. She glanced down at her clear desk, missing the messy disorder of her old one. She even found herself missing Rhys Edwards, her Superintendent, with his acne pocked skin and habit of scratching his beard with a pen. Her colleagues may not have been her best friends but she knew them well and would put herself out for them at every turn, as they would do for her. Now in Belfast she would have no one to rely on, no one to pick up the slack if she needed it, and no one to make her laugh when the day turned grim.

'So, first day then. What do you make of us?' Richard swung the car into reverse while Anna clicked her seatbelt into place.

'I shall keep my judgment until I have more to go on.'

'Wise woman.'

He hit the indicator stalk and pulled out on to the rain-washed road.

'So, what brought you to this part of the world?'

Anna paused, unsure of how to answer. 'Oh, the usual, bored really. Fancied a change of scene. The offer of the secondment came up. I thought now or never.'

He nodded as if to say he understood. 'Not many from your part of the world over here. Poles, Lithuanians and Romanians yes, but not many Welsh.'

'I guess you've been missing out then.'

They stopped at a pedestrian crossing. A child in a yellow raincoat skipped out and was hastily grabbed back by her mother as the lights turned amber.

'Well, have you had a chance to get up to speed with this Wells girl case?'

'I've read the briefing and looked at the press stuff. No leads yet?' she asked.

'Nada. You know what it's like at this stage – it's all about elimination. The volume of work on this one will be huge with so many wedding guests to talk to.'

'What about CCTV? I assume the hotel had cameras?' Anna said.

'Yep, but wouldn't you know they were down. There was a loss of connection which management had reported over a week ago, but they hadn't got around to fixing it.'

'Coincidence or just convenient?'

McKay grimaced, 'That's for whoever takes the lead in this case to decide. There's a lot of pressure riding on this case and my balls are busted if we don't come up with something double quick. I need a breakthrough and I need it today. Let's see what we can glean from the funeral goers.'

With the church car park overflowing, like the other mourners, they were forced to park some distance from the church. The black hearse sitting at the front of the church steps still held the oak wood coffin adorned with blooms of pink and white flowers.

Anna struggled to keep up with Richard's long strides. She silently cursed herself for wearing such high heels. She liked to think the added couple of inches made up for her small stature and she had been keen to look well presented on her first day. She'd revert to her usual boots and trousers when she settled in.

They left the brightness of the mid-day sun and entered the dark, hushed church. Voices mumbled quietly while an organist played a hymn Anna didn't recognise. The altar was opulent. A huge arrangement of yellow and pale blue flowers flanked either side of the marble altar table where the priest stood, arms opened and raised as the congregation stood on cue. The choir began to sing and the coffin was carried in. Anna watched as the mother and father followed it up the aisle. Isabel Wells was dressed in a severe charcoal grey dress walking slowly beside Declan Wells in his wheelchair.

Anna was used to religion and the rituals of mourning but the Catholic mass was not familiar to her. Her own family was Baptist. Their church a pale wooden construct, with little adornment and certainly no graphic artwork of the crucified Lord or the periwinkle blue clothed Virgin Mary statue, holding a fat infant Jesus.

As the congregation worshiped, kneeled, prayed, stood and sang, Anna allowed herself to drift off in thought. She wondered if Jon had sorted the leaking showerhead; if he had remembered to call the garage about the part for her car, and more importantly, if he missed her. She was still trying to work out her own feelings. The newness of her surroundings, the assault of the accent, the cultural shorthand – all of it was so different, and welcomed. Part of her expected to feel at home in Ireland. To have found herself in the greenness of the countryside, in the din of the city, in the rumble of Belfast. She had always felt something was missing, some unknown part of her she couldn't identify. Even with her brief time in the city every conversation was loaded. People weighed her up, assessed her, and she did the same too.

She glanced around at the congregation. The family sitting in the front rows, heads lowered as if the weight of grief was pressing down on them. The father, Declan Wells sat at the edge of the pew in his chair. That must surely jar, she thought, always being separate because of the chair. She made a mental note to ask Richard about him. The case notes mentioned he had been in a car bomb. She knew that he was a psychologist working in forensics and had been in the force for many years. He was likely to have been used to dealing with the murder of someone else's daughter or son and now here he was playing the reverse role.

Anna couldn't imagine it. She wasn't naive enough to think that she could understand the pain of losing a child.

The mother placed her arm around the other daughter who was crying freely, tears streaming like they would never stop with her new husband, Rory, sitting beside her. The case notes said the mother, Isabel, was a lecturer at Queen's University. She taught in the English faculty. By all accounts, they appeared to be the typical middle class, well-to-do family. Now they sat devastated and broken.

The priest was holding the white disc of communion high up, praying for the transformation of the bread into the body of Christ. The choir began to sing again, 'This is my body broken for you …' the words lilting and somewhat strangely joyful. Anna watched the congregation mouth the responses, and as they moved in unison to kneel, she caught sight of the new husband, glancing behind, scanning the crowd. Who was he looking for?

* * *

He held the bird in his hand, feeling its heart beat like a snare drum against his palm. The quickest and most efficient way to kill it, without damaging the specimen, is to compress the lungs. He repositioned it, making sure that its body was between his thumb and fingers so that it could gain no purchase with its talons on him. As always, he wanted to cause no impairment to the specimen. An intact creature was always preferable. For a larger bird, he would need to insert a sharp knife under the left wing, straight to the heart, making sure to plug the mouth and the wound instantly. This made him think of the girl, her gaping mouth lying wide in a silent scream.

Chapter 6

Declan made it his business to position his chair close to McKay at the entrance to the church.

'Where are we with forensics? No one has given me any details and I swear to God if something doesn't happen soon, I will crack heads.'

Richard was doing that awkward stance of being bent over to speak quietly to Declan as the mourners filed out of the church, seeking out the family to pay their respects.

'Declan, you know the protocol. You can't be too closely involved. We have little to go on but it's early days.'

People were waiting to speak to Declan. Izzy was being hugged by someone from the university, and Lara was talking to a one of Esme's school teachers.

Declan took the hand of a well-wisher and thanked them for attending, while Richard stood by. Aidan Anderson, the city's Lord Mayor approached them. 'Mr Wells my sincerest condolences,' he said.

'Thank you. Good of you to come today,' Declan replied.

'The mighty and good have all turned out,' McKay said.

'He knows my son-in-law. Now I need to know who you have working on this.' Declan spoke through gritted teeth. He could barely contain his anger.

'We've good people on it. Thomas King, the usual team and a blow in from Wales – Anna Cole. That's her over there talking to one of the mourners.'

'Get him caught.'

Richard nodded, his mouth in a tight line. He patted Declan's shoulder.

'How is Izzy bearing up?' asked Richard.

'As you would expect.' Declan released the brake of the chair and manoeuvred out of the crowd. He couldn't stomach another empty platitude.

* * *

The days after the wedding were a blur. Declan fought against the instinct to shut down, to allow the blessed numbness of shock to wash over him. He needed to stay alert. To question how the police were handling the case, keeping an eye on what was going on and who was in charge. He was desperate to have an insight into to pathology reports and to keep on at them to get the forensics back. Sure, they placated him. Told him that they would do everything humanly possible to get this monster locked up; that they had every man and woman on it. But Declan knew all too well that mistakes were made, people messed up, evidence was lost, tampered with, either deliberately or accidently, and that not every bastard out there got what they deserved.

He also knew that if they got who had done this, if they had them locked up in watertight evidence, then it still wouldn't bring his daughter back.

Esme. When he thought of her it was in movement. She was always rushing, a swirly mass of teenage hormones, long, tawny brown hair, and legs clad in skintight pale blue jeans. As a child she had been athletic, keen on running and good at gymnastics. Again, always moving, running, jumping. *Look dad, look at me. Look at what I can do!*

When he ended up in the chair something between them shifted. She wasn't so quick to show off her cartwheels, to ask him to take her to the Mary Peter's track where she would sprint and jump hurdles. He saw it for what it was – her way of protecting him. As if she was not rubbing his nose in her ability to be quick and agile while he had been left to rot in the blasted contraption. They never spoke about it in the way they should have.

Never acknowledged that he could no longer be the same type of father. Instead she went to fewer running events, collected fewer medals and certainly didn't share that part of her life with him. Izzy said it was her age – she was becoming more interested in her friends and boys than spending time with them. That it was only natural that she pulled away from them. Sure, hadn't Lara been the same? But Declan knew different. It was as if she decided not to excel at something beyond his realm of possibility.

The details of her death tortured him. It was an endless unease, like ants clawing through his brain, roaches scratching at his lungs. Every part of his being was affected. He had managed to protect Izzy and Lara from knowing the worse of the pathologist's findings. Head injury, impaling and strangulation. The words sounded clinical and removed from the reality of his daughter lying on a cold mortuary table.

He looked around his home office lined with dry tomes of psychiatric learning, books on every aspect of the criminal mind, dusty looking forgotten piles of academic research papers and journals stacked in the corner. All this knowledge, research and training, and yet he was prevented from using any of it to help find who had did this to his daughter.

Frustration tightened like a hard, tight knot inside his chest. He had to do something. To be part of the investigation, as being on the sidelines was doing his head in. He couldn't shake off the feeling of shame and blame. It was as if misfortune had sought him out. Again.

He had ended up working in the police by accident. The module he had wanted to do at Queen's was oversubscribed so as an afterthought he had ended up taking a two-term course on theories of criminal behaviour. That was it; he was hooked. By the end of his second year, he had ensured he was well placed to major in criminal psychology and to do a dissertation entitled, '*The applications of psychology to the criminal justice system; terrorism and political violence in Northern Ireland.*' Under the tutelage of Professor Bonham, he had found his calling and secured an entry-level job in the prison service before moving on to the police force a few years later.

His career path wasn't welcomed at home. His parents, both fearful for their Catholic son working for the prison service and even worse the police, hounded him to find a secure and safe hospital job. It wasn't so much the nature of his work that bothered them, though his mother found the idea of trying to understand the workings of the criminal mind to be a lost cause, it was more the worry of the sectarianism he would face, the outright hostility and the not insignificant threat of being a Catholic working for the RUC.

'Have you no sense, lad? They'll put a bullet in yer head as quick as look at you,' his mother said. She used every blackmail tactic she could employ. Her heart wasn't up to it. Didn't he care what he was putting them through? Did he not think he was putting them at risk too? How could they hold their heads up in the street when everyone would have him down for a turncoat serving the British? He would be a walking target for both sides of the divide.

But Declan had refuted their concerns and pointed out that his work didn't put him on the firing line, that he was seen as little more than a pen pushing academic who was brought in the to look at theories of criminal behaviour, causes of violent crime and offender typologies.

He was grateful they had both died before the bombing and now this, Esme's death. He was glad they didn't have to go through the living hell of seeing their granddaughter buried. A small mercy on a dark day.

Declan hadn't forgotten how it felt to be a new comer, someone on the outside. As a Catholic, fresh in from graduation, he knew he had lots to prove. Coming top of his year in a psychology degree meant sweet F.A. to his colleagues.

But Northern Ireland had been changing. Within the police force there was an undeniable air of fear. Power, when held for so long, is hard to relinquish even for those who understood the sense and the justice of it. Declan Wells made sure to prove himself. He didn't put a foot wrong. He respected the traditions, kept his counsel to himself and turned a blind eye when necessary. He deferred to his superiors and the old brigade without ingratiating himself. Enough to show respect and to make it seem like he knew his place. Really, he was marking time. Time when the politics of Northern Ireland could no longer sustain the bigotry and sectarianism of old. Declan had intuition, and a belief that the system would begin to change, and when it did, he was well placed to help make the transformation and benefit from being part of it.

Even after fifteen years with the service, he never relaxed, never let his guard down and never got too close. He knew he was respected. Declan Wells was sound, they would say, with the unstated, *for a Catholic*, left handing in the air. He didn't try to fit in knowing he was all right if he kept to the sidelines. Now he feared the depth of the unacknowledged trenches were apparent in the investigation. Esme was high up on anyone's radar. No one liked to see a pretty, middle-class, young girl murdered and not find the bastard who did it. McKay and his team wouldn't like it hanging around, sullying their statistics. But Declan was no fool, he knew that they would end up chasing this idea that somehow Esme had brought it on herself, that her attacker knew her.

Maybe that was his own bigotry talking – an occupational hazard of living in this place meant that sooner or later nearly everyone displayed a certain tribal instinct.

His daughter was dead and he couldn't be sure that they were doing enough about it. The acid taste of frustration overwhelmed him. He couldn't sit around doing nothing. Not even the wheelchair was going to stop him.

He needed an in. A way to get to the heart of the case. He thought of that woman, Cole. Richard said she had been seconded in from Wales. He liked the idea of someone from the outside being involved. Someone immune to the politics of this bloody country. Someone not cowered into thinking along the same old, tired lines. Anna Cole was fresh in from the mainland, and could provide the unclouded judgment he needed. He had to convince her and the likes of Thomas King to let him play a part in the investigation.

Declan needed to take control, to feel that he was in some part helping get the bastard who had done this. It was his only way to cope. Lara had Rory; she didn't need to pay witness to her father's grief. And Izzy? Well, Izzy would cope fine as far as he could tell. He wasn't so presumptuous to think that that was the full picture. Izzy would take her grief elsewhere. Where and to whom, he didn't want to dwell on.

Chapter 7

Two weeks from the murder and everyone was beginning to feel anxious. At her desk, Anna read through the report notes again. Victim Esme Wells, seventeen-years-old. Death by strangulation. Interestingly, her mouth had been stuffed with wood wool. The report described it as straw-like shredded wood used in hampers and storage facilities. It was graded as super fine and suitable for toy stuffing. The idea of having that stuffed in your mouth while you fought for your life, made Anna shudder.

She trawled through the statements taken on the night of the murder. The buoyant thump, thump of the music had not completely drowned out the cries, for those smoking on the back lawn had heard the screams. At the time, the cries had been dismissed as rowdy horseplay. A day of drinking champagne and cocktails had ensured that most of the guests were well liquored. So, Esme had managed to scream out before the wood wool was shoved in her mouth.

It had been an unseasonably balmy night. The report suggested that there were a group of smokers out on the lawn to the rear of the venue. No doubt couples were mooching off to find a quiet corner. Someone had to have seen something. A bridesmaid can't wander off and be murdered without someone seeing her leave.

The report stated that a group of teenagers were having their own underage contraband drinking session courtesy of a swiped bottle of wine and had been sat in the bandstand. Earlier in the day the bandstand had been the focal point for many of the official photographs. She could bet the bride and groom had stood in the mock eighteenth-century folly smiling at the bequest of a charming photographer. Had someone been watching the

wedding party from afar? The hotel was set in lush green grounds, .
complete with a river that ran around the perimeter, the long
driveway up was reached over a stone bridge. Had someone been
waiting for the right opportunity? Was Esme the target or was she
the one who presented at the right moment for her killer?

'Cole, can you come into my office? I need a word,' Richard
called from the doorway. She lifted the case notes folder and
headed in.

'Sit,' he ordered.

She took the chair at the side of his teak desk and placed
the folder down. The view from the window was bleak. Concrete
blocks of offices, surrounded by high security walls, cameras, and
look out posts from more troubled times, gave the impression of
a fortress.

'How are you finding it, so far? A bit different from across the
water, no doubt?'

'Yes, sir but I'm keen to get stuck in,' she was aware of sounding
over eager, like a schoolgirl trying to impress the teacher she had
a crush on.

'You saw the Wells family at the funeral, it's a heartbreaking
loss, so it is. The only solace we can offer them is to find the killer.
What have you come up with so far? Any thoughts?'

'I was just having another read through the report notes, Sir.'

'And?'

'From what I have seen of the briefing notes we have no sexual
motive since she wasn't sexually assaulted. That's not to say the
murderer didn't intend to assault her and for whatever reason
killed her before he managed to do anything. Thomas King has
spoken to the two teenagers that found her. But there isn't much
more to go on.'

The team briefing had been held that morning and had thrown
up little of use. CCTV was still being checked, as were mobile
records. The wedding guests had all been interviewed with no one
seeing anything untoward or noticing anything suspicious. They
needed a break and soon.

'So, what have you gleaned so far?' he asked, his tone, somehow inviting her to slip up. She was the blow in. The new girl, and she didn't want to wreck her chances of playing a lead part in this case.

'The alarm was raised shortly after eleven o'clock by two teenagers. A boy of sixteen, called Joshua, a cousin of the bride and a girl, Hannah, who had been invited as an evening guest. Hannah was connected to the groom's family, the daughter of a friend of the family.'

'What were they doing to be so far away from the wedding party?'

'It appears that Joshua had led Hannah to a quiet part of the grounds hoping to get more than a kiss and a feel.' She paused to look through the folder, 'I haven't spoken to them but from the notes it appears Joshua had spotted Hannah early in the evening and had made it his business to be introduced. They had quickly established a few mutual acquaintances, and that they shared mutual Facebook friends. I suppose that's how young ones connect to each other these days.' Anna glanced down at her notes.

'They had been out for 'a wander round the grounds', was how Joshua described it in his statement and had caught sight of the body in the undergrowth. He wasn't sure who saw it first, him or Hannah, but within seconds they realised that she was dead.

'He was asked: How did you know she was dead? And he said, *'There was blood, a lot of blood plus she was twisted as if she had tried to crawl on her back to safety. To escape. And there was a bloody big branch, which at first sight looked like it was impaled in her body. A gnarled branch, thick and long looked like it was sticking right out of her chest. It looked like someone had put a stake through her heart.'* Joshua's words,' she added.

'At first he hadn't realised that the dark wetness all around the body was blood. He took out his iPhone and clicked on the torch app.'

Anna looked up from her notebook, 'The girl Hannah verified what Joshua told us.'

She glanced down at the witness statement and read it: '*It took me a minute to work out what I was seeing. I thought maybe she was drunk and had vomited all over herself, but then I realised.*' The images came together to make the scene before them something much more sinister than a plastered bridesmaid falling down in a drunken heap.'

Anna read from her folder, 'He continued saying, '*It was like an image straight from a horror movie. Some blood-lusting thriller with vampires and zombies.*"

She was sure he wouldn't forget the bridesmaid, with a bloom of dark crimson blood radiating from her centre lying like a leading actress playing dead in a mess of moss, brambles and nettles.

Richard leaned back on his chair, 'So a walk around the perimeter of the hotel grounds, looking for a private nook to become more intimately acquainted with the pretty Hannah had turned into a gothic nightmare.

'I'm told that you have worked on cases similar in Cardiff. The Hawthorne case, right?'

She nodded. 'Yes, I was the arresting officer. Good old-fashioned police work in the end won the day.'

'I've been told it was more than that. You put yourself on the line according to your DSI.'

A young girl had been reported missing only for her body to turn up under her neighbour's shed. Anna had a crescent moon of a scar on her right breast, inflicted by a screwdriver, to show for her trouble. The murderer had panicked and rammed the tool into her as he tried to flee.

She shrugged.

'We had a couple of high-profile cases recently and were lucky to get results quickly.'

'How do you feel about working on this here case, then? I'm being pressed to get a result soon and it seems that the powers that be like the sound of you. You've got the experience, but those eejits out there won't thank you for being in the co-pilot on this. Can you handle a bit of whinging?'

'Goes with the job, sir. Can't keep everyone happy all of the time. I'm prepared to take a bit of flak.'

'Good. You'll be working alongside Thomas King. He's the lead so whatever he says goes. Is that clear?'

'Yes, sir.'

'Go track him down. He's expecting you. Keep me updated with any breakthroughs and get to work. Fast.'

Anna went back to her corner desk and found Thomas sitting on her chair.

'So, Tonto, we're to be partners on this here case. Are you up for the job?'

'Tonto?' she raised an eyebrow.

'Aye, my side kick,' he grinned, delighted with his joke. There was something warm and attractive about him. His smile was disarmingly wide and mischievous. His pale grey shirt looked like it had been hastily tucked into to his trousers, reminding Anna of a schoolboy, the class joker who always got into trouble.

'Yes, ready to hit the ground running,' she said, moving towards the back wall of the office where Thomas had already began cataloguing the details of the case. It was how she liked to work too. Piece by piece she would add to it until she had a kaleidoscope of information. Leads, people, places, and if she was lucky at some stage she would see a pattern, connections and links that would create a story. Known associates and incidental contacts all had to be identified, talked to, and ruled out or in.

The workload could seem overwhelming at this stage of an investigation. Anna knew from experience, that constructing a narrative flow, looking at relationships between the victim and her family and friends, finding potential witnesses, and backing everything up with physical evidence was the safest way of getting the job done effectively. There were no short cuts in policing.

Anna lifted an enlarged photograph of Esme Wells and placed it at the centre of the wall and stood back. It was the type of face she could paint. The skin was smooth and fresh, no hard angles and not much depth for shadows to rest. A high forehead and deep-set eyes, fringed with dark lashes. The mouth would be hard to get right. The top lip seemed too thin to go with the bottom on, making her look, somehow, vulnerable and childlike.

'Pretty girl,' said Thomas disturbing Anna's mental analysis of the face.

'Yeah. Wide-eyed and ready to take on the world,' Anna replied removing the last blob of Blu-tack from the board's previous incident display.

'The briefing is scheduled for first thing tomorrow morning. Let's see if we can unearth a lead of some sort before then.'

'I've already pulled Esme's mobile records. The only red flag was too many calls to Rory Finnegan, the brother-in-law. We need to chase that up and have a word with him. Her school records were good, solid exams results with the ability to go on to university,' he said.

Anna breathed in deeply and felt a sense of satisfaction of being immersed in her work. She was in Belfast. She'd done it. Jumped ship into the unknown but here in the station, whether it be Cardiff or Belfast, she knew what she was doing.

Thomas sat down beside her and unrolled a long piece of paper. 'Let's map out times and places of everyone we've spoke to so far then we can put it all in the system and see what continuity HOLMES 2 throws up. I take it you use the same system in Cardiff?'

Anna gave him a look as if to say, 'Do you think we are still in the dark ages?'

'Yes, we use it. TIE – Trace, Implicate and Eliminate. We look at those with access to the scene at the time of the offence; anyone in the vicinity of the scene at the time of the offence; those living in, or associated with the geographical area or the premises and anyone associated with the victim with previous convictions for similar offences. Does that cover the plan for you?'

Thomas laughed, 'Right, well done, Hermione Granger. You've done your homework. A plus.'

Anna took a black marker from the desk, 'Ok, let's start with the wedding venue,' she drew an outline of the venue and the surrounding area. She could sense Thomas relaxing into his seat. They could be at this all night. She didn't think either of them had any reason to rush home so it made sense to get started properly, checking and double checking, looking for patterns and strange occurrences, waiting for that one delicious lead to take them right to the killer.

Chapter 8

The university was situated in a leafy part of Belfast, not far from Anna's rented house by car. She studied the campus map before heading off, to work out where she would find Dr Isabel Wells. When she drove down Stranmillis Road she saw that the area was busy with students going to and from lectures, dog walkers heading to the nearby Botanic gardens, and mothers with young kids, and babies in pushchairs. Parking was difficult, but Anna eventually found a spot in Elmwood Avenue.

She crossed the road at the pedestrian crossing outside the student's union building and saw the gothic style red bricked university building with its quadrangle and manicured lawns. The department of English and Irish literature was situated on a street of tall, cream Georgian houses, running to the university's main building. It all looked typical of university style buildings designed to have the air of entitlement and superiority. The online brochure had listed Dr Wells' specialist interests and publications: Medieval Literature and the Role of Kinship, Hiberno-Norse Relations, Tales of Three Gormlaiths in Medieval Irish Literature and Pagans and Holymen.

Isabel Wells didn't look like Anna's idea of an academic. She thought of the austere woman at the funeral, tall, terribly thin and angular and somewhat hauntingly beautiful with her cool blonde hair cut short. The meeting place had been Dr Wells' choice. Usually Anna would have preferred to go to her home – you could pick up so much about a person from their personal surroundings. Then again, maybe there was something she could deduce from the fact that Dr Wells preferred her office.

'Dr Wells? Anna Cole, we spoke on the phone?'

'Yes, yes, I know, please sit down.'

She stood behind a tidy desk, clear apart from a computer, a pot of pens and a mobile phone. The room, by comparison to the desk, was full of clutter and piles of books, manuscripts and paperwork fought for space on shelves and even the floor.

Anna took the seat indicated, placed her bag on the floor and crossed her legs. A poster of a Celtic dragon on the far wall caught Anna's eye. 'The Welsh emblem.'

'Well it has become so yes, but the dragon symbol has roots further back. The English word 'dragon' and the Welsh 'draig' both come from the ancient Greek word 'drakon', which means 'large serpent'.

'To us, the Welsh dragon seems quite typical in its dragon-like appearance with four legs and wings, but in many cultures, what we call dragons were essentially large serpents, as found in iconography from ancient Mesopotamia, Greece and Egypt.'

'So, we stole our national identity,' Anna said smiling.

'Well, we were all a land of foreigners at one point. There aren't many countries not divided by its languages, politics, culture and even geography. Northern Ireland isn't the only region plagued by history.'

'True but Belfast seems to be healing its old wounds or at least making a brave attempt.'

'I assume you are here to speak about my daughter not have discourse on political emblems and sectarianism.'

'Sorry, excuse me. I know this is a difficult time for you and your family but I need to run through some questions.'

'I understand the procedure,' she sounded irritated. 'My husband worked for the force for God's sake, but I have told everything I can possibly tell you to your colleagues.' She remained standing. Her face was devoid of any make-up but that did not prevent her being an attractive woman. She must be intimating as a lecturer, Anna thought. She guessed the students wouldn't be late handing in their assignments to her.

'I can appreciate that it is troublesome to deal with us, but really it can sometimes help to run over the events again, to talk, and you never know what can be uncovered inadvertently.'

Dr Wells sat down. Defeated, it seemed, and tired. The creases around her eyes told of sleepless nights.

'What can I tell you? We were at our daughter's wedding. The band were playing, we were dancing and having fun. I can't remember the last time I saw Esme. It was possibly during the first dance, maybe later on. I don't know. She was floating around talking to guests, as we were.'

'One of the wedding guests said he saw Esme speaking to Rory, the groom. He thought they were having a heated exchange at 9.15 p.m. or there about. Any idea what that was about?'

'Who knows? They could have been talking about the wedding reception. Esme wanted to invite a crowd of her friends to the after party and Rory was perhaps reluctant to allow a bunch of teenagers to join his wedding reception. Perhaps Lara will know.'

It sounded reasonable enough but Anna had been in her job too long to accept reasonable.

'Did Esme have a boyfriend? Anyone special she talked about?'

'No, we have already said all of this. Like most teenage girls, she went from one boy to another – most of them simply friendships. There has never been anyone serious.'

'Could there have been someone you didn't know about?'

'No, Esme was an open book, especially to Lara. They are very close. Were.' She looked down at her hands. Anna noticed the thin silver wedding band, the pale unpainted nails.

'We'll need a list of her friends. Obviously, we will be going through her social media sites to see if there is anything worth following up there,' Anna paused looking at her notebook. 'We're trying to work out if, and why, she had gone with the attacker, apparently voluntarily. It is unlikely, given the setting, that he dragged her off. We are working on the assumption that it could have been someone she knew.'

'We have given your people the guest list. It was a big wedding – Rory's choice as he has so many friends and business associates. There were one hundred and twenty guests, but most were family, close friends and a few colleagues. I can't imagine someone we know having done this.'

'Yes, I realise that it is difficult to take in, but we have to explore every avenue.'

Dr Wells placed her hands over her eyes. She looked exhausted and worn out.

Anna felt for her. This was the one aspect of her job she didn't like, dealing with grieving families always felt intrusive.

'I'm surprised you are here – at work. Surely you should take some time out. It's only been two weeks.'

'I'm quite aware of how long it has been. It's easier being here. Here I have to face my own pain, no one else's.'

'Well take care. If you need to talk or you think of anything else at all give me a call. You have my number.'

As Anna stood to leave the office a tall, grey haired man opened the door. Anna noted he hadn't knocked.

'Sorry I didn't know you were with someone,' he said.

'It's ok Fintan, Detective Inspector Cole was about to leave.' Anna saw something flash across her face. Almost like she was alerting him.

Anna nodded hello to him, 'Well, I'll leave you to your work. Goodbye then and please, if we can do anything, call me or the Family Liaison Officer.'

* * *

When Anna returned to the station she sensed a heightened atmosphere. An almost tangible electric current in the air – something had happened. Everyone was busy, voices chattering into phones, people moving around with purpose.

'Did you hear?' asked Warwick, an acned-faced officer with a thatch of sand coloured hair.

'No, what's happened?'

'Shooting on the Ormeau Road. Looks like it was dissidents. One man dead at the scene, another injured.'

'In broad day light?'

'Yep, the shooter was on a motor cycle. Pulled up alongside the car at the traffic lights and let them have it at point-blank range.'

'Welcome to Belfast,' said Holly.

Chapter 9

Declan manoeuvred himself across the parquet floor into the living room at the front of their house. Someone, probably Izzy, had closed the tweed curtains halfway across the bay window making the room look gloomy. He looked out towards house opposite. One of the roof tiles had slipped. He made a mental note to mention it to Dessie next time they were talking. It was the neighbourly thing to do. That was the type of street he lived in, one where people kept themselves to themselves, but passed the time of day occasionally and looked out for anything suspicious should anyone be away on holiday. Good neighbours. The same neighbours who, now, found it hard to look him in the eye least they would catch the ominous cloud of sorrow that had settled on him.

Thomas King sat on the edge of the sofa, as if he feared the old velvet settee wouldn't take his full weight. King's sidekick, Manus Magee was standing by the blackened cast iron fireplace, flicking through his notepad. The room was once the heart of their home, where the girls did homework and wrote stories about fairies and unicorns at the old mahogany writing desk. But now it looked shabby and past its best. The paintings, by Basil Blackshaw and Gerard Dillon, which they had saved up for and bought in Ross' Auction Rooms, still stood the test of time. They had been delighted with themselves; taking great pleasure in bidding against others to claim the paintings they'd set their minds on. The artwork and the shelves of books lining the far wall were the room's only adornments.

Manus shifted from one foot to the other, waiting for Declan to position his chair.

'So, get on with it then,' Declan said. He was in no mood to make small talk but he almost felt sorry for them. How many times had he been the one asking the questions, trying to piece together the unfixable? He could remember King as a nipper in uniform, back when he was still working. Before.

'When did you last see Esme?'

'Sometime around eleven. She had come over to ask for money to buy a drink. I told her to go easy. I know she was only seventeen but I didn't mind her having the odd drink. As it was a family occasion, I didn't want her getting tipsy.'

'How did she seem?' King asked settling back into the sofa.

'Her usual self. Nothing untoward.'

'No rows with boyfriends or anything like that?'

'No. Nothing I wouldn't have known about anyway. What do teenage girls tell their fathers?'

'Sorry to be going over old ground, but you know how these things go. The DI wants us to double-check everything. How had she been of late? Any problems at school? Any history of trouble at all?'

'Fine, all fine. Look where's this going Thomas? If I had anything at all you know I'd have told youse. This is only time wasting.' Declan sighed. He was fed up with protocol, procedure and people ticking boxes. He wanted manpower on the streets, questions being asked of those who might know something. The days were slipping passed too fast.

'Declan, you know we have to go through the process. We have to build up a picture of Esme's life, her friends, who she knocked about with. Looking inwards, before looking out.' He was a big bulk of a man, the type who played rugby and ran 10k for a warm up.

Declan nodded. 'I know how it goes Thomas, but I can't help thinking we should be doing more than nit picking through her life when there is nothing to be found. Whoever did this could have been an opportunist. They may not have been at the wedding. For God's sake, it could be anyone out there,' he flicked his hand in a gesture towards the street.

Magee walked over and sat on the arm of the sofa. 'What about your own history? Anyone with a grudge? We know there was some aggro over the conviction of the men who blew your car up.'

'Well unless they are complaining about getting off on a technicality caused by the PSNI's own DCI Brogan I can't see why they'd come after me or harm my daughter.'

'Worth mentioning, that's all. We need to check it all out.' Magee said.

'It was a bad show what went down with Brogan.'

'You don't say,' Declan could barely contain his contempt. The Police Ombudsman had ruled there was a failure in passing on vital information preceding the blast and as a result the subsequent investigation tried to cover this up. Two detective superintendents and two detective sergeants, from the PSNI unit had been disciplined, with Brogan ultimately losing his job. Delays in assessing information obtained at the time of the booby trap car bomb had led to a loss of momentum. An informant had passed on information telling of the likelihood of an attack on Declan but Brogan had not acted on the information, claiming he thought a forensic psychologist was an unlikely target. Those who were considered the likely perpetrators had walked free.

'Hard to stomach the thought of it, I know, but we have to look at all avenues Declan.

'When we did the search of Esme's bedroom, a considerable sum of cash was found hidden in a jewellery box stashed at the back of her wardrobe. Would you know how she came by this money?' Magee asked.

'Maybe she saved it up,' Declan offered. 'How much was it?'

Manus checked out his notepad before asking, 'We aren't at liberty to say at the minute, but it was more than you would expect a teenager to have. Did she have a part-time job?'

'No. She helped out around the house for pocket money. She'd exams coming up.'

King shuffled in his seat, 'There is one other thing we need to ask you about. Your new son-in-law Rory? He's in property management, isn't that right?'

'Yes, he has his own company. Buys old houses and business premises, guts them before selling them on. I think he has a few rentals as well.'

King pulled at his earlobe, which indicated to Declan that he was uncomfortable, before saying 'We have some information that he may be involved in some dodgy dealings. We aren't at liberty to say what's involved as we're still looking into it.'

'I don't know where this is going, or what it has to do with Esme's murder. I don't exactly see eye-to-eye with Rory but he's got nothing to do with what has happened to Esme.' Declan could feel his blood pressure rise.

'Bear with me, I was about to get to that. What was his relationship with Esme like? Were they particularly close?'

'Not especially. They got on well, like you would expect.'

'It seems they were more than friendly. Esme's phone records show she received more than one hundred texts and calls from him in the run up to the wedding day. Wouldn't that seem a bit excessive to you?'

Declan flinched. 'I don't know what you are insinuating but I can tell you, categorically, that Esme was not in a relationship with Rory.' The accusation made him draw breath, but he wasn't going to let them see his doubt. Could Esme and Rory have had a relationship? How could have missed something like that?

Manus Magee stood up, 'One more question Declan, before we go. How well did you know your daughter?'

'For fuck's sake, this line of inquiry will lead nowhere. Now if you have nothing worthwhile to add, get the hell out of my house.'

Chapter 10

Anna kicked off her shoes beneath the desk and put her head back on the chair. She closed her eyes and let the day flow round her head. The latest shooting had been close to a primary school. The victim was on his way to pick up his ten-year-old son. The other man was in the passenger seat and had been shot clean through the shoulder. He wasn't talking.

McKay thought he would be 'good experience' for Anna to see a bit of 'real action.' As if they didn't have guns on the mainland. When she arrived at the scene she found skull fragments and brain mushed all over the windscreen. The ballistics team was doing their analysis and the crime scene photographer was doing her bit.

She had seen her fair share of splattered bodies. The Cardiff drug gangs had fought a turf war a couple of years back. A fourteen-year-old boy had been intimidated into putting a bullet through the back of the skull of one of the gang leaders. Anna had been one of the first officers on the scene. The boy had stayed, frozen stock still in either fear or horror. Still holding the gun, looking at it like he hadn't expected the bullets to be real.

There had been other murders that had got under her skin. The death of a heavily pregnant girl, beaten to a pulp by her boyfriend. They arrived at the scene to find the baby had been born while her mother lay unconscious. It had slid into the cold February morning with the cord wrapped round its neck, blue and rigid. The solicitor who had been embezzling his clients' money and butchered his wife and two children in desperation, rather than let them know that he was up to his neck in fraud and debt.

It was all part of the job.

Belfast was proving to be a different sort of challenge. She hadn't expected to find the sectarianism to be so obvious. Whole geographical areas were marked out as being unionist or nationalist. Union flags, hoisted up on telegraph poles, pavements painted red, white and blue, or murals depicting Gerry Adams as a legend. They even claimed allegiance with Gaza and Israel according to their nationalist or unionist persuasion. *Viva Palestine* was chalked out in huge letters on the Belfast hills, to be seen from all angles within a five-mile radius. Pick your side it all seemed to say. Like wild animals pissing on territory to mark it as their own.

Even the station, with its full-on security, felt alien to her. When she had mentioned it to Thomas, he had laughed and said she should have seen it before The Good Friday Agreement: twenty feet high concrete and metal walls, wrapped in razor wire, along with fortress observation towers to protect them from 'Barrack Busters' – IRA mortars.

Then there were the beautiful, more affluent areas. Leafy and suburban, genteel and orderly. It was as if the troubles never affected these areas or the professional people living there in their own little bubble of money and education.

* * *

She had spent the afternoon trawling through interview transcripts taken from the wedding guests, looking for something to latch on to. When she drew a blank she joined Thomas, who was working on the social media stuff. She plotted time lines of when people could recall seeing Esme. The last definite sighting had been her heated exchange with Rory at approximately 9.10 p.m.

'Anything of interest turn up?' Anna asked looking at his computer screen.

'I'm sorting through Esme's social media accounts – so far it's the usual selfies, gaggles of girls pouting for the camera. More make up on some of them than a tranny.'

He clicked through the Facebook feed. A world of teenage narcissism scrolled in front of Anna's eyes.

'Have a look at this one,' Thomas clicked on a photograph of Esme and made it bigger.

In it, Esme was dressed in a waitress outfit – a short, black, A-line dress, with a white ruffled apron over the top. She hadn't uploaded the photo herself but was tagged in it by another girl – Carly Moss.

'Where was the photo taken?'

'Hang on I can get IT to geo track it.' Thomas clicked on a few links and opened a file. 'According to this it's down at the docks. There are a lot of swanky apartments down there.'

'The family said Esme didn't have a part-time job. They'd said they wanted her to concentrate on her exams and take on summer work. If she was waitressing it would explain the wad of cash hidden in her bedroom. We'd better pay this Carly Moss a visit, see what she has to say.'

* * *

Carly Moss' home was in an estate, set high, back against the rugged hills of east Belfast. Anna got out of the car and noticed that the air held a promise of rain. Belfast wasn't so unlike Cardiff on the weather front. Damp and cold was standard for this time of year in both cities. Thomas slammed his car door. 'Look there's Samson and Goliath,' he said indicating with a nod of his head in the direction of the vast yellow cranes standing guard in the distance near the harbour. Their vantage point for seeing across the city was marred by the grey weather. Cloud hung low over the horizon. The faint outline of Parliament buildings sitting on the hill at Stormont was still visible. 'You know these hills surrounding Belfast were believed to be the inspiration for Gulliver's Travels,' Thomas said as they made their way up to the white uPVC front door.

'Is that so?' asked Anna. She appreciated Thomas's attempts of educating her about her new home. He had taken on the role of tour guide cum house mother.

The estate was a warren of grey brick semi-detached houses, each with a small rectangle of garden fronting them. Number 77 was rougher than the others. The front gate was hanging off and a child's rusted bicycle lay neglected on the scabby patch of grass.

Thomas knocked on the door with his gloved fist. The door opened and a woman probably in her thirties stood back. 'Yes, what do you want?'

'We were hoping to speak to Carly. We're from the police. Is she at home?' Anna asked.

'What's she supposed to have done?' They could hear a TV from the living room. The theme tune of some daytime show jangling in the background.

'She hasn't done anything. Mrs Moss I take it?'

The woman nodded.

'It's to do with Esme Wells. I believe they were friends. Could we have a word with Carly?'

'She's not eighteen yet. You can't be coming here, questioning an underage girl.'

'We aren't questioning Carly, as such, we only want to have a conversation with her.'

'It's all right Ma, let them in.' A tall girl wearing a navy school uniform had walked into the narrow hallway. Her willowy frame looked out of place in the cramped confines of the house.

The mother reluctantly held the door opened for them.

The living room was impeccably tidy. Mrs Moss turned off the large television that dominated the wall above the fireplace.

'Youse better sit down,' the mother said.

The girl, Carly, sat opposite them, her legs all awkward angles like a new born deer. 'What's this all about?' she asked.

'DI Cole wants to ask you a few questions about your friendship with Esme.'

'We weren't real friends or anything. I know her from Facebook.'

'Ok, but you did know her, didn't you?' Anna asked.

The girl nodded. 'I'd see her about.'

'How did you connect on Facebook with her?'

'Can't remember. Sure, everyone is connected on Facebook. The whole of Belfast is my friend on it.'

'Did you ever see her out at parties, clubs or anything like that?'

'We've been at the same pre's'

Anna looked puzzled, 'Pre's – drinks parties?'

'You know pre-loading – when you go to someone's house and have a few drinks before going out. It's cheaper to drink a carry out than buy in a club.'

'What about work. Do you have a part-time job, Carly?'

'Not really. I do the odd shift at the newsagents down the road when they are stuck.'

'She's got exams coming up so she's studying,' the mother interjected. 'She's hoping to go to Queen's to do nursing and make something of herself.'

'So, you've never waitressed, have you?' Anna asked.

Carly swallowed and glanced quickly at her mother. 'No. Like I said I do the odd shift at the shop.'

'You had a photograph on Facebook of you and Esme in waitressing uniforms. Do you know the picture I'm talking about?'

She nodded, glancing at the mother again. 'Oh that, yeah I did a one of job for Rory Finnegan.'

'Do you know the date of this job?' Anna asked.

'Sometime in the summer I think. Yeah it was August.' She put her hand to her hair, twisting a few strands as she spoke.

'And where was the event?'

'I'm not sure, some swanky apartment down at the docks.'

'Rory Finnegan, did Esme talk about him?' Anna asked.

'Not really like, we were getting on with the job.'

'Did you ever see him interact Esme? How did they get on?'

Carly looked away. Just a quick glance downwards, enough of a hesitation to make Anna wonder.

'She had a thing for him. I don't know if they were together or anything, but she definitely fancied him.'

Anna looked over to Thomas. 'Did she tell you that she was in to him?' he asked.

'Not exactly, just you sort of pick up the vibe, you know what I mean? It was all Rory this and Rory that.'

'Surely you remember the address?' Thomas asked.

'I think it was the Diamond apartments – in the Titanic Quarter. But don't tell Rory Finnegan I said that.'

'Ok, well that will be all for now.' Anna said standing up. 'If you can think of anything that might help us, give me a call, but you've been very helpful, thank you.' Anna passing her card to Carly.

* * *

'What did you make of that?' Thomas asked back in the car as they swung out onto the dual carriageway at Knocknagoney.

'Esme had the hots for Finnegan. But was it reciprocated?'

Anna was psyched up. 'She seemed like a good kid, but she's scared. Finnegan knew how to manipulate her and Esme too, most likely.'

Thomas turned the window wipers on against the sudden down pour. 'She's hiding something that's for sure. Let her sweat for a day or so and she might suddenly remember something of interest about the one-off waitressing job when her mother isn't around.'

As they drove out of the estate onto the carriageway her phone buzzed out a vibrating tune.

'Anna Cole.'

'DI Cole, it's Declan Wells here. I'm Esme's father – the murdered girl?'

'Yes, Mr Wells, I know who you are. What can I do for you?'

Chapter 11

Declan didn't know what to expect from this meeting, but he was sure it was the right way to go. Anna could approach the case with experience and open eyes not clouded by sectarian judgment. All he had to do was to persuade her to keep an eye on McKay and not let him direct the case in a direction it didn't need to go.

They had agreed to meet in the Refinery, a new pub that had popped up on the lower Lisburn Road. Declan knew it had good access for his chair.

He watched her walk past the window and come in through the double doors. It took a second for her eyes to rest on him, but when they did, she smiled a slow, easy smile and strode over to him. She had that young student look going on, all rough casualness as if she didn't want to be seen to be a grown up. He'd seen her at the funeral, but hadn't really taken her under his notice. Now he could see she was a good-looking woman. Small in stature but with an attitude that came from carrying a gun and knowing how to use it, that said don't mess with me.

'Dr Wells,' she said as she put out her hand to shake his.

'Please, call me Declan. Thanks for agreeing to meet me.' He noted her husky, slightly melodic Welsh accent.

'I'm intrigued Declan. But first of all, get me a drink; I'm not on duty. A white wine please.'

He liked that, how she expected him to get the drinks in, how she didn't automatically feel she had to take care of him because he was in the bloody chair.

'Sure. I'll be right back.'

When Declan returned with the waiter carrying their drinks, Anna began.

'Esme was seventeen. Still at school, no known boyfriend, no record and no reason to end up murdered in a ditch at her sister's wedding.'

'Correct,' Declan sipped at his cider.

'And in your earlier call to me, you implied you wanted me to keep an eye on Richard McKay while I am working on this case?'

'Correct again.'

'So why do you think Richard McKay needs watching? And why should I second guess my superior and report back to you?' she leaned back on the chair as if assessing him.

'McKay is barking up the wrong tree, he sent King and Magee round asking all sorts of questions. McKay has Esme marked down as a teenage tearaway. He is implicating my son-in-law, trying to say they were having some sort of affair. It's all bullshit.' His couldn't help his face contort in disgust. The idea of Rory touching Esme made him so angry he wanted to rip someone apart. If there was any truth in it, then … He couldn't go there, not yet.

'According to you it's bullshit. What if he's right?'

'If you examine the case and come to the same conclusion then fire away and pull Rory in for questioning. Besides McKay will be all over the shooting on the Ormeau Road. He is under pressure to keep the assholes up at Stormont all sitting round the same table. If the dissidents start playing up, the shit ricochets all over the place. McKay has been part of the transformation of the PSNI and he has too much to lose by not looking after his own interests. There is talk of a new wave of trouble starting up. New weapons on the street and new power struggles on both sides. Turf wars mean body bags and no one wants to see the return to the old days. McKay will be too occupied with licking the balls of ministers and keeping the peace on the street to properly investigate Esme's murder. I don't trust his methods and I don't trust his motives. Implicating Rory and suggesting they had a thing together is a convenient move on McKay's part,' he stopped to take a sip of his drink. He didn't want to admit to Anna that he had misgivings about his son-in-law. Misgivings that had caused him many an argument with Izzy.

'But I don't think you'll be so quick to jump to the same conclusion. Esme isn't who they think she is.'

'So, tell me who is she?'

Declan was taken aback. He thought of Magee's question. How could he describe Esme? That girl, like all teenagers, was an enigma. Surely no father could claim to really know his teenage daughter?

'She is, was, my daughter.'

He paused looking into his glass trying to find the words to convey the ball of light and energy that he knew Esme to be as a child. They may have grown apart in recent years. But that was to be expected, surely all parents experienced that rebellion, that pulling away. It was only natural, he kept telling himself.

'She was a great girl. Beautiful, smart. I know I can't bring her back, but the least I can do is to see that whoever did this is behind bars. You are all treating me like I shouldn't have a say in how this investigation is carried out. But don't you see, I can bring my expertise to this? Let me work with you. Let me find who did this to my daughter.'

She looked straight at him. 'Apart from a conflict of interest and a million regulations barring you from investigating your daughter's murder, I am sure you can see that your professional involvement is not productive.'

'I know the rules DC Cole. The PSNI may have pensioned me off and made me redundant, but I have made it my life's work to read and understand murder, to work out the patterns and see where it takes us.'

'But you are still involved in the field of forensic psychology?'

'After this,' he gestured towards his chair, 'I moved into academia. I'm a guest lecturer at Queen's, they provide teaching hours when it suits me, and I research criminal behaviour, the causes and effects. So yes, I'm still involved.'

'What makes you so sure there will be a pattern?'

'There is always a pattern emerging from a tumble of chaos if you know how to look at it. Have you ever heard of complexity theory?'

She shook her head, the light catching the soft curve of her cheek.

'It is the study of how complicated patterns can result from simple behaviours of individuals within a system. Chaos is the study of how simple patterns can be generated from complicated underlying behaviour. Chaos theory is really about finding the underlying patterns in apparently random data.

'It is unfortunate that science has chosen the word chaos to describe this form of order, because the word chaos is at odds with common usage, which suggests complete disorder. So, you see, science defines chaos as a form of order that lacks predictability.'

'The killer wasn't chaotic, he was methodical, precise and kept the scene clean. That doesn't help your little chaos and pattern theory.'

'From where you are sitting it looks clean and methodical, but from my viewpoint I am in a storm of chaos. Can you imagine how it feels to lose a child? To have them harmed in this way?'

Anna sipped her wine.

'Why don't I tell you what I know about the killer?' Declan asked, looking up from his glass, seemingly changing tack.

'All right, go ahead.'

'As I told Thomas King, the killing has all the hallmarks of someone who may well do so again.'

'Why?'

'There is a marked prevalence of strangulation in relation to serial killers. In one of my research papers on serial murderers, I suggested that ligature strangulation represents the killer's animated rage with a specific concentration on the victim.'

He paused to make sure she was taking this in and not merely humouring him as a bereaved father.

'That is not to say that the absence of ligature underestimates the rage. In fact, there's also an association of strangulation in serial killings with the need of psychopathic sexual sadists to have greater intimacy with the victim than a weapon would give. She may have been hit on the head initially to stun her, but he wanted that close proximity of having his hands on her when she actually died.'

'Go on,' Anna said.

'Esme was taken and murdered close to the scene of a family wedding. The killer was risking immediate exposure. There was no sexual assault, so we can assume he was getting off on the risk of being found out. He liked the immediacy and risk factor.'

'Being in plain sight?'

'Exactly. He wanted to rub our noses in it and it hasn't escaped me that he may well have known Esme was my daughter and that there were PSNI people at the wedding.'

'You think there is some sort of revenge connection?'

'Not exactly. Nothing as direct as that but we could be dealing with someone who wants to make a point, who wants to prove himself.'

'Esme may have willingly accompanied her killer to the scene of her murder. Do you think she knew him?' Anna asked.

'It's possible, but we can't rule out that she met him on the night and voluntarily went with him.'

'So, someone her age possibly?'

He shook his head, 'No, I can't make that leap yet.'

'You said he may have done this before and may strike again. Why?'

'There was planning involved. I'm sure you already know the CCTV was tampered with.'

'We've no evidence it was deliberately not working. The fault had been reported the previous week so it may be coincidence. We are trawling through staff lists and seeing who had access to the cameras.'

He paused, 'I know that the scene was clean; he left no footprints. No fabric snagged on the branches. That tells us he knows what he is doing. That he has knowledge acquired either through his diligent study or even someone with police knowledge.'

Anna swallowed more wine. 'Declan, you need to go home. Be with your wife. Leave this to us.'

He put his hand through his hair, desperation etched on his face. 'I can't leave it. Don't you see how hard this is for me?'

'Of course. It must be difficult to process and handle such a death.'

'It's bad enough to lose my daughter like this. Can't you see I have insight, some understanding of what is going on, yet I'm being kept out of the inner circle. It's fucking killing me! I can't sit on the side-lines waiting for your lot to mess up.'

'Who says we'll mess up?'

Declan hesitated before he replied, 'We both know it happens all the time. Let me in. That all I'm asking. Please?'

Chapter 12

Anna arrived at the City Hall Belfast council office and looked up at the building's pale Portland stone exterior, noticing its almost fairy-tale design in its grandeur, with towers at each of its four corners and a huge copper dome tarnished to a Tiffany blue colour in the centre. The Victorian buildings throughout the city centre echoed the city hall and also shared in the distinctive blue green-topped domes.

The phone call had taken Anna by surprise. The Lord Mayor's secretary wished to set up an appointment for Anna to meet the Mayor, Aidan Anderson. She flashed her identification to the security guard in the green painted hut and was directed to the office of the Lord Mayor.

Anna made her way into the grand entrance which was dominated by a huge red-carpeted staircase. Marble statues stood placed around the hall and stained-glass windows cast colourful pools of light on the black and white tiled floor.

'DI Cole, an honour to meet you at last. I've heard a lot about you,' the Mayor said, taking her hand.

Anderson was taller than Anna expected. Younger than he appeared in photographs. Anna guessed he was around her age – early thirties. He had an athletic build, lean and sculpted. He was known for his park run campaigns – trying to encourage local people to take part in weekend runs through the city's parks. He logged his running times on Twitter and posted selfies with kids and mums and dads out to get fit and take in the fresh air. He styled himself as a man of the people, but with a contradictory air of statesman-like superiority.

'Nice to meet you,' Anna replied. She could see what all the fuss was. He was good looking – dark hair cut close to his head and a rough covering of stubble as if he was in the throes of deciding to grow beard but hadn't fully committed. He wore a navy suit with a fine blue pinstripe that accentuated his broad shoulders. The white shirt provided a crisp stark contrast to his lightly tanned skin. He put her in mind of someone who had been up-styled, had taken advice on how he was perceived and had acted on it to the final letter.

'I felt it was time to meet you. I believe you are one of the officers leading this terrible case concerning Esme Wells?'

Anna nodded. 'Yes, I am. We have a good team working on it.'

They entered his office. Anna noticed the thick piled carpet underfoot and the large mahogany desk at the centre of the room. Photographs of Anderson meeting British and US dignitaries were displayed on a low mantle table. This was a man who enjoyed the trappings of his office and position.

Anna sat in the chair he pulled out for her. 'I believe you are a good friend and business associate of Rory Finnegan?'

'Yes indeed, Rory and I have been friends for years. I trust you will find whoever did this to his sister-in-law.' His slate grey eyes full of concern, held Anna's for a few seconds too long, making her think he was a skilled manipulator. His every gesture felt contrived and polished.

'We do things a little differently over here. This type of murder doesn't belong on our streets,' he said patronizingly.

Anna almost smirked at his comment. His dubious republican past was squared off in his mind as being rightful violence for the end result. She could imagine him holding court in some American conference talking of his childhood, fully blighted by British soldiers on the streets of his homeland and British occupation.

She noted the framed photographs on his desk, an attractive young woman and a small child. 'Your family?' she asked, nodding towards the photographs.

'Yes, my wife Joanne and our daughter Edie. When I look at them I can't imagine what the Wells family are going through. I wouldn't want something so evil to touch a hair on Edie's head. I'd do anything to protect them.' He stared intently at Anna. She felt that his words were almost a threat.

'You knew Esme, I believe?'

'Yes, a lovely girl. Full of promise. She would have had a bright future ahead of her. We need more young people like Esme to take this country forward.'

'It can't have been easy growing up during the troubles,' Anna said.

'No, there were difficult times. My own family was deeply affected.'

Anna had heard that his father had been one of the Hunger Strikers.

'I wanted a different future, a better one, but I learnt that I couldn't achieve it alone, I had to bring certain factions along with me. You can't just wake up one morning and declare everything your family and community has stood for is pigswill. I needed to give them a new narrative, to let them feel that they paved the way for me and those of my generation to take a stand and benefit from a new type of politics.

'It wasn't easy to get here.' He looked around the room, the Lord Mayoral chains sitting on display. This was his seat of power. 'But there is still much to be done.'

'It's good to see that Belfast is thriving,' Anna said, 'The interest from the film industry and the Titanic Centre has really made an impact.'

'Yes, they have been hard won successes. I was always impatient for a better Belfast. I knew what we could do if only the will was realised in practical action.'

He stood and walked over to the floor length window looking directly up Donegall Place, the main shopping street in the city centre. 'We had a problem of confidence. We needed to believe in ourselves and to visualise a different type of place.'

He turned to Anna, 'When I was a teenager, Belfast city centre was a no-go area at nighttime. We were barricaded into our homes by fear, British soldiers on foot patrol on our streets, a ring of steel around the city centre, bags searched every time you went into a shop. All of that is in recent memory.' He leaned in close to Anna,

'So, you see, we can't allow the likes of this murderer to stalk our young people. They deserve better.'

A diminutive secretary interrupted them with a reminder that he had another meeting to attend.

'Apologies for such a short meeting, but it was a chance to touch base,' he said, walking Anna to his office door. She left feeling he had been assessing her. Deciding whether or not she was up to the job. She was still unsure of what to make of him. He was full of charm but with enough edge to make you respect his power. The women on the street loved him, teenagers and grannies too. He was known for his entertaining tweets and was active on social media, making him a more accessible politician for young people.

But there was something about Aidan Anderson that bothered Anna. His face was all over Belfast promoting a peaceful and prosperous city. Thomas had said he was thick with Finnegan. They had a history of dealings and although nothing had ever stuck, talk had it that Finnegan kept Anderson in his back pocket. Sweeteners were assumed to have been passed on to ensure planning permission was granted when required for Finnegan's property deals.

He had been a guest at the wedding, but had left early to deal with official city hall business. His alibi was tight – witnesses said he left the wedding venue at 8.00 p.m. and he was clocked by CCTV arriving at the City Hall offices at 8.25 p.m., where he was in meetings until late that night.

Every time she tried to get an angle on Rory Finnegan's relationship with Esme, Aidan Anderson came up. Esme had applied to do work experience at the council offices and Finnegan had set it up via Anderson. There was a link but not enough to make anything of at this stage.

* * *

Anna left the Lord Mayor's office and called Thomas to pick her up. He wanted to show her something, he had said that morning and it wouldn't be far from the city hall.

The car came to a stop at the dockside. The dark, cold water stretched out before them.

'So, this is where the Titanic was built?' she said by way of starting up the conversation.

'Yep, it only took us a hundred years to be able to cash in on that particular disaster. Come to Belfast to see our peace line, our bigoted murals and the dock that built the biggest shipping disaster ever.' He mimicked in a good impersonation of Aidan Anderson's voice.

'What do you make of Anderson?' she asked.

'Jumped up wee shite from Beechmount. Got himself an education at Queen's and decided he was going to exchange his petrol bombs for votes and back-handers.'

'He seems to be popular on the street.'

'Yeah, everyone wants to hear that Belfast is booming in the economic sense. The people are fed up with the rhetoric of old, so Anderson represents a new breed of politician for these parts. He's selling them success, a peaceful prosperous Northern Ireland.'

The wind cut through them when they got out of the car. 'Where are we going? asked Anna.

'Over there,' King pointed towards a huge disused red brick building. 'We are going to have a look around to see Finnegan's most recent purchase and I'll bet Anderson is in on a cut.'

Anna looked up at the three-storey sandstone and red brick office block. There was nothing special about it. It stood on Queens Road in the heart of the Belfast docks, in the recently developed Titanic quarter.

King pushed through the door at the back of the block. It gave way. 'An old acquaintance is on Finnegan's security, he accidently left this open for us.'

Anna followed him through the metal door.

'This is where all the office work and drawing went on for Harland and Wolff shipyard. My grandfather, and his father worked here. The only qualification you needed to get in was Protestant birth. Right here was the control centre for the shipping empire.'

Anna looked around the old building. It was dilapidated and run down. The premises had obviously been vacated a long time ago, but the grandeur and craftsmanship of the panelling, the sashed windows and wooden parquet flooring spoke of a time long gone; of a time when the grand liner ships were dreamt up, and the walls echoed what they produced.

There was something tragic about its faded beauty. Anna could imagine sitting right in this spot for hours, painting the intricate stain glass designed windows, examining the wooden coving and tracing a soft lead pencil over a page to copy the swirl and glean of the banisters. She would love to lose herself in the process, to let the colours, the textures of the paint and contrast of light and dark to soothe her.

'Wait till you see the main drawing rooms,' King said. They made their way up the wide staircase and reached the main drawing offices. King pulled back the heavy double doors. Anna gasped as she walked into the wide ballroom like space. The domed ceiling was an ornate display of stained glass, creating a kaleidoscope of colour against the late afternoon sky.

'Finnegan reckons he had netted himself a little winner by stepping in and buying this building for a knock down price of a couple of million. Trouble was, planning was a bugger. No one was allowed to damage the architectural heritage, but low and behold suddenly they have found a way round it. Finnegan plans to develop the rest of the building as a hotel, five star all the way, with the assurance that this floor is maintained as city council property to be hired out for weddings, events and such. Revenue on tap.'

Anna considered what he told her. 'But how could he afford to buy the building in the first place?'

'A little bit of jiggery pokery. The building and the surrounding site were put up for auction at a reserved price of two million. No one wants to touch it with all the red tape regulations around a listed building. Finnegan is told on the quiet that should he raise the money; the red tape can be ticker taped away.'

'So, he gets investors on board knowing that they can't lose.'

'Exactly but not only that, once Finnegan buys the place, he can sell the top floor to the City Council to keep as a heritage site of interest. And none other than Anderson presides over the whole shebang.' Anna's phone rang echoing around the huge empty room.

'DI Cole.'

'There's a young lady here, Carly Moss asking to speak to you. She says it's in connection with Esme Wells.'

'Keep her there. I'm on my way.'

Chapter 13

The upstairs of the house was like a foreign country to Declan. A place he had once been and felt he knew, but no longer visited. Since the bomb, he had been confined to the downstairs of the house. The extension, purpose built with his own bedroom, especially wide doors and a wet room, so that he could sit while showering, had made going upstairs unnecessary. Slowly he had come to think of the first and second stories of the house as being the girls' domain. Izzy had chosen to remain in their master bedroom. That had been another nail in the coffin of their marriage.

All was quiet. Izzy was out at her sister's and he didn't expect Lara to call round until the evening. This was his opportunity to take some time in Esme's room. He wanted to conjure her up, to feel her presence and to find a release for the coldness that had gripped his chest for the past four weeks. He was exhausted, wrung out and the old pains were back. Usually he was resigned to his injuries. He lived with them the way someone lives with an annoying, moaning aged relative. Now they were flaring up like flames of hate. Angering him and jeering at his inability to get up and walk, to run, to be active and do something about Esme's death.

He had long ago accepted that the time of self-fulfillment and ambition was gone. Choice, action and movement were limited for him. In the early months after the bomb, he would lie awake wondering what would happen if an intruder broke into their house. He was denied the ability to physically protect his daughters. He had to settle for financial security for them. That was his hope, to ensure a good education, and if he were to die, leave enough to help them build a life.

Now as he manoeuvred upstairs, slowly and painfully dragging himself on his front, his arms taking the strain, he wondered why he had allowed so much of his life to slip away from him. The bomb had taken more than his legs.

The sweat broke on him. The effort to pull himself up, stair by stair, was huge. His arms were strong from using the chair but now he was using muscles in a different way, and he felt every sinew ripple with the strain, feeling old and helpless. He thought about how his lead doctor, a man called Solomon, had tried to push the use of prosthetic legs on him, and how he had preferred the truthfulness of being confined to the chair.

'Think of walking your daughters up the aisle,' had been the refrain, a painful echo now. In the end, it came down to some things weren't meant to be, and that the damage went much deeper than his flesh.

At the first landing turn, he paused, lay back on the gold coloured carpet and closed his eyes. Light from the tall, stain-glassed window on the landing poured down on him. He could feel his pulse thumping and his chest heaved. He hoisted himself up thinking, knowing, that he had only a short flight of four stairs left to crawl until he reached Esme's room on the right. The door was closed and he reached up with a final heave of effort and pushed it open.

The room was dark. The curtains, a pale pink and green check, were closed. Light crept in under the drapes, illuminating the double bed pushed against the far wall, the desk under the window and the tall white wardrobes. The scene reminded Declan of all the mornings he had popped his head round the door when she was little, cajoling her to wake up, and get herself ready for school. Those days seemed so fleeting. He hadn't grasped how quickly children grew up, instead, looking ahead, not realising, one day, he would look back and wonder what was the hurry.

He leant against the wall to catch his breath and looked around. The room had been thoroughly searched. Declan hadn't been privy to what they had found of interest, except for the cash, but he knew they would have been looking for drugs and anything which would implicate Esme in her own death.

The floor was scattered with the detritus of her life. He knew the police wouldn't have messed up the room, this was all Esme's doing, the normal rushed about mess she would have left. The chest of drawers stood detonated with the drawers half open, clothes spewing out. A pair of silver high-heeled sandals lay casually at the wardrobe door as if she had kicked them off moments earlier. A rolled-up ball of a T-shirt lurked under the desk and he caught sight of a peach coloured thong, ridiculously grownup underwear for a young girl, he thought, but no doubt, it was what they all wore.

Her bed was roughly made, as if someone had thought to pull the duvet cover over as a last-minute gesture. Two plump pillows sat one on top of the other. A collage of photographs was stuck up on the wall above her desk. He recognised many of the faces, all teenage girls he had seen coming in and out of the house over the years. Some he knew he should know the names of, but after a while it was hard to keep track of who was who. The hairstyles, the makeup and the clothes altered them completely.

Her life was reflected in the mess around him. Her friends, all attractive girls, posing for the camera, appeared way too provocative for their age and upbringing. Their clothes, cut-off jeans, shorts, and skirts that couldn't even pretend to be much more than a slip of fabric, all said the same thing. The half-opened drawers, the clothes, probably only stepped out of and left where they fell, the makeup powder dusting everything on the dressing table, and the brown bottles of HeShi tanning lotion, both with their lids left off, all careless, reckless and chaotic. Did the room represent Esme's life? A life he knew nothing about. Did he know his daughter at all? A poster of Ed Sheeran with his shock of orange hair looked down on him. The corners peeling away from the wall, as if it too had been haphazardly stuck up. Everything about Esme seemed to be in a rush. A rush to get to school; a rush to go out; a rush to grow up.

Makeup spilled out of an oversized polka dot makeup bag across the desk where a couple of textbooks and a file of school notes were pushed aside. The entire room had most likely been photographed and catalogued by McKay and his team.

He leaned against the bed.

It was the stuffed rabbit that did it. She had carried it everywhere until the age of six. The sight of the now faded to grey cuddly toy, one ear threadbare and pathetically hanging off, unlocked his grief and left him reeling. At first the tears rolled silently and then his entire body convulsed, anger, hurt, the ache of longing, all rising up and reaching a crescendo, leaving him gulping for air. The crushing pain inside his chest was so strong he didn't think he could survive it. The agony that he had so far kept at bay, kept tamed deep inside of him, could be contained no longer. He tried to get control, to steady the heaving of his stomach and the violent shaking but there was nothing he could do but ride it out. He drew his useless deformed stumped legs close to his chest. Tears pooled onto his shirt leaving a damp stain. He brought his hands to the hallows of his eyes and wept. He allowed the tears to fall but he needed to be clear in his thoughts, to use the grief to propel him forward.

Chapter 14

Carly Moss sat at the desk, scrolling through her iPhone. Anna noted her mother was tight lipped beside her, obviously agitated, and in no mood to be in a police station.

'Mrs Moss, Carly, I believe you wanted to see me?'

'Tell her,' the mother said. The girl looked up from her iPhone. 'It's no big deal.'

'It might not seem important to you, but if you can tell us anything, it might help.'

'Esme and me did the odd waitressing job for her brother-in-law. It wasn't a one off, like I said before.'

'What kind of waitressing?'

'High-end parties, he called them. He had business contacts he wanted to impress so we got all done up and wore the uniform and served drinks. That's all.'

'Tell her,' the mother said again. The girl rolled her eyes.

'He told us that the parties were secret. We weren't to go telling anyone.'

The mother sighed. 'They'd other girls at the parties – prostitutes.'

'Is that right Carly?' Anna asked.

'I don't know if they were prostitutes. Most of them were from Eastern Europe or somewhere. I only spoke to one of them, a girl called Sveta.'

'Tell her how much he paid you,' Mrs Moss said.

'We got £300 a night.'

'I knew nothing of this. Something was going on if that's the kind of money he paid schoolgirls to pour champagne. I only discovered this today, I found the last of her money.'

Anna decided to change track, 'What about Esme? Were you two friends?'

'Yeah, she was nice. We didn't hang out or anything, but we got on.'

'Did she tell you anything about Rory Finnegan?'

'No, like I said before I know she fancied him. But there was one time I saw them, or I think I saw them, kissing. He had his back to me and I walked into one of the rooms in the apartment, the room where we put the coats and for a second I thought I saw him with his hands on her face, as if they'd been kissing. But I couldn't say for sure. It was just a moment. They saw me and we all went about as if nothing had happened.'

'These parties, can you tell us who attended them?'

'Businessmen mostly. I don't want to get into trouble. He made us sign confidentially forms,' she paused, 'non-disclosures, he said they were called. He said that we couldn't tell anyone who the guests were or he could sue us.'

'Carly, you aren't going to get in to trouble if you tell us what you know, but if you hold back, you have to realise, that later, you could be prosecuted for withholding information.'

The girl stared down at her hands. The phone now silenced on the table in front of her.

'There was one man I recognised.'

'Who?'

'I know him from the pictures that are everywhere.'

'I'm listening, Carly.'

'Yer man, Aidan Anderson.'

'The Lord Mayor?'

'Yes.'

* * *

Anna noted the strain on McKay's face as he watched her scrawl on the whiteboard:

No CCTV footage;

A strong possibility that she was too close to brother-in-law Rory Finnegan, 'Though he's accounted for at the time of the murder.'

Worked as a waitress at Finnegan's parties, 'The family was unaware that she was working for Finnegan.

No secret online contacts, but plenty of texts to and from the brother- in-law.

'There's the usual Facebook, Instagram, Snapchat and Twitter stuff that young ones go in for,' she said, tossing a sheath of papers down onto the table, looking towards Manus Magee who was tasked with trawling through the victim's social media and liaising with the software specialists.

'Not a lot to go on, and not a lot to bring before the superintendent. We are painstakingly talking to all of the guests and hotel staff, which takes time and resources that we don't have.' She directed her point to McKay, who was sitting on the edge of desk. His face darkened.

'And to make matters worse,' he replied, 'that jumped up wee shite, McGonigle, from the Irish News is saying that there's a killer on the loose and that we are out of our depths. They got wind of Cole's posting, and decided she'd been brought in from the mainland to save our arses.'

Anna felt the full weight of that opinion rest on her, as if she had somehow brought the investigation into question. She looked around the room,

'There's speculation that it was someone the victim knew. That she had friends outside of school and outside of her normal circle known to the family. King is working on that now, speaking to the school and any girls she hung around with. There wasn't a boyfriend on the go and we are still trying to work out what was going on between our victim and her brother in-law Finnegan. We need to know what went on at these parties.'

She paused and looked at the assembled room of colleagues. 'We need to think beyond the normal remit, examine previous unsolved murder cases, anything with a possible link to this case. We are day thirty-two. This isn't good enough, we have to get a break.'

'The intelligence analysts people haven't come up with anything historic, so I suggest we treat this as a one off,' McKay said, quickly slapping Anna down.

'What if he strikes again?' Holly asked.

McKay shot her a grim look. 'We have to make bloody sure that doesn't happen.'

* * *

He dressed carefully for work, black trousers, a white freshly ironed shirt, and his black fleece. He liked to take care with his appearance, always clean shaven, with a hint of fragrance, something citrus and fresh. His dark blond hair kept neat and short, the way he liked it. The girls appreciated it. Funny how his looks made people feel predisposed to like him. He hardly needed to say much at all. Look the part, be presentable, turn up on time, do the job and no one thought to look beyond his pleasant exterior.

It was one of those private party nights down in the Titanic Quarter. All flash professionals with balding heads, designer suits, silk ties and too much money. They tipped well to buy his silence, so he couldn't complain. Discretion was the buzzword. Not that he had too many people to spill their dirty little secrets to.

He liked to watch their every transaction. The girls, drugs – pills and lines of coke, drink, it was all subterfuge while deals were done on the side. At first, how they talked was strange to him – it was all contractual obligations, loss leaders, gross development value, growth strategy. They liked to talk big, throw in the odd comment about stashing away a hundred thousand here and there. Throwing down a deposit on a new build holiday home in the Algarve, buying a new Mercedes kitted out with all the toys. Over time he began to understand some of it. He began to see who was winning and who was there trying to keep the façade in place, desperate to be given a kick back from the big players. Hoping to hear about a possible deal worth risking it all on.

The champagne flowed. Bottles of Grey Goose vodka, Copeland gin and Moet and Chandon were littered around the room. The girls drinking it like it was going out of fashion. They were told to drink, to make the men feel like they were simply being entertained at a private house party. It was all an illusion, which the participants willingly and eagerly bought into. It was easier to take a girl by the hand and lead her to an upstairs bedroom if you thought she was into you and not being paid by the hour.

By midnight the sofas, deep and low, were littered with warm bodies turned into each other, faces being snogged before moving on to the bedrooms. Some of them didn't take it beyond the living room, enjoying the thrill of a pretty girl giving them attention but not wanting to jeopardise the family at home.

They were gorgeous girls too; handpicked and brought in to entertain the professional palm slickers. Most nights there were a few politicians too. He recognised the faces from the television. The Lord Mayor was one of them, though he looked a bit different in real life, younger and less cocky. He had a preference for the blonde girls; Lena and Svetlana from Lithuania were his usual choices. They would lead him to the upstairs rooms, away from the drinking and drug taking. White powder divvied up on silver trays with snorting straws provided. Strange how if you dress a room just so, expensive grey leather sofas, subdued lighting, sheepskin throws and oversized velvet cushions, it all looked so acceptable. Respectable even. Money could buy anything.

He was paid to watch the girls, make sure no one got rough with them and keep any eye on the security cameras too. Easy money and the work suited him.

Chapter 15

Lara Well's swanky, newly built house in East Belfast, sat nestled in a development of similar homes, all redbrick and neat, with mock Georgian windows. Anna rang the doorbell while King finished off a call on his mobile. It sounded like he was getting domestic grief from his former wife.

'Sorry about that,' he said to Anna as the glossy blue door opened. Up close Lara Wells looked younger than Anna expected. She had the same glacial blondeness as her mother, but her doe-like, soulful eyes, were most definitely her father's.

'Come in,' she said, opening the door wide enough to usher them into the black and white tiled hallway. A huge display of flowers sat on a highly polished console table, the scent, slightly cloying, wafted around them as they followed Lara into the kitchen. It was large, with designer, painted cupboards finished in pale grey. A ginger cat slept on floral cushions crammed into a deep window seat. The double patio doors looked out over a neat square patio area, leading to a circular lawn edged with shrubs. Lara indicated for them to take a stool at the oversized, marble topped island.

'Coffee, tea?'

'Coffee would be good please,' Anna answered shrugging off her charcoal wool coat.

'Sorry, give me your coats and I'll hang them up,' Lara took both of their coats and disappeared off into a back hallway. Thomas raised his eyebrows to Anna as if to say, would you look at this place.

Lara returned and busied herself with a coffee machine, recessed into the one of the cupboards.

'So, how have you been doing?' Anna asked.

'You know, not good. How can any of us get over this? Esme was my wee sister. I loved her to bits.'

'None of this can be easy,' said Thomas.

'I still can't take it in. It was supposed to be the happiest day of my life, and look how it has all turned out. Esme was so excited about it all. She helped me sort everything, she went with me to pick out my wedding dress, and she couldn't wait for it to happen. There were times I thought she was more excited about it all than me.'

She handed them their coffee and placed a jug of milk on the marble island worktop.

'Thanks,' said Anna, taking the cup. 'You work for Norcott Laboratories, don't you?'

'Yes, I'm a PhD research candidate part of a team looking at equestrian drugs. Rory and I are supposed to be on our honeymoon,' she sighed, 'So I'm not worrying about work at the minute. Besides, the lab can wait. Esme's more important. I keep racking my brain trying to think who could it have been. Who could have done this to her?'

'You hear things about murderers being known to the family. It makes it worse to think it could be someone we know, someone who was a guest at the wedding, even.'

'We know you spoke to our colleagues last week, but we would like to talk to you about Esme. Get a sense of who she was and what her interests were, who she hung out with, that kind of thing. The kinds of things sisters tend to tell each other. Would that be ok?' Anna asked.

She nodded, 'It's awful. The thought of someone doing that to Esme. I can't get my head around it. I keep going over it. Who would want to hurt her?'

Thomas set his coffee cup down onto a coaster, mindful of Lara's marble work surface, 'I know this can't be easy, but anything you can tell us about Esme helps. It allows us to piece together her character, work out her interests, who she might have come into contact with on a day-to-day basis. Or even online. You might think something's not relevant but honest to God you'd be surprised how many cases are cracked with a throw away remark that somehow lets us piece it all together.'

'Sure,' Lara said, taking a sip of her coffee as she sat down. 'Esme was the princess of the family. We all spoilt her. She loved her clothes and makeup. Getting her hair done, shopping with her friends, all the usual for a teenager, you know. But there was more to her. She was caring too. She would do anything for you.' She cried softly, taking a tissue from her sleeve to blow her nose.

'I'm sorry,' said Anna, 'Could she have had a boyfriend on the quiet? Someone that she wouldn't want your parents to know about?'

Lara sniffed and dropped the used tissue into a stainless-steel bin beneath the worktop.

'No. Honestly, I think Esme would have told me. She wasn't one for secrets. She was an open book with me. If something had been going on, I think I'd know.'

'What about school, was she happy at school, any issues there?' Thomas asked.

'She could have worked harder for sure.' Anna and Thomas both turned to see Rory Finnegan standing in the doorway. He was wearing an expensive looking grey pinstripe suit with a pale blue shirt, open at the neck. His hair, thick and dark, was slicked back. He looked like the type of man who spent time at the gym; caring about the impression he left on others.

'She was doing her AS levels – English, history, French. She wanted to go to Uni to study French and business. She was a smart one, our Esme.'

'This is my husband, Rory,' Lara said. He strode in, his hand outstretched to shake first Anna's and then Thomas's. His clasp was over firm and hard, as Anna knew it would be. He held her hand for a few seconds too long, and gave her a once over glance, as if assessing her. Anna was suddenly conscious of the top two buttons opened on her blouse.

'Some house you got here. Not many newly married couples get a starter home like this,' Thomas said.

'We like it. It's a good area. Great neighbours too.' Rory helped himself to coffee.

'Lucky for some. Mr Finnegan, we believe you and Esme got on well.'

'Yes, she was the wee sister I never had.'

'Rory was always spoiling her. He doted on her.' Lara offered, looking to her husband.

'Well, what can I say? We liked to treat her from time to time.'

Anna saw a look pass between them. Just a moment of something acknowledged.

'We believe Esme did a bit of waitressing for you at private parties. Can you tell us who attended these little get-togethers? We're going to need dates, locations, names of those attending.'

'Parties? No, I think you've been misled. Esme helped serve food and drinks at business meetings, maybe on a couple of occasions.'

'Well, like I said, we need details.'

'I'd need to check with the office, see the files.'

Thomas leaned across the island, 'You do that Mr Finnegan. In the meantime, we might have to get a warrant and help ourselves to your files.'

He glared at them, obviously rattled, 'I don't like your attitude. We are trying to come to terms with Esme's death.' Finnegan said, his voice low and quiet, moving towards Thomas.

Anna stood, 'We'll be going now, but if you can think of anything at all you think we should be aware of, you know where to find us.'

Lara showed them to the door. 'I'm sorry that Rory is a bit off. He's as upset as I am about Esme. You will let me know if there is anything I can do, any news …' her voice trailed off.

'Of course,' Anna replied, 'Take care. We'll be in touch.'

* * *

'Well, what did you make of Finnegan?' Thomas asked as he manoeuvred the car out of the driveway.

Anna frowned, 'Smarmy, arrogant, and a bit too sure of himself. What's the story with his business?'

'Not sure of the full picture yet, but we might be able to link Finnegan to a couple of brothels operating out of the Holylands area. His da built half of the new homes in Belfast in the eighties and nineties. He saw off plenty of racketeering, boys with guns looking for protection money, that kind of thing.

'Finnegan junior got to hold the reins as the property bubble burst, which we think may have led him to diversify. Then a few months back, a young Lithuanian girl got a bad battering from a client. Except when it came to charges, she wouldn't press, saying he was her boyfriend. The address she gave was one of the houses linked to one of Finnegan's companies. It appears he may have even brought the girls over from Lithuania. Magee is running the data through this morning. The house isn't in his name, registered under a company called Acorn Management, but Magee thinks it might be a front.'

'Finnegan was definitely at the reception when the alarm was raised. Several witnesses placed him at the bar with his best man. We don't believe he murdered Esme but what was going on between them?'

'If we can get to the bottom of that, then maybe we can get the full picture of what Esme was up to.'

'What makes you so sure she was up to anything?'

'Teenage girls are always up to something Cole, trust me.'

* * *

That evening Anna looked out over the small patch of garden stretching out from behind her house. The grass had been recently mowed, probably the last cut of the season, and a lone blackbird was pecking for worms in the dusk. The bird took off as soon as the grey and white cat made an appearance. He was back for a prowl around. She assumed he came from next door.

He didn't look like a stray, but she like to throw him the odd scrap of leftover chicken or ham.

She sighed, thinking about home. It was scary how easily she had packed up and left. The sense of belonging she had looked for upon arriving hadn't come, but she did feel comfortable and at ease. As expected, she hadn't missed Jon. In fact, she had been so busy settling into work and getting to grips with her new surroundings, she barely gave him a second thought.

Her dad was another matter. She couldn't help feeling bad about leaving him. The thought of him bumbling along at home trying to sort out the laundry and making his 'frozen meals for one' broke her heart. She knew he had friends and neighbours who would rally round him, but for how long?

Camille's death had been a long time coming, and the support which had been so plentiful in the first months of her diagnosis, soon waned as people got on with their own lives. Jimmy said he didn't need anyone, and that his own company suited him fine, but Anna knew he would be lonely and had a tendency to fall melancholic, playing his old vinyl records while sitting staring into the burning fire. She couldn't afford to think about it - to let her mind return to her mum's last days. The searing guilt, which she tried so hard to keep suppressed, would bubble up, threatening to overwhelm her. It was just too painful, too raw.

Anna pulled out her manila folder of notes. There wasn't much to it. A birth certificate, some doctor's notes detailing the birth and that was about it. The research she had gathered on her birth mother was patchy at best. Anna had been born in a convent home for unmarried mothers. It was ridiculous to think that even in the late seventies such shame and banishment was still part of the norm in Ireland. She knew her mother was seventeen, and part of a large Catholic family originally from Keoghill, a market town outside Newry. Anna, while only weeks old, was transported to a sister convent in Dublin, and then on to Wales. She was four months old when her adopted parents, Jimmy and Camille Cole had been presented with the bundle of a screaming infant.

All red faced and indignant, her dad had always said. Furious at the world, for no good reason.

They had cared and nurtured her, never denying the adoption, so that Anna had been brought up knowing she had been specially picked by them and for them. That her life with them wasn't a biological lottery but instead one they had worked hard to fashion. Anna was never in any doubt of their love.

It was thick and smothering.

She was watched carefully her whole life. Protected and cared for in ways she could see her peers didn't have to put up with. It was as if Camille and Jimmy had been desperately aware that she wasn't truly theirs, and that one wrong step would mean that fate would snatch her back.

Watching Camille fade away to skin and bone, eaten up by the cancer had been hard. The sense of frustration that they couldn't help her more, couldn't ease her suffering, was what haunted Anna most. The well-meaning hospice nurses and the GPs were all well and good up to a point, but really when all was said and done, none of them had the balls to do what was the kindest thing – to help her on her way. Anna squeezed her eyes shut trying to preempt the tears. She couldn't cry about it; couldn't allow herself to think about what she had done.

It was time to start looking. To instigate what she had come here to do. Camille's death, at the age of sixty-eight, had awoken something in Anna. She knew the time was right to search out the mother who had given birth to her, and handed her over to the nuns in dark habits, only to be ferried away to another country, and a different life. Jimmy understood. Said he knew the time would always come when she would go haring off to Ireland. They both knew that Camille wouldn't have approved; that she would have found the process too hurtful, too tremulous.

But here Anna was, miles away from home, and everyone she knew and loved, seeking out a mother who had given her away, and a family who might not know she existed.

Chapter 16

*H*e liked running at nighttime in the rain. The feel of the wetness against his face, the squelch of each foot as it pounded the muddy ground. The moon gave enough light to illuminate his way. He continued on down the steep bank, slowing, each footfall taken with care, bringing him closer and closer to the special place. The distant rumble of traffic mingled with the sounds of the forest around him. Twitches of animals, lurking in hidden dens, a call of a bird, definitely not an owl, something else he couldn't identify.

He adjusted his backpack, releasing the light pressure of the straps sitting on his shoulders. The gentle weight inside felt good. He liked the thump of it against his back, now slick with sweat. It was important to stay fit and strong. To be ready to run, at any given moment. To be agile and alert. He had trained himself over a period of six months. Tracking his speed, knowing the area, reading the weather and being prepared. He knew that his physique helped him in other ways too. The girls liked to see his hard shoulders, his well-defined arms; to caress his chest and taut stomach. They liked how he looked, always commenting on his eyes and his cute mouth, teasing him about his hair, which curls if he lets it get too long. All bullshit. He was expected to respond in kind, to admire their beauty, to talk of gorgeous skin and amazing hair. They were easily pleased.

He hadn't always got the girls. When he was younger, at school, he was the outsider. The one on the edge of everything. Never invited to the big parties with the good-looking girls. He was too quiet, too reserved. Never quite getting the joke. He knew he was partly to blame. His tight little gang of three was enough for him. Dan, Vincie and Glenn. It was easier to be the watcher, than to be watched.

The earthy ground gave way to the footpath. He slowed his speed to a jog. Took a swift look around to make sure there were no late-night dog walkers, or cyclists knocking about. All clear. The break in the hedgerow was coming up. If you didn't know where to look you would easily miss it. He stopped, took a breath and looked around again.

The copse of trees had provided the perfect spot. Malone House Manor was built on the site of a seventeenth century fort at the edge of the copse. Now it was a National Trust property, maintained by the council. The surrounding footpaths, and river walks all open to the public. Access to the copse was easy from the back of the hotel grounds. His exit had been through the copse onto the path running adjacent to the river Lagan – the path he was now on. He slivered through the hedgerow opening, trying not to damage the bushes any more than he had to, ensuring that he adjusted the branches and brambles so that they didn't look altered. He clambered up the bank on the other side and reached his destination. The area had been cleared. A remnant of police tape still flickered in the rain, but other than that, there was no evidence to suggest what had occurred. He liked that.

Amongst the trees the rain was reduced to the odd splat, the ground beneath his feet almost dry. He breathed in deeply, feeling the night air fill up his lungs, clean and pure, despite being so close to the city. It was darker in here with the trees covering the moon but he could see enough. He took his backpack from his shoulders and took out the package. It felt cold through the plastic bag. Gently he unwrapped it. The feathers were slick and wet, its bill slim and pointed. He placed the little bird on the place where she had laid. The eye sockets now rendered to blind, black holes. It would watch no more.

* * *

'Daddy? Are you home?' Declan heard Lara call out from the hallway. For a split second, he allowed himself to think it was Esme. His mind was treacherous, waiting to catch him out and to floor him with the full force of his grief.

'I'm in here,' he called out. Lara came in looking drawn. She usually had her shiny blonde hair tied back, neat and preppy, but today she wore it loose, reminding him of when she was little. It didn't seem that long ago that she was playing dress up as Cinderella and insisting Esme take the part of the ugly sister. Esme, only too pleased to be included in her older sister's game, always went along with it. There was a photograph somewhere of her dressed in an old silk blouse of Izzy's, her hair piled high on her head, red blotches of lipstick staining her cheeks and a scowl to make her look ugly. God, he'd have to find that photograph. That was a good time. When they were a young family, with life's possibilities stretched out before them like a promise of summer in springtime.

'Dad? Are you all right?'

'Sorry love. I was thinking of Esme. Remembering when you two were little.'

She looked stricken, 'It's so awful. Can you believe this has happened?'

'I know sweetheart. It's impossible to wrap your head around. Should've been your special day and now we're left with nothing but heartbreak.'

'Rory said they'll catch whoever did it. They will, won't they?' her voice was breaking, wanting him to reassure her, make it all better. Except he couldn't. Life would never be the same again.

'They better. If I have anything to do with it, they bloody will.' He saw a flicker of something pass over her face, that old look of pity, or maybe it was disbelief. He paused, feeling embarrassed that in front of his daughter that he appeared so incapacitated. He knew what she was thinking, that he was fuck all use to any of them.

'Your mother's gone into the university for a couple of hours. She didn't want to leave her students high and dry.'

'For God's sake, she should be here, not going to work. I told Rory the same thing, but he said the business won't wait for him to pick himself up, that he's no choice but to get on with it.'

'I want to talk to you about Rory,' Declan said.

'What about him?'

'His businesses. How much do you know about what he's involved in?'

'What's that supposed to mean? Where's this coming from. He isn't *involved* in anything he shouldn't be. I know you don't like Rory but you need to accept we're married now. You can't keep being like this.'

'Like what?'

'Finding fault with him, making little digs about his work. He works hard and makes sure we have a good lifestyle.'

'We brought you up to be your own woman. You've a great career. You don't need his money.'

Lara sighed, 'Dad, please.'

Her tone was a touch too defensive for Declan's liking.

'Just be careful. The police mentioned something about his business connections. Watch what you sign, that sort of thing and if you are ever worried, you can come to me, you know that don't you?'

'Of course, Daddy, but you're being silly. Rory's a good businessman, nothing more than that and I trust him so you should too.'

'Ok, pet. Let's leave it at that then. But be careful, you know your old man can't help worrying about you.'

Chapter 17

It was Saturday and Anna was lost without the routine of going to the station. They had pulled a double shift the previous day, going through CCTV, pulling phone records and talking to Esme's school, so she needed a bit of time to clear her head. The day stretched out before her. She had agreed with Thomas to take the morning off and to reconvene in the late afternoon, should anything come up. They were still waiting on the tech people to come back with anything gleaned from Esme's computer and phone.

The grey and white cat was back. This time he came up to the back door, meowing for attention.

'Hey puss,' she stroked his fur and was rewarded by him butting her hand with his head.

'You hungry, boy?'

She found a tin of tuna in the cupboard, and put it out on a plate, placing it on the back step for the cat to eat. He ate hungrily, rewarding her with a final head butt and full body rub against her legs before she closed the back door.

It was clear and dry, though cold. She didn't fancy sitting around all day waiting for Thomas to ring, so with nothing better to do, she decided to take herself off on a walk. She threw on her wool coat, grabbed her backpack with her sketchpad and pencils in it and headed to Shaws Bridge. It was a known scenic spot in South Belfast, and backed on to the hotel grounds where Esme was murdered. The forest edged trail ran around the river Lagan, making it a popular spot for dog walkers, runners, cyclists and families out for a stroll. It was busy. Young families were out in force keen to get the last of the fading autumn sunshine before the rain came. Dog walkers nodded hello in that companionable way of Belfast people.

She decided to go off track and climbed up the through the bank of trees and hedgerows into the field to the left of the riverbank. A walk without a purpose was a waste of time in her mind so she might as well revisit the scene of Esme Well's death. The site had been cleared of all evidence of the murder, although she had been told a make shift shrine had been created with a few bunches of flowers wilting at the foot of a tree not far from the crime scene.

She stumbled over a gnarled root of a tree. Her navy, suede boots were not a great choice for roaming around river banks. She continued on, steadying herself, fearful that one wrong step could see her falling face first into the sludge at the river's edge. The scene was picture perfect. The autumn sun, though weak, glinted through the just-turning burnished gold leafed trees and reflected off the gently flowing river. It wasn't wide, little more than a deep stream in parts, but at its centre it could be deep and dark. Why not throw the body in? Why leave her lying to be found? Why was concealment not an issue for the killer? Or was he disturbed?

They had tracked down all the sex offenders known to them and a good few of those who had managed to escape conviction but were worth keeping an eye on. There was no evidence to suggest the killer was sexually motivated. Esme's body hadn't been violated in that way. Everything about the murder, the location, the fact that she had apparently willingly gone with her killer all spoke of a different type of crime.

A clearing had been made where the body was found. The forensics team had created a defined workspace. Anna looked out across the river. She could see a middle-aged woman walking a spaniel on the path on the far side. A robin flew down and sat close to her. She thought of the victim – young and vulnerable. How easily had she been led away to her death? There was no indication that she had gone against her will. Anna's mind was sifting through the possibilities, and the questions that kept nagging at her.

What was going on with the victim and Finnegan? Was there something Esme knew about him that made her a threat?

Anna lowered herself down on to the mossy ground, with her back against a huge sycamore tree for support, and took out her sketchpad and pencils from her rucksack. Maybe it was macabre to do this, to sketch the scene of a murder, but it was a habit Anna often relied on to help clarify the details of a case. She needed to methodically look with the clarity of an artist's eye, to place the soft lead pencil on a blank page and trace out the scene line-by-line, shadow-by-shadow until something beyond the sketch appeared.

The undergrowth was dense and foreboding, yet almost ethereal. It was a perfect spot to hide away. It would have been very dark under the cathedral-tall canopy of trees. The moonlight would have failed to shine through the overlapping branches. The river, down from her spot, was sluggish and she used a burnt umber watercolour pencil to capture its dankness. The bank, a tangle of brambles and weeds, she scribbled in viridian and Windsor green. She worked fast, wanting to capture the shades in the fading mid-morning light.

As she directed the pencil over the page, twisting and turning to mimic the branches, gnarled and entwining, each reaching for the other like lovers, she thought of Esme and her last minutes. The choke of fear, the buckle of panic clawing at her insides. She felt edgy thinking of Esme. Not all cases had the same effect. Some you could cope with easier than others. It wasn't always fair but someone like Esme Wells, pretty, well liked, from a good, loving family, demanded more sympathy than the long-time drug dealer who had his brains bashed in by an associate.

Esme was at that golden age, about to gain real independence, experience the wider world and begin her adult life. Anna could remember the headiness of it all – the teenage years when you lived with the sense that at any minute, you could take flight. That anything and everything was possible. The monotony of school punctuated with banter, roaring laughter, and delicious flirtations. The love for friends you probably wouldn't recognise in twenty years. The teachers who inspired you, and the ones who irritated you by simply speaking. The parents who infuriated you and made you feel suffocated and misunderstood. Didn't they know you were fully formed and ready to take on the world? Or was that only Anna who experienced that particular strain of growing up.

McKay and some of the others couldn't see past the fake tan and make up. They thought Esme's life was all Facebook statuses, selfies and Snapchat. They didn't know what it costs emotionally to be a girl in the throes of becoming a woman: to be heckled by random men, *gizusasmilelove,* to be judged by your peers – too fat, too skinny, too smart, too stupid, to open a magazine and see image after image of how the world wanted you to be.

Her pencil flashed across the page, seeking out light and shadow. Adding detail to the outline, filling in the precise twist of a root, the dangle of a leaf, hanging from a branch. She had almost finished the sketch when she caught sight of something in the undergrowth. The police tape was still flickering in the breeze, outlining the exact spot where Esme had been found. In the middle of the site Anna thought she could see something, lying on the fallen leaves. From where she sat it could be an old black purse or something. Moving closer she realised it was a bird. A dead bird. It was mainly black with white patches on its wings, distinctive red legs and webbed feet. She supposed it could have died and just happened to end up there. Or a dog or fox could have carried it. But just in case it was of significance, Anna took her phone out of her pocket to photograph the bird in situ. She then reached into her rucksack and grabbed an evidence bag. With her blue latex gloves slipped on, she picked it up, feeling the wing unfold under her fingers. Its head flopped forward as if the neck had been broken, its eyes a dead blackness.

Up close it was beautiful. Fragile and contained. Hard to imagine it flying high above all of this. It was then that she noticed that the eyes weren't a dead blackness at all. They were absent. Both sockets were small empty pools. The eyes had been removed. Plucked by another animal? She didn't think it was likely. The vacant sockets stared blankly creeping her out. She sealed the bag and looked around. The dog walkers were long gone and the low, grey-clouded sky threatened rain. Not many people passed by this part of the path.

Later, when she came back from the station having handed the bird over to be analysed, she looked at the sketch. She had captured something of the atmosphere of the place, but something about the scene still eluded her. Something was out of reach. That old gnawing feeling of frustration and anger sat in the pit of her stomach. She recognised it like an old friend. The anger that would propel her forward, would help her be relentless in her search for answers.

* * *

That evening Anna walked through Belfast's Cathedral Quarter on her way to meet Holly, Thomas and a few other colleagues for a drink. A pink bus passed by with the advertising slogan 'Take Back the City' blazing out. It was clear that promoting Belfast to its own inhabitants was on the council agenda. At every turn, there was a poster shouting out catchy Belfast propaganda or the grinning face of Belfast's Lord Mayor declaring Belfast as *the place to be.* In spite of the weather, there were plenty of pavement cafés and a sense of cloning continental café culture. Obviously, heavy investment had gone on and it was time to cash in on the dividend of the peace process.

It wasn't natural for Anna to be sociable, but McKay had made it clear, the little gathering had been in her honour, a belated *welcome to the neighbourhood* sort of thing. She didn't think she could get away with declining. She would have preferred to sit at home going over her case notes, finishing the sketch and trying to get a hold on the case. But she had to admit, she didn't have much else to do on a Saturday night.

The city streets were lively with early evening revelers. Music spilled out of bars, people chatted animatedly in their smoker's huddle. It definitely felt that Belfast was full of itself, delighted to be out of the wilderness years of bombs and bullets.

'There she is. What are you having? This rounds on King,' Holly shouted over the noise. A band was playing Whiskey in the Jar, every man in the place singing along to the guitar riff.

'White wine, thanks,' Anna replied, raising her voice above the din.

She shuffled into the leather banquet where the rest of their crowd sat.

'Nice place,' she said looking round. The bar was kitted out to look like an alternative gothic cathedral. The high arched ceiling, decorated with fallen angels getting up to all sorts of debauchery. The walls were painted blood red and seemed to pulsate under the lighting, while the antiqued style mirrors reflected the girls with made up faces and men with the flush of their second or third pint in them. A couple sat in the corner huddled together. 'Well what do you make of us so far?' King asked. His brown eyes merry with the buzz of a few pints.

'You're a sarcastic lot. Prone to look on the negative side of things and quick to judge.'

He roared laughing, 'You got us down to a tee, Cole. Guilty as charged.'

She looked down at his hands, noticing the absence of a wedding ring. Holly had said he was separated from his wife.

'We're complicated people, Cole. Nothing is ever as it seems.'

He had a small scar above his right eyebrow. Anna found herself wanting to trace her finger over it. His eyelashes were dark and surprisingly long.

'C'mon and dance.' Holly pulled Anna up towards the dance floor in front of the four-piece band, who all looked as if they weren't long out of school. They were playing Kings of Leon's

'Sex on Fire.' Anna looked back and saw King's eyes follow her to the dance floor.

* * *

The night seemed to move too fast. Someone suggested another bar. They moved like a pack, swaying drunkenly into each other. Thomas holding her up when she felt she could dance no more. The lights in the bar coming on too bright, the bartender calling 'time please'. She was drunk and didn't want to go home to the rented house. Thomas pulled her in close to him, whispering in her ear words she couldn't distinguish but she had got the gist of it. His flat was close-by in the docks area. They both jumped in the first taxi, which drove past a statue looking out towards the harbour. Thomas told her it was known locally as 'Nuala with the Hula'.

'It's made of stainless steel and cast bronze,' he said, as he rested his arm over her shoulder. Anna looked out at the tall, metal structure standing illuminated against the wet, dark sky, lengths of metal spiralled upwards culminating in outstretched arms holding aloft a ring, symbolising thanksgiving and unity.

He paid the taxi driver and took Anna's hand.

* * *

The flat had all the hallmarks of a single man's abode, sparsely furnished with an oversized flat screen on the wall. A soulless bachelor pad, from the pale grey walls to the Xbox console, it smacked of microwaved dinners, cold beers and loneliness.

The open plan living room looked out over Belfast lough, the city lights glimmering against the rain soaked night. The only thing giving the place a bit of character was the record player and the pile of vinyl albums stacked beside it. Anna noted he had Blondie's 'Parallel Lines' on top. She approved. Though she'd bet he wouldn't have anything as cool as the Ramones, preferring something like the Smiths or Kraftwerk or maybe even the Pet

Shop Boys. He looked like he'd dig the eighties. She'd have to enlighten him, educate him a bit.

'Can I get you a night cap?' he asked, holding up the half-full bottle of Bushmills whiskey. There it was, that slow sexy smile enticing Anna to let go of her inhibitions and the nagging doubts of not getting mixed up with a colleague.

'Sure, with ice, please.'

* * *

He stood to the side of the hall, taking in the scene. Clusters of girls had gathered in intimate huddles, admiring each other's dresses, squawking in that annoying way they had, hugging and posing for endless photographs. They were made up to look like garish versions of themselves, toxic coloured skin, shaded cheekbones, over-thick eyebrows and shimmering eyelids. Their dresses were an array of jewel colours, flashing sequins, silk or satin. They bustled round, checking their phones, taking endless selfies.

He had trained himself to look slightly disinterested, as if his feelings were buried deep and he was unreachable. People who knew him sometimes thought he was cold, unfeeling even, but the truth was he felt too much. Every emotion was intensified, every touch an exquisite sensation. There was nothing unfeeling about him. He had worked hard at creating a façade, an image that helped him achieve what he wanted. The key was to not give too much away, and to project what they wanted to see. Once you know what they want from you, it is easy to give it to them.

It helped to have the right look, to have that fresh faced, approachable yet reserved exterior. Attractiveness made all the difference. If you look a certain way you can get away with murder.

* * *

When he saw her his heart leapt. She was perfect. Pale skinned, with a smattering of light freckles, long copper-red hair, kitted out in a beautiful green dress. He could imagine her choosing the dress, dreaming of this night, and the buzz of getting ready. The anticipation of what was to come tasted like nectar in his mouth. Adrenaline surged through him, firing up his muscles, putting every cell of his body on red alert. He felt wired knowing he had found his next kill. Even the colours and sounds in the room became heightened. He was jacked up with the thrill of it, and the glorious foreplay of what was to follow. It was a pure, natural high, better than the hum of any speed bought on the street.

Then there was some sort of altercation between her and one of the boys. Their heads were close together, but their body language suggested that they were fighting. The date, no doubt. He watched it unfold, knowing he could step in at any point and play the bouncer card at any moment; to be her protector. He followed them out to the main hallway, hanging back so that he was out of sight, hidden by the huge palm tree standing in a massive clay pot. The DJ was playing a slow set, Adele followed by Ed Sheeran. It was that time of night when couples pair off in the hope of kissing and more.

From his vantage point, he could hear snippets of their argument, 'You said you were ...'

'I didn't mean it ... sure you know ...'

It was as if they were kids play-acting. Making a whole drama out of nothing. She would be recounting to her friends, word for word what had happened. Posing with tearful eyes and a dropped bottom lip on Snapchat. The boy would play it cool with his mates, say she was too clingy, too needy.

Her hand reached up and she pulled her hair round to the side, exposing her pale neck. She turned and he saw that her dress was backless. He took in the devastating nakedness of her back, the pale sun-starved skin like a blank canvas. He could see the small bumps of her spine rising towards her hairline, the tendons stretching as she turned her head away from the boy. How amazing it was - the intricate network of tendons, muscles and veins beneath her pale skin, how the skin contained it all, yet was so vulnerable to a knife's edge. How easy it was to slice through, to puncture a vein or artery to release the life-giving blood and watch it drain out of her.

He liked to think she sensed him watching, that some deep primeval part of her knew she was prey. Did the tiny hairs at the back of her neck stand to attention? Did her heart beat a little faster and her pulse quicken? He watched the sinews of her neck move and stretch as she continued to talk to the boy. The gestures, and her expressions told him to get ready. With a final word, she flounced off, ready to run to her friends and be consoled while the boy in the formal suit, stood impassive and fed up.

It was game on. He followed her, primed like a boxer in the ring. He walked quickly out from behind the palm tree and placed himself in her path. 'Woe there! You nearly mowed me down. Are you ok?' he asked, his voice all concern.

'Sorry, I didn't mean to bump into you,' her eyes were filled with unspilled tears.

'Oh now, whatever is wrong can be sorted out. No need to cry, sweetheart,' he took her by the arm and directed her to the doorway. She was unsteady in the high-heeled strappy sandals, swaying slightly as he placed his arm around her.

'Come on, a bit of fresh air will sort you out.' She went like a lamb. Meek and gentle. All he had to do was lead her, like an obedient dog.

Chapter 18

Anna woke with the buzz of hangover. Her mouth was arid and her eyes stung against the dim morning light. It took a few moments for her to realise that she wasn't in her rented house and she wasn't alone. Thomas was already up and in the shower. She could hear the drone of the shower water. With relief, she found her clothes were still on. She was in the middle of putting on her shoes when he walked in.

'I was going to bring you some breakfast.'

'Thanks, but I should get home,' She could barely look him in the eye. He probably felt let down. They had both expected to have sex when they left the bar. It was that kind of vibe, but nerve had deserted her almost as soon as they arrived at his apartment. Now though, he looked as though he expected to pick up where they had left off last night.

'Hey, what's the hurry?' He strode towards her with nothing but a towel around his waist, his chest hair still damp from the shower, smelling of fresh pine needles and mint.

'Aren't there rules about shagging staff,' Anna made a flippant attempt to joke away her embarrassment. What seemed like a perfectly reasonable thing to do in the easy, relaxed haze of a night out, now seemed sordid and pathetic, made worse by the fact he was in the throes of a separation, and she was supposedly still in a relationship of sorts with Jon.

She was saved by his phone buzzing. 'I have to take this,' he said. He turned away, giving her a view of his tight ass clad in the still damp white towel, as he answered the mobile. She heard him reply to the caller with an urgency in his voice.

'Where was she found? Secure the scene, I'm on my way.'

* * *

They pulled into the wide driveway of the impressive looking Culloden Hotel. 'Wow, what is this place?' Anna asked.

'It was originally built as an official Palace for the Bishops of Down, no expense spared, but these days it's a five-star hotel and spa.'

The grey stone building stood proud on the slopes of the Holywood hills, overlooking Belfast Lough and the rugged county Antrim coastline.

'Nice setting too, acres of secluded gardens and woodland, the perfect spot for a murder.'

Anna knew he was thinking about Esme Wells.

The techs, in their white suits, looked like ghouls emerging from the trees. The previous night's rainfall had been off the charts and now the ground was slick with mud. The killer's shoes would carry plenty of mud from the scene but unfortunately footprints would be hard if not impossible to read.

'Where is she?' Thomas asked the spotty faced uniformed officer at the entrance. 'Round the back sir, through the trees.'

They drove the car around the grounds of the hotel property and pulled in. Manus Magee was stood talking to a man in a dark suit. The wind whipped Anna's hair as she climbed out of the car. She pulled her leather jacket around her, hoping no one would notice she was wearing last night's clothes. Within a few strides they had reached them, Magee speaking before they had even time to say good morning.

'Eighteen-year-old female, at her school formal. No one noticed she was missing, and she wasn't found until a dog walker came across the body this morning,' he said as they walked towards the back of the gardens. A few SOCO officers were shuffling about in their white paper suits, working the scene.

They crossed the lawn and headed towards the tented area, approaching PC Dodds, the uniform standing guard, 'Detective Cole and Detective King,' Thomas said, 'What have we got?'

'The site has been secured, Sir, but the man who found her, moved the body. Said he thought she was drunk and asleep. His dog ran all over the scene too.'

'Right.' Anna could tell Thomas was seething. 'McKay will go ape shit and we're to somehow magically ensure no press,' he said. A tampered crime scene was not going to help anyone.

'And there's something else, Sir,' Dodds said.

'What?' Anna asked.

'You'll see,' he said, he shuffled as if uncomfortable, his eyes watering in the cold morning air.

Anna looked to Thomas and raised her eyebrows.

They made their way down the gravelly path where the white tent had been erected, sheltered from the wind by the copse of trees.

A woman with a protective white suit on strode up to them.

'This is Dr Margaret McCann, the FMO,' Thomas turned and said to Anna. 'What have we got?'

She nodded to Anna, 'Probable cause of death, head injury, though there is some light bruising on the neck. Once I've done the autopsy, I'll know more. Right now, it's a preliminary assessment, nothing more. I'll run the usual blood tests too, but the toxicology results will take time.'

'How long?'

'Forty-eight hours at least. It's looking more complicated than a bashed in head and tox screens. This one's a bit weirder than normal, you'll see for yourself what I mean.'

'Jesus, are they trying to put us off before we go in here?' Thomas said to Anna.

They reached the tent in a few short strides. Anna could feel the acid of last night's alcohol slushing round her stomach. She willed herself not to throw up like a rookie. Her palms sweated in response, in an effort to control her hung-over stomach.

They stopped at the tent. 'Are you ready for this?' Thomas asked. Anna nodded, biting back a retort, wanting to slam him for thinking she needed to steady herself before entering the tent. She had seen plenty of dead bodies, in all conditions, but she said nothing, taking in a lungful of the early morning November air. There was an uneasy quiet in the tent; techs getting on with the job, all chat murmured in respective tones.

The girl lay on her back, with her head facing away from them. It was clear that her head had been bashed in, the blood coagulating in thick, glistening, dark gobs around her red hair. She was dressed in a long, dark green formal dress, all silk and lace. She wore a corsage bracelet of diamante stones and faded and crushed cream roses on her wrist, the petals already browning at the edges. One strappy sandal was hanging from her pale ankle, while the other was discarded close by. Anna could picture the anticipation of the formal, waiting to be asked by a boy, the choosing of the dress, the getting ready. The night of excitement and fun turned into the most horrific nightmare.

Thomas spoke first, 'How was she found?'

One of the techs looked up from his position kneeling close to the girl, on the opposite side of Anna and Thomas, 'Face down. The walker turned her over thinking she was asleep. You need to see this, come round this side,'

Anna and Thomas walked around the body. The first thing that hit Anna was how pretty the girl was, her skin so fresh and clear. Her hair, a crown of burnished copper curls. Then she saw it. The girls' mouth was stuffed with something. Anna bent over to get a closer look, her gloved hand reaching down. It was a bird; small, brown tail feathers were sticking out of the mouth like a feathered tongue.

'Christ, is that a bird?' Thomas asked.

The Tech nodded. 'Sick bastard, rammed it into her mouth.'

Just then Margaret returned, 'You've seen it then?'

'Yeah, what do you make of it?' Anna asked.

'Until I get her on the table I don't want to disturb what's in there too much. I can't say if the bird was inserted after death, during or before. But give me a while and I will hopefully have something for you to go on.'

Anna thought of other cases where victims had been mutilated, foreign objects inserted into orifices, usually indicating a regressive necrophilia. There was something so sinister and weird about the bird in the victim's mouth. The killer was making a point. She was sure Declan would have a theory relating the bird found at Esme's death site and to this one. What was the killer's behaviour telling them about his personality? She thought of the eyeless bird left, as if to torment them after Esme's murder. They were still waiting on the results from the first bird to come back, but in all likelihood, with the eyes removed, it looked like it had been left as a token. A marker of sorts. The cruel hand that had chosen to maim that poor creature and use it as marker for his crime, could be the same one at work here.

There was another case, years ago in Llantwit Major, where a murderer had left a trademark slash on his victim's chests. She hadn't worked on that case but she remembered the lessons learned for it. Afterwards they realised that the killer was mutilating the bodies as a warning to others – leaving his trademark V cut into the skin of male prostitutes. It was the trademark that eventually led them to the killer. The V was his sign for victory over the young men who he saw as an aberration of nature. His twisted religious undertones helped the detectives on the case to pinpoint a religious sect set up in the Vale of Glamorgan.

The dead girl's features were soft and still childlike. A scattering of freckles danced across her now pallid face. Anna could smell the blood, coppery and sickening. Her stomach heaved and she was glad she had eaten nothing for fear it would come back up.

'No ID yet. Obvious struggle, one of her nails is broken, torn right off, so she fought back. Too early to say whether or not we are looking at the same MO. It is possible. Her dress hasn't been ripped, and rigor hasn't set in yet,' said Dr McCann.

'Has her bag or phone turned up?' Thomas asked.

'Nothing, sir.' Replied one of the officers.

'There's evidence that this was the primary scene, blood on the rock to your left,' Margaret pointed with her torch towards the rock. The blood stains still evident.

'Any prints yet?' Anna asked.

'No. A few smudged marks, could be gloves. Other finds are a couple of cigarette butts and a beer bottle but they could have been here for some time by the looks of it.'

'We'll get them checked out,' Anna said.

'Did you say she was found face down?' Thomas asked.

'Yeah, the walker turned her over. We haven't moved her yet,' the tech said.

'Make sure we get the walker's fingerprints, shoe prints, and clothing logged to rule them out of any evidence found,' Thomas barked at the SOCO.

Anna noted the left arm, flung across her chest. She was slight, delicate even. Blood was congealing on her top lip, along with the blush of a fresh bruise.

'Too much of a coincidence, don't you think?' Anna said quietly to Thomas.

'It's possible, they're separate. Until we get the PM, we can't assume anything. But we need to act fast,' he replied with a deep sigh.

Anna nodded. 'And keep the site secure in case he turns up later with another memento for us, but the bird, it's too much to be a coincidence. We didn't go public with the one found at the first scene murder.'

The sight of the girl made Anna feel weak and unsteady. She'd seen plenty of bodies before but the pretty dress, the idea of the prom, the preparation, the fussing over dresses, hair styles and hoping to be asked by the right boy made this seem particularly sad. A videographer was filming the site. A SOCO was setting out white marker cards on the ground, indicating spots of interest where the undergrowth had been disturbed. The air tingled with a nervous energy. A bird squawked as if indignant that they were disturbing its peace.

'Are you ok?' Thomas asked.

'Hangover. I just feel a bit shaky.'

There were plenty of detectives you couldn't admit feeling off colour to at the scene. They'd hold it against you, and make sure the entire squad knew you couldn't stomach the job. Anna was sure Thomas wasn't that type of knobhead.

She willed her stomach to steady, and felt the stirring of the silent rage, a disturbance of any peace she'd hope to claim leaving Wales. But she welcomed it; she needed the white-hot molten lava of anger running through her centre, keeping her lit with an urgency to catch the killer.

There was much to be done. They needed to ensure the entire area was well secured. The press would be clambering all over the place given half a chance. A second body would heighten speculation about the killer and they had to act fast to obtain as much information as they could, to look for connections between the two cases and to make some sort of headway. They would also need more manpower. It was cases like this that made Anna wonder how anything got solved before the HOLMES system. The data and information from each case could be logged and compared. It helped to ensure nothing was missed or overlooked. A batch of new officers – floaters – assigned to help with the case, would have to be briefed and assigned tasks.

* * *

'What's happened? What's going on?' they turned to see a girl, running towards them.

'Miss, you can't go down there,' a uniformed officer was shouting.

She pushed past the cordon; her face flushed as she was grabbed by one of the techs.

'This is a crime scene. You can't be here.'

'Oh my God, it's Grace, isn't it? It's Grace!' A flutter of birds rose up from the trees, disturbed by her screams, and flitted into the sky. Anna walked up the small hill towards them.

'It's ok, I'll speak to her,' she said to the officer. 'Come on, come with me.' Anna directed the girl away from the tent over towards a low stonewall which wrapped around the lawned gardens of the hotel.

'Why are you here? Who were you looking for?'

'Grace, my friend she was meant to stay at my house last night, only she had gone off in a huff. So I thought she had gone home. I've tried calling and calling and texting but she hasn't replied. I phoned her house and her dad said she wasn't home. I lied to him, told him she'd gone to stay with Hannah instead. She was meant to be with me. Oh my God.'

She was shaking, her voice rising higher. 'One of my friends saw a post on Twitter about police being all over the Culloden grounds and that a body had been found. I had to come down. Please tell me it isn't Grace. Look, this is her.' She thrust her phone at Anna, showing her a photograph of two girls. There was no mistaking the dark green dress and red hair.

'We have found the body of a young girl but she hasn't been identified yet.'

The girl sobbed.

'What's your name?'

'Rachel, Rachel Rafferty.'

'Okay Rachel. I'm going to need to get you home. Do you want to call your parents? Let them know where you are and that we will be in touch?'

She nodded and let Anna lead her to the car. 'We will get one of the officers will look after you. We will need to talk to you later, is that ok?'

The girl nodded and let herself be handed over to one of the uniforms. 'Tell the parents we will be in touch soon,' Anna told the pink-faced sergeant.

* * *

In the car on the way back to the station Thomas was quiet.

'What are you thinking?' Anna asked.

'Two murders, both at hotel venues. McKay is going to want something by the time we get back to the station. What did you get out of the friend?'

'Looks like our victim is the girl she was worried about. She showed me a photograph from her phone. Formal identification won't happen until later when we contact the family, but it seems the girl is called Grace Dowds. Rachel said they had a falling out last night over a boy and Grace left the formal early, about eleven. She was supposed to stay over at Rachel's house.'

'We'll need to get the boy in and anyone else who was party to this fight.'

* * *

At the station, the incident room was bustling with activity. The clack of keyboards, the busy hum of conversation, the sound of panic, trying to catch up with the day's events. There was a feeling of anxiety in the air, a sense of desperation too.

Anna watched Thomas stride into the room. He stood at the front and the noise died down. 'I want CCTV from every available angle. There's a garage on the road into Holywood, check out their cameras too, and any local businesses on the road in or out of the town. Get licence recognition on any vehicles in the vicinity as well.'

He looked tired. Anna knew though that the swell of adrenaline would carry them through the next twenty-four hours.

They would dig down and find the energy required to propel them on.

'Come on Tonto, we are heading back to Holywood to talk to the family.'

* * *

Thomas automatically took the driving seat. She'd assert her right to drive another time, but for now she was still feeling unwell and welcomed the opportunity to relax back into her passenger seat.

'What do you know about the family?' Anna asked as they set off.

'Father owns a chain of car sale showrooms. Big money people, but nice with it, by all accounts. They are well known – Stephen Dowds had stood for the local council elections last year. He was on an independent ticket, trying to get the new wave of voters too young to be branded by the bigotry of old.'

'Did he win?'

'No. When it comes down to it, people here tend to vote along tribal lines. It'll take another couple of generations for the ingrained hatred to bleed out.'

Anna laughed, she was starting to get the underlying humour. The dark and telling.

They drove out of Belfast towards Holywood again, heading on to Craigavad. She saw the tall, yellow gantry cranes, Samson and Goliath, standing proud over the shipyard where the Titanic had been built. On past the Odyssey, an out of town entertainment complex – home to the Belfast Giants ice hockey team, a cinema and concert venue, and further on out, leaving the city behind, past the George Best airport and the signs for Ikea.

'That was some Sunday morning wake up,' Thomas said.

Anna hesitated, searching for the right thing to say. 'Look Thomas, I don't want to give you the wrong idea,' she opened her window to get some air as he pulled into the outside lane.

'I'm sort of coming out of a relationship and I'm not looking to get involved right now.'

'Sure, no problem,' he looked out the window.

Anna cursed herself silently for getting into this predicament. She needed her colleagues to respect her as a good detective, not see her as an easy lay. What was she thinking of running around like a teenager, kissing a man she hardly knew and going back to his apartment? Thank God, he had been happy to let her fall asleep in his bed. She shuddered at how irresponsible she had been. It wasn't like her to act like this. When she thought of Jon she blushed with shame.

They passed a huge sign congratulating Rory McIlroy on his latest win. Holywood, his hometown, proud of their talented golfer.

'The papers are going to have a field day with this,' Thomas said.

'All we can do is catch the bastard, before it happens again because as sure as night follows day he's going to strike again.'

Holywood proved to be a small, wealthy town full of coffee shops, nice little boutiques, and gastro pubs, all edged by the beauty of the coast. Anna watching out the window, thinking how pretty the town was, as Thomas took them to Craigavad Grace's family home. They pulled into the driveway of a large Georgian style pile. Anna couldn't help thinking that Northern Ireland had some beautiful houses.

At the top of the asphalt driveway she saw four cars neatly parked, two BWMs, an Audi convertible and a C class Mercedes. Serious money. Money could be a buffer to all sorts of problems. Unfortunately, not in this case. Her heart contracted for them. Their daughter murdered not more than three miles from their home.

Thomas reversed the car to park alongside the other vehicles and they took in the view. The house was three stories tall, looking out across an immaculately manicured, wide front lawn, which sloped away to the view of the grey watery lough in the distance. The stone house was framed by fading clematis and oversized clay pots grouped in clusters near the front steps. Before Thomas had a chance to ring the doorbell, an older man opened the heavy wooden door.

'Police, I take it?'

'Yes, we're here to speak to the Dowds family.'

'Come in. They are expecting you. My daughter and her husband are in here waiting,' he said. Anna and Thomas went through.

The man was probably around seventy and looked beaten. His shoulders hunched up towards his excessively large ear lobes and his head of thinning silver hair. He indicated for them to follow him down the long hallway. As she followed, Anna caught her reflection in a huge gilded mirror that was hung above a long, dark-wood table. Everything about the house, from the driveway to the curved staircase, felt grand and opulent. The Dowds were obviously loaded. They were shown into one of the doors to the right of the hallway, where the Family Liaison Officer, greeted them. 'Joanne Dixon,' she said. 'The family are in here.'

'DCI King,' Thomas said as he strode purposefully into the room. Anna entered behind him taking in the scene. It was like something out of an interiors magazine, with thick Persian rugs covering the gleaming wood blocked floors, a huge chandelier hanging from the central ceiling rose, and a deep bay window, draped with heavy tapestry curtains, providing views over the Lough. Anna stopped herself from gasping at the opulence of it all.

'I'm Grace's father, Stephen.' The man stood up from the wine coloured velvet chair he was sitting in and reached to shake their hands. 'Have you heard anymore?'

Anna shook her head, 'No, I'm afraid we have nothing new, but we would like to ask you some questions about Grace's friends, who she was with last night, that type of thing.'

The woman, obviously the mother, hadn't yet spoken, sobbed quietly. Her shoulders moving rhythmically with every breath she took, were draped in a pale blue wool cardigan. Anna would bet her week's wages it was cashmere. You could almost smell the money, or maybe that was just the scent of the Diptyque candles. Tuberose and fig type smells that made Anna feel like she had walked into a luxury hotel.

'Mrs Dowds, I am so sorry for your loss. I can't imagine what you are experiencing, but I need you to know, we are doing absolutely everything we can to find out who did this, and get them off the street.' Anna felt her stomach roil. It was always the same for her – the crime scene felt like work, she could go into overdrive and see it as a formula to be untangled but this – dealing with the grief up-close, was agonising. There was no escaping behind evidence, SOCO reports, and corpses. This part of the job was what made the murder real to her, to see the pain of loss first hand.

'If you lot had done your job right the last time, Grace would still be here,' Stephen Dowds said, striding over to the marble fireplace where he lifted a photograph. Grace in her school uniform smiled out from the silver frame. He stared at it before placing it back again. Anna could feel the resentment sizzle off him.

'While we are looking at every possibility, there is nothing conclusive to connect the two girls' murders at this time.' Thomas spoke in a low voice, respectful and gentle. Anna could tell he had experience of dealing with this type of raw grief. He struck just the right tone.

'Jesus, I can't take this in. I can't listen to this. It can't be real,' Maureen Dowds looked exhausted. Her sobs returned and Anna placed a tentative hand on her shoulder. Murder was the great leveler. All the success and hard earned wealth couldn't protect the Dowds from the agony of this.

The grandfather returned to the room with a tray of tea things. 'I'm trying to keep busy,' he said, almost as if apologising, as he set the tray down on the side table.

Anna accepted the cup of tea and added a little milk. 'Thank you.'

'Grace was at a school formal, isn't that right?' Anna sat down and took out her notepad.

'Yes, it's a big deal nowadays. She has talked of nothing else for weeks,' Stephen said. 'We had a bit of a party here to see them off, like. We took pictures of all the girls standing on the staircase and the boys posed for their photographs too. We must have had forty people here, teenagers and their parents all dressed up, full of the excitement for their big night out. Who'd have thought ...' he looked out towards the velvet green lawn and the grey Lough as if contemplating what he couldn't bring himself to say.

'They left here at seven o'clock, in a specially hired party bus. I gave the company name to your colleague.'

'Did you hear from Grace again during the evening?'

'Yes, she sent me a text to say that the food was awful and that one of the boys had thrown up on the bus on the way there. Too much to drink, I'm sure,' Maureen said. 'That was at 10.40.'

'After they left we over saw the tidying up – our cleaner Martha was here to lend a hand. Then we went to bed and the next we heard anything was when the doorbell rang the doorbell at nine this morning.'

'Did you expect Grace home?'

'No, she had arranged to sleep over at her friend, Rachel's house. They all wanted to make the night last as long as possible, so we didn't expect to see her until today.' Stephen Dowds said.

Anna noticed another photograph on the mantle place. Two tall boys flanking the redheaded pretty girl in the centre. A typical family portrait.

'Are these your children?' Anna asked lifting the heavy silver framed picture.

'Yes, the boys are both at university over in Bristol, they are on their way home as I speak. Terrible to give them such bad news over the phone, but we couldn't risk them hearing it on the news, or seeing something on Facebook.'

'No, it's impossible to contain anything these days. The press will be all over this I'm afraid, but Joanne, the family liaison officer, will advise you on how to handle any unwanted enquires.' Thomas said, getting up.

'We'll leave you in peace now. Let us know if we can do anything more and rest assured we are going to get whoever did this.'

* * *

Back in the office Anna called the techs dealing with the two birds but she was told they needed more time. Instead she focused on the social media sites to see if there were any mentions of Esme and Grace. Naturally, they both came up with hundreds of references to what had happened along with condolences from friends. It was likely most of the so-called friends were virtual, friends of friends, but every possible connection had to be examined. The IT department would be on to it, but Anna always liked to get a feel for the contacts in any cases like this. Sometimes it felt like crawling through a sticky web of possibilities to get to the creep at the centre.

There were several photographs of Grace at parties, one arm draped around a boy, another dressed in her school uniform looking young and serious. Richard McKay appeared in front for Anna's desk looking like he was about to murder somebody.

'I want an update, with King too,' he said, his eyes boring into Anna's computer as if he half expected her to be sitting playing solitaire.

Anna found Thomas helping himself to a coffee. 'McKay's looking for a briefing. Come on.'

Anna sat at Richard McKay's desk feeling like she had been called to the principal's office.

'So, brief me, what've we got?' McKay asked.

'Grace Dowds, aged eighteen. Daughter of prominent business man Stephen Dowds. Out at her school formal at the Culloden Hotel. Seen leaving the hotel at 11.03 p.m. on CCTV – alone. Found dead this morning by a dog walker.'

She noticed Thomas fiddling with his watch, anxious and keen to impress.

'We are going to have to move fast on this. Stephen Dowds has friends in high places. Cause of death?'

Anna shifted in her seat. The inference, that the Dowds girl was of more significance because of her daddy's powerful connections, rankled.

'Obviously, we'll have to wait on the autopsy report, sir, but looks similar to the Esme Wells case – head trauma and asphyxiation. No sign of rape or sexual assault,' she said.

Thomas took over, 'We've two primary lines of enquiry: first a disgruntled business associate of Mr Dowds – he's plenty of enemies out there. Rory Finnegan, Esme's brother-in-law – has featured in our research and he has business links with Mr Dowds.' Thomas looked to Anna to continue.

'Second, we are looking at connections between the two scenes of crime – the venues, both girls were found within close proximity to the hotels. Significantly, we have evidence of the killer leaving a trademark tag. In both cases, birds have been found at the site. In Esme's case, as you know, a dead bird with its eyes removed was found after the site clear up and in Grace Dowds' case, a bird had been inserted into her mouth.'

Thomas says, 'We are still waiting for the findings on the birds. Who knows what might turn up? With regards to the hotels, we're looking closely at staff lists and taxi drivers in the area.'

'And third?'

'Actually sir,' Anna said, 'This one's a bit off the wall. We would like to have a look at the Declan Wells car bomb file. Just to make sure there's no connection.'

'Connection? What sort of frigging connection?'

'Who's to say it isn't some sort of revenge motive?'

'Cole, I think you'll find that when we close a case here it's for a reason. The Declan Wells car bomb was dealt with at the time and I sincerely doubt you'd find anything trawling through all that again. Don't be wasting time.'

Chapter 19

The night before had caught up with her. She showered and got into her tracksuit bottoms and her old Zeppelin T-shirt, glad to have the grime of her day washed away. Her hair hung damp around her shoulders. She debated whom to call first, her dad or Jon? She had put off both calls for days, not wanting to be interrogated about when she would be going home for a visit, nor did she relish the idea of talking to Jon, having spent the night at King's apartment, even if she hadn't done anything to regret.

The doorbell rang, making her jump. It wasn't as if she expected to have visitors.

She opened the door and was surprised to see Declan Wells. She looked down on him, parked at her front door in his wheelchair. His dark hair falling in an unkempt mess about his face. He looked wrecked.

'I told you this would happened. What have you got on the second girl?'

'Declan how did you know where I lived? You shouldn't be here.'

'Do you think I'm going to sit back on this fucking chair and let him slip away to do this again?' He was seething. There was a white-hot rage emitting for his every movement.

'You better come in,' she hesitated, unsure of how she would get his chair through the door. 'Round the back, there's a patio door.'

* * *

He was barely in through the door when he started, 'Two girls, both young, both out at private events. I knew it would happen again. I told you.'

'Declan, it isn't as if we have been sitting around doing nothing. We are scanning CCTV, interviews with every guest at the wedding have been conducted and now every attendee at the formal. It all takes time.'

'You don't have time,' he said manoeuvring the chair into the living room. 'He will act again.'

'We've no reason to think so.'

He took a deep breath if as readying himself for battle. 'You need to construct a profile. To start thinking of this as part of a larger plan. Not nit picking through Esme's life.'

Anna didn't like being door-stepped, let alone being bullied about the case. The last thing she needed was a distraught, grieving parent trying to hijack the inquiry.

'Dr Wells, I can't make this any clearer, if you have concerns you need to talk to the Family Liaison Officer, she will be able to reassure you that we are in full control of the investigation.'

'Hardly,' he said, manoeuvring the chair, 'You can't brush me off. I've been around the police too long to know how things get done and how things are missed.'

Anna was certain she was in for a long night. He obviously hadn't been sleeping well, dark shadows under his eyes and his dull complexion gave it away. He was still handsome though. He needed a haircut and a shave and he was way too old for her, but there was something about him that attracted her. It was his command, the fact that he was imposing, almost in spite of the chair. She could imagine he would have been a force to reckon with before the incident. Thomas had told her about the car bomb. How he had been very lucky not to lose his life, and how there had been repercussions for the force when it had been discovered a tip off had not been passed on.

He sat in his chair looking fired up, as if he could move mountains to prove his worth to Anna, 'If I were part of the investigation,' he said. 'I would have access to the crime scenes to be able to gather information from the source. Cases are solved by putting all the information together, clues, patterns, theories and hypotheses.'

She knew there was little point in arguing with him.

He went on, 'Think of it this way: I'm trying to uncover a cancer. If I were a medical doctor, treating a patient, I would ask for a case history, lifestyle, previous illnesses and such; I would examine the pathology as it presents before me and make my diagnosis based on my findings. All I'm asking for is to have insight.'

It was impossible to resist Declan's insistence. No matter how many times she protested that he shouldn't be there or working on the case, he shot her down with the logic that no one wanted to find who did this more than him. He would do whatever it took, and he had been proved right so far. The killer had an agenda. Two dead girls and the threat of more, if they didn't get a result fast. She had divulged more than she intended to, like the information on the birds, but she figured that it wouldn't hamper the investigation. He was so focused, so knowledgeable about how to create a psychological portrait, and so convincing.

* * *

By midnight they had drawn up a profile. Declan was sure that the killer was mid- to late twenties. He had a grudge against young girls, possibly spurned by an ex-girlfriend.

'All we know about the killer is based on aspects of his crimes. Unfortunately, the more crimes he perpetrates the more we learn about him,' he said sighing.

'Do you think there is possibility he has killed before?' Anna asked, studying his face, noticing for the first time the shadows and lines, sure she could commit his profile to memory and sketch it later if she wanted to.

'He may have, but I think Esme was his first.'

'Why?' Anna thought of all the reported sexual attacks that had gone unsolved, the incidents considered one-offs that perhaps didn't have the full attention they should have received.

'He's been building up to this. Maybe he has stalked girls before, made a nuisance of himself and got off on frightening them. Just because we don't have proof that the girls knew him doesn't mean that they hadn't come across him somewhere. Esme wasn't his starting point, but she was his first murder.'

Anna watched him in the dim light of the room. He looked beat, yet there was a spark in his eyes.

'The killer sees the victim as an object. He has some degree of control; we know this because he's careful with the scene. He thinks he hasn't given too much away because the scenes are relatively clean of any trace of him. But the birds are his trademarks. He is telling us plenty. The sadistic nature of the removal of the first bird's eyes has shock value. That was him signaling that there was more to come.'

Anna's jaw tightened, 'Go on.'

'Typical motivation for serial homicide is often described as being either sexual or internal psychological gratification. We haven't evidence of the perpetrator's bodily fluids, most likely if it were sexual he would have assaulted the girls in that way or left evidence of masturbation. So, we need to ask what is his internal gratification?'

'Motive?'

'Not exactly. Sure, motive comes into play, but I'm thinking more along the lines out what does he get out of each kill in the heat of the act.'

Declan's face looked flushed. He continued, 'He's self-assured in his behaviour, appears to operate a con and ploy approach – dupes the girls into accompanying him away from a place of safety into the forest. This shows he can maintain a superficial relationship. He is charming, flirtatious even. They don't feel threatened by him, which tells us he's probably young. Young enough for them to feel safe with. Teenage girls still think of the dangerous man as being older. The victim is a prop to him, he doesn't form attachment, no sexual interference.' Declan paused, he was watching Anna intensely as if to make sure she was taking in what he was saying.

Anna said, 'If what you are saying is true, he must have built up a rapport with the girls. Chatted them up, or maybe knew them prior to the murders.'

'Yes, quite possibly, he knew them, or at least was able to make them feel that he knew them. Kids nowadays are on Facebook with every Tom, Dick and Harry. It could be an online connection.

'It's significant that the murder happened in close proximity to the wedding reception. He is letting us know he isn't frightened. He's enjoyed the danger of possibly being caught. Somehow I feel that he wants to show us he's capable of doing something heinous within near reach of safety.'

'It's a desire for power then?'

'Yes. Power and dominance. Superiority even. He's asserting his power, proving what he can do this under our noses, and maybe, he knows there were significant authority figures at the wedding.' She could hear the frustration in his voice.

'And the birds?'

'I was getting to that. The bird left at Esme's site was a calling card. He had probably watched from a safe distance, knew the site had been cleared and went back to mark the scene with his docket. He's intelligent, or at least thinks of himself as being so and wants to play with the investigation. Show his ability to stay one step ahead.'

Anna says quietly, 'There will be more won't there, if we don't catch him?'

'I think so. The bird could be symbolic; it suggests he sees women as passive creatures, delicate and easily crushed. The insertion of the bird in Grace's mouth shows he's getting brasher and sicker and suggests that there is more to come. It's staged.

He is getting a kick out of setting the scene. The birds are props he is using to create an added dynamic.'

They talked some more, going over the details again. The venue, the wedding, the guests and Declan's PSNI past.

Declan sighed and looked weary. 'We are looking for someone relatively young – young enough for Esme to feel an affinity with. Someone who has access to the event – so that he can operate under the cover of a big event like a wedding or a prom night.'

'We're already checking security, bar and catering staff, but someone might have been brought in on a freelance contract to do the job for the night, giving him access to the event and time to pick out his victim,' Anna said. 'We have all the staff from both venues on the interview lists. If anyone isn't accounted for, we will know by Tuesday at the latest,' she added, aware that she wasn't telling him anything he didn't already know. It was crazy to have allowed Declan to come in and to start down this path of going over the case, but she had been careful not to disclose anything he shouldn't know, or anything he couldn't have gleaned from the press. Still, she knew if Thomas or McKay were aware that she was allowing Declan to be involved on any level, her job would be on the line.

He leaned back against his chair, his hands rubbing at his eyes. She recognised the pain etched on his face and something in her stirred in response. It was late and she was tired, but Declan was easy to work with. She liked how his mind was firing off in all directions, leaving no possibility unexplored. She could imagine he had been good at his job. He was wasted in academia. She would have liked to work with him under different circumstances.

'How are you and your wife coping?' she asked pouring another glass of red for them both. Her resolve to keep it professional had ended sometime around midnight. Neither of them mentioned how he would drive home after drinking the best part of a bottle of wine.

He shrugged. 'Izzy and I aren't exactly together. We haven't been, not really since this happened.' he looked down at his legs.

'I can only speak for myself and right now I'm wrung out. I'm at an impasse, until we get this bastard I can't grieve, not properly. Every time I think of Esme, I think of him. Of his hands around her neck, of what she felt, of how frightened she must have been.' He looked down into the glass of merlot.

Anna could see the impact of his suffering in the way he held himself, on the defensive, ready for combat, unsure what was to come next. Anna figured that surviving a car bomb would do that to a person, leave them fragile amongst the wreckage. Now he had to deal with the devastation of losing his daughter in the most awful of circumstances as well.

She recognised something of herself in him. She knew what it was like to lose someone close. First her birth mother; in some deep recess of her being, she knew she bears the wounds of that loss and then, the desperate agony of witnessing Camille's suffering when death was the kindest release of all.

There was something in the quiet dignity of the way he conducted himself, how he contained his pain that made her want to reach out and comfort him. He was methodical in his approach; every action was deliberated and considered. She could see that it was an effort for him not to bow under the weight of the grief. But like the bough of a tree he could only bend so far before breaking. Without giving it too much thought, she placed her hand on his face. He moved towards her, as if her touch was balm to his pain. He went to speak, to protest probably. 'Shsssh,' she said, leaning into him, her lips finding his.

Anna woke first, her neck sore from the position she had been lying in. Declan was still asleep, spread out in front of the dying embers of the fire. They had made a makeshift bed on the floor of pillows and a duvet, while they lay talking into the small hours of the morning. Anna smiled at the memory of him. His touch had been so tender and gentle she had barely felt his hands wandering over the contours of her body. He kissed her with such reverence at first and then desperate passion, as if he couldn't get enough of her.

She had taken the lead, moving fast before either of them gave it too much thought. As her hand had reached down to undo his belt buckle he had stopped her, held her by the wrist and asked if she was sure. She answered by pushing her hand roughly down his trousers and reaching for him, neither was turning back after that. He had surprised her by staying. The downstairs cloakroom meant that he had no need to go upstairs, and they had managed to sleep well enough on the made-up bed of pillows and duvets.

Later, when she pulled his trousers off, she looked at his legs and saw the scars and the crumpled stumps patched together by the surgeons. Her hands moved over them as if needing to understand how they had been damaged, and how they had been put together. He kissed her long and hard, pulling her faded T-shirt over her head. Now she turned into him, feeling the rise and fall of his chest as he breathed deeply.

He stirred. 'Hey, you,' Declan said turning to her.

'You were sleeping so soundly I didn't want to disturb you.'

'I haven't slept like that for weeks, not since ...' he drifted off not wanting reality to ruin the moment. 'My back is going to kill me,' he said smiling.

'I hope I'm worth it,' Anna joked getting up.

'Totally.'

Anna felt herself blush. It was the way he looked at her, like she was salvation.

Chapter 20

Anna watched from the side of the conference room as Thomas sat down beside Richard McKay, facing the bank of reporters and television cameras. The initial awkwardness between them had dissipated and Anna was relived to be focusing on the case. Cameras began whirring into life, flashes of light and the chatter quieted down.

'Thank you for joining us today. I am Detective Inspector Richard King. I will provide you with some information of the what has happened in the two cases, and then you will hear from Mr Dowds, father of murdered girl, Grace Dowds.'

Anna watched the hacks scribble their indecipherable shorthand in their notepads. She knew they had a job to do but once too often she had seen first-hand their intrusiveness and their lack of respect for the due process of the law. She had a mistrust that they would spin these murders into something salacious, as if the death of two young schoolgirls wasn't bad enough, they would look for the worst possible angle. Trawl their Facebook pictures to find the most suggestive one, and all the time manage to look like they are taking the higher ground, hounding the police to do more, while badgering the girls' poor, heartbroken relatives. She thought of Declan and his desperation to ensure the murderer was caught. The memory of his hands all over her body flit through her mind before she dragged her thoughts into the present moment and focused on Richard's words.

'... We have a double murder inquiry with the second body, that of Grace Dowds, aged eighteen, found in the grounds of the Culloden Hotel. I can tell you that both girls died as a result of strangulation. The PSNI Serious Crime Operations are, of course, doing everything possible to ensure the killer is apprehended.'

He paused to allow questions. Immediately a tall gangly man stood up, 'Is it true that you have brought a detective over from Wales because your people aren't used to dealing with crimes of this nature?'

'No, most definitely not. The detective you refer to was here on a planned secondment, but of course we welcome her input.' His eyes met Anna's across the room.

'Can you say if either of the two girls were sexually assaulted?' a female reporter this time, who remained seated.

'No. There was no evidence of sexual assault.'

'If there was no sexual assault, would you say you are struggling to find a motive?'

'We can't say anymore at this point. Now, Mr Dowds would like to speak.'

The room fell into a hush again.

'I would like to appeal to anyone who may know anything which can help bring this killer, or killers, to justice to come forward. I am putting up a reward of £100,000 to help find who did this.' A buzz went around the room, the reward hadn't been mentioned to them before this. Anna knew too well they weren't going to gain anything from it. Often, such rewards caused more harm than good. They would need extra officers just to man the phones. Every crank and his aunty would be calling the hotline with their own personal take on the case and possible sightings and theories.

Dowds waited until hush fell over the room again, before he continued, 'Grace was a beautiful, loving daughter and we are heartbroken that this has happened.' He bowed his head.

'That brings our press conference to a close,' King said, standing and leaning in to talk to Stephen Dowds.

The rumble of voices in the room rose and they all began packing up. They had been thrown their tidbits for the day; it was back to the newsrooms to make something of it.

* * *

His hand automatically reached to stroke the dog while he watched the local news programme. 'Good boy,' he said, smiling to himself. The collie, as always stood to attention, the best dog ever. He had named it Odin, after the one-eyed Viking god of gods. Odin liked to meddle in affairs in order to stir up the mortals, encouraging violence and war. By doing so he increased the number of warriors in Valhalla that would be there to fight with him in the final battle.

They were talking about the murders on the television. The screen was filled with an image of the river Lagan, flanked by the grassy banks, teaming with wildlife if you knew what to look for, and the woodland behind. The reporter was talking about Esme, her life taken from her in the picturesque setting on the day of her sister's wedding. Then they switched to the scene at the Culloden, the hotel manager speaking to the camera, saying that they were all shocked by what had occurred.

His girls. How he had taken them from the hotel venues and led them to their deaths. The press conference was shown. Police were appealing for witnesses to come forward. The chief detective was doing the talking, but off to the side of the conference table, he could see that female detective, the one they had sent over from the mainland. Anna Cole. The papers said she was Welsh. She was interesting, attractive, in that easy way some women had of not trying too hard. He liked that. She was looking to the male detective doing the talking and then her gazed moved to the audience of reporters, poised with their notebooks and microphones.

He thought of a line he had read and liked, 'The man who knows birds by both sight and song has a tremendous advantage over him who does not.'

He stroked the black and white pelt of the dog, thinking of the work involved. His latest creation. Like all good collectors, he liked to keep a notebook of his finds, data and projects. He enjoyed the skill involved, the development of his learning. How each project taught him something new. From discovering the best mount for supporting the structure, to selecting the perfect eyeball, to achieving an accurate head shape. It was all so rewarding. He even enjoyed sewing thousands of tiny stitches, painting beaks, and each of the individual transformative tasks.

As always, he had taken careful measurements before the skinning. There was no room for error.

'You're a good boy, Odin,' he said. The dog had been a good specimen, just like the girls.

* * *

Anna was still thinking about the birds. She was sure the first one had been deliberately placed at the site, and that Declan was right. It was a macabre tribute.

'Hey, Thomas, any word from the tech guys on the birds?'

'No, nothing yet. Could we be dealing with a twitcher with a passion for killing young girls?' he said.

'Twitcher, as in a bird watcher?'

'Yeah, hard to know, but the bird angle has to be explored.'

Anna looked down at her notes. She had been looking up bird symbolism. Trying to see if there was some sort of hidden message. So far all she had turned up was a whole heap of possibilities and nothing concrete.

'Esme's murder site had been cleared days ago so whoever had left it must have been watching to make sure we'd cleared off,' she said.

'Yeah, I was thinking that, but until we know more about bird, how it died and how it links up with the one found Grace's mouth we can't run with it.'

Thomas moved across the incident room and sat on the edge of her desk. His face over-eager as he said, 'Give the tech guy a ring. Put a rocket up their arses. Your Welsh accent'll charm him into getting us the job done.'

Anna rolled her eyes at him but picked up the phone.

'PJ, Anna Cole here any news on those birds yet?

'DI Cole, I was just about to give you a call. Saved me the bother of dialing your number.'

Anna could hear the smugness in his voice. He obviously had something worth sharing but was playing up his role. Tech guys could be the biggest assholes.

'Well, I've had a good examination of your first wee birdy. It's a black guillemot. It wasn't hard to identify – black and white plumage and bright red feet. I took the liberty to speak to an ornithologist. He says you find guillemots in the larger sea lochs of Scotland, and the northern and western isles, but it's also found in here in Northern Ireland and the Isle of Man.'

'And, any idea on how it died?'

'I found a tiny fragment of netting embedded in the bird's throat which would suggest it was caught in some sort of trap. Its neck has been wrung. A quick twist and it would snap easily enough. So, whoever left it there probably left you a wee message, all right.'

'Any chance of tracing the netting fragment?'

'I'm on to it. Should take another couple of days, could have been something the bird picked up from a trawler net so I have to rule out if it's been an incidental find. I suspect not though, so I'd say look at trappers, wildlife experts that kind of thing. The Royal Society for the Protection of Birds might help you out.'

'Right, thanks PJ. If anything comes through on the netting let me know straight away. What about the second one?'

'That one's still with the pathologist. Since it was found in-situ on the victim, she deals with it so you'll have to chase her up.'

Anna thanked him. Thomas had heard it all via speakerphone. 'So, the killer is definitely in the know about how to capture and handle a bird. He has trapped it and left it for us to find.'

'Yeah, so it's over to Margaret McCann now to see what the second bird tells us.'

* * *

The office was still busy. Holly was up to her eyes trying to organise the extra hands that had been called in. The reward would be nectar to every idiot seeking attention but they needed to follow up every single call.

Anna let the buzz of voices fade behind her as she added her sketch to the wall of maps, scribbled notes, photographs and time lines. The photograph of Esme caught her eye. The image didn't convey the sparkly girl Declan had portrayed her to be. He had said she was bright and articulate, never slow to speak her mind and quick to point out injustice. She was mad about animals and longed for a dog. Declan said he'd wished they had given in and got her one.

Now Grace's picture was added to the wall. Her photograph placed beside Esme. Her family feeling the same agony that Declan told her of. The frustration, rage and desolation that sat like a boulder on his chest. She reached for her phone.

'Hi, it's me.

Chapter 21

Mortuary suites didn't bother Anna. She always found the scene of the crime more disturbing. The body, sometimes still warm to the touch, the air only recently expelled from the lungs. Here, in the sterile world of stainless steel and over bright lighting, the body was reduced to physical parts: flesh, bone, sinew and muscle, carefully examined to give up the clues and secrets of death.

Dr Margaret McCann looked up and nodded as Anna entered the room. She was instructing her assistant to place her instruments in a precise order, left to right.

'She's over there,' Margaret said, indicating with a nod of her head. Anna walked over and offered up a silent prayer. Grace Dowds looked so young as she lay stretched out on the steel table. The skin over her cheekbones appeared stretched, highlighting her fragility, the freckles appearing even starker than when Anna had first seen the body. Her strong brows, which in the photographs, framed her pretty face, looked too heavy and dark against the blue, waxy paleness death had reduced her to.

'Did you see the strangulation marks, here and here?' Margaret asked as she put on her Dictaphone to record her every cut and finding. Anna nodded looking at the angry, purple and red welts around the girl's delicate neck.

'Same as Esme Wells?'

'Looks like it. No fingerprints, though. He definitely wore gloves. SOCOs have recovered some fibres – leather, and although there was no wood wool this time, as you know, we have this.' She held up a plastic bag containing the bird. 'The SOCO team said they have a trace of wood wool on one of the feathers.'

Anna caught herself holding her breath. There was something unsettling about the smell – the gassy smell of death and rubbing alcohol, mixed with an unpleasant undercurrent of disinfectant. She never voluntarily attended autopsies, but like the crime scene, they too, offered up morsels of information. Each fact or suggestion helping to paint shade and light onto the larger picture.

'As you can see, it was a robin,' Margaret removed the bird from the plastic bag.

It lay on the table, small and still. Anna moved over to look closely at it. It was small and slightly plump, with tawny brown feathers slick with some sort of coating. Its distinctive orangey red breast was flattened into its chest so that it looked like it had been punctured, knocking all of the air out of it. The thought of it being inserted into Grace's mouth made Anna want to be sick.

'Do we know how the bird died and if it was alive when the killer struck Grace?'

'Hard to say, but I think it was alive when it was put into her mouth. I can tell you that it died from being crushed which suggests it was alive before being placed in the victim's mouth.'

Margaret adjusted the microphone attached to her lab coat, 'I will be checking the teeth and mouth to see if there are signs that she clamped down on the bird, that would be consistent with the fractures in the bird's bone structure as seen in the X-ray. The material coating the bird is residual vomit. She most likely gagged as it was put in her mouth.'

* * *

Anna left the mortuary before Margaret began her post mortem. There were some things she didn't need to see. She made mental lists on her way back to the office. The feather and the fibre played on her mind. They had enough to think it was the same killer. They assumed the wood wool found in Esme's mouth was from packaging – a crate of wine, or something fragile that needed to be encased to protect them. But maybe they had got that wrong. What if the wood wool was used as stuffing? The idea of the fibres being forced into Esme's screaming mouth made her stomach heave, but the bird was a step further. As if the sickening violence wasn't enough.

At the office, Anna called up the profile notes on her computer. The killer was beginning to feel real. Someone presentable, good looking even, not old, maybe twenty-five to thirty years old, charming and persuasive enough to lead two girls away from a busy venue to their deaths. They must have felt comfortable and relaxed with him. Anna sat at her desk staring at the open file. She had mapped out narrative sketches – lists of known associates, places of interest where they would be travelling to school, for both girls. She was looking for similarities, cross over points, anything to link them but so far nothing solid. They didn't know each other, either in the real world, on Facebook, Snap Chat or on Twitter. But she couldn't ignore that they were both young women, out celebrating. Pretty girls with everything going for them. Education and the comfort of wealth behind them, especially in the Dowds' girl's case.

She had an unnerving feeling of having missed something tangible but she wasn't getting anywhere sitting there.

'Holly,' she called across the room, 'Do me a favour, ring the school and tell the head I'm on my way to pay them a visit. I want to talk to some of Grace's friends,' Anna said as she grabbed her jacket, the pool car keys and headed off.

* * *

Grace's school was the closest thing Belfast had to a posh public school. Drummond House was a co-ed grammar, situated on the edge of Belfast city centre. Like Esme, Grace's school was elite. The use of academic selection at the age of eleven had created for a number of grammar schools in Belfast. Each offering a first-rate education to any pupils who had met with the entrance criteria.

Anna drove through the wide gates at the bottom of the driveway, taking in the trees at either side and the brilliant green lawns, immaculately kept and edged with rhododendrons and azaleas, before going around to the back of the building. An old, distinguished looking red brick building housed the main school with smaller buildings around an internal courtyard at the back. It all smelt of money and privilege.

The pupils all wore a uniform of charcoal grey blazers over sharp, bright white shirts, with dark green ties and grey pleated skirts for the girls and black trousers for the boys. There was little to differentiate them apart from school bags, hockey sticks and swathes of long hair on the girls. The boys moved in clumps together, jumping on each other in horseplay and firing a rugby ball back and forth between them. They moved in a mass, like a flock, all on the same path to whichever class they were heading to next.

Anna parked and made her way into the main building, following the sign for visitors. She showed her ID to a secretary seated behind a glass partition. 'You'll want to speak to the principal Mr Collins, I assume?'

'Yes, he should be expecting me, can ask him to give me a few moments please?'

The principal's office was panelled in dark mahogany with an oil painting depicting the school building hanging above his highly-polished desk.

'Mr Collins, this is Detective Cole,' the secretary said as Anna made her way forward into the room. Anna held out her hand. 'Sorry for the intrusion, but would it be possible to speak to some of Grace's friends?'

A group of students had been gathered in to the common room. Some of them had been crying. One girl was still sniffing into her balled up tissues.

'I'm sorry and I know this is a hard time for the school. You must all miss Grace and feel really upset about how she died,' Anna said sitting down in front of them. A few of them nodded in agreement. 'I need you to think carefully. If there is anything which may be of help, you have to tell us. Did Grace have any friends outside of school? Any boyfriends or acquaintances that she kept from her parents?'

Anna knew that she should have structured the interviews, selected the girls and boys close to Grace and brought them in for questioning, but experience told she would hear more if they weren't intimated and being made to answer questions with mummy or daddy listening in.

She took a list of their names. Six best friends, and several who were said to be good friends but not 'best'. Anna hated the whole ranking of friends that went on. The inner circle and those on the fringes competing to be accepted by the 'in' crowd. Grace appeared to be popular and well liked.

'Mia, can you think of any reason why Grace would have left the hotel on the night of the prom?'

The girl shrugged. 'She might have gone out for a cigarette, or she might have felt sick. She had been drinking a lot.'

'Does anyone remember Grace saying she was going outside?' They all murmured 'no.'

Anna was able to identify the boy who had been Grace's date for the night. Ben Radcliffe spoke quietly, 'We had a fight. Grace wasn't happy that I was spending most of the night with my mates at the bar. She wanted me to dance with her.' He looked grief stricken. His clean shaved skin, made him look even younger than his eighteen years.

'And this was at around eleven you said?'

'I think so, I can't be sure. She stormed off and I went back to the party. I didn't see her after that,' he said looking down at his hands.

'Has anyone any idea of if she would have gone off with someone?'

'Do you think it was someone at the formal?' a girl called Ashleigh asked.

'We have to consider every possibility. We will be talking to everyone who attended on the night and hotel staff. You can imagine it will take time to interview everyone, so we need you to think carefully, and if you can think of anything give me call.' She handed each of them her card.

* * *

Holly was pouring coffee when Anna returned to the office. 'Want one?' she asked.

'Sure, white, no sugar.'

'King was looking for you earlier.'

'He probably wants an update before the main briefing. I'll get to him in a minute.' Anna could see the trace of a smirk play at Holly's mouth. She didn't need the whole place thinking she had shagged a colleague. If he has said anything, she'd be pissed off. It was hard enough gaining their trust and respect as the outsider. She cursed herself again for being seen heading off with Thomas on the night out. She wouldn't make the same mistake twice.

The briefing meeting had been set for 2.00 p.m. McKay strode in with a thunderous look on his face. He'd probably been getting flak from above, Anna thought. The powers-at-be were keeping the pressure on, and as the press had used Grace's death to run with a double-murder angle, the force risked looking slow and incompetent.

'Let's get started. As from today the two cases will come under the code name Operation Ophelia. We don't choose the name but it isn't the worst they could come up with. DI Cole, update us on the Esme Wells case and what we have so far on Grace Dowds?'

'Yes sir.' Anna stood at the white board and clicking on her laptop, displayed the first photograph – Grace Dowds lying in-situ.

'PM is back and cause of death for Grace Dowds is the same as Esme – strangulation. Unlike Esme, there were no other major injuries except for bruising and marks, which suggest she fought her attacker. DNA samples are not back yet, we're still hopeful that we'll find something, though it appears our attacker is careful.'

She clicked the mouse again and a new photograph appeared of strands of fabric. 'Significantly, with both girls, traces of this fibre have been found. In Esme, the fibre, called wood wool was stuffed in to her mouth.'

Thomas King spoke, 'In Grace's case, SOCO found a few stray fibres. Possibly transmitted to the victim from the perpetrators clothes. At the first crime scene, seven days after the murder, a bird was recovered. Apparently placed as some sort of marker.' He clicked on the picture, showing the dead, black guillemot. 'As you can see the eyes have been removed. There is evidence that whoever removed the eyes knew what they were doing, the eye sockets remain intact with no damage and this apparently takes a bit of skill and practice.'

Anna continued, holding up some wood wool, 'This is an example of the fibre we are talking about. It is used for stuffing toys and certain types of packaging. It is coarse, dry curls of finely serrated wood, almost like a thick papery texture. As Thomas said, it is also used in taxidermy. We are looking at all of those angles.'

The room murmured.

'And going back to the first bird,' Anna clicked on the link and a photograph of the dead, eyeless bird flashed up on the screen.

'This was found at the first scene, a week after the murder of Esme Wells. As you can see, the eyes of the bird have been removed. It's a strange finding. The site had been cleared days before who ever left it must have been watching to make sure we'd cleared off. We have a report from a forensic entomologist, which is on the system so have a read. Basically, they told us the bird had been dead for a while, probably a few weeks and stored.'

She went on, reading from her notes, 'The feather mites usually die off after the bird is dead and don't cause any further damage to the feathers. The bird has also been soaked in a mild detergent, which would get rid of them anyway. What usually eats the feathers away, later down the road are moths or larvae. This tells us that, whoever left the bird, knew how to work with wildlife. And of course, it is also significant that the eyes have been removed without damage to the socket.'

Thomas took over, 'In the case of Grace Dowds, a bird was placed inside her mouth. We now know that the bird was put into Grace's mouth before she died, and that the robin was alive. The robin died through the force of Grace's mouth clamping down on it. There was residual vomit on the bird, and its neck bones were crushed along with some of the skeletal bones.'

The room murmured.

'Sick bastard,' Magee said.

'Yes, we are dealing with someone who has a penchant for the ghoulish,' Thomas paused, letting the room settle down again. 'He obviously knows the sites well, has access to the girls, is perhaps familiar with them or is confident in chatting with them and leading them to their place of death. He also knows his way around wildlife, so we may have some sort of a specialist on our hands.'

Anna clicked on to the next picture, 'As you can see the scene where the body was found is mainly a small woodland in the hotel grounds. She was covered in trace elements from the environment, soil composition and twigs, debris of the natural habitat. All pointing to the fact that this is the primary scene. Footprints are of no use – possibly covered up by the attacker.'

Anna turned to Thomas, 'You have the PM report.'

He stayed in his seat and read from his file. 'Time of death in Grace's case is estimated at sometime between midnight on Saturday and 2.00 a.m. Sunday morning. Contents of her stomach were consistent with the meal she ate at the formal, and toxicology reports show she had drunk vodka, quite a bit.'

'Was there a sexual assault?' asked Holly.

'Again, like the Esme Wells case, no sexual assault.'

'Tox screen was negative for drugs, although she had been drinking, she was in no way out of it and we can assume she went willingly with the killer,' Anna added.

'We're looking at the same man then?' asked Conlon.

McKay turned to the room. 'I don't want the press getting wind of the fibres or the dead bird. Until we have more to go on we tell the press to treat this as a separate case.'

'Could she have been targeted because of who her father is?' Holly asked. 'He's pretty high profile.'

'Mr Dowds has already asked if it could be connected to him standing for the elections. He's worried dissidents had something to do with it. Previously, threats had been made against him and his family, but at this point we aren't convinced there is a connection.'

'Where are we with staff interviews?' McKay asked. Manus Magee had been tasked with over seeing the painstakingly work of collecting information on the staff lists of the two hotels.

'I was getting to that. The regular staff all checked out, nothing of interest but both venues hire in extra bouncers and security staff for big events and significantly, both use the same company. There are a few names on the list that weren't scheduled to work the night in question so we have ruled them out but we need to go back to them.'

'Right get on to it and obtain a comprehensive list of anyone working for the two venues, whether they were scheduled to work or not.'

'Already on it, sir. Esme's phone records are still with the IT department and we need to see if she had any unusual activity on her Facebook – any new friends, secret messages that kind of thing.'

'Chase them up,' McKay said, bringing the briefing to close.

The morning briefing lacked the eagerness and excitement of the week before. There was an eerie hush in the incident room. New back up staff brought in to assist, were methodically sorting the extra paperwork, thrown up by the reward. Calls were coming in, mostly crank, a few promising possibilities, but they all needed to be checked out. Half-finished coffee mugs and the remains of hastily eaten lunches sat giving off a stale odour that they were all too preoccupied to deal with. The team was deflated and quieter than usual. There were significant links between Esme Wells and Grace Dowds. What DNA samples they had from Esme, hadn't matched anything in the system. Hundreds of police hours had been spent interviewing the wedding guests, examining the CCTV and generally picking through the detail of the two cases.

* * *

The day had drifted away from Anna. She had spent it following up phone calls, checking on data the floaters were logging. The higher the stakes, the quicker the days seemed to rush past as if time was speeding up. Anna was lost in thought, thinking about Grace Dowds and the moments before she died; the squirm of the bird being shoved into her mouth, its beak hitting the back of Grace's throat, making her gag, its heart thumping against the roof of her mouth, the dry desiccated feel of the feathers. How she must have bit down in pain, trying to fight back, feeling the crush of the bird's brittle bones underneath its flesh. Anna took a swig from her bottle of water, her throat parched, almost imagining how Grace had felt, when Thomas came careering in.

'Grab your coat, Cole, let's get out of here,' Thomas said.

'Where are we going?'

'I need substance, a dinner that doesn't come served in plastic from a microwave and a drink. You don't mind driving, do you?' he replied, feeling in his jacket pocket for his keys and then tossing them to Anna before she could respond. They headed to the Botanic area of Belfast. At that time of the evening, workers were heading home and students where queuing up for Boojum, the burrito bar. They parked and made their way through the rain-drenched streets to The Empire Music Hall, a church like venue with stone steps leading up to the first-floor entrance.

'This used to be a Victorian church until it became a comedy club and concert hall. I've had some great nights in here, back in the day,' Thomas said, getting himself a pint and Anna a coke.

'I saw Snow Patrol here before they made it big. Great gig. And Ash too – local band. Ever heard of them?' He led Anna over to a round table with two wonky looking chairs.

'Yeah, I've heard of them. Some hit about a girl from Mars? They were cool for about five minutes when I was at uni'

'That's them. Classic tunage!'

'So, what have you been thinking?' Anna asked taking her coat off. The rain had soaked right through, leaving her feeling chilled and miserable. It had been that kind of day.

'About the case or Ash?'

She laughed, 'The case you muppet. Where are we going with it?'

'Statistically, we both know we should be looking at someone close to the girls – Finnegan fitted that bill with Esme. Young, male and with a possible motive.'

'Motive being they had something going on, or that she had seen or heard something at one of Finnegan's little exclusive soirées. Except he's placed at the wedding venue at the supposed time of death – with at least twenty witnesses saying he was on the dance floor giving it his all to 'Mr Brightside', followed by a trio of *Blur*, *Oasis* and the *Libertines*.'

'*Blur* and *Oasis*? Really?'

'I know criminal, but we can't arrest him for bad taste in music or dubious dance moves.'

'That's a pity.' Anna studied the menu. 'I'm going for the Cajun chicken.'

'A dirty burger for me, extra onions and fries, thanks.' The waitress took their orders and Thomas waited a second until she had left their table, 'Perhaps our lad Rory had someone do his dirty work for him. He's not the kind to get his hands dirty. I'm still pressing to get a warrant to search his offices.'

'But his new wife's sister? At his own wedding?' 'Not our problem. Ours is not to reason why, ours is but to suggest he could have, and then find the evidence to support the crazy theory.'

'Mmm,' Anna said taking a sip of the coke. 'Yes, we know that his business isn't clean. He's dodgy for sure, but to take a hit out on his sister-in-law? It's a bit of stretch. Don't you think if it was Finnegan then it would be more a crime of a passion and he would have done it himself? Our killer shows evidence of being considered and thought out.'

'Maybe Esme was blackmailing him, threatening to tell her big sister what kind of man she was marrying.'

'What about we take Finnegan out of the murder equation for a second. Our killer could be someone else in attendance at his business parties. Maybe Esme, who we can assume wasn't all sweetness and light, had seen or heard something and was using it to blackmail them?'

'Phone records and internet searches would have thrown something up to suggest another player involved.'

'It's an angle we need to explore all the same. And just because she had a crush on Finnegan, and was seen kissing him, according to Carly, doesn't mean she wasn't led on by him and seduced into some sort of relationship. He had all the power and control,' Anna said as the waitress set down her plate of food. She felt defensive of Esme, on behalf of Declan.

After dinner, they went outside for Thomas to have a smoke. Anna leaned against the cold stonewall, feeling the damp from the earlier rain seep through her coat.

Thomas blew out a stream of smoke into the chilly night air, 'We still have the problem of why did both girls willing leave the safety of the two venues? That suggests they knew the killer or were at least familiar with him. If they had been forced to leave with him, someone would have seen something or heard a protest. Could the meetings have been planned?' he said.

Anna watched people go past, students on their way out for the night, professionals coming home late from work. 'Or our guy knew where to find them and got lucky. Could he have been after any girl who fell for his chat-up lines or the promise of drugs?'

'We've no proof either girl was into anything stronger than a Bacardi Breezer or vodka. There were only kids, still hoping they can get away with a few drinks.'

Thomas flicked the ash from his cigarette, 'Dirty habit Tonto, don't ever let me see you suck on one of these cancer sticks. I only ever smoke when I'm on a big case that fucks up my mind.'

'Understood. I'll confiscate them as soon as this case is over.'

'Theories, theories and more damn theories. None of this says they knew him for sure, and we can't totally rule out a stalker, even without Internet evidence. He could have been watching them from afar.'

'Don't forget the clean-up – this was strategic. He knew what he was doing, had planned it even.' Anna paused thinking of the birds – how theatrical it all was. She could still recall the smell at both the scenes of earthiness and damp mildew. She thought of the birds and their delicate, fragile bones.

She continued, 'This isn't some love-struck teenager with an obsession, carrying out a crime of passion. He's too organised and controlled in what he does. Think of the guillemot bird, left like a sick love token at the scene and then the robin, euugh, I'll never get that image out of my head. He knows the areas and the venues. We also need to remember the close vicinity of others. He was taking a big risk of someone hearing something in both cases.'

Her mind turned to Declan. Her instinct was telling her that he was right; whoever was carrying out these crimes had some sort of personal vendetta. While she didn't want conjecture and theorising to cloud good judgment based on hard evidence, she couldn't help but think of these girls as the *post-troubles generation*. To them, the violence of the past was little more than a history lesson.

Sure, Esme had dealt with her father's injuries, and had grown up with the outcome of the bomb, but like Grace, she had opportunities and a different way of life without a sense of what it had been like to live in a time of conflict and daily civil unrest. On the surface, life for them was all about Snapchat, Facebook, school, filling out university UCAS forms and nights out. It was a different time. Belfast wasn't on its knees with regular bombings and execution style shootings.

There didn't seem to be anything random about the killings. She thought of the sketch she had done of Esme's murder scene. The velvet dark depths lurking in the undergrowth, the shade and light of the stream below reflecting from the sun. From the victim to the setting, all appeared staged and theatrical. Last night she had spent hours sketching guillemots and robins, trying to get a handle on the killer and his MO; playing it over in her mind while each feathery stoke of the pencil drew another form, the wing, the legs, the beak.

But until she had something concrete to offer, she wasn't going to share her half-baked psychological assessment of the killer. While she didn't want to tell McKay that she was looking into Declan's car bomb case, she did tell Thomas. He remembered the case, even though he was barely out of Garnerville Police Training College when it had happened.

The rain had started back up again as they made their way down the road to another pub. It was good to have this time to kick ideas about the case back and forth. Anna was glad there had been no awkwardness between them. Thomas had proved to be a good partner to work with, and she was relieved that they hadn't become involved in a relationship together. Life was complicated enough.

'It was just another car bomb, as I remember. They weren't so rare in those days,' he said taking a sip from his bottle of beer. They'd moved outside so Thomas could have a smoke. The rain stopped and the sky, inky black, was streaked with ribbons of cloud.

Anna was trying to get a handle on the timeline of Northern Irish politics, 'Wasn't the ceasefire in place then?'

'It was. We'd the Good Friday Agreement in place by 1998 but dissidents were still making their own noise and trying to make sparks fly by targeting police and those connected to them.'

'But for the target to be a forensic psychologist, surely that was different?' Anna asked. She couldn't imagine a world where she would have to check her car for devices before going to work every morning.

'Yeah, I suppose so, but in those days, even those who did building work for the police were considered legitimate targets. We were all under threat one way or another.'

'And Brogan – the DC in charge, did you know him?'

'Nah, before my time but from what I've heard about him he was your typical old-school bigot. Red, white and blue through and through. His type don't exist in the force anymore, well, if they do, they keep their opinions to themselves.'

'So, Brogan was implicated in the enquiry – he didn't alert Declan Wells to the fact that he was at risk?'

'Appears so,' Thomas said with his mouth set in a grimace. Anna hadn't worked with him for long, but she had already ascertained he had a strong sense of justice and a moral imperative to do the right thing.

He continued, 'I've done a bit of digging and Brogan was pensioned off on ill-health but essentially it was a cover up, to prevent the RUC looking bad. He was a staunch unionist with a penchant for Fenian bashing back in the day. His type are a dying breed, thank God. Holier than thou, while breaking every moral code there is in the name of justice.'

The notion of a police force divided was an anathema to Anna. Sure, she had encountered racism. One of her Welsh colleagues from Penarth had told her of snide comments and being passed over for the better jobs because of the colour of his skin. She couldn't imagine a hatred within her colleagues so entrenched, that it would result in someone being almost killed. She thought of Declan and his pain, the way he tried to downplay his injuries.

She felt a hot flush of rage on his behalf. That Brogan had withheld significant information resulting in such horrific injuries, all because Declan was from an opposing side of the community. It bothered Anna on a deeply personal level.

Chapter 22

The RSPB pointed Anna in the direction of local taxidermists. There weren't too many taxidermists working in and around Belfast. A few calls helped Anna narrow her choice down to Jude Collins who offered workshops, as well as made-to-order, stuffed wildlife. Manus Magee had been speaking to a few wildlife specialists and had visited one taxidermist in the area, leaving Anna to follow up Jude Collins. Apparently, there were a few disreputable means of catching birds in order to stuff them and place them on a mantelpiece. A piece of carefully placed wire netting, sitting inconspicuously high up in a tree, could trap a bird easily enough. A carefully handled, stuffed and mounted bird like a guillemot, could fetch up to £250 on some of the auction sites. A quick check on EBay showed that there was a market for all sorts of stuffed wildlife. There was no accounting for taste.

She knew she shouldn't have told Declan about the birds. It was like throwing him a crumb from the banquet table; he was starved for information about the case. Anything at all that he could use to track the killer. He was certain the killer was using the bird as tag, a marker.

'The insertion of the bird into Grace's mouth has a ritualistic element. It shows premeditation before the killing and a certain viciousness. I am looking for a pattern of evidence, working out the killer's modus operandi.'

'Well, we can assume that he selected both of the girls and lured them to their deaths,' she said.

'Yes, but it is significant because that tells us what the killer is like. He must possess a certain attractive charm that the girls find relatable to or attractive even. There is a suggestion that his actions show a cognitive thought process.'

Anna frowned, 'What do you mean?'

'Well, he is showing forensic awareness in the clearing of the scenes. He adapts a ploy approach to lure them away. He is methodical and calculating, and he has shown a unique signature behaviour model.'

She asked, 'You mean the birds?'

'Yes. That's his signature. His calling card. He's ritualistic, has certain habits and behavioural patterns. He knows the localities, he feels at ease with the girls, confident enough to approach them in public places and is charismatic enough to lure them away.'

Anna took a breath. 'What's the difference between the modus operandi and the signature?'

'The pattern of evidence suggests it is the same killer. The modus operandi is learned behaviour, he has worked out how to approach the girls, what works to remove them from a place of safety. He can adapt his MO according to each killing, adjusting his technique. The signature is his personality stamped on the victim, in this case the wood wool in Esme's mouth, the mutilated bird left at the scene and with Grace the bird inserted into her mouth.'

Anna stayed quiet. Declan's eyelids twitched, 'It gives us something to work on. We can look into the use of netting to catch birds. Check out wildlife specialists, anyone working with birds.'

'I'm on it Declan. We are already talking to wildlife and bird organisations.'

'Please Anna, let me do this with you,' he pleaded. His voice was raw with desperation to be doing anything related to the case.

She knew he needed to move one of the pieces of the chessboard, to feel some sort of control over the chaos of his life. If Richard knew she was considering allowing him to accompany her to speak to the taxidermist she would be in deep shit, but right now she didn't care. Declan inspired something in her. She could barely think of him without a need she didn't know previously existed. Being with him felt right even when every molecule of her being told her she was playing with fire. Her career was in jeopardy, but for once she didn't want to put it first.

* * *

She wasn't sure what she wanted to get out of the meeting with the taxidermist, but the killer's calling cards were pointing her in this direction. Like all these fact-finding missions, you never knew what it would throw up. Besides, Thomas was bogged down with chasing leads from the reward phone ins and they were in a cul de sac going nowhere fast.

Jude Collins worked from her purpose-built workshop at the back of her home in Ballygowan, on the outskirts of Belfast. Her stone house stood at the end of a lane, big and bleak with small picturesque square windows looking how Anna imagined traditional Irish houses would be. The front door was painted a bright canary yellow, cheerful and welcoming. Before they could knock the door opened.

'Hello, DI Cole and my colleague Dr Wells. We spoke on the phone.'

'Yes, of course I was expecting you. Come on through, ignore the mess.' The slightly built woman, welcoming them into her home, didn't look like Anna's idea of a taxidermist. Her blonde hair, curly and long, was pulled back into a messy ponytail. She wore tight, skinny jeans with a green baggy jumper and well-worn trainers.

'Access for yourself is going to be round the back,' she said to Declan as he directed his chair to where she indicated. Anna followed her inside.

'Sorry I haven't tidied up,' Jude said as she led the way down a low-ceilinged hallway through to a large, square kitchen furnished with a black Aga and pale duck egg blue painted wooden cupboards. A terrier dog, lying in a wicker basket by the stove, lifted his head to check them out.

'Don't mind him,' Jude said, 'he's so old I wonder how long it will be before he finds himself in the workshop.' Anna laughed. A rectangular, oak table stood in the middle of the room flanked by wooden benches. It all looked cozy and homely.

'My workshop is through here, just out the back.' Anna saw Declan make his way over the courtyard toward them. Outbuildings and a stable block surrounded the courtyard. A black Volvo jeep was parked at one side next to a trailer. Jude unlocked the wooden door and switched on an overhead light. Anna scanned the workshop. A large metal-topped table took up most of the space and was cluttered with tools, fabric and pieces of straw. Shelves lined the walls where various woodland creatures sat staring out with dead, glass eyes like something straight out of a child's nightmare.

Jude cleared away a space for them to sit down.

'So how does this work? Do you get commissions or do you work on your own projects and sell them on?' asked Anna, looking round the cramped space. Hares, squirrels and birds sat watching with dead, beady eyes on the shelf closest to her.

'A bit of both. Sometimes someone comes across a dead animal that they'd like to keep as a taxidermy item, or a beloved pet dies and they contact me. We have to assess how the animal has met its death. Illegal hunting and killing happens and any suspicion has to be reported to authorities.' Anna looked at a life-like tortoiseshell cat sitting on the lower shelf. Its fur looked inviting, as if it had been made to be stroked, but the sight of it made Anna squeamish. She didn't understand the desire to stuff a dead animal.

'So, what happens if you find a dead animal?

'Once you've established that the animal has died a natural death, even road kill if it's not too damaged, you put it in a plastic bag and freeze it until you are ready to work with it. You work to halt the decay. Although it's often hard to tell how long ago the animal died, the eyes are usually a good indication. If the eyes are still rounded it's reasonably fresh, but if the eyes have dried out a little and show wrinkling, or worse a complete indent, it's a bit older. You must decide if the animal is still salvageable or not. No one wants an ugly mutated looking thing. Mind you, there is market for two headed cats and dogs with a head at each end. Some weirdos like that kind of thing though I don't work like that.'

'Your website mentions workshops. Do you train other taxidermists?' Declan asked.

'Yes, there's good money in running workshops. I usually do three or four every year depending on the demand.'

'We could do with having a look at your records, names, addresses, that sort of thing.' Anna said as she made her way round to the shelf full of specimens, rodents and birds. A crow looked down on her with its black, unblinking eyes and yolk yellow beak. Then the tortoiseshell cat shifted its position and curled up on the crowded shelf. 'Shit its real!' Anna jumped back.

'That's Heathcliff, he likes to keep me company. I keep telling him one day he'll end up just like the rest of them,' Jude laughed.

'So, explain to us how you work and how you go about preserving an animal?' Declan asked.

Jude sat down on the tall stool stroking a mousey grey pelt laid out on the table, 'Once you do a quick check on the animal to see if there are no oddities, you write it up into the register. Then you put the animal or bird into the project freezer. I don't always work on them right away.

'When the time comes to start work you remove its skin and wash it thoroughly. The anatomical structure of the animal, along with other measurements such as eyes and key feature placements are carefully noted. You can't take it apart and not understand how to put it back together,' she showed them her workbook. Each page was labeled with a date and a description of the animal and the measurements noted beside a pencil sketch of how she intended to present the finished piece.

'Before I begin, I make a mock up – it's called a voodoo doll. This is a version of the creature, made out of cotton wool and string.

Like this …' she reached over to a shelf and showed them small field mouse fashioned out of cotton wool. 'This has to be the exact shape and size of the creature being immortalised.'

She continued, 'Here, I'll show you something I've been working on.'

She moved over to a wooden block where a brown field mouse lay.

'So, I start by making an incision along the back of the mouse using my scalpel, and then the skin is pulled away from the body in the same way a butcher would skin any animal.'

Anna watched fascinated as the skin peeled back from the tiny frame of the mouse.

'Borax powder, which is a compound of boron also known as sodium borate, is often used to help preserve the skin and the fur – particularly from insect infestations. You don't want the creature rotting on you. Formaldehyde can also be used to preserve the specimen, but it's a harsher chemical to work with.'

Jude indicated to the bottle of Borax sitting on the shelf. 'The body and the insides are dispensed with, and the legs are removed and replaced with wires. Or you can use acetone to clean the bones if they are to form part of the final mount. Once the pelt has been cleaned and dried, it is placed around the cotton wool 'voodoo' version, and sewn up. One technique of cleaning pelts involves corn flour.

'Rubbing cornstarch to clean pelts with a damp cloth draws moisture and dirt from the inside of the pelt.'

Anna peered over her shoulder to have a closer look.

'Then when it's dry, the cornstarch can be brushed or vacuumed off the skin, and I use a baby toothbrush to comb the fur into place. It's more or less the same process for most mammals.'

The cat stretched and jumped down from its shelf. Jude went on, 'In the Victorian times, animals were gutted and tanned and then stuffed with straw and sawdust, before being sewn back up. There were no preservation chemicals or techniques used, and the animals eventually rotted away. In the 1970s, the stuffing technique stopped, and taxidermists began to stretch the animal's skin over sculpted moulds, or mannequins, made from foam. It's becoming a popular art form again.'

Anna couldn't see a stuffed animal as art. She thought of an exhibition she once saw as child, at Bristol museum. Cats and rabbits and birds had been fashioned into human-like poses, wearing clothes and hats, having tea and playing cricket. She'd had nightmares afterwards. Camille had to let her sleep with her for a week. Her poor dad, relegated to the spare room.

'What if someone wanted to remove an eye from a dead bird. How do they go about it?' Anna asked.

'It's easy enough if you know what you're doing. I use a flat blade screwdriver and insert it at the top of the eye between the eyeball and the orbit, like this,' she demonstrated holding a screwdriver.

'Push the screwdriver all the way to the rear of the eye socket, working it down to the back of the eyeball. There's a knack to it. You have to push in and pry down at the same time, and then if you are lucky, the eyeball comes out in a pop, with no bursting. After that you trim the fatty tissue that holds it to the skull.'

Jude continued, seemingly delighted to have someone interested in her work, 'When you are working with a body, it needs to be re-sculpted, either by a foam cast of the original body, wood wool or a combination of both. The measurements made earlier are carefully followed while making the replacement body. Once the skin has been washed, treated and tanned, it goes back over the new form.'

Anna shifted from the far end of the table away from the glassy eyes of a stoat, 'You mentioned wood wool. Is it a common material for stuffing?'

'Yes, most taxidermists would use it,' she said.

Anna fingered a small metal scoop, 'So what kind of tools would you use?'

'That's a brain scoop, you're looking at.' Anna placed it back down, and resisted the urge to wipe her fingers on her skirt.

'Don't worry its clean,' Jude said. 'I also use bone cutters, skin stretchers, clamps.'

Anna shuddered. The tools were like torture implements.

'Have you seen anything like this used to capture birds,' Anna showed her the clear plastic evidence bag containing the tiny fragment of the netting removed from the guillemot's throat. 'It is part of a plastic net found around a guillemot,' Anna said.

'Can't say I have seen anything like it, but yeah, I'm not surprised you get people keen to work on a particular bird so they go out of their way to hunt it down.'

'Anyone come through your workshops who you felt was a bit off? Maybe overly involved, standoffish or just different?' Declan asked. 'Anything out of the ordinary could help us.'

'Plenty would say I'm a bit of a weirdo. Not many appreciate the art and craft of taxidermy.'

'No one stick out?'

'Maybe. There was this one fella, a while back. He was only interested in working with birds. Kept to himself didn't want to be part of the group workshop, asked for one on one tuition.'

'That wouldn't necessarily be enough to make you wary of him. Was there something else?'

'Well, I was pretty sure the birds didn't meet their deaths naturally. Besides he was pretty intense. Seemed to enjoy the process a bit too much. Was really into the slicing up and skinning. An older guy, maybe mid-sixties, religious and serious like, you know the type.' She looked at Declan as if he could read the shorthand.

'Do you have his details?' Anna asked.

'Sure, it will be on the computer but I remember his name – Cunningham. Josh or Jason, I think. I can check it out. But really, anyone can teach themselves taxidermy these days there are plenty of tutorials online. Trial and error and a few books and your half-way there.'

* * *

'You're quiet, what are you thinking?' Anna asked in the car, driving back to Belfast.

'Those stuffed animals unsettle me. Why anyone would want to keep a stuffed cat is beyond me. And the birds, so beautiful, their wings fanned out as if about to take flight, yet stone cold dead.'

'I know. It's creepy as fuck.'

'What do make of the Cunningham guy? Might be worth paying him a call.'

'Possibly the wrong age for the guy we're after, but yeah, check him out.'

* * *

That afternoon Anna sat at her desk and trawled through the HOLMES system. The floaters had been updating it with their enquiries and she needed to catch up. She couldn't help thinking about Declan's comments on the theatrical mastery of the scenes. The killer had control over the girls, over the crime scene and how he presented it to them. Declan said he showed a heightened self-awareness. Knew how to work the girls, lure them away from a place of safety. Both had been murdered at a social event, in the grounds of hotels, only thirty or so feet away from help.

The lines of investigation were a tangle of loose threads. With no sexual assault, or robbery they were lacking a clear motive. Both girls' phones had turned up in their handbags – Esme's found at the scene and Grace's recovered from the hotel. Grace's bag, a silver clutch bag had contained her phone, a Mac lipstick and her purse. Why had she left it behind?

They appeared to be popular girls. Both intelligent, attending good schools with every intention of going on to university. Esme had completed her UCAS form and had hoped to go to Edinburgh or Liverpool to study. Was her choice of university applications a reflection that she wanted away from Finnegan? Neither had boyfriends or at least no one significant. Anna thought about the kiss that Carly had thought might have happened between Esme and Finnegan. She didn't want to tell Declan about it. Not yet.

Thomas and Manus were digging around, looking for any common business associates between Dowds and Finnegan. They needed to rule out the possibility of a deal gone wrong and a revenge motive. So far, they hadn't anything substantial to put to Richard McKay. Thomas had warned Anna that McKay considered a half story to be worse than no story.

There was little evidence of a forensic nature. Anna had seen other cases where the weight of evidence was heavier in the exchange of fibres found on the suspect, transferred from the victim. Hair was the most common element to be found. Footprints had been either washed away by the night's rain or the killer had been very careful in both instances. A large branch had been used to sweep away tracks at the scene of Esme's murder. Even the most thorough of clean ups will leave some small trace.

Internet histories had shown no red flags of significant persons. Neither girl had a stalker known to their friends or families. Only Rory Finnegan's many telephone calls to Esme ticked that particular box.

Anna flicked to the photograph of Grace Dowds. Her red hair had fallen over the side of her face. Her uncovered cheek, translucent under the light of the photographer's flash. Her lips full and opened slightly, were tinged a violet blue. If Anna were to paint the scene, it would look pre-Raphaelite, like Ophelia lying in the river. Hastily, she googled Ophelia to see the painted image. She read that the scene depicted was from Hamlet. Ophelia, driven out of her mind when her father is murdered by Hamlet, drowns herself in a stream:

'There, on the pendent boughs her coronet weeds Clambering to hang, an envious sliver broke;

When down her weedy trophies and herself Fell in the weeping brook. Her clothes spread wide, And, mermaid-like a while they bore her up;

Which time she chanted snatches of old lauds,

As one incapable of her own distress,
Or like a creature native and indued
Unto that element. But long it could not be
Till that her garments, heavy with their drink,
Pulled the poor wretch from her melodious lay
To muddy death.'

There was no drowning in a river, but Grace's death felt like a muddy death. The prom dress, like a costume from another time. She itched to draw what was in her mind's eye. To try to make sense of the crime scene, through shade and shadow. Esme's crime scene photographs had the same eerie feel – the young woman returned to nature, lying on the forest floor surrounded by moss, twigs and tree roots. Anna couldn't recall another case that had her returning to the crime scene photographs so much. It was as if she was trying to read the images, to extract information from what was captured in the frame of the camera. Maybe it was her artist's eye drawn to the macabre images of beautiful girls in dark woodland settings.

* * *

'Hey, Anna, nothing on that Cunningham fella you asked me to check out. He seems legit and he's been living in Canada for the last six months,' Thomas said scratching his eyebrow with the lid of a pen. The office phone rang and he picked it up. Anna heard the delight in his voice. 'Great, exactly what we need.' He hung up and spun round on his chair to face Anna. 'That was the data trawl people, Rory Finnegan's little empire isn't so clean after all.'

'What have they found?'

'Esme's bank account shows deposits that are coming from a company linked to Finnegan.'

'Well we can start by having little chat with him again,' Anna said. She thought of Declan and how he had told her that he didn't like Finnegan, son-in-law or not, he wasn't happy with Lara's choice. According to Declan she had had her head turned by Finnegan. Anna didn't think Lara would have been so easily impressed.

'That's not all,' Thomas said grinning, 'Finnegan uses the same security company as the hotel group. One of their men hasn't turned up to work for the past week. No sign of him and not answering phone calls.'

'What's his name?'

'Luke Nead.'

Chapter 23

Declan felt guilt. Not over Izzy, no, that sense of duty had passed long ago, but guilt that he could experience the euphoria of being with a woman like Anna and be experiencing the sweet joy of sex again, while Esme was cold in the ground.

He was in his office responding to work emails. Research that he was heading up had come to a crashing halt. He had neither the time nor the inclination to put the work in. His students, some he was supervising thesis projects for, would have to be assigned new supervisors. Focusing on Esme's case and being close to Anna was all that mattered to him. Izzy had found a way to go back to her students, but he couldn't face it.

Ever since the bomb he felt like he was living on borrowed time; that the ground beneath him was on a timer, waiting for a precise moment of complacency to go off. Now it had happened. Esme's death was the explosion he felt in his bones, the curdling of his insides and using up of his reserves. Yet he also experienced a sense of relief, not that Esme was dead. God no. But relief, that the awful feeling of foreboding, had caught up on him. He knew what he was dealing with now, and his purpose was to catch whoever had done this. He had nothing left to fear and nothing left to punish him.

There was little he could do for Esme beyond finding who had done this, and his instincts had proved right so far. The killer was in an active phase; he would act again given the right circumstances. Declan's job was to read what those circumstances would be and pre-empt him. As for a profile, he needed to look beyond the obvious, explore his potential background. It was likely that he was someone with an abusive childhood, even someone under the radar – not so abusive as to attract attention of the authorities, but enough to do damage. Possibly even a parent in a position of power and respect, a teacher even. Someone who was in a trusted position, that wouldn't be questioned. If he found the source of the evil, maybe he could be led to the killer. For the assaults to be made in a public, close to crowded venues, suggested snatched opportunity. Yet, something nagged at him, telling him these girls were not mere objects to the killer. They were not mutilated, not sexually assaulted. There was a sick care in what the killer did. So clean and clinical in his execution.

The mysterious bird theme suggested a sacrificial element. His mind kept going back to the idea of the destruction of life, and how easy it would be to kill a bird. Fragile and helpless in the wrong hands. Just like the girls. The birds were objects that had to be related to the killer's behaviour. There was a message in what he was doing. There was a definite cognitive thought process at work. Planning and exactitude of what he was doing. A bird might be easy to kill but not so easy to catch. The killer had gone to a lot of trouble.

Much of the legwork was routine, basic investigative policing. Forensics, detailed examination of the crime scene, thorough interviews with all at the venue. But sometimes the grind of police work was not enough. Sometimes it required thinking like a killer, finding their motivation and working backwards. He felt an uneasiness lying in the pit of his stomach. They were missing something. He was sure of it.

Two girls murdered both in a short period of time of each other was unusual especially for Northern Ireland. Geographically they were not far apart, a mere ten miles. Everything would suggest that the perpetrator was a lone male – his strength in over powering the girls suggested as much. Declan couldn't help thinking that there was something in the murders that was deliberately designed to taunt the police. Making them look inadequate and out of their depth. The press leak of Anna's involvement only strengthened the media's perception that the PSNI were struggling, that they were forced to bring in an outsider from the mainland.

Esme could have easily been dumped in the river Lagan, which would have helped wash away some of the physical evidence. Instead he left her on a mossy bank, as if he wanted her body to be easily discovered. There was research to suggest that failure to hide the body or bury it indicated the desire to send a message of shock to the community. A warning almost.

Declan leafed through his research papers trying to find one in particular he remembered explored crime phases. His clinical mind was looking for patterns, for configurations that might help illuminate something vital to the case. He found the paper and read: *We can glean insight into personality through questions about the murderer's behaviour at four crime phases:*

The Precursor Period: What fantasy or plan, did the murderer have in place before the act? What acted as a trigger for the murderer to act one particular day? Could the wedding somehow have been significant in triggering the killer?

Approach, method and manner: What was the deciding factors in the type of victim or victims, which the murderer selected? What was the method and manner of murder: shooting, stabbing, strangulation or something else? Is there an indication of personality in anything left at the scene either deliberately or accidently? They could assume the girls hadn't felt threatened by the killer. It appeared that they either knew him, or were relaxed enough to feel it was okay to go off with him.

Body disposal: He didn't hide the bodies or cover them so there was a sense that he was flaunting his crime.

Post-offense behaviour: Is the murderer trying to inject himself into the investigation by reacting to media reports or contacting investigators? Is there a return to the primary scene? Well, they had seen evidence of this with the bird left at the scene after the clear up.

He had called in old contacts at the office of the State Pathologist to get hold of a copy of Esme's autopsy report. It was gruesome reading but he felt that he needed to understand exactly what his daughter had endured. It was also important for him to learn as much as he could about the killer through his methods.

Esme hadn't died from the blow to her head though it did significant damage. She had died through being strangled. Declan knew that the usual clinical sequence of a victim being strangled is one of severe pain, followed by unconsciousness, and then brain death. Esme would have lost consciousness due to the blocking of the carotid arteries which deprives the brain of oxygen, blocking of the jugular veins which would prevent deoxygenated blood from exiting the brain, and closing off the airway, causing her to be unable to breathe. Only eleven pounds of pressure placed on both carotid arteries for ten seconds is necessary to cause unconsciousness. The report showed impression marks where the killer's gloved fingers pressed into the skin. The report also stated that erythema – redness – was present on the neck demonstrated in a detectable pattern. He knew from previous autopsy reports that these marks may or may not darken to become a bruise after death. Her fingernails were intact. She hadn't had chance to fight back. The image of the penetration of her chest cavity by the branch sickened him so much that he had to take a break from reading it.

The precise nature of the killing suggested to Declan that the killer had a fundamental knowledge of what he was doing. It was as if he understood the clinical features and had ensured the head injury was enough to stun her, slow her down and make her compliant so that he could perform the strangulation. The hyoid bone, a small horseshoe-shaped bone in the neck, helps to support the tongue. The larynx, made up of cartilage, not bone, consists of two parts: the thyroid cartilage, which is next to the thyroid gland and the tracheal rings. The killer had pressed exactly on the spot where compression was needed to induce asphyxiation.

* * *

He heard the front door open. Izzy, had returned from the university. He could hear her set her keys on the hall table, the tap, tap, tap, of her heels on the wooden floor.

'Declan?' She called, 'Are you home?'

'I'm in the office. Catching up on work emails.'

'I'll sort out something for dinner but I'm going up for a shower first.' she replied from the hallway.

At times Declan could feel Izzy's pain as keenly as his own. It bothered him on some deep level that she should suffer like this. The death of a daughter, so cruel and brutal, had felled them both. Somehow, he was able to contain his grief. He kept it wrapped up tight inside of himself like a cold piece of granite lodged in his chest. His focus was still on getting who had done this. Grieving would come later. When he thought of Izzy and Lara, his heart contracted and missed a beat. The knowledge that he wasn't alone in this desperate well of pain made it harder to bear.

* * *

Later that night Declan downed two painkillers and a sleeping tablet. He needed something to force his mind to still itself. Dinner had been strained. They hardly knew how to talk to each other. Now he desired nothing more than to drift away and find a temporary relief in sleep. His mind had other ideas.

After the bomb, they had fought their way back together again. Slowly their love had been diluted from a passionate certainty to something convenient and routine. The light of their love gradually faded. They had done their best to make it work and to an outsider looking in, it did. But both of them knew that family was all that was left between them. If he had given it any thought back then, he would have accepted the status as being a natural progression, parenthood and approaching middle age did nothing to flame the embers of love. But after the bomb he watched as Izzy threw herself into her work, and into caring for the girls with a renewed energy.

His lower legs had been 'wrangled', that was the word the consultant used. An image of his grandmother's mangle compressing the sudsy water out of clothes came to mind. The semtex bomb attached to the undercarriage of his Volvo, had ripped apart metal and flesh, creating a dulled symphony of explosion. He never knew how long he had been conscious for, but lying face down on wet muddy grass, he remembered the moment before the pain and horror took over, causing his mind to black out. Unable to appreciate what the bomb had done, his brain was incapable of understanding his life would be changed forever, and in ways he could not foresee.

All the main political parties, labelling it an attack on efforts to build peace, condemned the car bombing.

Dissidents, as far as Declan was concerned, were little more than fascists, a group whose fundamental mindset is molded rigid in the certainty of their validity, so certain they feel they have the right and a mandate to maim and kill others. In a time of political stability and an uneasy peace accepted by the majority of people in Northern Ireland, what they stood for defied logic. But Declan appreciated that it was this narrow view that made them particularly dangerous and unpredictable. It was their intolerance that galled him the most. Their inability to accept a middle ground.

He missed his height almost as much as he missed his ability to walk. At 6 foot 3 inches tall he had possessed an easy authority that had helped him throughout his career. People looked up to him, literally. His frame was strong and wide, crafted through years of playing Gaelic football in his youth. The skills of which he seamlessly transferred on to the rugby pitch to accommodate his Protestant work colleagues in later years. He was respected, on and off the pitch, as someone who would initiate, lead but always remember he was part of a team, working as a collective whole. His role as psychologist and his Catholic background marked him out as separate. At times, he felt like a different breed all together.

Declan was not one for introspection, but eight months of rehabilitation had forced him to think, if not analyse all that had gone before. Rehabilitation did not begin to describe the hard work and pain he had put himself through rebuilding what was left of his body. The mind was another thing all together. He had been made to speak to psychiatrists, those well-intentioned professionals who repeatedly reminded him that he had been through an ordeal, that he would feel anger, shame and grief for the life he no longer had. But he refused to be button holed. Life throws curve balls at you and the mark of a strong person is in how they deal with them. Declan wasn't going allow himself to play the victim. His body might have been banjaxed, but almost perversely he wasn't about to give in graciously. A fat pension and a life of watching the local news bulletins was what the majority of them dreamed of. No more back room politicking and no more front-line action. Sure, he had to make adjustments and to work bloody hard, but what else was there if he couldn't work? He made do with private consultancy work and lecturing at Queen's but even that took a long time to build up.

Declan had learnt the hard way that life could have moments of pure beauty within times of desperate sadness. After the bomb, he had spent months being rehabilitated, tortured by well-meaning medics and physios who, despite his bad temper and frustration, kept on his case and didn't allow him to wallow in his depression. There were times when he wanted to give up. Let the bastards win and just drift away in self-pity.

Visits from his family were not always pleasurable. It was too hard to see the concern and fear etched on their faces. But sometimes they managed to lift his spirits to levels he didn't think he would feel again. Fleeting moments that told him he would be okay. He would make it back from this godforsaken hell on Earth. Especially his girls. The first time Izzy had brought them in, he could tell they had been well warned what to expect. Their faces pale, and their eyes wide with fear, told of half-truths and overheard conversations.

He had joked that they couldn't finish him off, made out that he was some sort of war hero who had crawled from the rubble of his bombed-out car. 'They got my legs but they didn't get me!' he had said, smiling with as much commitment as he could muster. Esme had asked was he only 'half a daddy now?' He had laughed at her directness, her quick summation of events.

But when they saw he was still daddy, they relaxed a little and Esme had happily climbed on to his bed. Lara, always so self-contained, had taken a bit of coaxing. They accepted his new status as 'half a daddy' quicker than he did. And more so than Izzy ever had. Now, having spent the night with Anna, he had such a moment of joy.

Declan could remember when he first set out on his career. Psychological profiling was relatively new and there were many in the RUC who doubted its place in policing. It didn't help that he was a Catholic, fresh in and keen to make his mark. There were plenty like that old bastard Nelson Brogan who took every opportunity to mock Declan and his statistics, profiles and graphs of probability. Dicky, he used to call Declan. When Declan corrected him and said his name was Declan, but that he was often called Deccy, Nelson Brogan replied, 'I don't speak the Pope's Irish Dicky.' Declan thought *so that is how it is going to be.*

* * *

His thesis had involved the notorious Shankill Butchers. He examined the connections between mental illness and terrorism. Up until that point, the psychology of terrorism was expressed in the language of mentalisms, and theories of pathologisation. He was looking at behavioural psychology, and the connection between an individual engaging in terrorist activity and developing a mental disorder. Certain stressors that occur because of terrorist activity, could result in psychological disturbance in terrorist individuals. These factors could explain terrorist group instability and how it should be taken into account when detaining and interrogating terrorist suspects. All theory and trajectories that the government was hoping to use to their advantage. The Shankill Butchers were thought to be the case to prove the point.

There were plenty like Brogan who didn't want a snotty nosed graduate interfering in their police work. For Brogan, the job of the police force wasn't to *understand* the criminal mind, just to bang them to rights.

Declan opened his eyes and estimated from the dim blue light behind the curtains, that it was not yet 5.00 a.m. He had eventually drifted off.

Sleep was a necessary torture. Sometimes he craved it as respite from the pain of life. Other times he thought if he could survive without it, he would gladly give up the mockery of retiring to bed and tossing and turning through the night, catching wisps of sleep, before it was acceptable to abandon all notion of sleep and rise again for another day.

He reached over to check his phone out of habit. No new messages. The house was quiet. Izzy was probably still asleep. He hoped she was, that she could find some rest even if it was induced by a sleeping pill. He wished he could offer her some comfort; some sort of acknowledgement that he understood her pain too, but the gulf between them was as wide and deep as the Atlantic Ocean.

His thoughts lingered over the case. He found it easier to think of it in work terms. It was the only way to keep the grief dampened. Work terms. That phase played around his mind. There was something about the murders that made him feel that the killer was familiar with police procedure. It wasn't only that the crime scenes were relatively clean. There was so much information online these days that anyone could ask Google to fill them in on protocol and how to leave no clues. There was something else. The selection of the victims. Both born in a new era of a post troubled Belfast. They represented the hope and prosperity previous generations had been denied. Had someone been trailing Esme? Had they known her every move intimately? Had his whole family been watched? The questions tormented Declan until he could take no more.

He reached for his phone again and hit the number.

'Anna,' he said, 'I've a theory.'

Chapter 24

Anna and Thomas were itching to get Finnegan into the interview room. There was enough of a dodgy whiff about his businesses to make him worth pressing on; businesses, owned by holding companies, properties in untraceable names, planning applications for buildings that were never finished and re-zoning of plots of land inexplicably free for development when once they were out of bounds. It was clear he had friends in high places with the city council planning office in his back pocket. There was enough to justify calling him in and to see how he reacted to questions about his relationship with Esme.

Anna followed Thomas along the pale green painted concrete corridors down to the interview room. The whole station was buzzing. They had at last brought a suspect in and even if Anna had doubts about Finnegan's part in Esme's murder, she wasn't going to pass up interviewing him. Right now, she wanted to focus all her energy in getting the most out of Finnegan and seeing how he reacted under pressure.

The Belfast Telegraph's front page had forced their hand. 'Dead Prom Queen' was how they had described Grace Dowds and they were quick to point to Stephen Dowds' political campaign last year as being bank rolled by Finnegan.

Rory Finnegan could be connected to both victims. Anna could remember her instant dislike of him, his slimy manner and his arrogance, but that wasn't enough to bang him up. If she cuffed every misogynist she came across there may be a shortage of men.

Finnegan had come in prepared with his solicitor, Paul Murphy, a notoriously sharp man known for his big cases and ability to weasel his clients out of anything. Thomas had told her of Murphy's reputation, how he was well known for conducting his business in the best restaurants in Belfast, and how he was considered the best by Belfast's most disreputable crooks.

'Murphy,' Thomas said nodding as they entered the room. The solicitor nodded a greeting in return. He was dressed for the part with his white, crisp shirt cuffs showing beneath the wide pinstripe suit sleeve, finished off, Anna noticed, with gold cufflinks in the shape of a rugby ball. Next to him Finnegan looked like a carbon copy. They both had the same arrogant pose, sitting well back on their chairs as if being called into a police station was of little concern. A waft of cologne, a woody and pine fragrance was hanging in the room. Anna guessed Murphy was the culprit. He looked like the type to splash it on too heavily.

'My client wishes it to be noted that he has voluntarily offered to assist you with your enquiries and to point out that he is free to leave at any time should he so wish.'

'Duly noted,' said Thomas taking his seat and staring at Finnegan.

'Officers, what can I do to help you?' Finnegan asked opening his blazer button as he moved forward in his chair.

'For the record we're detectives, Mr Finnegan,' Anna said placing her folder on the table in front of her. 'We have asked you to come to discuss your relationship with Esme Wells, among other things.'

Thomas leaned back in his chair, mirroring Murphy's body language, letting Anna kick things off, as planned.

'Mr Finnegan, you are in property developing, isn't that right?' He nodded.

'Business can't be good these days for property developers. People are still cautious after the recession.'

'We deal with student rentals and high-end properties. The students have got to rent somewhere and the recession didn't harm those who were smart enough to cushion the blow.'

'So, what's your business model then? Do you build houses, sell them or rent them out?'

'All three on a good quarter. I buy anything that I think I can turn into a good profit plus I have some properties that I rent out, and some we manage for others.'

'Sounds like you're raking it in. Good for you.' Thomas was playing it well, taking on the role of us lads in it together. He continued, 'Hard to make a quick buck flipping houses these days though. Aren't I right? Not like it was before the crash. But no worries, we'll come back to your business dealings.' Thomas made a flourish of shuffling Inland Revenue headed paper.

'Would you say your relationship with Esme was good? You two were particularly close?' Anna asked.

'Yes, we were close but I don't like what you're implying.' he stared at Anna, his grey eyes piercing, cocky, as if he was so sure of himself that he was daring her to go further.

'We have Esme's phone records. They tell us she called you a fair bit in the days leading up to the wedding. Would you normally have so many calls from her?' Thomas asked.

'What can I say, we're a close family, so we are.'

Anna considered this, from what Declan had told her there was no love lost between him and Finnegan. She decided to change tack. 'Esme worked for you on a few occasions, waitressing, isn't that right?'

He looked at his lawyer. 'She stepped in to help out a couple of times, yes.'

'You recognise this girl?' Anna placed a photograph of Carly in front of him. He shook his head.

'For the record could you answer, please?'

'No, I don't know the girl in the picture.'

'So, you've never met her?' Anna asked.

'I can't say if I have or haven't but she doesn't ring any bells.' Anna leaned back on her chair, 'Let me jog your memory. This girl, Carly is her name, worked for you, at one of your little soirées. She was able to tell us the nature of your parties and name a few of your guests too.'

Rory's face was unreadable, as if he'd known this was coming and he'd prepared himself. Silence. Anna could wait all day. Let him sweat in his own juices a bit.

After a moment, he says, 'What can I tell you? They were business meetings. There's no law against entertaining associates.'

'You are aware of the newspaper reports linking you to Grace Dowds' father Stephen?' Anna asked going straight in as planned.

'Yes, Stephen and I have worked together in the past.'

Thomas leaned in close to Finnegan across the table, 'You see our problem is that we have two dead girls, and you are showing up as a connection in both cases. Help me out here Rory, help me understand,' he placed another photo of Grace on the table. It was from the crime scene, her head twisted away from the camera at an unnatural angle. 'So, you've definitely never met Grace, is that right?'

Finnegan looked down at the image of Grace in her prom dress. 'Possibly. I couldn't say for sure.' He leaned back on his chair and appeared cocky, a bit too relaxed and sure of himself. It was an act. Anna could put money on the fact that inside his mind was running on over drive and he was panicking, hoping Murphy would dig him out of whatever hole he was headed for.

'You won't mind if we take a closer look at some of your little business parties? CCTV cameras, that sort of thing. To check that everything is kosher, like?' Thomas said with a smirk.

'You have nothing on me, and there is no reason for you to be looking into my business. Now if that is all officers, I need to get back to my grieving wife, if you don't mind leaving us to it.'

'Oh now, sure, we've just a few more questions and then you are free to go. What's the harm in helping us out Mr Finnegan? Surely you are as keen to help us out as much as possible?' Anna said, keeping her voice pleasant and neutral, as if they were all good friends, on the same side.

'These parties that Esme waitressed at – we'd like a full list of anyone who attended as a guest or employees who worked at them.'

Finnegan looked to his lawyer.

'Something that's been bothering us Rory, as you know, Esme's phone records show that you and she conversed a lot. Would you care to share with us the details of your conversations?' Thomas put the question to him. 'I'm sure you will want any suggestion that you may have been having an affair with your wife's younger sister explained away.'

Anna watched him look to his solicitor for guidance again. Murphy gave a slight nod of his greying head. Finnegan's expression changes, it alters his whole being. He's no longer the swaggering professional out to give a helping hand in getting justice for his wife's baby sister; now he's eagle sharp, his eyes steel, and his shoulders hunched as if he is a tightly wound up spring ready to throw the first punch. Not someone you'd want to cross. Definitely not someone a seventeen-year-old girl could handle if things got out of hand.

Thomas leans forward, 'Perhaps Esme came on a little too strong. You felt what? Threatened? Under pressure? Hard to resist and when it all goes down she starts to feel guilty. Cries that she can't bear sharing you with her sister, can't live with the betrayal.'

'Esme had a bit of a crush on me. What can I say? I tried to let her down gently but you know how young girls get.'

'No, I'm not sure how young girls get. Maybe you would care to fill me in?' Anna said.

'She looked up to me, and I suppose, I spoiled her a bit.'

'Did you give her money? Buy her gifts?'

Finnegan looked to his lawyer before answering, 'On occasion yes. But it was all harmless. She was like a little sister to me.'

'That sounds a lot like grooming to me,' Anna said sitting back.

Murphy glanced up sharply from his notes and cleared his throat, 'I don't like allegations being tossed around. Watch what you say to my client Detective.'

Anna ignored him.

'Did you ever have sex with Esme?' she asked, leaning in closer to Finnegan.

For the first time, he seemed rattled. A shine of sweat coated his forehead.

Murphy piped up, 'My client does not have to answer that question.'

'Sounds to me like you were grooming her, buttering her up before getting your end away. Have a thing for sisters, do you?' Thomas said.

'I love my wife. Esme was only a kid, a teenager.' He looked to Thomas, 'You know how girls are these days, all short skirts and flirting. She might have chased after me, but I didn't do anything wrong.' He wiped his hand on his trouser leg. They had him over the ropes with this.

Thomas leaned back on his chair, 'You see, Rory, here's the problem, too many phone calls, buying her gifts … and then we get wind from a reliable source that you and Esme may have shared a little bit of nookie. What was it? A kiss and a fumble? Or did you have sex with her?'

Murphy looked apoplectic, practically rising up from his chair in rage, 'My client does not have to listen to this nonsense.'

Anna decided it was time for another change of tack while he was vulnerable.

'Well, back to Stephen Dowds, how well do you know him? Is it purely business?'

'He's a business associate. I buy my cars from him.'

'Papers are saying you helped to get his political career off the ground. That you bank rolled him all the way to the city council and beyond before he fell at the last hurdle.'

'People in this place still vote according to how their grannies and grandas voted. Green or orange. I'm open to change, to see things done differently.'

Thomas shifted on his chair, 'Wouldn't hurt to have someone close on the planning committee if you are looking to buy land and develop it.'

Finnegan shrugged his shoulders. 'No crime in having friends in high places.'

Anna closed her notebook, 'I think we're done here, Mr Finnegan but we'll most certainly be in touch. Go home to that wife of yours and maybe have a little think about your dead sister-in-law. If anything should come back to you that you think might be relevant, let us know.'

* * *

Later Anna and Thomas watched the tape back. 'Do you believe him?' Thomas asked.

'What?' Anna asked turning towards him, 'That he didn't have sex with her?'

He nodded.

'He didn't out right deny it. He's hiding something, but we can't know for certain if it was a full-blown relationship. Did she hit on him or did he lead her on? He could have had a hold over her in some way. A young girl with a major crush on her sister's husband-to-be – could have the potential to blow up.'

'He knows we can't hold him. His lawyer is one of the best and if we set a foot wrong he'll be down on us before you can say guilty as charged. What do you make of him?'

Anna considered his arrogance, the way he had looked at her when they first met as if he routinely assessed women to decide whether they were worth his time.

'I certainly don't like him. I'd say he is full of himself, and that he is one of those men who thinks he loves women, but really, he is only interested in how good they make him look. I don't know if I see him as our killer though.'

'He is definitely hiding something. We need surveillance on him and maybe with enough rope he'll hang himself.'

Anna agreed, though she doubted McKay would sanction surveillance. Finnegan was hiding something all right but she couldn't decide if he was trying to protect his marriage or his business.

* * *

Anna headed back to the office to track down Russell and Manus. They were in charge of logging every member of staff working at both events. So far, one still eluded them, the man called Luke Nead.

'Where are we with the search for the rogue security guard?' Anna asked.

Manus Magee stood up, 'So far we've drawn a blank. He wasn't working that night and none of the other security staff recall seeing him.'

'What about the wages clerk, did she have anything of interest to say about him?' Anna asked.

Russell shook his head, 'Genevieve's her name, and she didn't give us anything worthwhile. He was always paid cash in hand, same as other casual staff. He had no address logged with them. If they needed him in, they called him on the mobile number,' he paused to stretch and yawn, 'We've put a trace on it but it's been either switched off or conveniently disposed of.'

'Did the firm say if he usually went AWOL?'

'Yeah, they said they weren't always able to use him. Apparently, he takes himself off on hikes up the Mournes. No signal. Camps out for a couple of days and then collects his messages when he's back within signal.'

'Keep on it. We need to track him down. At this stage, it's the best bet we have,' Anna said.

Manus scratched the back of his thick neck, 'No mention of family or girlfriend, even though he's supposedly a good-looking fella. They seemed to like him well enough. No concerns. Always did his shift and gave them no trouble.'

Anna sighed, 'Why keep such a low profile, no known address, and not responding to calls? Something's going on with him. Get Genevieve from the security firm, to come in and give a description. Make it official, see if she suddenly remembers anything that might be of help.'

* * *

Seeing Declan was a mistake. She knew that much, but when he came calling, she always let him in. Tonight, was no different. She could smell whiskey on his breath. His shoulders looked lost in his jacket and she could see that he was wired. There was a restlessness about him that she recognised in herself – that sense of need to crack the case, to be one step closer to finding the killer.

'You brought Rory in for questioning. Why? I've told you they are looking at the wrong man. He's my daughter's husband For Fuck's Sake! I might think he's a prick, a jumped up little asshole but he didn't kill Esme!'

Anna tried to push past his wheelchair to block his path into the living room. 'You shouldn't be here. We shouldn't be doing this. It's too dangerous. My frigging career would be over if this got out.'

'Don't, Anna. What we have, has got nothing to do with the case,' he said softer. Anna felt like she was pouring acid into an open wound, but she needed to wake him up to the fact that his son-in-law wasn't all he seemed.

'Look Declan, I know you don't want to hear this, but Finnegan may have been depositing money into Esme's account. Something was going on.' Anna could see this was torturing him.

'Why didn't you tell me earlier?' he asked quietly.

She knew he would ask that. 'Declan, you know why. You shouldn't be involved as it is. Even though this case has brought us together, if there is anything real between us we have to draw a line. It's a murder investigation and I'm breaking every rule ever written by letting you in on what is going on. It has to stop.'

'Rory isn't the link. You said yourself you don't think he's guilty of murder.'

'Yes, but you have got to question why he was paying Esme, and we can't ignore the link to Grace's family.' She let her words seep in. Carly's description of seeing Rory and Esme together in a possible embrace was always at the back of her mind. While she longed to tell Declan, to make him see the possibilities, she knew she had to hold back. Not for the first time she wondered how she had allowed herself to become entangled with Declan. She was compromised, and if McKay or Thomas got wind of the relationship she would be off the case and disciplined to boot. She didn't need internal investigation. Not again. The fallout from her mother's death had left something of a black mark on her record. Anna didn't think her career would survive a second strike.

'I'm not saying Rory is the murderer, but he is up to something and we need to rule him out. You know that most murder investigations get murky, things are thrown up that may have absolutely no link to the main crime, but if you lift a rock and dig around with a stick you find all sorts.'

She didn't want to hit him with the double blow that his wife was having an affair with one of her colleagues. Dr Fintan Swanton, from the QUB modern languages department. Anna had seen something pass between them when she had spoken to Isabelle in her department office. Thomas had done a bit of digging, or flirting more like, with the Dr Isabelle Wells' department secretary and had been told of the little inter-departmental relationship.

It was more than obvious that the marriage wasn't exactly happy, but she didn't think he'd welcome the knowledge of Izzy's affair, even with his entanglement with Anna. Spouses could lead separate lives, but at the end of the day they were still connected on a deep level.

He reached over and took her hand, 'I'm sorry. This is all so ...' he searched for the words, 'fucking crazy. I'm going out of my mind with frustration.'

Chapter 25

Genevieve Marston didn't look happy about being brought into the station at six o'clock in the evening.

'Look I've told your lot already. I don't know much about him. Nice enough fella. Polite and well turned out. Likes his clothes I'd say, always dressed smart, like. Never gives any lip like some of them.' She sat forward on the chair as if she was frightened to make herself too comfortable.

Anna folded her arms, 'You said he isn't always easy to get hold of. Did he ever give an explanation for this?'

'Sure, he likes to go camping. Said he likes hiking in the mountains, nature and all that. No harm in getting your head showered every now and then. Except I'd prefer to do it on a beach with a cocktail in my hand, not up Slieve Donard on a blustery day getting the head blew off me.'

'Did he go on these trips alone or with anyone?'

Genevieve shrugged, 'How should I know? We scarcely pass the time of day with each other. He calls in to collect his pay and we have a bit of a chat. That's it.'

Anna was frustrated. They desperately needed to talk to Luke Nead. 'You don't have an alternative number or address for him?'

'No, like I said before, I send out a text to the casual workers and if they are free they text back. First to come back to me, are the first to get the job. Simple.'

There was one aspect of Genevieve Marston's description that niggled Anna. Luke Nead liked to go hiking, enjoyed nature. It wasn't a wild leap to think he might know a thing or two about wildlife and birds.

'Genevieve, we are going to need a detailed description of Luke Nead from you.'

She rolled her eyes, 'Fine, I can't promise it'll be perfect, but I'll do my best.'

* * *

The vigil was planned for 8.00 p.m. at the front of the City Hall. The organisers were handing out candles while a group at the front began singing hymns. Anna and Thomas pushed their way through the crowd.

'Bloody fanatics,' Thomas hissed, 'Nothing like a rally to get the good people of Belfast out on the streets.' The crowds were gathering, awaiting the orchestrated mourning and candle-lit vigil organised by Aidan Anderson, the city's Lord Mayor and self-appointed Belfast saviour.

They were standing in Donegall Square, part of a quadrangle of the city's main shopping area, where Belfast City Hall stood at its centre, headquarters of the city council. The City Hall building looked splendid with the Continental Autumn Market wrapped around the front of the building. It was decked out with twinkling lights and aromas of roasting chestnuts, crusty bread and baked potatoes. A girl pushed past eating a burrito; Anna's stomach rumbled. It had been another long day, with uninspired canteen sandwiches and coffee being their only food.

Thomas steered Anna towards the back of the crowd. 'They eat this shit up. One minute they are out protesting over the right to fly a flag and the next they are holding paper cones with a candle lit in memory of a dead girl they have never met.' Thomas said, his mouth close to Anna's ear in a conspiring way, as they pushed their way through the crowd. It was a cold, sharp, clear night. The town was full of shoppers and the decision to call a vigil in memory of the dead girls hadn't gone done well with the Superintendent. Their officers were out in force to deal with the crowds.

* * *

The City Hall looks like something from the front of a Christmas card, all twinkly lights and packed full of shoppers and those wanting to take in a bit of the festive cheer. The continental market was pulling in a good crowd. The stalls were full of craft tat, silver bells, autumn harvest wreaths, scarves and hats. Burritos and marshmallows on sticks dripping with lilted chocolate. Kids were whinging at their mas and das for chocolate covered crepes, a bag of Turkish delight and another go on the merry-go-round. Jesus, his head was splitting just listening to them.

The crowd seemed to swell and he found himself caught up in a riptide of people before a pretty girl smashed into him.

'Oh, sorry, I near took the legs off you with my bag. Swear to God, I don't know my own strength!' She smiled at him, her blue eyes, behind a pair of oversized geeky glasses, flashing with merriment. He could tell she was appraising him, taking in his Lacoste shirt, his North Face padded jacket and his freshly shaved face. He never had any problem attracting girls. They all seemed to like what they saw.

'Sure, no harm done. Can I help you?' he asked, giving her his smile. The special one, the girls all liked. He took the over-packed Topshop bag from her, while she steadied herself, rearranging her other bags of shopping and positioning her handbag across her body, the strap sitting between the velvet clad swell of her breasts. She clocked him noticing her breasts and gave him a half smile before automatically drawing her parka coat tight around herself.

'Aww thanks, you're so kind after me near taking you down with my shopping. I've been in town all afternoon and I think I've near enough spent all my wages!'

'You're just right, pretty girl like you deserves to be spoilt.'

She blushed, as he knew she would, smiling shyly as she took the Topshop bag back from him.

'Are you here for the vigil?' she asked.

'Nah, not really, but since I'm here, I might as well stick around to see what the craic is.'

'It's awful, what's happening – those poor girls being killed. Me and all my friends are scared to death to go out on our own.'

'You should be careful, right enough. Stick together, I'd say that's the best idea.'

'That's what my mummy says. She texts me all night until I'm back home safe and sound.'

It was then that he caught sight of her – the Detective. 'Sorry, I got to go, I've seen someone I know.' He pushed through the crowd, leaving the girl behind, her mouth gawping wide as if in mid-sentence, as he tried to reach the other side of the steps outside the City Hall building. He was sure it was her – Detective Anna Cole. He recognised her from the televised press conference, the curve of her jaw, the swish of her dark hair as she turned her head, scanning the crowd. Looking. There was another detective with her. He could tell from the way he carried himself, that squat ready for anything stance, that he was police. There was something so satisfying about seeing them, of being close enough that he could almost reach out and touch the back of her silky dark head.

* * *

A hush settled over the crowd as Aidan Anderson walked onto the stage, flanked by his minders. His hands out stretched to quiet his audience. He had the swagger and presence of an American Evangelist.

'Total wanker.' Thomas said. 'Jumped up wee hood from West Belfast who talked his way into politics and now thinks he owns the city. Loves mixing with the great and the good in America. Probably raising funds for the IRA should they need to start buying arms again.'

Anna nodded. She had read plenty about Anderson since she met him – it would've been hard not to. He seemed to be everywhere, all over the media, bigging-up Belfast and bringing in new business and big events like the MTV awards. He obviously liked the publicity and never shied away from his past, saying that men like him had sacrificed so much to bring about the new Belfast. 'Keeping 'er lit for the future' was his slogan.

'People of Belfast,' he began, 'it is with great sadness in our hearts that we gather here on this cold autumn night to mark, not one, but two deaths, of young girls in our community.' A murmur of agreement went around the crowd. Anna watched as the swelling crowd huddled together, hoods up against the sharp biting cold, looking up, transfixed by Anderson.

'We have fought hard to gain peace, and we are not about to give up that fight. Someone must know something about this evil murderer in our mists. I ask you, to search in your hearts, to find the strength, and the courage to speak out.' The crowd clapped in appreciation. 'Now I ask you all to bow your heads and hold a minute's silence as a mark of respect and remembrance.' The crowd obeyed, united in their mawkish outrage. Heads hung down and a hush fell over the assembled mass.

After a moment's silence, he raised his arms to quiet the crowd further.

'On this autumn night, we have come out in force to show that we will not be cowered into the shadows. Two young girls have had their lives taken in sickening violence, and we will not stand by and allow a third to die.'

The crowd cheered in agreement.

'We will not allow Belfast's daughters to die in this brutal way. Whoever has caused the death of these two beautiful young girls, we urge you to hand yourself in to the police. If you know anyone who has been acting suspiciously, do not hesitate to call the incident room number.' The police number flashed up on a screen behind him.

McKay had asked Aidan Anderson to abandon the idea of the vigil. They didn't want any more of a media circus than they already had. The Irish News had run with the headline

'*Gate Crasher: Strike Two.*' People were scared. City pubs and restaurants had reported a twenty per cent drop in takings. Dissident republicans had issued a veiled threat that if the police didn't find the killer soon, they would be prepared to dole out their own kind of justice.

Anderson had been insistent that the people of Belfast needed to see that the city's leaders were not sitting back allowing a killer to prowl the streets. They needed to feel safe and what better way to show the killer that he wouldn't be tolerated than a mass rally. Anna wasn't so sure of his motives. From what she saw of Anderson, he enjoyed the media attention. He styled himself as some sort of local hero, out to do good for the whole community.

Anna and Thomas scrutinised the crowd, watching for that imperceptible moment, a flicker of interest to alert them. Anna thought about how some killers often bask in the fallout of their actions. They seek out gravesides, they watch the family. Their killer could be part of the vigil, holding a candle up high, and pretending to pray for the souls of the murdered girls. He could be enjoying the outrage manifested by the people of Belfast. For a second she felt unnerved, as if someone was watching her. She turned but could only see the crowd, which had begun to disperse. There was no one keeping an eye on them. She was rattled by tension. Crowds made her uncomfortable too, there was always that sense that catastrophe could strike, one false move and panic could erupt. She was relieved when Thomas suggested they head back to the car.

Thomas took the driver's seat, 'It feels like we are no further forward Tonto. For fuck's sake, this one is going to get the better of us,' he said, banging his palm on the steering wheel. They'd both been there before; cases that failed to give up their secrets easily, dead-ends that wasted precious time and resources.

'McKay is going to start drawing back the extra man power. Before we know it, this one will be consigned to the back burner and we'll be shifting through paper work and logging boxes of evidence for storage.'

'Surely not?' Anna asked, 'there's too much at stake. Two girls, brutally killed and the threat of further victims.'

'We don't know for sure we are looking at a serial killer. What if they aren't related?'

'Copycat, you mean?'

'Why not?'

'No, there's an undercurrent, I'm sure of it. Something links them.'

Thomas pulled out on to Chichester Street.

'Well, you better pull something out of the bag soon or we're both in trouble.'

They knew that a case like this needed a break. Something to drive the momentum forward, and to keep the powers-that-be happy enough to sign off on the much-needed resources. Anna sighed. She had poured all her energy into this case and she didn't need distractions like Declan; but yet, she wanted him. The case offered respite from her life, the stuff she didn't want to deal with. It was all she thought about. This is what she loved about the job – the necessity to let it consume you, emotionally and physically. Until there was nothing left for anyone else.

Chapter 26

"DI Cole. Can we speak to Mr Brogan?' Anna flashed her identity card to the care home manager.

'You can speak to him all you like, but I doubt you'll get much of a reply.'

She led Anna down a corridor, which reeked of institutional living.

'This is Mr Brogan's room.'

The door was open. Mr Brogan sat in an old faded green armchair looking at a portable television, which had the sound turned down. A small cupboard sat squat beside the bed and a dark wooden wardrobe lined the far wall. The room, though small, was personalised with furniture that looked as if it may have come from his former home rather than belonging to the care home. The man sat in a wheelchair looking out towards the manicured lawn. He had thick eyebrows, incongruously dark against his ham pink complexion and thinning, steel grey hair. His hair was slicked down with what could be grease or an old-fashioned hair cream. He wore polyester, fawn coloured trousers, with an elasticated waist. A stain of what looked like porridge sat at his crotch.

'Mr Brogan, I am DI Cole. I am here to ask you some questions.' No response.

'The third stroke left him without speech and his hearing isn't good at all. You'll be lucky if you get any kind of response. God love him. Stuck here all day. Doesn't like the recreation room. Gets agitated easily if the other residents make too much noise I can tell you who comes and goes, we keep a log. Usually, he only sees his son, Robert. People have to sign in and out.'

'Does he have any other visitors?'

'No, that would be his lot.'

'Mr Brogan, your son, Robert, have you seen him lately?'

Anna noticed a slight stiffening of his shoulders, a barely perceptible change in his alertness.

Still no response.

'The son hasn't been here for a few weeks. Mr Brogan's sister used to visit the odd time. I don't think they're close; her visits seemed to be more out of duty than anything. She lives in the Glens of Antrim somewhere. I expect the journey is too much for her these days.'

'Would you have a name and contact details for the son and the sister?'

'I'm sure we do. I can check the records in the office.'

'Thank you, that would be great.' She turned to the old man, noticing his incongruous box-fresh Adidas trainers, 'Mr Brogan, thank you for your time.'

Back at the station, Anna found herself cornered by McKay coming out of the canteen. The smell of something meat and tomato-style made Anna realise how hungry she was.

'Update?' he said, through a mouthful of sandwich. She followed him along the corridor and up the stairs into his office.

'Take a seat. I heard you went looking for Brogan. I thought I made it clear, there isn't a link.'

'You did, sir, but sometimes you have to explore all avenues just to rule them out,' she had to appease him or risk getting a bollocking.

'Did you speak with Brogan in person?'

'We tried, but he was no help. Appears to be incapacitated by a stroke. All picture and no sound, but it could have been an act. The staff say he doesn't communicate, but he flinched when I mentioned the son's name.'

'I doubt that that means anything of use for now. So you're still determined to chase this line of enquiry?'

'Sir, we have Brogan's name on the list as a person of significance. His connection with Declan Wells can't be ignored. We have to talk to him if only to cross him off our list.'

'No visitors coming and going from the nursing home?'

'Not of late. His son, Robert usually checks in and a sister from Glenarriff used to visit him. Might be worth a chat with both of them.'

'Fine, get on it but keep me in the loop,' he said, finishing the last of the sandwich.

* * *

Anna had spent the evening at home, tidying up, catching up on chores and just pottering. All the while her mind was mulling over the case. The girls, all too young to remember the bad times in Belfast; now all part of the new nightlife. Days of the city centre shutting down at five had past. No more security searches for explosives going into shops, no ring of steel surrounding the main shopping street of Royal Avenue. No routine shootings, bomb explosions or reign of terror. Instead, that Belfast had been replaced by one trying to assert itself as diverse, culturally rich, with high educational attainment, a country wanting to embrace the endless possibilities of life not dictated by the troubles.

At one time Belfast was supposedly one of the safest places for a woman to walk the streets at night in the UK, if not in Europe. Sex crimes were not tolerated by the paramilitaries and as long as you didn't stumble into a riot, you were pretty safe.

Her phone rang. 'Hello stranger.'

'Dad I was going to call later,' her heart lurched at the sound of his voice, all so warm and familiar.

'Yeah I'm sure you were. How are you?'

'Good, busy, you know how it is.'

'I read last week in the Echo that police officers are more likely to develop stomach ulcers.'

Anna rolled her eyes, 'Is that right, well no symptoms yet Dad.'

'That job's brutal for stress. Don't know why you don't pack it in and do a nice quiet job like teaching, or working in a library – now there's a job with no stress.'

'Dada we both know I'd never be happy sitting in an office all day, even if there were lots of books to read.'

'Time you settled down girl. I don't know why Jon puts up with you.'

'Well maybe he won't have to for much longer.'

'Why? What's that supposed to mean?'

She hadn't the heart to tell him that she wasn't in love with Jon any longer. 'Oh you know I've been thinking, maybe it's time to move on.'

'Anna, don't be making any rash decisions. Think about it.'

'I will. I have to go.'

'Nos da.'

'Night Dada.'

* * *

Anna set off early. The case was swamping her every thought to the point where she couldn't think straight. She needed clarity and experience taught her that a break away from the minutiae of the crime work could help her see things better.

She planned to do some groundwork and knock on some doors in Keoghill to see if she could find any leads on her birth family. It was time to face what she had been putting off for weeks.

When she woke at seven to a sharp drop in temperature, she considered rolling over and going back to sleep on her Saturday off but she knew that if she did, it might be a few weeks before she would get the opportunity again. Work was crazy busy and she daren't put this off any longer. Besides she was only making a tentative step to have a look around and maybe ask a few questions. She wasn't ready to go wading in at the deep end.

The roads glistened from a light frosting of ice as she eased the car on to the main roads away from the city. She spotted a sign indicating filming going on. Probably, *Game of Thrones*. The signs were all over the place and Belfast had certainly made sure to cash in on its newfound status as a film production site. Everyone in the office watched it and many knew of someone who had been cast as an extra. Anna never seemed to have time to commit to a series. It was all she could do to keep her eyes open to catch the headlines of Newsnight.

Once she had passed the giant canary yellow cranes of Harland and Wolff the city roads gave way to green fields. Belfast was a city of contradictions. Industry snuggled against the dark green hills and bled into the coastline. If it had a better climate, it would probably do all right as a holiday destination. Mind you, she thought, there was no shortage of tourists.

Anna had put off this visit for long enough. She had instigated the move as a part of her grand plan to make contact with her real family. Not that she could ever call them that in front of her dad. It was just that since she had arrived and taken on her work, the desire and energy needed to track them down had seemed to wane. Now she was living in Belfast and working here, she didn't feel the same urgency to find them. It was as if being here, in Northern Ireland, was enough.

Her Saturday morning jaunt to Keoghill was her attempt to start the ball rolling. She knew that these things took time and perseverance. All she wanted, for now, was to see the town where she had been born and to perhaps ask a few questions.

* * *

An hour later Anna pulled into the main street of Keoghill. She hadn't expected it to look so pretty. A row of ice cream coloured houses edged the main road looking out over Strangford Lough. It was the superficial kind of postcard pretty – beneath the peeling façade she could sense the hardship. Some of the shop fronts were boarded up with 'to let' signs buffering the wind, announcing their downfall. It was the type of town dependent on tourism and fishing, and neither seemed to be bringing in big money. She could smell the salt in the air and the undercurrent of fresh fish. A small, grey stone-wall ran along the length of the main road, separating the town from the green-grey lough.

Anna wanted to get the feel of the place so she decided to head towards the town square. Getting out of the car she felt the bracing wind whip around her. It was bloody freezing. She pulled on a navy wool hat she kept in the car and her thick Barbour jacket, zipping it up to keep the chill out.

She hadn't bothered with breakfast before setting off, so her first stop was a cafe situated on the main road.

'That's some morning,' the café owner said as he set out pastries and croissants in the glass covered counter.

'Yeah, it's freezing out there,' she scanned the blackboard menu behind his head. 'I'll have a latte and one of those croissants please.'

She took a seat beside the window and watched the road come to life. A man was walking his dog, a terrier that didn't seem to want to be going anywhere. He dragged it along, looking behind every few minutes to give the dog some encouragement. A couple of kids rode bicycles on the footpath followed by their mother. The place was slowly starting the business of Saturday morning. A local newspaper lay on the table and she noticed it carried an article about the reward for information on Grace's murder. They had been inundated with crackpots as expected. Those wishing to cash in on the money, and those looking for attention. So far, all of them wasting time and manpower.

Thomas was spending the day at the station. They were well suited in that regard and proved to be a good team. Her initial longing for the easy camaraderie of her old office had been assuaged by Thomas' supporting role and his easy-going way. They had progressed beyond the awkwardness of the *almost sex night* and Anna was relieved to find him to be a good partner, conscientious and loyal. When she pushed for the Brogan angle to be investigated he didn't stand in her way.

The last few days in the office had been grim. A large percentage of police work is pure drudgery, laborious and time consuming, fuelled on coffee and pre-packed sandwiches. Much of this case had rested on elimination. The spikes of interest threw out connections and possibilities, and helped to propel them onwards.

* * *

'Are you here for the farmer's market?' the café man asked, setting the latte and croissant down on the table in front of Anna.

'No, I'm trying to track down some family members. Maybe you could help? Would you know where I could find the Keiltys?' She'd thought about flashing her police ID, but in Northern Ireland that could go against you as easily as it could go for you.

He looked at her as if to weigh her up. 'Well as long as you're not from the Inland Revenue or something equally dodgy?'

She sipped the hot, creamy latte, and said, 'I promise you, I am not from the Inland Revenue.'

'I know a fair few Keiltys,' he answered, as he wiped down the counter top. 'Don't know if I want to go giving out information to strangers, no offence like.'

She hesitated, 'Honestly I'm not after them for anything. They are long lost family. I'm over visiting from Cardiff and I would like to meet up with some of them.'

He smiled, 'Ok, then. Martin Keilty runs a bric-a-brac shop up on the Shore Road, you might want to start with him.'

She finished her breakfast, paid her bill and dropped a generous tip into the jar at the counter and headed off. The Shore Road was short walk away. Anna pulled her hood up over her hat and braced herself against the bitter sting of the cold air. She had no idea if Martin Keilty could help her. But it was worth a shot. In a place as small as this, there was bound to be a connection.

The shop turned out to be off the Shore Road, down a little entryway. The signage looked freshly painted, gold lettering against a sage green background - *Keilty Refound*. The bay window was full of bric-a-brac, an old typewriter, a brass trombone, ornaments and a few depressing looking prints depicting hunt scenes. She pushed the heavy door open and an old-fashioned bell jangled overhead. Inside the floor space was limited as heavy dark furniture took up most of the room. Sideboards, occasion tables, bookcases. The tick of a tall grandfather clock punctuated the silence. Anna almost tripped over a stack of paintings waiting to be hung, lying cluttered against the wall.

At the back of the shop, a man was working on a faded gold wingback chair.

'That's a lovely chair,' Anna said.

'Victorian, walnut and velvet but threadbare and coming apart at the seams. Not beyond repair though,' he said looking up at Anna for the first time.

'What can I do for you? Would you like to make me an offer? It's a great wee find.'

Anna hesitated, 'Sorry, I'm not buying. I'm trying to track someone down and I believe her name was Keilty, though she could have married. Would you know where I could find Kathleen Keilty?'

'Who's looking for her?'

Could it be so easy? A quick computer search, an hour's drive, and few inquiries? Anna paused. 'I'm a relative.'

Her phone rang with McKay flashing up on the screen.

'Sorry, work,' she mouthed to Martin, before turning away.

It was Thomas, 'Anna, I need you back in today. A twenty-year-old girl's gone missing. A student called Emma Casey, friends say she should've returned home last night and her phone just goes to answer machine. The parents are in a bad way; terrified she's been taken by the killer. McKay's here, ready to smash heads.'

Anna hung up. Her family reunion would have to be stalled for another day. She hastily scribbled her contact details down for Martin, 'Please, would you pass this on to Kathleen Keilty? Tell her Anna Cole is trying to track her down.'

Chapter 27

Declan knew that his involvement could cost Anna her career, but he was convinced that given the opportunity, the killer would attack again. He couldn't afford to be principled and play by the rules. It was time to do something other than grieve.

He moved a pile of papers from the table. During the day, when Anna was at the station, he developed his own working pattern. He had forgotten how satisfying it felt to be working a case. If only it wasn't the killer of his daughter and another young girl he was investigating.

The odd evening, he headed to Anna's house and ate a hastily made supper, usually something easy like cheese on toast or if they had time, a chilli.

The night before, Anna had draped herself across his sawn-off legs. 'You look tired,' she said, kissing him lightly, her lips dry and soft.

'I could say the same to you.' She had that drawn look of a detective knee deep in a case. Over-worked, and unable to take her foot of the pedal, for fear of missing something. He'd seen it in others and knew what it cost them – relationships, family, friendships. This job came with a price.

Part of his work on the force had been rebuilding damaged police officers, wounded on duty. Long after physical injuries healed, the mental scars would weep and fester. There had been some who'd, while never injured in the line of duty, simply lost their nerve and found themselves paralysed with a stomach-churning fear of what could happen.

Anna was the type who would keep going. Case after case, losing a little bit of herself, with each conviction. It would be the unsolved ones that would steal her sleep; the ones who were out of reach, in the shadows of her dreams, slowly sucking on her soul, until one day she'd wake up and find she'd nothing left to give.

He read through his notes: charting time lines, aerial site maps, Venn diagrams of possible connections and then trawled through his knowledge of criminal theory. Rational choice theory is grounded in free will – the man who discovers his wife is cheating on him with his business partner, shoots them both – he has made a rational choice to do so and after weighing up the consequences of the deaths, decides the risk is worth taking. This theory emerged during the eighteenth century and asserted that people have free will; Declan didn't buy into this for Esme and Grace's deaths. He was sure that the killer's upbringing had to have an impact.

His mind flitted to something he remembered reading – the idea of definitions of success, Albert Cohen, the great American criminologist's argument, that gangland culture emerges in economically deprived areas of cities because working-class males, frustrated by their inability to compete successfully with middle-class youngsters, set up their own norms. They, in effect, redefine 'success' in ways that to them seem attainable, creating their own rules of morality.

He'd seen this in Belfast. Communities living in bleak poverty, with low educational attainment, no hope of jobs, and no vision to see a different kind of life. They inverted the moral norms and began policing their own communities. Racketeering - seeking so-called 'protection money' from local businesses in the promise that they wouldn't be burnt down, by the same individuals collecting the pay off. Punishment beatings for anti-social behaviour, like joyriding, had to make Cohen's definition laughably accurate.

* * *

Anna feared the long drive to Glenariff with Thomas would be a wild goose chase. She couldn't help feeling that they were missing something. There was more information coming in than they could handle, yet not enough substantial leads.

'Aww wait till you see Glenariff Forest Park, it's a pretty special place. Lots of riverside walks and three spectacular waterfalls. Glenariff – Queen of the Glens – is the most beautiful of the nine Antrim Glens.'

She let him keep chattering away to give her mind time to reflect.

'It has a waterfall walkway that opened eighty years ago and has been upgraded all along the three-mile stretch that passes through the National Nature Reserve,' he went on.

'Give it a rest you,' she finally joked. 'You sound like the bloody tourist board.' They were both tired. The case was taking its toll on everyone. The past forty-eight hours had been a mass of interviews and following up leads of sightings of the missing girl, Emma Casey. Anna was frustrated. They were still hoping she would turn up of her own accord, surprised at all the fuss, but they couldn't take any chances. She had Declan on the phone, desperately seeking answers she didn't have. He'd begged to see her last night but she'd told him it was too dangerous. She needed to concentrate on her job. Now she feared this road trip to check out Robert Brogan's aunt's house was taking her off track.

'Well it's pretty special. You'll see what I mean.'

They drove on up the M2 leaving behind the grey mist surrounding the hills of Belfast.

'So, Tonto, you've definitely given me the blow off then,' he said switching lanes.

'Sorry?'

'Ahh the old lingo problem – blow off, kicked to the kerb, all hope lost.'

Anna sighed. She'd hoped that Thomas had decided to forget about their near encounter and her misjudged night.

'I don't think it's a good idea – technically you're my boss. The lead detective on this case.'

'Us Ulster men not good enough for you, then?'

'That's not fair. It would be awkward. We were both hammered and I'm sure you can see that it definitely doesn't make sense to mix business with pleasure.' She dreaded to think of how he would view the hypocrisy of her involvement with Declan.

'Don't worry, I'm only pulling your leg. Last thing I want is another bloody relationship.'

Anna took the opportunity to change the conversation, 'So, what do you know about Nelson Brogan and the son Robert?'

'Brogan senior's reputation went before him. Back in the day he was one of the old brigade. Not the type of man you'd want to cross, if you know what I mean. There were plenty who feared and hated him but he got results and in those days, that was all that mattered.'

They pulled off the motorway onto a slip road.

'And the son, Robert? Do you really think he could be a person of interest?'

'Who knows, you wanted the Nelson Brogan angle checked out and as old man Brogan isn't capable of wiping his own ass, let alone hunting two girls and killing them, then it makes sense to check out his son. Plus, he's proved tricky to track down so that in itself creates an itch that needs scratched. Maybe he's our Luke Nead fella.'

The address they had been given at the care home had been found to be empty. Neighbours hadn't seen him around and the telephone number he had left with the care home wasn't being answered.

'What about Declan Wells, did you know him when he was working?'

'Not really, before my time. It was a travesty what happened to him then, and now. Bad times to live through.'

The sky hung bleak and low as they passed along roads of hedgerows, fields and scattered houses. A road sign announced a nearby pub was being auctioned off. They drove past a sign for Tor Head and a friary named Bonamargy. The radio station lost signal and Thomas, impatient with the need to reach their destination, turned it off. An hour later the satnav instructed them to make a U-turn. They were lost, when suddenly Anna caught sight of an opening in a hedge.

'Look,' she said, 'go back.'

The road they were looking for was little more than a dirt track. They were driving through a valley, the Glens rolling up and onwards on either side of the road. Hedgerows scored along the sides of the car until they reached a clearing. Gnarled trees flagged the opening to the main driveway giving way to a view of the old stone house. It stood surrounded on three sides with run down outbuildings looking inward onto a courtyard. She imagined the setting would have been pretty in its day, cobbled stones and a central well, with a view across the deep green swaths of the Glens. At first glance it was dilapidated, but there was evidence that work had been done to start fixing it up; fresh pointing outlined the windows which bowed in places, looking like they were in danger of sagging under the weight of the stonework. Part of the yard was run over with weeds and the remains of old farm tools – a wheelbarrow rested on its side, and a scythe stood rusted against the cable wall. The overall impression was one of piecemeal work. Someone had tried to keep on top of the repairs. Potted plants were gathered around the stone steps leading up to the forest green front door.

'Here we go then,' Thomas said, snapping off his seatbelt. 'You take the lead and I'll try to get a look around.'

The woman opened the door before they had time to knock. 'Yes, can I help ye?'

'DI Cole and DI King. We would like to have chat with you, about your nephew, Robert Brogan,' Anna said as she reached the front door.

'Rabbie? What do you want with him? He's done nothing wrong.'

'We need to eliminate him from our enquires.'

Maude Briers looked directly at Anna with a touch of arrogance. Age hadn't withered or weakened her. She was a broad woman with a tight, contained bust. Her hair, steel grey and wiry. Anna doubted she had ever dyed it or indulged in anything so flippant as a blow dry.

'You better come in. But I've nothing to tell you. He's a good boy, so he is.' They stepped into the small hallway. Coats were hanging from wooden pegs and an assortment of boots sat below. Two pairs were men's boots. Anna noticed a framed tapestry handing on the wall: *Happy shall he be who taketh and dasheth thy little ones against the stones. Psalms 137:9.*

Christ, and religion was supposed to be about love, she thought.

They followed the woman into the living room. It was dark, yet cosy with a low ceiling and a small window looking out over the green swath of the Glen. A fire glowed in the hearth, flames licking through the turf stacks, filling the room with a peaty scent. The furniture, although dated looking, was well polished. As well as the turf, Anna could smell beeswax, and something else, maybe lavender. Maude Briers appeared to be house proud, everything in the room looked cherished and well cared for. A dark oak table gleamed, surrounded by four upholstered chairs, while two comfortable looking armchairs sat at angles by the fireplace. On the far wall of the room stood a dresser, which held an assortment of crockery, an ornate soup tureen and an old Victorian-looking doll. A religious scripture plaque sat in the middle of the first shelf. Anna wasn't close enough to read the verse this time. A door leading into the kitchen was open, showing an old range and fitted cupboards.

Thomas sat at the oak table without waiting to be asked. 'We need to speak to your nephew as a matter of urgency. When was the last time you saw him?' he said getting straight to it.

'Last week sometime. Maybe Thursday. The days roll into one another, I don't always keep track.'

'You don't have any children yourself Mrs Briers?' Anna asked, touching the doll. Its face was bisque, the surface covered in small hairline cracks, the painted features faded to a dull grey. Anna's fingers stroked the matted thatch of golden brown hair, which felt strangely human. She couldn't imagine any child wanting to play with something so creepy.

'No. Not that it is any of your business and if you don't mind, I'd rather you didn't touch that. It's precious to me and very delicate,' was the terse reply. Anna removed her hand from the doll at once. She resisted the urge to wipe her hand on her trousers.

'You must be very fond of Robert. Spoil him as a child, did you?' Anna asked, watching the woman's tight mouth soften ever so slightly.

'Rabbie was a good boy. Still is. He always goes to church with me when he is staying here. Whatever you want to speak to him about, I'm sure he has nothing to do with it.'

'Would you say you're close to your nephew, Mrs Briers?' Thomas asked. Anna could see the arrogance wane a little. Maude Briers obviously had a soft spot for Brogan. 'As close as an aunt should be. What is this all about?'

'How long have you lived here?' Anna was keen to press on; keep her talking in the hope that they could glean something that would help them.

'Going on forty odd years. It was my husbands' family home before we took it over. Originally an old school house.'

'So, you never moved up to Belfast like your brother then?'

'No, I'm from the Glens and I'll stay in the Glens till they carry me out in a box.'

Anna noticed a framed photograph of an angelic looking child sitting on the stone well in the courtyard. On a side table near the fire she noticed another photograph. This one was more recent. In it stood a young man, with his arm raised, holding a dead hare. He was smiling, as if delighted with his kill. Anna couldn't be certain but the young man in the photograph fitted Genevieve's description. Could Robert Brogan be Luke Nead?

Anna turned away from the photographs. 'How was your relationship with your brother Nelson?'

'It's no secret we didn't get on, but I fail to see what business it is of yours.' Her jaw tightened and Anna sensed she was close to telling them to leave.

'Mrs Briers, is this Robert in the photograph?'

'Yes, that was taken a few years ago. The place was near run over with rabbits, we had to cull a brave few of them.'

Anna gave Thomas a look. 'I know you care for Robert, so I need you to know that by helping us find him, you are helping him.'

'Any chance of a cup of tea?' Thomas asked. Anna knew he was trying to buy them time before they were told to leave.

'If you want.' She went into the kitchen and they could hear her fill the kettle and arrange the cups.

'As I said, Rabbie was a good boy. I don't know how you think he could be involved in any trouble.'

She returned with the teacups, saucers and a jug of milk, waiting on the kettle to boil.

'Thank you,' Anna said, taking a cup and opening her notebook. 'Did Robert stay with you when he was little?'

'Yes, he used to spend the summers here. Got him out of Belfast, away from the troubles and all that. His father was always busy over the twelfth so he was better off here with me.'

'You didn't get on with Nelson and his wife Bridie?'

'Nelson was a hard man to get on with and Bridie was a mouse of a woman, just let him do what he pleased. Never stood up to him. She didn't go to church either, if she'd had a better relationship with the Lord then maybe her marriage would have been better.'

'Had she reason to need to stand up to him?' Thomas asked.

'Oh, I'm not saying he beat her if that's what you're getting at. He was a bully. Liked things his way. But then pressures of the job probably took their toll. The police force wasn't the easy ride it is today,' she added looking at them with contempt. Anna let the last remark pass without comment as the older women returned to the kitchen to finish making the tea.

When she returned, Thomas asked, 'What was Nelson's relationship like with his son?'

'As I said, Nelson was a bully.' she set the teapot on the table and offered to pour for them.

'Rabbie took the brunt of his father's temper. That's why I loved to take him down here. Spoil him a bit and let him have some fun. Loved the animals he did. Always finding some half dead creature and bringing it back to look after it.'

Thomas walked across the room and looked out over the yard, 'Does Robert have a girlfriend?'

'For the love of God, what's this about? I'm not saying another word.'

'Mrs Briers, we are investigating a serious crime,' Anna spoke softly, 'and at this point we need to eliminate Robert from our enquires. You are helping him by giving us this background information.'

She saw the woman relax a little. 'Rabbie has never been in trouble. He's not that kind of man.'

Anna glanced at her notepad, 'We have an address for him in Belfast, 56 Tildarg Street, Cregagh Road. Is that right?'

'Yes, he bought that house when his father had to move into the nursing home.'

'No sign of him at that address. Neighbours say he hasn't been around much. Comes and goes, but keeps to himself. Any idea where we would find him?'

'No, maybe he's gone away for a few days.'

'Would that be usual for him?'

'I don't know. I don't keep tabs on him. When he turns up I'm delighted to see him, but there's no reason to say he can't head off somewhere.'

'If he were to head off, where do you think he'd go?'

'I honestly couldn't say, I haven't a notion,' she said her lips pressed tight together and looked towards the fireplace.

'Ach, I'm dying for a cigarette. Would you mind?' Thomas asked. 'Was a long drive down, sure I'll just pop outside.' Anna knew he was offering to get off side, to let them chat one on one, while he took a nose around.

Anna took a sip of the weak tea, 'So, no girlfriend?'

'Not that I know of. But he's a handsome young man. Plenty of girls have tried to catch his eye,' she lifted her head, as if proud of Robert's good looks. 'But he isn't ready to settle down yet. It would have to be the right woman. And sure, why would he tell his old aunt? It's not like I'm desperate to see him marry.'

'What about work? What's he do for money?' Anna asked.

'He works for some property developer in Belfast, maintenance like. Helps fix up this old place too, when he gets the chance. Rabbie can turn his hand to anything. This'll all be his one day,' she said, looking out of the window across the fields.

'Did he mention the name of the company he works for or the names of any of his colleagues?'

'No, not that I can think of.'

'What about work for a security firm. Did he ever mention doing doorman or bouncer for events?'

'No, for goodness sake! Can't a man have a job and go about his business without people asking all sorts of questions. I told you, Rabbie is a good lad.'

Anna had a feeling she knew more than she was saying. There was something unsettling about the house. Maybe it was the location, low down in the Glen, it felt as if darkness was never far away. The sinister doll seemed to be watching from the dresser. Anna suddenly felt too hot. The fire crackling in the hearth emitted a fierce heat.

Maude suddenly turned and looked directly to Anna, 'Tell me detective, have you tasted the promise of the Lord?'

Anna raised her eyebrows, unsure of how to reply.

Mrs Briers continued, 'We can be purified by our sacrifices, you know. It's not too late to repent and rejoice in the light.'

Anna instinctively flinched. The old woman was making her feel uneasy. There was something sinister in the way she was looking at Anna, as if she could reach in and rip out her very soul and dash it into the fire.

'Deuteronomy 27:16,' she declared, "Cursed is anyone who dishonours their father or mother.' What do you say to that?'

'I don't actually have anything to say to that Mrs Briers. I'm here to ask some questions and then let you get on with your day.' Anna decided to go softer on Maude. She could easily tell them to leave. Maude Briers appeared to be the type of woman who spent too long alone with nothing but her own thoughts and the bible for company. Anna looked down at her notebook, wondered where Thomas had got to and tried to get back on track, 'How did Robert do at school? Did he have friends?'

'Well, he often kept to himself, but that was because his da was in the police, you were told to keep your business to yourself in those days. Not like nowadays when everyone flaunts everything for all to see and hear.

'Besides, Nelson wouldn't have let him bring friends home. I think that's why Rabbie loved the animals so much.' She smiled, as if remembering him as child. 'We'd a goat once that he took a shine to. He'd a piece of string, he tied round its neck and took it on long walks with him, like it was a dog.' The smile faded and her face darkened. 'One day the poor thing was found hung. Jumped over a fence with the string still on it and got caught. Poor Rabbie found it. But he didn't cry – knew better than to let his da see that kind of weakness.' The woman shifted on her seat as if to say she'd said enough and began tidying up the teacups. 'Can I help you tidy up?' Anna asked. Without waiting on a reply, Anna carried the teapot into the kitchen with Maude following after her. She placed the still warm teapot beside the sink when, in a sudden swift movement, Maude grabbed Anna's wrist, 'You know, the law of the Lord is the final stand. We will look to him for judgment on the last day.'

Anna freed herself, feeling uneasy, 'Thank you for your time Mrs Briers. If you can think of anything else, give me call. We'll be in touch, and if Robert contacts you, let us know.' She stared at Anna with suspicious narrowed eyes, as if to say she knew she carried sin deep in her heart. Anna placed her card with her contact details on it on the windowsill next to an earthenware, blue jug filled with drying lavender and left to find Thomas.

* * *

'Well what do you make of her?' Thomas asked as they headed back up the country roads towards the motorway.

'Obviously protective of Robert. Definitely a paid-up member of the scary God squad. It seems that Robert is as close to a son as she has ever had. The father, Nelson seemed to be a big problem, reading between the lines. The photograph though – that could easily fit the description Genevieve gave of Luke Nead.'

'Yeah, I caught that too. Plus, he knows how to handle wildlife. Robert Brogan is becoming more interesting by the day.'

'Did you see anything of interest outside?'

'Nothing much. One of the outbuildings though had the windows whited out with Windowleen,' he looked out the side window, 'Managed to get a glimpse through the side door, which was near hanging off its hinges, seemed to be some sort of storage place. Looked like a barrel of potatoes, some animal feed and some old tools.'

* * *

It was going on for seven o'clock when they arrived back at the station. Anna had met plenty of eccentrics in her line of work but there was something about Maude that had made her feel uneasy. It must have been the combination of the desolate farmhouse; the creepy Victorian doll and her religious fervor that made her feel unsettled.

'I'll put a call in to the local police see if they can keep an eye on the place and watch out in case Brogan pays his aunty Maude a visit,' she said to Thomas. She wanted to ask about Maude as well, see if there was anything they may have missed. Local coppers were often helpful when a case brought them out of their usual locale. In a place like Glenariff everybody was bound to know each other's business.

* * *

She got through to Donald Montgomery, the local Glenariff officer, on the second ring. 'Aye sure I know old Maude Briers. She's a harmless aul being. Keeps herself to herself, apart from her church that is. She's well known among the Protestant churchgoers down here. Her church is the Baptist Christ Covenant Church, but I'm positive you'll only hear good things about her from them. She plays the organ and sings a bit I believe as well.'

'What about her nephew Robert Brogan, have you had any contact with him?' Anna asked.

'No, can't say I have. I'm aware of him. He stays with Maude from time to time so I've seen him about the town. The girls all fancy him, right enough but I don't think he's much interest. Probably has himself a Belfast belle to keep him company.'

'We are looking into one line of enquiry – that he uses another name. Luke Nead, ring any bells?'

He thought for a moment before saying, 'Nope. Nothing familiar about a Luke Nead. We can run it through the system but I'm sure you've done your own checks.'

'Well, thanks Officer Montgomery, you've been helpful. Keep an eye on the Brier place for me. Drive past the odd time and if Brogan should turn up let us know ASAP.'

Manus came bounding into the office, making Anna think of an over excited puppy. 'Hey, Emma Casey's been found, safe and well. The mother's just off the phone,' he said.

'That's music to my ears,' Thomas replied smiling. Emma Casey, had crashed at her ex-boyfriend's house in Limavady and had failed to tell anyone. Her phone had been dead and she didn't realise that her family and friends were frantic.

'I hope she realises what a fuss she created. We have had manpower stretched looking for her while we've a double-murder investigation on our hands,' Anna said.

'Ah, now Tonto, let's just be happy she's turned up and all is well,' Thomas said, still grinning as he headed out of the office. His relief was genuine and Anna liked him all the more for it. She was being churlish. It was the stress of not having that break they needed.

'Right, that's me away home,' Manus said, 'Unless you need me for anything else?'

Anna shook her head, 'No, we're just finishing up here ourselves. Get some rest and be in early for the briefing tomorrow morning.' She was thinking of shutting down her computer and heading home when Thomas reappeared and threw a file on her desk. 'The Nelson Brogan – HR file,' he said.

She knew it was pointless to resist. If she left, she'd probably be up all night turning the case over in her mind torturing herself until she came back in to dig around again.

'Anything of interest?'

'All exemplary stuff. Except for one incident. 1987 call to his home. Boys in dark bottle green turn up to find his missus in bits and saying Brogan had threatened to kill her. All retracted the following day.'

'He roughed her up?'

'Seems so, and most likely not a one off.'

'Ha, so as old Maude said, Brogan wasn't so perfect. An abusive husband.'

Thomas leaned back on his chair, putting his hands behind his head, 'Yeah, so the big question is what affect did all this have on little Robert?'

* * *

The morning briefing had an edgy feel to it. Everyone was getting irritable. The team was deflated and quieter than usual. Forensics had failed to link Finnegan to Grace and what samples they had scraped, were not matched in the system. Hundreds of police hours had been spent interviewing the wedding guests, and the prom attendees, examining the CCTV and generally picking through the details.

'Where are we with staff reviews?' Richard asked. The team had been working its way through the staff lists of the two hotels.

'Nothing of interest except for the security details. As we know both venues hire in extra bouncers and security staff for big events and they often use the same company.'

'Check it out and don't miss anything.'

'Already on it, Sir.' Anna said.

'We've a couple of guests at the Wells–Finnegan wedding who have reported seeing Esme and Rory Finnegan arguing in the hotel foyer. Apparently, they had words, no one caught what was said but he did grab her arm as she tried to walk away. One of the guests said she thought Esme was crying but she couldn't be sure. We suspect he and Esme were in a relationship.'

McKay raised his eyebrows. 'Keep the pressure on him. No evidence on her phone or laptop of their relationship?'

'No, they were all clean, other than lots of phone calls to Finnegan, no texts of particular interest.' He picked up the newspaper left on the desk, and threw it in disgust. 'That jumped up wee shite McGonigle is getting off on this. Can you believe he is calling the killer the Gate Crasher?

'We have the First Minister breathing down our necks to get this maniac off the streets. Young women and girls are frightened to go out, and we are chasing our fucking tails.' He looked stressed and pissed off.

Anna had seen the news story online – 'Who will be the Gate Crasher's next victim?' The scare mongering had started. Photographs of Grace Dowds and Esme Wells staring out, the archetypal tabloid victims.

It was true they had come up against a wall. The numbers of people at both events hampered the investigation. People were unsure of what they heard, if they had seen the victims leave the hotels and at what times. There was plenty of talk, conjecture, but nothing solid.

'There are to be no leaks to the press. If Communications and the PR department want to pander to them that's their problem, but they are to get nothing from us. Is that clear?'

Anna picked up the newspaper. 'Sometimes the press can be helpful in a case like this.'

'It isn't helpful to be scaring people and saying we have a Jack the Ripper type scenario on our hands,' Richard fumed.

* * *

Later that evening Anna and Holly were alone in the canteen.

'Rough day?' asked Holly, helping herself to coffee and a blueberry muffin, her make-up as perfect as ever.

'Yeah, could say that.' Anna took a chair and Holly sat opposite, stirring her coffee as if she hoped to find salvation at the bottom of the cup.

'I don't know what's happening to this country. At least during the troubles, you knew who was what, and who to keep an eye on. This pervert makes a change from dissidents and flag protestors getting out of hand. Any firm leads?'

Anna shook her head. 'We keep chasing ghosts of leads.'

Holly took a drink of her coffee, 'We've seen a rise in the number of sex crimes, in keeping with the national figures, but this killer doesn't have a MO for sexual assault, does he?'

'No, that's the thing, the girls are murdered, brutally so, but there isn't a sexual assault.' Anna paused, 'All this talk of a new dawn for Northern Ireland and a workable 'shared future,' do you think the murders could in any way be linked to the past?'

'How do you mean?'

'I don't know. It seems as if the killer is trying to prove something. It's a feeling I get, but maybe it's this place – Belfast.

You all seem so hung up on the past. Sure, there's plenty of talk about the new order and peace and all that, but every which way I look there's historical inquiries, flag protests, marches and meetings about banning marches, riots about the marches being banned - the lot. For an outsider, it doesn't look so harmonious.'

'We don't let go easily, that's for sure,' Holly said, picking at her half-eaten muffin.

'Maybe that's it, our killer doesn't want to let go of the past.' Anna placed her hands around the hot cup of coffee.

* * *

Anna hadn't seen the little grey and white cat for a few days. The weather had turned cold so she assumed he was keeping himself in doors. But she missed seeing the swish of his tail and the interaction. She called Declan. 'You said before that you didn't think the police would take Esme's death seriously. That it wouldn't be a high priority.'

'The peace process is a fragile beast. The Executive is at an impasse yet again. The balloons sitting up in Stormont can't make a decision that doesn't involve name calling and point scoring, so keeping them happy and preventing all-out war on the streets is the bigger picture for the PSNI.' Declan sighed.

'What if our killer is acting politically?'

'Where are you going with this?'

'What if he has an agenda? That he didn't like the new status quo and he wanted to make a point?'

'Angry with the state?'

'Yes, or the police. Someone with a grudge and an agenda.' She heard Declan breathing down the line, thought of his warm breath caressing her neck and shivered, 'Could he be trying to tell us something, or teach us a lesson?'

Declan sighed, 'Do you think the girls were singled out?'

'Not necessarily. They may have been planned locations but chanced encounters with each of the victims. It may have been enough that they were young girls with everything to live for. The first generation to have lived free of the bombings and shootings.' Anna said.

'What has made him hate like this, who is he angry at – the police or the state?' Declan asked.

'Or is it the new order? Belfast is 'buzzing' according to all the marketing hype maybe our killer doesn't like this new way of life. Not everyone wants to let go of the past.' She could sense him thinking.

'Their bodies weren't posed in any way but it is possible that they were staged,' he said.

'What's the difference?'

'To pose would suggest sexual gratification for himself, whereas to stage it, is sending a message to us.'

'So, what's his message?' she asked, 'That's where we need to go with our investigation.'

* * *

It was dusk. The sky had settled into a violet hue, edged with pink and orange. He loved this time of evening when he could go out trapping without fear of running into to anyone. Usually the Giant's Ring, a henge monument at Ballynahatty, near Shaw's Bridge, was free from walkers at this time of year. The odd car would be parked in the Minnowburn car park, ostensibly just sitting there but, those in the know knew that it was a gay pick up point. Most men parked up there where either married or had yet to come out, so they had no interest in his lone figure walking along with his leather satchel draped across his body.

He walked across the grassy circular enclosure, sunken into the ground and surrounded by its earthy bank, and headed towards the river where he hoped to find prey. Something different, like a stoat or an otter. He had trained himself to walk with care, making as little noise and movement as possible. His eyes peered through the falling darkness, alert to subtle movements and the flash of bright eyes.

He was near the river when he smelt it. A fox den, that pungent musky odour of their urine. The burrow was deep into the ground with the first couple of feet of the main entrance enlarged and dug into an oval shape to allow the fox to bolt out if it needed to. He reached into his satchel and pulled out his leather falconry gloves for protection, along with the plastic bag of raw meat. If the fox was at home he could entice it out with some fresh meat and be ready to strangle it with his length of wire.

* * *

He remembered his first fox, caught in the Glens while staying with Maude. He found it wounded, most likely hit by a car. The sinews of its left rear leg were exposed, raw and gristly. He could remember the saliva gathering in his mouth. The beautiful anticipation. He bundled the creature in his coat, being careful to cover its snout so that it couldn't bite him. He carried it back across the field and when he reached the outhouse he laid it down. The stupid beast had looked at him with something close to longing, begging for water, or relief from its pain. He smiled and watched it, its heart visibly pumping beneath the orange coat and listened to it whimpering. Low and snivelling.

When Maude found him, lost in the pleasure of the kill, she stopped in her tracks, absolutely still. He felt the horror of what was to come wash through him. She would punish him; beat him even, just as his father would.

She raised her arms and he before he could take the first strike, he ducked down, holding his head in his hands for protection. But no, she didn't hit him. Maude took him in her arms, and cradled him; carrying him home where she bathed him, washing away the blood. All the while singing hymns to him in her beautiful voice.

'Veiled in darkness, Lord we pray,
Take us back before we stray.'
He could still remember the words and the haunting, sombre melody.

Chapter 28

The next day, after work, Anna pulled into the narrow driveway running up the side of her rented house and was shocked to see Jon sitting on the front step.

'What are you doing here?' she asked, none too pleased.

He rummaged in his rucksack and pulled out a clutch of envelopes, 'Delivering your post.' He grinned, almost disarming her with his good looks.

'I said to forward my mail, not hand deliver it. You better come in.'

He followed her up the narrow hallway through to the living room.

'I'm serious Jon, what are you doing here? Is my dad ok?'

'Yeah, yeah he's doing ok. I wanted to see you. We should talk.'

Anna sighed. She had spent the day trawling through CCTV footage, trying to identify anything that could possibly put Rory Finnegan in the vicinity of Grace's murder. Lara had supplied him with an alibi – they had been attending a charity dinner and CCTV proved she wasn't covering for him. She had a headache and she suspected Richard was pissed off with her for raking over the Brogan case file. The last thing she needed was a heart to heart with Jon.

'Come on, I'll buy you dinner,' she said keen to put off the inevitable.

They headed over to the Lisburn Road and chose a small Italian restaurant decked out with early Christmas lights.

'So, how have you been?' Jon asked, lifting his eyes from the menu to look directly at Anna.

'Busy.'

'Nothing new then. Still using work to hide behind.'

Anna wanted to tell him to fuck off with his amateur psychology, but she was hungry, and didn't have the energy required to fight. She could still recognise Jon as being attractive. His hair, shorter than he normally wore it, was starting to turn grey at the sides. He was clean-shaven and as always, dressed casually in a preppy style, which she often playfully mocked him for. His eyes, intensely dark and prone to looking melancholy, until he smiled, were what first attracted her to him when they had first met in Cardiff's Yard Bar on St Mary Street. They had both been out with their respective group of friends, drinking and enjoying the live band, Roosevelt. The tall good-looking guy in a brown jacket had asked to buy her a drink and for once she didn't decline and shoot him down with a withering look. They talked and before she could convince herself it was a bad idea, they had agreed to move on to somewhere quieter. They'd dated casually for six months, gradually spending longer and longer together before, almost without a discussion, he moved in.

'I thought we agreed, no visits.'

'I think you'll find I didn't agree anything.' They placed their orders and resumed the conversation.

'So, Anna, are you going to tell me what's really going on with you?'

'What do you mean?'

'You run off to this place,' he looked around, as if to say this dump, 'Barely three months after your mother dies. Never mind that we had even skirted marriage. I did think that was where we were headed. It feels like you're running away.'

'I never promised you anything Jon.'

'No. That's true you never did.' His tone was sad and resigned.

The food arrived, allowing Anna a few minutes to avoid conversation as she began eating.

'So, you are staying here then?' Jon asked.

'Looks that way,' Anna replied sipping her mineral water. 'Why did you come Jon?'

'Call it concern. Call it courtesy,' he hesitated, taking a drink from his glass before saying, 'I am seeing someone at work. Nothing serious, its early days but I wanted to see where I stood with you before taking it further.'

Anna couldn't blame him. The writing had been on the wall for some time, but she hadn't felt strongly enough to end it either. She had sort of hoped it would fizzle out naturally. The coward's way out of a relationship.

'How gallant of you.' She hated herself for sounding so bitchy. He didn't deserve it.

'You've no business getting snarly with me Anna. If you wanted me, we wouldn't be sitting here. We'd be back home building a life together. Instead you decide to go off and find yourself. How's that working out for you, by the way?'

She was stung by his comment. Somehow, she had always believed he understood her; that he got her need to do this, to try to find out more about where she came from.

Jon looked at her with something close to pity. 'I was there, when your mother was dying, I was there for you. Don't forget that it was you who ran out on me, on our life together. Did you expect me to wait until you'd figured out whatever is going on in your head? Because I can tell you, there's no figuring out what you went through. What you did.'

Anna froze. How much did he know? How much had he worked out? She spoke but barely trusted her voice not to give her away, 'I don't know what you mean. I'm doing just fine.' Images flashed through her mind, the quick sharp thrust of the screwdriver in that dank shed. The pain shooting through her breast, the metal taste of fear.

Then later, with Camille, the smell of death on her skin, like lilacs and over-bloomed lilies. The bones of her face protruding, making her look so different. The heartbreaking sound of her father crying.

'You got what you came for, permission to move on.' Anna got up and grabbed her bag and coat, not caring about the dinner she'd been served moments ago. 'Where are you staying tonight?'

'I've booked a room in a hotel near the airport.'

'Good. I'll get my dad to call you to arrange packing up my stuff at the house.'

Outside in the rain, Anna tried to compose herself. It was churlish to take offence, to be hurt, after all, she lay no claim to him, had made him no promises to stay faithful herself. Somehow, she still felt the sting of betrayal. It was easier leaving him, if she could think of him waiting for her. So that part of her life was over. Two years spent playing house and pretending to be grown up. It hadn't suited her, not enough anyhow. Anna had reverted to type. If home life is messing with your peace of mind, throw yourself into work. The hopelessness of remaining in a relationship with Jon seemed clearer now that she was away from him. She was overcome with relief. It was done.

Chapter 29

Declan was past making excuses for his wife. The months had slipped into years and here they were together but apart. Izzy had her own life.

He recognised that he had messed up; that he had been going through the motions of family life and turning his head from what he had known for the longest time. That she had someone else to love, to turn to. The pain of that knowledge had burned low for so long and was now extinguished, drowned out by the pain of losing Esme and quenched by finding Anna. The need to know who Izzy was sharing her life with and how long it had been going on, what they did – he felt he was over it. He was past caring.

What frightened him was how he felt about Anna. Her skin, so translucent and pale, all the more so against her dark hair. Her lack of self-consciousness when she undressed, the way she didn't mind if he watched her. He wouldn't be enough for her, but it was partly the fact that she didn't need him, yet wanted him, which aroused him so much. And that voice; sounding like poetry, folk songs, honey and cream.

* * *

Somehow it was easier to be naked in front of her than Izzy. Anna had never known him before the car bomb; she had never known who he had been. The first time he had been with her he had carefully avoided letting her see his broken body, his ragged scars and the tightened atrophied muscles. She had shushed him and had taken over, her hands trailing where he hadn't been touched in years. *Years.* God, he could have cried with the pleasure of her mere touch, if it hadn't been for his self-consciousness and his sheer embarrassment.

He waited for her to say, 'It isn't that bad' or 'you don't need to be embarrassed with me.' But she didn't. Instead, she reached out and touched him; her kisses raining down on him like a benediction offering solace. He knew that somewhere in the shadows of love you find fear. The knowledge that if you surrender to it, you can only get hurt. Anna wasn't some fantasy he had dreamt up to the pass the hours lying in a hospital bed. She was skin and flesh and bone with that moon shaped scar on her breast. He couldn't wish away how he felt, even if he wanted to.

* * *

The first year after the bomb had been about being alive. In spite of the horror of his damaged body and the loss he had experienced, he could appreciate a deep respect for life and he was determined not to abuse what was left to him by being bitter and full of anger and regret. He could sense that there was nothing to gain in anger; it was wasted energy that he didn't have to give. The perpetrators weren't even on his radar. That was for others to worry about. He needed to focus all of his strength and abilities on recovering and trying to make the best of what was left of him. Through the pain, the agonies of skin grafts, rehabilitation, and infections, he had held fast to his determination to not be the one who made this bad situation worse. He could see that for Izzy, and the girls, life could get back to some sort of normality, provided he allowed them to. If he acted like some crazed King Lear, full of the injustice of his life, they would suffer along with him. So, he buried whatever bile of emotion threatened to rise to the surface, and after a while it became easier to act the role of someone who had resigned himself to a lesser life.

He could see now that in doing this he had given Izzy permission to move on without him. By keeping her out of his head and his torment, he had cut her free. He hadn't counted on her abandoning him. She had outgrown him. He had closed the door on any hope of tenderness for fear it would be pity. When they had first married, he enjoyed the idea of them being a tight unit. A team, as clichéd as that sounds. When the girls came along he felt relegated to the sidelines. He was the protector, not the nurturer and that was fine. He understood his role and his part in it all. He was prepared to work hard, to provide for them and to be whatever they needed him to be.

When the house was being remodelled to accommodate his reduced state and his need for a wheelchair they had argued over pathetic details like handrails and bath chairs. He had sensed Izzy's frustration of having her choice of designs and her inherent good taste reduced to the practicalities of the disabled. The builder would arrive with brochures of grab bars and hand rails, expecting decisions to be made and all Izzy could do was to sigh. At times, he wanted call her out on it. To make her feel small and guilty for showing such disdain for practicalities. He couldn't of course.

To have a woman like Anna want him and enjoy his company was more than he could have ever hoped for. He didn't think he could have borne the past two months without her to lean on. She accepted so much of him without question. His grief and his disbelief at losing Esme had been so awful yet amongst the trauma and pain was this need to rise up and grab what pleasure he could find and Anna had offered him that glimpse of tenderness.

Chapter 30

'They're at it again,' Richard said as he dashed through the office. 'Riots on the lower Newtownards Road. I'm heading out there but stay put.'

'I'm coming,' Anna said grabbing her jacket.

'No stay here, that's an order. The roads are gridlocked so you'll not manage to get home for hours and there's no way I'm letting you anywhere near it without an armoured jeep.'

She saw Holly and Russell share a complicit look. Richard had been emphatic about Anna not accompanying him but she wasn't about to sit around waiting to be told she could have his permission. Thomas was off supposedly chasing up IT reports but Anna knew he'd had a meeting with his divorce mediator.

She gave McKay a five-minute head start to get out of the building before she grabbed her keys and left. Richard was right. The traffic was slow. Five o'clock rush hour was bad enough on a normal day. It was Halloween, a big event in Belfast. As Anna drove by the houses in the more up-market end of East Belfast, she could see carved pumpkins glimmering on doorsteps and kids dressed up in elaborate costumes to go trick or treating, were passing by on the streets.

Another vigil had been announced to commemorate Esme and Grace's deaths and it appeared that the riot had broken out as the vigil had begun to disperse. Community leaders were calling on the people of Belfast to come out in droves and pray for the swift incarceration of the perpetrator. Social media pages had been set up to register interest in the event. Thousands had signed a petition to put pressure on the PSNI to do more, causing Richard to seethe for two days and give everyone an extra hard time.

Politicians, keen to be with the swell of public opinion, were taking the opportunity to ask what the police were doing and could the case be handled better?

Aidan Anderson had told the press, 'dark deeds need to be met with light and that the spotlight of justice must be strong and uncompromising.' He was quick to suggest that perhaps the PSNI were out of their depth and that perhaps now was the time to have stronger cross border links with the Garda Síochána. Anna could sense the tide was turning and that they needed to assure the public and the politicians, that they were making progress. But progress wasn't enough, they needed an arrest.

* * *

Not for the first time, Anna thought how divergent Belfast was as a city. Those with jobs and money seemed to live in a bubble of harmony and normality while only a few streets away those with no prospects clung to the old violence and bigotry. They had been trying for a week to contain the outbreak of rioting plaguing East Belfast, close to a notorious interface. Talks with community leaders had broken down and they were calling for the head of the PSNI to resign with the second murder victim barely buried. Belfast people liked to deal their own type of justice and if the police weren't coming up with the goods they had decided to show their anger. The report had come in that one hundred youths, some aged as young as twelve, had been involved in fierce clashes.

Additional police had been deployed in the east of the city the previous night in an effort to quell tensions after officers were pelted with petrol bombs and bottles. The homes of petrified residents caught in the middle of the disorder had also been targeted with two cars set alit. Missiles raining down on them had damaged attending fire engines. There were skirmishes between rival groups in the vicinity of the nationalist enclave of the Short

Strand, with much of the violence appearing to have been pre-arranged on social media. The most recent trouble involved sustained attacks on police officers by loyalist gangs, hell bent on voicing their discord and frustration that a killer was at large. They failed to see the irony of their outrage when Belfast had more convicted killers at large thanks to the Good Friday Agreement than any other UK city. But this was a new type of murder. Belfast was used to its blood being spilt for political reasons.

Loyalist community representatives had met earlier in the day to discuss the powder keg situation, with further discussions between political representatives and the police due to take place in the coming days. The talks had obviously broken down and the power hold over the young of the community had failed to contain their lust for street violence. It seemed to be any excuse to take to the streets with a make-do balaclava and half a brick to lob at any moving target.

Anna knew that summer riots around contentious parades and flags were common and were even known as 'recreational rioting', as if it was a perfectly normal occurrence for teenagers to take to the streets for entertainment. To come out on the dark, cold wet nights was something else. That showed commitment and anger.

The rain pissed down as the car crawled through the traffic. At the junction of Bloomfield Avenue, a road known for its upmarket boutiques, she turned on to the Newtownards Road and heard the first thunder clap of violence. Sirens cried out in the distance as a blaze of indigo and amber fireworks rose up against the petrol blue evening sky. Since it was Halloween, the shops were full of fireworks – the riot weapon of choice.

Anna drove on through Belfast's bleak rain soaked streets. The orange glow of the street lights glinting off the black roads. She saw a shopping trolley filled with bits of wood and set alight as it rolled across the road and stopped at a cable wall. The siren of an ambulance whirled close by and she watched as a hooded figure stretched his arm back to hurl a petrol bomb into the crowd. Smoke rose up from the crowd along with a cheer of 'Yeeeooo.' The battle cry of victory.

The side roads were jammed with traffic. People trying to make their way home after doing a day's work. Anna kept to the main route but found the car engulfed by rioters and on lookers. She edged the car, inch-by-inch, slowly through the crowd, as hands slammed on to the car, and abuse spat out of angry mouths. Hate and violence unleashed like a raging epidemic. She turned into the street to her left, glad to have got out of the worst of it and turned her lights off. She looked around and saw that she had pulled into one of the back streets of red-bricked terraced houses. Youths were running past the top of the street brandishing any weapons they could get their hands on – metal pipes, pieces of masonry and bottles, some of which were filled with sloshing petrol, corked with a rag to catch the flame at the opportune moment.

Two frightened faces peered out from behind a curtain window. Anyone with any sense would be hiding out until the worst of it died down, but several residents were standing in their postage stamp sized front gardens, as if this was a spectacle not to be missed. One of them was drinking a can of Budweiser. She thought it odd that he seemed to be looking on as if this was entertainment.

Anna had experienced street violence before. She was used to unrest, but the burly rugby players littering the city streets after a match in the Cardiff Arms Park or the newer Millennium stadium seemed like harmless rogues compared to this lot.

* * *

Suddenly, she heard a roar of, 'PSNI scum.' Some of them were so obviously kids. They should be safe at home, doing homework and playing video games, she thought. They looked barely thirteen as they ran wild with their misplaced sense of vengeance.

Why did everyone blame the police for everything in this town? Anna wondered.

She watched as hooded figures with scarves tied round their lower faces, to prevent being caught on camera, gathered in a huddle at the street corner, apparently planning their next move. A police Land Rover took position on the road opposite and Anna watched as the youths roared back into life, bottles and bricks in hand ready to cause trouble. A firework shot up into the police barricade to shouts and whistles. It was like sport to them. Anything to bait the police, and give them an excuse to interact on an aggressive level.

The next thing Anna knew her car was surrounded. They were pushing it from side to side, causing it to rock back and forth. She revved up the engine, glad she had the sense to lock the doors in advance. Faces with rubber Halloween masks pressed up against the windows, some comical and others grotesque. As she managed to get the car going she heard a deafening crack. They had smashed in the back window. Within seconds she was being pulled from behind, dragged through the broken window. This is it she thought; fuck they are going to kill me. She tried to reach for her Glock but her hands were dragged behind her. She had to get away. She had to fight back.

Thrashing and kicking, she fought them but there were too many, and they were stronger than her. Hands grabbed at her clothes and her hair, yanking her through the back of the car. Hands tore at her, dragging her through the broken back window and she felt her shoulder pop in a scream of lightning bolt pain, rendering her dizzy and sickened. Bile rose up into her throat, acidic and viscous, burning as she swallowed it back down her gullet.

She thought of the two British soldiers in the late eighties, taken from their car in the midst of a funeral cortège, stripped and mutilated before being murdered. Wrong place, wrong time and wrong nationality. What was she thinking driving into this? Had she been trying to prove she didn't need to be nannied to do her job? How bloody wrong she was.

'Get her identity card out, she's an undercover cop, so she is.'

The noise was deafening. Somewhere far off she could hear a siren. A whoosh of flames. A roar of chanting, indecipherable words. A blow to the front of her head was the last thing Anna felt. Cold and sudden it smashed down on her skull. And then, velvet blackness.

* * *

The heat made her think of Camille. The fevers that had raged for days, though it felt like months, were impossible to control. Anna had sponged her down with cooled water, gave her slivers of ice which melted immediately on touching her lips, and kept two fans whirring, constantly, at each side of the bed. The morphine never seemed to do enough.

Her mother would alternate, from being lucid and clear in her desire for it all to be over with, to raging in a haze of madness. Using language Anna had never heard uttered from her mother's lips. Asking for her own mother, and crying out that the cat was scratching at her feet, that insects were eating at her, that the fire had burned down and where was the coal? All ranting lunacy, yet so apparently painfully real to Camille. Then begging forgiveness for being a burden, for not coping with the pain. Both versions of her mother terrified Anna.

Usually Camille was such a contained, controlled person, that this loss of all sense of decorum made Anna feel her mother had only ever presented a shadow of herself. It was as if she was always on her best behaviour, should anyone doubt her ability to be the perfect mother, for fear they would snatch Anna away.

Despite Camille's readiness to tell anyone how close Anna and she were, that they were so alike in their personalities, and even mannerisms, it was her father whom she truly felt closest to. He accepted her without any desire to assert his ownership over her. To let her be his daughter rather than Camille's need to always be recognised as Anna's mother. As is always the way with children and parents, the more Camille needed her, the more Anna pushed her away.

But that was over. Camille was gone.

Anna wanted to crawl out of her own skin. The heat was searing now. Burning down on her face like a laser, warming her blood to boiling and drying her skin to a leathery parchment. Somewhere at the back of her mind she sensed she was safe. In a bed, probably a hospital, beyond that she didn't dare think.

* * *

When Anna came round, she was aware of a blinding pain caused by a bright light shining in her eyes.

'Steady now.'

'She's conscious.'

'Anna, it's ok. You're safe. You're at the Royal Victoria hospital. You have some injuries, a concussion, some cuts to your face and a bashed-up shoulder, but really you've been lucky. Your shoulder will hurt a bit, but we have given you some pain medication that will kick in real soon. You're best trying to sleep for now.'

Sleep. She wanted to fall into the blackness of sleep, but something was bothering her. She couldn't remember what she was supposed to do. She had something important to focus on, but what was it that was out of reach?

* * *

Later she woke, hearing herself moan. Pressure on her shoulder was causing pain to radiate out in jagged spears across her chest and down her arm. She tried to move it into a better position but the pain was more intense and she just about stopped herself shouting out. She steadied her breathing in an attempt to gain control. Beyond the hospital room she could hear the murmur of voices, the clink of a tea trolley and a distant telephone trill.

Her tears threatened to spill over. She was so stupid to have put herself in that situation. Who did she think she was, stumbling in on a riot like some sort of tourist voyeur wanting to see a bit of Belfast action? She knew the score, knew the risks yet thought she could sit on the side of the road and watch it.

She was in pain, laid up for God knows how long but at least she was safe. It could have been so much worse. Carefully she moved her good arm and wiped at her tears. She tentatively felt stitches across her cheekbone and the soreness of bruising beneath her eye. She didn't want to know what she looked like. Not a pretty sight.

The Halloween mask clad faces, the angry chants of 'Get her, get her. PSNI scum!' clawed from her consciousness, making her gasp at the memory. She had been terrified. Somehow on a primitive level she had fought them, kicking, scraping at them with her nails, biting, but she was powerless against their strength and numbers. The Land Rover had rammed at them, barely in time, but not before hands had grabbed at her breasts, in lurid aggression. Her body dragged by her limbs from the car, she watched them torch it, petrol and fireworks creating an explosion of Technicolor splendour. Almost beautiful, amidst such ugliness.

Chapter 31

The next day Anna checked herself out of the hospital. Thomas came to pick her up and greeted her with a bollocking.

'What were you thinking off? Have you any idea how fucking dangerous your little stunt was?'

She still winced from the pain in her shoulder, but she figured she would be recovered enough to drive in a day or so. In the meantime, she would be out of the office - Richard had insisted she take a few days off, despite her protests.

'Please, no lecture; take me home and fill me in on the case on the way.'

'We're still chasing up that one name on the security staff list who we haven't been able to contact.'

'The Luke Nead man?'

'Yep.'

'Have we anything to connect him to Robert Brogan?'

Thomas pulled out into the outside lane, passing an Ulster bus. 'Not as yet, but he's definitely worth chasing up. We know it's the same security firm Finnegan uses from time to time so we desperately need to speak to him. He worked various sites around Belfast and Holywood so he would have known the venues and crime scenes well. He wasn't booked to work the nights of the murders, but that's not to say he didn't turn up and blend into the background until he chose his moment.'

'That's as good as a lead as we've had. Any address to check out?' Anna asked.

'The security firm was sketchy. Looks like he was paid cash in hand and didn't work regular shifts. If they needed him they gave him a call. The payroll girl gave a description; medium height, clean cut, good dresser, but wasn't sure she could give a good enough description to help get a photo-fit drawn.'

He must have felt bad, for he swung the car by Tesco's and said, 'Sit there, I'll get you some supplies.' She didn't want to think about what Thomas considered essentials. A frozen pizza and four bottles of Magners, no doubt. But still, she wasn't complaining.

The case was shifting. She could feel it. They had reached that almost imperceptible moment when it stopped dragging its heels and began to pick up some momentum.

Her phone buzzed. A text message from Declan, checking to see how she was. She had managed to convince him that she was well enough, that she'd merely had a scare and that wasn't worth the risk of visiting her. He could be seen by one of her colleagues or even the press.

Thomas returned carrying two plastic bags with groceries. 'I hope you're not expecting me to cook for you as well,' he said, starting the engine.

Anna opened the front door and breathed in the familiar scent of the house. Now that she had been here a few months, the place had begun to feel like home. She winced with pain as she took her leather jacket off and left it on the banister before making her way through to the kitchen. Thomas followed with the shopping.

'Will you be all right for a bit? I'm heading back to the office,' he said looking at her with a mixture of pity and frustration.

'Yes, I'll be ok.' She wanted him to leave. She felt so vulnerable and close to tears. She needed to weep and get rid of the emotion threatening to choke her.

'If you need anything, let me know.'

'Call me if there's anything of interest,' she said, though neither was holding out much hope. It felt like a stalemate scenario.

'Sure. Get some rest and I'll see you in a day or so.'

While Anna appreciated his gruff kindness, she was relieved he hadn't hung around.

The time passed in a blur of rubbish daytime property programmes, eating cheesy Doritos and drinking Lucozade – Thomas's idea of supplies. By evening she was feeling stir crazy. Her facial injuries had turned fifty shades of purple, while the stitches felt tight and itchy. The shoulder pain was eased by the codeine and ibuprofen, but going out was not an option. She was still feeling a little delicate and queasy, though that could have been from the pain meds.

She decided to call Cerys. It had been a few months since they had spoken. They were both so busy that they had relied on sending texts. Brief updates that didn't required too much thought. After the past few days, she felt like she needed to hear a friendly voice.

'Hey you!' Cerys said on answering. 'Hang on till I put Gethin into his high chair so I can talk in peace.' Anna lay on the sofa, listening to the sounds of domesticity that had become her friend's way of life. She could picture Cerys' homely kitchen, the hand painted kitchen cupboards in some ridiculously named shade of Farrow and Ball, like Elephant's Breath. The Emma Bridgewater pottery and the Cath Kidston tablecloth. The perfect scene of family life, a silent rebuke to Anna's existence of take away suppers and half empty bottles of wine.

'So, how are you? How's Ireland?'

'Yea, it's all good.' There was no point in telling Cerys what had happened. She didn't need another lecture and she didn't want to worry her. 'It's different in so many ways, but I'm adapting. This case I'm working on is driving me mad.'

'Nothing new there then,' Anna could sense Cerys smiling at her, and probably rolling her eyes. It didn't feel right to lay all the shit of the last few days on Cerys. Not for the first time, she considered how her job made her feel apart from normal life. No wonder cops tend to get together with other cops, she thought.

'How's motherhood?'

'Tiring. No strike that – exhausting! You would not believe how little sleep I get and I haven't even got you here to moan to.'

'I'm sorry. I've been a lousy friend. Have you seen Jon?'

She heard Cerys draw a breath, 'Ben took him out for a pint last week. He said you guys had spilt. Ben thinks he's seeing someone else. I'm sorry Anna.'

'No, don't be sorry. It's ok, really, he told me.' A sudden painful, loneliness grasped at Anna.

Cerys said, 'So come on, when is your time up? I need my friend back home to keep me sane and take me on the odd night out before I morph into one of those zombie mummies who only talk about cracked nipples and baby poo.'

Anna laughed, 'I'm not sure, there's a lot to do here.' How could she begin to explain how Belfast had got under her skin or maybe it was the pull of being with Declan. Either way she was in no hurry to go back to Cardiff.

Maybe it was the warmth in Cerys' voice, but she suddenly and unexpectedly found herself crying.

'Hey, Anna. What is it? Tell me,' Cerys demanded.

'I'm sorry. I'm just feeling a bit low. It's good to hear your voice.'

'You're still in the throes of grieving for your mam. It was too soon to go haring off to Northern Ireland. You need to be here, with your friends and family around you.' The baby cried in the background. She could hear Cerys shushing him.

'Honestly, I'm fine. It's been a long day. Go to Gethin and give him a big kiss from me. I'll call you again soon.'

'Are you sure you're ok?'

'Definitely. I promise. All's fine.'

There was no point in telling her about the riot. She didn't want her dad hearing about it.

'Ok. Well make sure you are looking after yourself. No living off takeaway meals and coffee. That's an order!'

* * *

It was late when Anna woke to find herself on the sofa. Something had disturbed her sleep. She had taken two painkillers around seven o'clock and they had helped to take the edge off the injuries and let her sleep. Now her shoulder ached. A deep burning pain that only a large whiskey could touch. She heard it again, a soft knock on the back door.

Dragging herself of the sofa, she headed to the kitchen and checked through the side window. It was Declan. He'd come after all.

* * *

Later that evening, relaxed, having drunk a bottle of good wine, they lay wrapped into each other when Anna said, 'So explain it to me.' She rolled over on to her side, placing one hand on Declan's bare chest. Her head was fuzzy with the alcohol and the pain medication. She'd probably have one hell of a hangover in the morning but for now she didn't care. She could feel Declan's heartbeat, strong and steady, beneath her hand. Neil Young was singing about the needle and the damage down in the background. Declan's choice. They had drunk a bottle of red and had explored each other until they were both satisfied and tired.

'This place has some psychos running around. You've seen for yourself,' he gently traced a finger across her stitches at the side of her face.

He continued, 'Some of these kids have been brought up on a diet of brutality. Every day they are fed hatred, bigotry, the likes of you couldn't understand. They were educated in separate schools, lived in sectioned off estates defined by peace walls and kerb stones painted with the tribal colours. And when they weren't being spoon-fed hate at home, it was painted on the gable walls where they played football. Smashing a ball against a propaganda slogan, so carefully crafted and presented that it was almost like art. Banksy had nothing on them.

'Then they would hear the news, another victim, another shooter. Knee cappings up dark entries, punishment beatings for dealing drugs or pulling someone else's girl. Hit a woman or sexually assault her and she doesn't bother with the police. Too long and drawn out and not even the certainty of a conviction in a court system she has no faith in. So, she has a word with a friend of a friend and before you know it *he* gets a late-night call from six men with balaclavas and hammers. Justice is dealt. Everyone knows the system.

'So, ask yourself what happens when so-called peace comes along. The control and the power seep away, to be replaced by normality and civilised living. There's a vacuum, a well of hate and anger and violence that needs to find an outlet.'

She pondered his words; it sounded so cynical, to think that a peace process could have given rise to an undercurrent of unfulfilled anger and violence. 'So, are you saying all the suicides you hear about on the news, the senseless violence we see on the streets, and the girls' murders are all directly linked to the troubles?'

'Who's to say for sure? In years from now, they will look at the stats and some professor will publish a research a paper, and we will know for certain – that Belfast was a torch paper waiting to go up, all over again. Until then, we are rummaging in the dark trying to find sense and reason where there is none,' he sighed.

Anna thought of the threads, all failing to be tied up neatly. Experience had taught her that police work is largely the gathering of information, shifting through the fragments to find the connections and to painstakingly sew it all together into a tapestry of evidence. She thought of Robert Brogan and their theory. How could she tell Declan where the case was leading them? It would break him into a million pieces. She had a sense that he was holding it all together to see the case through to the end. To see the murderer caught; thereafter, she didn't know what would happen to him. Some tragedies are too painful to live with.

He sighed, 'We can't risk another girl's life. I'd give anything for this to be just another case. Someone else's daughter. I'd be shocked and concerned, angry at the senselessness and the savagery, and I'd do anything to catch the bastard. I only wish to God, it hadn't been my girl.' Anna placed her head on his chest and held him tight.

Chapter 32

The next couple of days were hazy. She slept a lot. Fitful, feverish sleeps, from which she woke uncomfortable and dry mouthed. It was like waking with a hangover without the fun. She'd dreamt a lot too, waking sometimes with a sickening guilt all intertwined with thoughts of Camille and Declan. She dreamt of trying to save Camille only to realise that it was Declan she was rushing to save.

By day three, she realised she needed distraction and when the call came from Martin in Keoghill, inviting her to meet a member of her birth family, she gladly agreed. Showering made her feel better. Her shoulder was still sore so dressing had been hard. She cursed the painkillers for not working quickly enough and threw back another to help her through the drive to Portaferry. A strong coffee would hopefully keep her alert.

The journey allowed Anna time to think and she tried to prepare herself for the meeting. After all this time to actually meet her mother would be pretty momentous. She thought of herself as a young girl, how if she had been pregnant, Camille would have swaddled her in love and support. To keep the baby or to have an abortion, Anna was certain that either way, her parents would have been there for her, without hesitation. The scenery passed her by without much notice.

An hour later, anxiety and nervousness made her stomach quake, as Martin led her into a dark passageway, cramped and narrow with boxes, discarded pieces of old oil lamps, an old long forgotten typewriter and a mantle clock. It all looked precarious, as if it could all crash over at the slightest touch. Light came from a door at the end of the corridor and there, sat on a wooden chair, in what looked like a make shift kitchen was the woman she was so anxious to meet. Martin cleared his throat, 'Anna this is Maura.' Anna looked confused; she hoped he was taking her to meet Kathleen.

The woman stood to greet them, hesitant and unsure of herself, so that Anna felt she had to make the first move and speak. 'Hello, I thought I was meeting Kathleen.'

The woman examined Anna's features as if looking for some sort of hallmark of family. Proof.

'I'm your aunt, so I am. Sure you are, you're the spit of the Maguire's, my mother's side of the family.'

Anna gave her a quick awkward hug and noted that she was exactly the same height and similar in build to herself – compact and lean.

'Thanks for agreeing to meet me.'

'We knew you'd show your face, sooner or later.'

'I'll leave youse to it,' Martin said. 'There's a kettle and some tea bags if youse want a cup of tea. Help yourselves.' He headed back to the shop.

Anna looked at the woman in front of her, searching for her own proof of ownership. The faded brown eyes and the over bleached hair didn't have anything of the familiar about it. But the build, the size and the shape were replicated in her shoulders and her neat waist.

'So, tell me about yourself. I take it you travelled over from across the water?'

'I'm here on secondment with the PSNI. I'm staying in Belfast.'

The woman laughed. 'Well that's a good one. Wait till they hear that.'

Anna didn't know how to take her. It certainly wasn't what she expected.

'Well what did you come for? What do you want to know?' her tone was defensive.

'I don't know. I suppose I just wanted to meet my biological mother. See if there was any connection. It sounds stupid now.'

'No, not stupid. We all said it would happen one day. Did you have a good home and a good up bringing?'

'Yes. I'm lucky I suppose but there was always that sense of wanting to know where I came from and what my birth family were like.'

'I'm sure you did but it's not like a soap. These things are never as clear cut as you think.'

Anna sat back on the chair and sighed. All the tension, the anxiety and the up build had made her feel wrung out. And now she wasn't even getting to meet her mother.

'Why didn't she come?'

'As I said these things are complicated. You can't just waltz in and think it'll be all happy families.'

'I never thought it would be easy, but do you not think she owes me a conversation at least?'

Maura reached forward, and in almost a hiss, said, 'We don't owe you anything *missy*, so you can get that into your head straight away.' The quiet aggression took Anna by surprise. The words had been spoken quietly but there was mistaking her tone.

'Does Kathleen not want to meet me?'

'What Kathleen wants isn't at issue here. You're coming back is like raking over old scabs. Sometimes the past is best left long buried.'

'I'm sorry you feel that way, but surely you can agree that I deserve to meet my birth mother.'

Anna couldn't believe that after all this time she was face-to-face with a blood relative. Yet she wasn't surprised that she was being met with open hostility. She thought she might be seen as an unwanted intrusion. The antagonism was in the snarl of her expression, the hands twisting at her coat, the eyes narrowed in suspicion, as if Anna was there to claim some part of them.

'I've come this far, surely Kathleen would like to at least meet me once? I'm not asking for a relationship. I had a great mother and I'm not looking for another. All I want is to know a bit about my background.'

'There's not much to tell. Kathleen had you and put you in a safe place to be adopted and by the looks of you, you've done all right.'

'I know what it was like back then for unmarried girls, that they were ostracised and treated badly, but that wasn't my fault.'

'What would you know coming here with your fancy clothes and your designer handbag? Let me guess, Mummy and Daddy lived in a nice detached house with lovely dinner parties and trips to the library and the zoo,' she sneered, looking Anna up and down as if she despised her.

'Holidays aboard to France or maybe it was a nice part of Spain or Italy for the culture. You went to a good school, got yourself a first-rate education, on to university, student parties and posh boyfriends. Well missy, life wasn't quite like that for us growing up, so don't come in here telling me you understand what Kathleen or any of us went through.'

Anna was taken aback. 'You aren't being fair. I didn't mean to suggest that I understand, just that I'm not naïve; I know Kathleen probably had it hard to find herself pregnant. I don't even know how old she was,' she sighed. 'If I can't understand then why don't you tell me?'

'It isn't my story to tell. It's down to Kathleen. I'll speak to her and get back to you. If she wants to meet you, or for me to tell you how it was, then so be it, but if you ask me, some stories are best left untold.'

Chapter 33

Memory was a treacherous beast. After the car bomb shards of information pierced through the fog of disbelief and horror. Now, he was experiencing the same functional amnesia. He could gather partial visual images of the wedding day: seeing Lara walk down the stairs of their family home, looking beautiful in her wedding dress, his gasp at the wonder of how his daughter had grown from a child to this sophisticated young woman. The ride to the church in the car and the heavy weight pressing on his chest, of wanting to say the right thing, to let her know that if it should all fall apart, she could always come home, but biting the words back because she would interpret it as another dig at Rory. He had promised Izzy that going forward from the wedding day he would set aside all his doubts about Lara's choice and accept Rory into their family. What choice did he have really?

He understood what his brain was doing. It was shutting out that which he couldn't bear to recall. The prefrontal cortex, responsible for focused attention and rational thought was impaired because of the high stress, fear and horror of what he had endured. Every now and then, he would remind himself that it was Esme who had faced the sheer terror, not him, but then the idea of what she endured only served to make him feel worse. In her final moments, it was likely that her prefrontal cortex had shut down, effectively drowned in stress chemicals. She would have literally been frozen in fear, with little ability to fight for her life.

The worse had happened and his brain could barely cope with it. Just when he needed to be rational and clear thinking, he found that his thoughts were sporadic, firing off in a hundred different directions, trying to grasp on to the truth, but feeling it evade him, slipping away like a handful of dry sand. At times he felt shut down, unresponsive and passive. Then the fog would lift, rise up like the mist at dawn, and for a short while he could be active, making some sort of headway, working with Anna to form theories and seek a path towards finding the bastard.

Rather than spend another night tossing and turning in bed he decided to watch the wedding DVD. It must have been the tenth time he had done it. It was helping him piece together the day, to create a timeline of who was where and at what time. He knew the police were doing the same thing. Anna had told him that they were clocking every frame for the time period Esme had been likely to have left the venue and met her fate. Declan was looking for something else. What that was he couldn't say. Glimpses of his daughter laughing, dancing, sitting at the top table to the left of the best man, lifting her champagne glass for the toasts. All of the scenes were played out in front of him as if he was watching a drama of someone else's life.

He could see himself, the brand-new suit, made to measure, sitting in his wheel chair, making conversation and preparing to make his speech. He watched himself pull at his shirt collar, nervous and anxious to get the speeches over with, knowing that there was a weighty expectation for him to strike the right balance between humorous and moving. That he should give Lara some sort of wisdom about married life, to reminisce about her as a girl, to talk about her faults – nice, funny things like the time she had taken up cooking and nearly poisoned them all by putting lavender in the casserole instead of rosemary.

He continued watching: the first dance, an Elton John cover by Ellie Goulding, the cutting of the cake, the wedding band playing the crowd pleaser songs like Galway Girl and The Gambler. It was almost 1.15 a.m. and he was about to call it a night when he noticed something in the background of the television screen. The camera was focusing on Lara, the bride surrounded by her girl-friends as they danced to Ed Sheeran, but in the background Declan could see Esme. She was upset. He froze the frame trying to catch the exact expression on her face. There was no doubt she was crying. She was reaching for someone off camera, her arm outstretched. Frame by frame, Declan watched and then he saw him.

Chapter 34

Anna was on the road back to Portaferry and was trying to focus on the case but her head was swamped with thoughts about her birth mother. The press was full of stories of the Magdalene laundries, homes for unmarried mothers who were forced to hand their babies over to the Catholic church who, in some cases, sold the children on to wealthy Catholic families aboard. Families they knew would protect the church with their silence and continue to contribute financially. Jimmy and Camille weren't Catholics, so how Anna had ended up being placed with them she had no idea. As far as the paperwork was concerned, Jimmy had said, they had acquired Anna through the regular channels. Social workers and home reports all being part of the deal. Beyond knowing they had been matched with a healthy baby girl, Jimmy and Camille had been told no more, nor did they care. As far as they were concerned, Anna was theirs and her life began the day they were handed her.

This country is fucking crazy Anna thought, squinting against the low November sun.

It was definitely cold enough for snow. The forecasters had been predicting flurries in the high ground and Anna had noticed a white cloak of frost lying on the Black Mountain hills overlooking Belfast. Now, driving to Portaferry for the third time, she noticed the beauty of the coastline, which was verdant and woody, looking out over a bleak slate coloured sea. The gales had whipped in the previous day and Anna could see branches and debris littering the roads. She passed the small Portaferry castle, little more than a tower house.

She was heading to Kathleen's house.

The call from Maura had been short and direct. 'She will meet you as a one off. You are to go to her house. Don't expect too much and if she says the conversation is over, then accept it – leave and move on. She wants no follow up visits, and no on-going contact.' Anna had no choice but to agree to the terms.

Kathleen's house was part of a row of terraces, known locally as the ferrymen's cottages. Anna parked the car in front of the houses and made her way to the yellow front door, number seven. The stone houses each had a small bay window downstairs and two small, rectangular windows upstairs, nestled beneath a blue slate roof. Her mother's house had a front garden – a well-kept patch of lawn, with what looked like a freshly raked border punctuated with purple and pink heathers.

As Anna approached the door it slowly opened and there she was, her birth mother. After all this time, the wondering, the imagining as a child daydreaming her to life, there she stood – real and alive. She was about Anna's height, though Anna appeared taller in her high-heeled boots, with a similar build to Maura – the same slope of the shoulders, the neat waist and the soft swell of hips beneath a dark green wool skirt. There was familiarity in the grey of her eyes, the lashes curling upwards and the pinch of her mouth, drawn into a tight line.

'So here you are at last,' she said, 'You better come in then.' There was no hug or kiss by way of greeting. Anna followed her into a tiny hallway where she took off her coat and hung it over the bannister.

'Through here.'

They went into a small living room, furnished with a small two-seater sofa, covered with a crocheted blanket in colours of teal and purples. An open fire flickered in the stone hearth.

'Sit down and I'll get you a cup of tea. Or would you prefer coffee?'

'Tea will be fine, thanks. Milk no sugar.'

While Kathleen busied herself in the kitchen with the kettle, Anna looked around the neat little room. The house looked out towards the lough. The view from the net curtained window was dramatic on such a windswept day. The fireplace mantle held a clock and a couple of tall brass candlesticks, no photographs or trinkets to hint at the person living there. A small television set was nestled in the corner of the room next to a neat pile of newspapers and magazines.

'Here you are. Help yourself to a scone.' She set a tray of tea things down on a low footstool and handed Anna a cup. The cream and jam scones and bite sized tea cakes suggested she had gone to trouble.

'Maura was right, you have a look of the Maguires about you.'

'Your mother was a Maguire, isn't that right?' Anna asked.

'Yes, she was Ellen Maguire from the Markets area. A good woman who reared nine children when times were hard.' They both sipped at their tea. Kathleen took a drag on an electronic cigarette, puffing out the vapour.

'So, you grew up in Wales then? Your accent has a lovely ring to it.'

'Yes, in Cardiff but I went to university in Bristol.'

Kathleen raised her eyebrows.

'I read Politics and Criminology, before joining the police when I graduated,' she continued, rambling because she was nervous.

'Maura said you were working with the police over here for a while.'

'That's right. I'm on secondment for six months.'

'Well, I'm sure you don't want to be sitting here making conversation all day. I'll tell you what you're after.' Kathleen sat her cup down on the low tea tray, clasped her hands together and took a deep breath.

'We were living through bad times in those days. You can't even begin to imagine what it was like growing up back then. We'd no money, none of us had, so that wasn't an issue; you just got on with it and accepted your lot. We knew no different. Jobs were scarce for Catholic men, good paying jobs and apprenticeships for the shipyard and Shorts went to the Protestants and we were left to sup the rest. The jobs no one in their right mind would want. Still my father worked hard and we got by.'

'By the late sixties things were changing. People got fed up being told they were second class citizens, if you were on a housing waiting list you automatically went to the back of the queue if you were a Catholic. You could hardly blame the young lads, agitated, standing on street corners seeing no way out. Plenty of them had reason enough to join up, my brother Jamesie was no different. He liked his history books and before long he was reading up on what was going on beyond this wee country of ours. He knew everything there was to know about the blacks in America and their fight for rights and the early civil rights movement here. Half the time my father would say what have the blacks got to do with us and our Jamesie would launch into one of his speeches. He could see plain as day that what was happening in America needed to happen on the streets of Belfast. Before long he was part of a group organising rallies and marching down the Botanic Avenue into the town. It was all about equal rights, socialist slogans, nothing sectarian. He ended up getting himself a good job working as a trainee paralegal. Not many round our way had jobs like that. He didn't have a law degree but he was well read and worked hard. He could've gone far.' She paused putting the electronic cigarette to her lips again.

'You are probably wondering what our Jamesie has to do with you, but I'll come to that. I just want you to know what it was like and how it all happened, like.'

Anna sipped at the weak tea. The fire settled in the hearth, burning low, while rain began to fall softly outside.

'The seventies and early eighties were brutal times. The likes of you, living across the water, and being so young, wouldn't know what it was like to have our streets patrolled by soldiers. Never mind that wee boys acting as hard men, ruled our communities. Wee boys who grew up to have access to guns and too much power. It seemed that one day they'd be out playing with a make shift go-kart, and before the week was out they'd been fingered to come in and talk to one of the big men. Flattered, to be asked to do a message, they felt important and in the know. But they soon found themselves delivering bullets and throwing petrol bombs.'

'They knew how to work them, bring them into the fold and brainwash them into thinking their way was the only way. And if anyone stepped out of line, they answered to the same boys they'd looked up to sitting in a darkened back room in a pub. They just had to say the word and then they were summoned up to some piece of wasteland to get a bullet in the back of their knees. Rough justice dealt out by a pack of power mad, self-appointed crime lords. Fear and power are a heady combination. They got off on it.'

She paused to poke the embers of the fire, placing a log on it to keep it going. The rain had turned to sleet and the afternoon light was ebbing away.

'Our Jamesie was seen as a bit of a mouth piece. They wanted him to front their campaign, to speak to the papers and the television crews. They sent reporters from all over to film the civil rights marches. For once, our wee shit-hole of a town was on the big map, and as far as Jamesie was concerned, all we had to do was to speak out and be heard while the spotlight was on us. He thought if the rest of the world saw the conditions we lived in, heard the injustices of the voting system and knew that Catholics were being downtrodden then they would have to intervene and fix it.'

'My mother always said he was a dreamer. *If his head isn't in a book it's in the clouds,*' she'd say.

'God, my tea's stone cold, do you want a top up?' Before Anna could respond, she poured more tea into her cup from the pottery style teapot. 'Well Jamesie wasn't one to bow down to anyone, so when the big men came around demanding that he stuck to their script, our Jamesie told them where to go. He wasn't interested in playing by their sectarian rules. He was out to speak up for anyone treated badly by the system. Even though it looked plain as day that Catholics were put upon, he didn't have a bigoted bone in his body, and saw it as a working-class struggle. He was peace loving. He had no time for guns and bombs, and even though Bloody Sunday made many a young fella join up, he knew violence wasn't the solution.'

'So anyways, I was fourteen when all this was going on. We'd been burnt out of our house, forced to move back to the Markets where my mother had come from. I was at an age when the boys start to notice you. I'd hair down to my waist and a great wee figure. Me and Rosie Curran, she was my friend, would go out walking the streets knowing full well we were turning heads.'

'Trouble was, I caught the attention of the wrong one. One of the fellas our Jamesie had talked back to, over the civil rights marches, took a shine to me. Sean was his name. Sean Healy. He'd a reputation as being a bit of bad fella. Course I knew very little of this then. Alls I knew is that the best-looking fella from the road had asked for me to meet him. Never mind that he was nineteen and I's only a slip of a girl. You nearly got a crick in your neck looking up at him, he was that tall. Even in heels I barely reached his shoulder. He had eyes that smoldered, burnt right through you, they did.'

'Before I knew it, he was buying me presents, perfume, a wee silver necklace. Turned my head, so he did. Then within three months I was pregnant with you. Scared out of my wits. Thought it was the end of the world. Little did I know it was to get worse.'

Anna could scarcely breath. Her shoulder ached from the long drive, and she felt like the room was closing in on her. As if ghosts from a past she didn't know she shared, were standing nearby, listening.

Kathleen took a sip of her tea and went on, 'Word got out that Sean had been seen getting out of an unmarked police car. He was being watched, in case he had turned informer.'

'He told me he had been lifted and asked for information but hadn't gave them anything. They'd pictures of me and him and said they would charge him with being with a minor if he didn't bring them something – names, times, places.'

'You couldn't understand the fear of being caught like that. If his own ones thought he was passing on information, he would have been taken away and shot without a second thought. It was only a matter of time.'

'So, he tells me he has to go away for a while over to England or maybe America, he didn't know. Lay low until it all dies down. Course little did I know in order to get out of the country, he had to give the peelers something to go on. So what did the bastard do but tell them our Jamesie was involved. Told them that he had moved guns for the Ra back in November, and that they could find the stash in blocked up walls of the place Jamesie worked.'

'They came and dragged Jamesie from his bed in the wee small hours of a December night. Beat him badly, my ma and da begging for mercy, the wee uns all howling and me clutching at my belly, barely three months gone and somehow knowing deep down that this was my doing, that Sean was behind it.'

'We never saw Jamesie again. He was found hung in his cell two weeks after they lifted him.'

Anna sensed the pain of Kathleen's story. It was a world so far removed from her childhood of warmth and safety, love and security. Yet this is what she had come from. These were her people.

The light outside had faded away to an indigo darkness, illuminated only by snowfall. Kathleen got up to pull the curtains and switch on a lamp that sat on a small table at the side of the fire.

'That's a bad night out there. You better watch driving back to Belfast in that weather.'

'But what happened next? What did you do about the baby? About me?'

'Another day child, I'm passed myself with emotion. I feel like a wrung-out dishcloth.'

Anna tried to hide her disappointment. To have come so close to knowing the full story, but she could see Kathleen was worn out.

'I can come again? Next week maybe?' Anna asked, not even trying to hide the pleading in her voice.

'I'll call you. See if I'm up to it. I haven't been too well. Heart trouble. I had stents put in a while back but the doctor says they need to take me in again see what going on,' she spoke as if she was frightened, of what may lay ahead. Anna thought of Camille and the long days spent in hospital wards. The waiting. The uncertainty.

They said their goodbyes and Anna faced the bleak drive home, her head full of the intimidation, terror and trepidation of the late seventies in Belfast. Questions burning in her mind and her biological family and thinking of the spectre of Sean Healy, and what happened to him when he left Belfast and Kathleen behind.

She called up Thomas' number on her phone.

Her voice was wavering with pent up emotion, 'Tell me we've had a break. Anything at this point would do.' She needed cop talk to ease the pain she felt, pain for Kathleen, Jamesie and herself.

* * *

He made notes as he worked. Taking measurements: length, breadth, recording the thickness of the muzzle and the limbs. His journal was full of such projects, carefully recorded over the cream pages. How he would love to have such a record of the girls but it was too risky. He wouldn't give them anything so tangible to use against him should they get close.

The fox was laid out on the bench, primed and ready. Using calipers and a sharp knife he began the skinning process. He worked the blade under the skin, continuing to cut on up to the first rib being careful not to slice the flesh retaining the bowels. The skin of the fox was thin so he needed to be careful to not allow the knife to slip through. He sliced the ears off exposing two lumps of gristle beside the hole and set them aside for later. He rubbed the beast down with preservative making sure to reach all the crevices.

He worked through the evening with the fox taking care when removing the pelt and ensuring it was well, dried and prepared. The head had been skinned, the brains and eyes scooped out and the skull poisoned to prevent growth of any nasty unwanted bacteria. Finally, the legs had been drilled for the wiring and the rods to be inserted and he was now choosing the eyeglasses. Then all else was done, with a deft hand he had sutured the skin back in place. It would make a beautiful piece when it was finished. The dark orange pelt was soft to the touch and the ears sat alert as if it was listening carefully, ready to pounce.

How he longed to have a better facility, a workplace purposely designed. The old barn had been sufficient up until now, but really, he needed better refrigeration, metal shelving, a good work surface for skinning and place to hang hides that wouldn't risk stretching. A place to create his final masterpiece.

Chapter 35

Five days' recuperation had been Anna's limit. By day four she was itching to be back at the station, whether her injuries were better on not. Thomas filled her in on what had been going on in her absence. Another punishment shooting in North Belfast, a fifteen-year-old boy taken up an alleyway to have his knee caps blown off. His girlfriend had been at the scene. There was a feeling of frustration and anger that the cycles of old were replaying like a record that just wouldn't come to an end.

The night before, she had had to deal with Declan's insistence that they weren't doing enough.

'What was he saying to her to make her cry?' he asked, the urgency and stress showing in his face.

He was frantic, his eyes imploring her to look at the screen. They were looking at video footage from the wedding. 'Look, she is pulling at his arm as he tries to walk off. It has to mean something, doesn't it?'

'Please, Declan, calm down,' Anna said. 'They had an altercation, we already know about this. Finnegan claims Esme had too much to drink and he told her off. Told her to behave as it was a family wedding, not a night out with her friends.'

'That doesn't add up. Esme had a few drinks but she wasn't doing anything to draw attention to herself. Izzy or I would have noticed. And Rory wouldn't be telling her off, that wouldn't be his way. He'd be more likely to have a word with Lara and tell her to step in and talk to her sister.'

He rewound the video again.

'Can't we isolate the sound, hear what they are saying?'

'No, it was a long shot, but we've already tried. The tech guys said the microphone wouldn't have picked up their voices. There was music playing and one hundred and twenty odd people mulling around.'

She could sense that Declan was feeling the tightening grip of frustration.

'I've seen Esme and Rory interact hundreds of times and never once considered that anything could be going on. Now, I'm not so sure. Why else would they be quarreling at the wedding? Had Esme threatened to tell Lara what Rory was really like? Had that been why she had been killed? Had Rory been the one to take her life? To squeeze her last breath from her body and leave her on that damp mossy ground?'

Anna took his hand, 'Declan, I know this is over-powering. You are desperate to get answers, but you have to trust me. We are on this. Let us do our job.'

'Listen to me Anna, you need to bring him in for questioning,' he said.

'Declan, please I know what I'm doing. We've already talked to him. Our inquiries are ongoing. That's all I can say at this stage,' she could hear how hallow her words sounded. 'I'm sorry, but we've already crossed too many lines here. You shouldn't be this involved in the investigation.'
'Fuck's sake, Anna this is my daughter we are talking about!'

* * *

Declan opened his eyes. *Esme.* She was always the first thought. The knowledge of her death lay lurking in his consciousness, never far from the surface and rarely silenced totally by sleep. But something had woken him, a dark dream, a fleeting thought in his sleep. Whatever it was, it now evaded him.

It was becoming easier to fall asleep at night – the couple of sleeping tablets helped - but increasingly, he was finding himself awake around 4.00 a.m. He needed to pee, but he couldn't be bothered with the effort of getting into the chair. His hip ached and his shoulders hummed with pain. Low and deep but nearly always present. He doubted anyone realised he still experienced pain from his injuries. Pain clinic doctors didn't offer much hope of it ever being fully resolved.

The house was still. Izzy had gone to bed around eleven. She had cooked supper for them both, and they had eaten in companionable silence. Neither wishing to talk about Esme. They had watched the local news, an ammunition haul in County Tyrone, a major drugs find in Coleraine and an item on organised dog fighting.

As they sat in the living room with the curtains drawn against the autumn night, watching the fire glowing in the hearth, he was almost tempted to ask about her insistence on going to work, the weekend spent at her sister Caroline's, the self-assured way she carried herself, and the containment of her grief; all of it told him she had someone else to cry to. He was surplus to requirements.

All those years together, and he still couldn't figure her out. He knew many considered her cold and distant. His mother had never thought much of her. She thought Izzy was too self-involved, too caught up in her career. He hated how she was always so quick to judge the way they had brought up the girls – relying on a series of child-minders and crèches in the early years. Declan used to defend Izzy, telling his mother that she was a great mother to his girls and why shouldn't she have her career. But part of him had always hoped she would stay at home, write academic books and become the sort of wife his father would have thought was perfection, dinner on the table, the children freshly bathed and in their pajamas – something very far from their normality.

Later, when he'd come around from the shock of his injuries and was working hard at his rehabilitation, Izzy had been there for him, but he saw something die in her. He had often thought of what she had lost that day.

He checked his phone for the time. 4.17 a.m. He wondered if he would see Anna today. His emotions were all over the place. He knew he had no business getting involved with her, but felt helpless to resist. Being close to her was like having a stake in life again. To feel emotions and sensations he hadn't allowed himself to feel for years. He also had to admit, being with her was like having a foothold in the investigation. Not that she gave too much away. He was aware of the risks she was taking in being involved with him. The cost could be her career and he had the feeling that without the job, like him, she'd be lost.

He sensed she was holding out on him. That there was something of significance she wasn't telling him. It was in the way she had asked about the car bomb and the aftermath, how she had questioned him about old Nelson Brogan. Did he have any contact with Declan after he had left the force? Was there unfinished business? Questions that if a shrink had asked him, he'd shut them down. But he'd humoured her, kept her talking, hoping he'd find out what was behind the questions. Nelson Brogan, last he'd heard, was putting time in at a nursing home. He was hardly in a position to be out murdering.

Something funny was going on with Rory too. He couldn't pretend the logs of calls between him and Esme had meant nothing. Yet he was frightened and didn't want to acknowledge, even to himself, that Rory may have meant more to Esme than simply her sister's husband. Property developers in this place were notoriously shifty. Belfast had so many back-room deals being done with repossessed property being hocked off to the bidder offering the biggest back hander. Could he see Rory being guilty of greasing some council officials palm? Yeah, he had to admit, in a heartbeat. But hurt Esme? He couldn't be so sure, now that the he had time to process everything.

He thought of Esme's plans. She'd talked about going to university and then moving to San Francisco for a year. Maybe work in marketing or the media after travelling for a bit.

See the world. Big plans all laid out in front of her. When she was little, maybe seven or eight, she had loved *Little Mermaid*. He remembered her singing 'Under the Sea', so many times that he'd find himself humming it while at work. Then he'd smile to himself, as it would make him think of his little girl shimmering and sashaying in her mermaid costume while she sang along to the song.

At one point, she had wanted to be a vet, to tend to injured and sickly animals and set up an animal hospital and a dog-grooming business. Or had that been Lara? He hated that sometimes memories between the two girls became intertwined.

Chapter 36

Anna would never get used to seeing a dead body. Some were more upsetting than others. Some were even mundane – the old woman found after a fall on her doorstep; some were gruesome – the carnage of a car accident, the stabbing up an alley way following a Friday night scuffle on Churchill Way, the drug over dose in a squat in Cathays, the child drowned in the Wharf. None were pleasant, but there were definite degrees of distress and disturbance.

Aisling Mackin, a student, had been reported missing less than six hours ago. Her housemates had alerted the police saying that it was out of character for her not to come home. If she had decided to stay out or gone on somewhere else, then she would have contacted them. It had been too early to consider her a missing person; the police expected her to turn up like the previous missing girl.

Aisling never made it home to the student house she shared with her cousin and four other girls. Hysteria over the murders had rendered the city a jumpy mess, parents demanded that their daughters be home early and to keep in touch at all times. But for Aisling's parents, it looked like the worst fear possible had happened.

And now, in East Belfast, another girl had been found murdered.

* * *

'I'm not making any official statements on this one yet, but you can assume time of death was around five hours ago. It's recent.

I'll need to take her in to get further answers,' the state pathologist, Professor Ciaran Tohill took a few steps back from the corpse. The wheelie bin reeked of fish, rancid fat and dead flesh. Anna fought to suppress the need to gag. A large Belfast City Council sticker was peeling away from the plastic bin. With a bit of luck, it would have captured something of use to the techs.

Thomas was speaking to Manus Magee and technicians at the far end of the alleyway. They were in a busy part of the city, the rush hour was under way and crowds were starting to gather on the other side of the cordon, mobile phones at the ready to take pictures. Anna glared at them; sightseers looking for drama in someone else's trauma. They needed to make the alley way secure, and to alert the family, before some dickhead uploaded a photo on social media and did it for them.

'Watch your step, it's very icy,' Anna said as Thomas approached.

'Is it her?'

'Looks that way. Blonde hair, early twenties. Obviously, we haven't got a formal ID on her, but when we get her out of that bin, I'd put money on it.'

Aisling had last been seen at a 'wrap' party, celebrating the end of filming of a period drama in Belfast. She had bagged a small extras part in the production, the money helping to supplement her student loan. The party was held in Saffron, an upmarket restaurant and bar, and had finished just before two in the morning.

Anna shoved her hands deep into her coat pockets. It was freezing. Belfast had been in an icy grip for over a week. She heard Thomas on the phone calling in a full team of technicians. They couldn't risk missing anything.

'What's happening?' asked Russell coming over to them.

'You tell me. Who found her?'

'A fella opening up the café around the corner. Came out the back of his premises here for a quick ciggie, and caught a glimpse of the red coat hanging out of the bin. Thought he'd found a present for his missus, but I guess he discovered more than he bargained for.'

'Why stuff her in the bin?' asked Anna.

Russell blew on his hands to warm them, 'Who knows? Rushed job or perhaps someone came along and interrupted him.'

'It isn't as staged as the other two victims,' Anna said as much to herself as to Russell. 'Maybe we are looking at different killer. What state is she in?'

'Pretty bad. Her face has been messed up. Evidence of bruising around the neck.'

'Well, that is similar to the previous girls ...'

'Appears so,' he said. 'Press are going to have a field day.' He indicated with a nod of his head the direction of the group of people gathering at the end of the alleyway. 'The wee spivs are already sniffing round.'

She looked at Russell, and could see he was shaken. Their breath rose in celestial ribbons as they stood guarding yet another dead girl. Three in four months.

'I take it we are linking the three deaths?' asked Russell.

'Looks that way, but keep it in-house for now, until we know for certain.' Anna felt the cold nip at her nose and ears and felt such a sadness come over her for the dead girl, lying in a dirty bin. There were times she seriously questioned her judgment in her career choice, there were surely easier ways to earn a living. She should have gone into marketing or PR, except she forgot she wasn't so good with people. Her diplomacy skills were lacking for those sorts of jobs. Anything was better than this. She heard her father's words from before.

'Right,' she said. 'I'm heading to the station.'

* * *

In the station, Anna called Declan. 'Listen I don't want you hearing this on the news, but there has been another one.' She spoke quietly, not wanting anyone to overhear.

She heard his sharp intake of breath and then the low, 'Fuck. Is there a bird at the scene, a calling card like before?'

'No, but it looks like he was disturbed. The girl appears to have been dumped, maybe he was planning on coming back. But you know we can't be sure it's him again, not until we do the autopsy ...' she trailed of.

'Bullshit, you know it is. We need to move faster. Anything of use?'

'The girl is slightly older this time, not a school girl, maybe early twenties. We haven't got a full ID yet. Facial injuries and strangulation marks.'

She thought she ought to say something to reassure him, to make him believe they were close to catching him. But what could she offer? Declan was every bit aware that the bastard was still two steps ahead of them.

* * *

Chief Superintendent Richard McKay knew how to hold an audience. Anna watched as he perched on the side of the desk and cleared his throat. Immediately, the room fell quiet.

'As you probably know, we have the body of another young woman in the mortuary. Aisling Mackin, twenty-one-year-old student and aspiring actress. Pathologists are working to ascertain the cause of death, but initial thoughts are that we are looking for the same person who killed Esme Wells and Grace Dowds. Much of the investigative work is routine, we know what we have to do, forensics, CCTV, talk to the last people in her company. There's a lot to be done, but routine inquiry is not going to solve these cases alone, we need to think outside the box.'

A murmur rose up.

'Look for anything unusual, anything that might link them. Aisling's body was deposited in a wheelie bin; the bin was located two streets away from where it should be. We need to trawl CCTV footage in the area, and look at the reasons for moving her body.

She was wearing a distinctive red wool coat so we need to see if anyone spotted her. Was the murderer taking her somewhere else, or had a different party moved her afterwards? We need to look at all options.'

'Any definite link with the other girls?' asked Magee.

Anna responded, 'Nothing beyond the obvious – that they are young girls on a night out. We are still keeping Rory Finnegan in our sights though.'

She felt the cold dread of another long drawn out murder case. Sure, the adrenaline would kick in and they would put in the conscientious hours required to examine all the possible leads and specks of evidence but at the minute all she could think of was the victim. Did fear paralyse her or had she fought for all she was worth? Not for the first time, Anna vowed she would never have children. She couldn't bear the fear and the responsibility, and the terror of failing to keep them safe. Maybe this time he had made a mistake, something that would help them nail him.

'Whoever we are looking for has good geographical knowledge of the scenes. Probably lives and works locally. He knows his way around the venues.' Thomas said.

'Magee is in charge of reviewing all CCTV. We've already spoken to staff working near where she was found. Nobody saw anything strange when they headed into work this morning,' he took a deep breath, 'we need to talk to anyone in the vicinity last night. Take a look at all the regular customers; get access to credit card records. We don't have a primary crime scene at the minute. The wheelie bin had been moved, so there's a lot of work to be done.'

'CCTV covers the front of the entrance, but not the back alleyway,' Anna said.

'Why move her? Where was he taking her?' asked Thomas.

Anna felt uneasy; the little hairs on her arms were standing on end. She thought of life being as insubstantial as a candle flame, one flicker away from extinction.

'We need to focus on that alley way – did he have a vehicle waiting to take the body somewhere else? Was he disturbed, and had to leg it?

I want answers to all these questions,' McKay looked defeated. This investigation was catching up on all of them. Even Thomas, normally so fit and healthy looking, was showing signs of eye bags.

McKay started wrapping up the meeting, 'Get to it.'

'Holly, you can go on this one with Anna, I want you two to speak to the university. Find out if Aisling had any problems, and talk to the girls she shared a house with.'

Anna noticed a vein on his left temple pulsing. 'I want every fucking thing you lot are doing summarised and on my desk at the end of every bloody day,' he stormed off with every officer in the room breathing a sigh of relief they hadn't been singled out.

Thomas looked pissed off. 'What more can we do?' he asked Anna as she headed over to her desk.

'Keep the investigation moving. We don't stop. We don't doubt we'll get him; otherwise, the bastard has won. We've lots of areas to cover, some of it might overlap with previous evidence, but we could find that one piece of information to make this kaleidoscope of fragments fall into place, giving us that perfect picture of truth.'

'Poetic, Cole,' he smiled. 'I'll head back down to the crime scene have another chat to the fella who found her.'

'Ok, I'll catch up with you later. Let's see if Holly and I can find anything out from Aisling's housemates.'

A few calls later and Anna had learnt that Aisling was a good student, full attendance, marks on track for a high 2:1, her part-time filming work hadn't encroached on her studies and she had no issues requiring counseling or assistance from the university welfare office.

'Right let's go,' she said to Holly, grabbing her coat as they made their way out to the pool car.

Within half an hour, they had reached the university area where Aisling lived. Holly turned the engine off and they sat for a moment taking in the view. During term time Aisling lived in Jerusalem Street, a tightly knit street of red brick terraces each with a tiny handkerchief sized patch of garden at the front. At the bottom of the rows of terraced houses, separated by a road, the area was edged by the banks of the River Lagan, a slow and sludge-like river that ran through the city and was known to have had a tendency to stink like a witch's commode in the heat of the summertime before it had been given an environmental make over. Anna couldn't help making a mental note of the colours, the shadows and shades. Habit. She'd maybe put it down on paper later.

'Why's it called the Holylands?' Anna asked as they parked in the tightest spot imaginable.

Holly reached for her bag, 'It was something to do with a fella called Sir Robert McConnell.'

Anna watched as a couple of students ambled past, obviously in love, holding hands and hanging off each other's words. She envied them and their ability to close the world out and focus solely on their love.

Holly opened her door, continuing, 'He was a devout Christian and a Victorian developer. He'd gone to Palestine and Egypt so he named the streets after the places he had visited, leaving a legacy of street names like Cairo Street, Jerusalem Street and Palestine Street.'

'And there was me thinking some wit in town planning had the foresight to see that the Middle East and Belfast would have much in common,' Anna said, closing the car door. Just then Anna's phone buzzed. 'It's Thomas, hang on.'

She answered the phone, 'What's up?'

'Guess who Aisling's landlord is?' he paused for effect, 'Rory Finnegan, no less.'

'Shit.'

'Exactly. Talk to the girls in the house, and I'll meet you back here. See what you can get out of them.'

Chapter 37

The student house reeked of Chinese takeaway, stale beer, mildew and cigarettes, with a faint undertone of perfume. It was one step up from a squat, yet there was nothing hard up about them – nice clothes, a good TV, laptop sitting on the sofa. A make-up bag lay opened on the coffee table spilling its guts of Urban Decay and Mac make up – none of it cheap.

Caroline McGinty had obviously been crying. She sat on the black leather sofa, looking down at her hands shredding a damp tissue. 'We can't believe it, like. She was so lovely.'

They could hear the tech guys walking around in the room above, still searching Aisling's room. 'How long are they going to be up there?' Caroline asked.

'Not long. I know this is hard to take in, but we need to ask you some questions about Aisling's friends. Let's make you a cup of tea.' Holly went through to the kitchen and opened and closed a few cupboards looking for cups and tea bags.

Anna waited a few minutes to let Caroline stem her crying. 'Did Aisling have a boyfriend?'

She sniffed loudly and blew her nose, 'No and I would have known, we were very close.'

'Was anyone bothering her, hassling her or making her uncomfortable in anyway?'

'No, not at all. Sure, it can be a bit mad round here with parties and stuff, but we had done all that in first year. We've all settled down a bit now. Aisling was so easy going. Nothing ever got to her. She didn't even fight about the cleaning rota.'

Anna looked around the living room. It was cluttered with mess – magazines, a few coffee cups and a half-full wine bottle. The usual mess of student life. A coat lay over the back of a chair and a pair of boots lay casually on the fireplace hearth. It was a dark room, overlooking a tiny, high-walled, backyard.

'How long have you been living here?' Anna asked gently.

'From the beginning of term. End of September. We all shared a house last year too.'

'And who do you share with?'

'There's three other girls. Two of them have gone home and Maggie is at her boyfriend's house. I'm not going to stay here tonight either.'

'Probably a good idea to get away. The press might try talking to you, but just ignore them. If they hassle you, let us know.' Holly said, handing Caroline a mug of tea.

'Your landlord is Rory Finnegan. Is that right?' Anna asked.

Caroline nodded, sipping the tea.

'Would you say he's a good landlord?' Holly asked.

'Yeah, we met him when we were signing the rent documentation in his office. Everyone round here knows Rory – he owns half the Holylands. If there's a problem we call his property management company.'

'Has there been any need to call them?' Anna asked.

'The cooker wasn't working when we moved in, but he got it sorted for us. Oh, and Maggie's bedroom door wouldn't close properly, so a joiner came around and fixed it.'

'Have you ever had any reason to think Rory Finnegan was especially interested in Aisling?'

'No. We've seen him driving around in his fancy car, but she never said anything about him,' she stopped, her eyes wide, 'You don't think Rory Finnegan did this, do you?'

'No, but we have to keep all lines of enquiry open,' said Holly.

'Do you know when the funeral will be?'

'Her family will probably let you know.'

Caroline nodded.

'I know it's been a long day for you, but if you can think of anything, anything at all,' Holly said.

She nodded again.

* * *

Back in the car, Anna said, 'So we have a link with Rory Finnegan again.'

'He keeps popping up like a crooked jack-in-the-box,' agreed Holly pulling out on to the Ormeau embankment. 'Maybe we have enough to scare the shit out of him, and make him think we know more than we do.'

'Let's see if McKay agrees.' Anna thought of Declan and felt sick. She didn't like Finnegan. There was something off about him that was for sure, but the thought of him being responsible for the murders made her shudder.

Chapter 38

Anna pushed the food away. Neither she nor Declan had eaten much. She felt queasy and pumped up on adrenaline. Declan was setting up their make shift office in the living room while she cleared the dining table.

'What's this?' he called.

'What's what?' she asked walking back into the living room, carrying two wine glasses and another bottle of pinot noir.

'This,' he held up one of her sketches.

'Oh that. It's a drawing. I sometimes sketch the scene to help clarify things.'

'What? You draw the crime scene?' his tone was incredulous.

'Yeah, it's no big deal. It can help me figure things out, work through the tangled mess that's in front of me, and try to make sense of it.'

'There's no sense to be made out of a murder.'

She could hear hurt in his tone. 'I'm sorry, you weren't meant to see that.'

He removed another from her pile of paperwork. It was a watercolour painting of the Lagan towpath, the place where Esme had been found. She had worked on it at home using her initial pencil sketch to create the painted image, heavy with atmosphere, a lone rook standing on the lower branch of a tree, looking towards the river.

'And does it work, do you find *meaning* in painting the scene?'

'Yes, I mean, no. It's neither science nor magic. It's merely a way for me to process my thoughts, to contemplate what I've seen.'

He looked down at a different charcoal sketch, one of a lane leading up to Maude Brier's house. It was little more than an old cottage, an outline of a run-down shed-like building off to the side and an old well in the foreground. Anna looked at Declan as he placed the sketches on the table. Scenes and drawings she had done of each of the murdered girls. All young women starting out – opportunities, university, travelling aboard, working, relationships – all ahead of them, like a promise to be fulfilled.

She began gathering her drawings and paintings together, away from him.

'I can't bear the thought of you casually painting the scene where she died. It's not right.'

She wanted to say, it's nothing to do with you, it's the investigation, how she worked, but how could she?

He mumbled something and then Anna saw he was crying.

'Sorry, Declan I shouldn't have left those drawings lying around,' she said sitting on the chair near him.

'It's not the drawings. I need to know – did she suffer? Was it quick?' He hadn't asked her that before. She had expected him to; loved ones nearly always do.

'Declan, I can't know for sure, you know that,' she reached for him, her arms reaching around him, pulling him into her embrace, and all thoughts of ending it drained from her mind. His fingers reached for a photograph sitting on the pile of documents. His fingers lingered over it – Esme, at an end of term party. Her face aglow with fun and optimism. The coffee table held the newspaper clippings, pictures of the girls and an assortment of post-its marked out a time frame. A map spread out showing a dark blue line outlining each of the places the girls were found. Anna lowered herself on to the floor beside Declan's chair, 'There has to be something in the localities – why does he choose these places? What is his knowledge of the areas he operates in?'

'We have to assume he is working in some capacity that brings him into contact with the venues. Doorman, barman, waiter.'

'We're still chasing the elusive security guard. He could just be someone doing the double, claiming benefits and getting cash-in-hand for working the odd shift but we need to rule him out,' Anna said.

'And then there's me,' Declan said.

'You, what about you? We don't have you down as a possible suspect if that's what you're thinking.'

'No, that's not what I was getting at. My case. My history,' he looked down at his stumps. 'I've tried not to bring this up but could there be any link between what happened to me and Esme's murder?'

Anna sighed. She didn't want to tell him that they had been digging. That they were already considering this angle. 'It doesn't fit any possible motive. If someone has a vendetta against you, why kill the other girls?'

'Copycat? Maybe he's had a taste of it and wants more? I'm not saying this makes sense, but I don't want you to exclude anything.'

She thought about the crates of catalogued evidence they had rummaged through, the evidence boxes pertaining to his case. Four boxes labelled with a reference code: EA/454 737 8. Evidence sheets, statements, photographs of the wreckage and of Declan's mutilated body.

He placed his head in his hands as if despairing, 'Anna, in this country, it's always about politics and religion. That's the beginning and the end of everything here.'

In the boxes, there was nothing to hint at wrong doing on the part of Brogan. Conveniently, three months later he retired on medical grounds, as Thomas had told her. According to an old station hand, that Thomas had tracked down, Brogan was asked to go quietly.

Later on, Anna lay in bed alone. Declan had gone home. Something had soured between them when he'd see the sketches. She considered their future. Could they possibly have one? The spectre of Esme's murder always lay between them. Could they survive beyond it? Declan had recognised something in Anna. Being with him was like looking into a fairground mirror, reflecting back a warped image of each other, each damaged. But she knew the risks; she was jeopardising her entire career. Everything she had worked for. If she didn't have this job, what would she have left?

* * *

The cat came easily enough. Stupid, trusting creature. All it took was a piece of fish, fresh and meaty, the scent pungent enough to give off a whiff. The fur was grey and white, a good coat. It rubbed against his legs as if to thank him for the morsel of fish, looking for more. He lifted it and placed the sack over its body, holding it close to him as it began to cry in protest. Its body arched and wriggled, while its sharp claws pierced through the sackcloth. It meowed, a howl of despair.

The light went on at the back of the house, illuminating all for him to see, like a cinema screen coming to life. He watched her through the kitchen window, filling the kettle at the sink, turning to reach for a cup from a cupboard. He stood, cloaked in the darkness of the garden. He liked that, the feeling of being in plain sight, if only she knew where to look. The moon, shrouded in cloud, spilled no light. He had learned that it is important to always pay attention, to watch and see what is in front of you. She was as dumb as the cat. He felt the animal begin to settle against his chest, giving up its idle fight. He thought of his work, out capturing wildlife, the stealth required, the slow patient prowl. Yet often nothing is gained in waiting. If you hesitate the creature will inevitably take flight. Sometimes you have to act in the moment, take what is in front of you.

Chapter 39

"This is it, the break we need,' Thomas said to Anna, pleased with himself. Forensics had picked up a soil sample from a boot print in the alleyway where Aisling's body had been found, and the results of their analysis had come in. Anna allowed herself a smile.

'At last,' she said, 'but is this enough to give us the link back to Brogan?'

Thomas placed his hands on her shoulders, 'Yes, it does. We can't trace Luke Nead and we now have a positive ID of the photo-fit Genevieve gave us. The care assistant at the home says it's a good enough resemblance to Robert Brogan, so this soil sample places Aisling's murderer as having been in the Glen's area, which brings us to Maude Briers and Brogan's connection.'

Anna nodded, 'Yes, and the CCTV captured inside Saffron shows Aisling interacting with two men. One of them has to be our guy.'

Holly approached the desk, 'We've got a license plate match. A camera, attached to a garage near to the restaurant, clocked a small white Ford van. The plates match those seen on ANPR cameras on the night of Grace Dowds' murder, travelling from Holywood to Belfast passing by George Best airport – the same small white van.'

'Who is it registered to?' Anna asked.

'The previous owner – a Jason McAuley. He sold it on a few months ago. Didn't have the fella's name or number. Paid a grand in cash.'

Thomas smashed his fist into his palm, 'Looks like we are getting somewhere. Right, let's keep this moving.'

* * *

For all the divorce drama Thomas seemed to be dealing with, Anna noticed that he was never far from the case. He lived and breathed it just like she did. They had put in another long day, and now, before heading home, they were making sure everyone was up to speed.

Thomas suppressed a yawn, glanced at the screen set up in the room and took to the floor. 'Right, you lot. Let's recap where we are to date.'

They were all tired. The entire team had been pulling long days, but Aisling's death had made everyone extra edgy. Thomas shushed the group of uniforms, and a few detectives.

'We have failed to locate Luke Nead, and now believe Nead is an alias being used by Robert Brogan.' A murmur went around the room.

'Going with Genevieve's description and the photo-fit image, we have managed to get a positive ID from the care home assistant. She says that the image does indeed look like Nelson Brogan's son Robert.' He paused to let Anna come in. She stood and held up the photo-fit image.

'We are working with the theory that Robert Brogan, working as a security guard under the pseudonym, Luke Nead, had the opportunity to know the venues where the two girls were killed.'

Manus Magee shifted in his seat, 'What's the bird angle? Have we anything to link that back to Brogan and to the murder scenes?'

Anna sighed, 'Up to this point our only link has been that we know from the payroll clerk, Genevieve, that Luke Nead talked of hiking, that he enjoyed wildlife. The aunt of Robert Brogan said something similar. It's tenuous, but we went with it and now with Aisling's murder we've had a lucky break.'

Thomas turned the screen on the wall and opened up the computer file on his iPad. 'With this we have something more substantial tying it all together. At the scene where Aisling Mackin's body was found in East Belfast, forensics picked up an interesting soil sample.' He tapped on his iPad and part of a shoe print flashed on the screen. 'We have secondary transfer of a small amount of soil that was likely to have been lodged in the assailant's boot. Soil material on the suspect's shoe can have material coming from many locations.'

Anna took over, 'But we sent the sample to forensic geologist, Hannah Burton, and she believes that the soil composition, pH levels, texture and chemical make-up, along with traces of sheep faeces, all suggest that it came from the Glens of Antrim area.'

'So, Brogan has been using his aunt's house as a base?' Russell asked.

'We have eyes on the house and there has been no sign of Brogan but he knows the area well. It looked like Aisling's body was being moved and he was disturbed; was he taking her to another location to stage it and leave us another calling card or was he taking her somewhere in the Glens?'

* * *

Declan woke with a jolt. His body was slick with sweat. His muscles, sore and tight. Sleep wasn't worth the turmoil. He reached for his bottle of codeine tablets, found it lying empty beside his bed. In frustration, he threw it towards the wall where it landed with nothing more than a soft thud and rolled mockingly away.

Fuck, fuck, fuck. He couldn't take any more. Sleep was lost to him now. He thought about the paintings he'd seen in Anna's house. The crime scene rendered to a palate of colour, greens, browns, purples, all depicting something he couldn't respond to. Yet, he could see that the formation of the scene, the examining of the light and shadow, the choices that Anna made in deciding where to place the brush, could help sort through the murkiness. When he looked at the drawings he felt angry, hurt even, that she would be able to take the scene of such evil and turn it into a piece of art.

He thought of the previous night's dinner. Izzy had instructed him to be present. Lara and Rory were visiting and he had to behave, she'd said.

'They need our support too. Lara says the police are hassling Rory over his business and finances, using the pretext of Esme's death to dig into his companies. It isn't right. You should have a word with Richard McKay or someone higher up,' Izzy said, setting the table. She went about putting together the meal; the smells of garlic, lemon, and roast chicken making him feel nauseous. The idea of having to sit through the farce of a family meal made him want to heave. How could they play at being some sort of family unit? But deep in his bones he knew whatever Rory had been up to, it couldn't have anything to do with Esme's, or the other girls', deaths.

He had failed to get much out of Anna regarding Rory. He knew she was keeping something from him, and part of him didn't want to know. Whatever it was it wasn't likely to be good for Lara, or any of them.

'Set the table, would you?' Izzy said, her voice low and strained. He couldn't think why she was putting them through this bloody charade. He dutifully did as he was told, maneuvering the chair around the table, setting cutlery at each of the place settings. There were plenty of things he loved about the life he had created with Izzy and her family dinners had been one of them. He grew up in a household where you ate as and when it suited. Usually sitting with your plate on your lap watching Star Trek. Izzy's way was more refined. Nice napkins, good crockery and proper conversation. Now, though, he was sickened by the pretense of it all. There was something false about it. He could barely manage to eat these days let alone talk about world affairs while passing the gravy boat.

And then there was Rory. He'd been avoiding him. Lara tended to call in while Rory was at work. She kept her own hours at the laboratory but like Declan, she couldn't focus on anything other than Esme.

* * *

They arrived on time. Lara went straight into the kitchen to help her mother finish the cooking, leaving Declan and Rory alone.

'So, any updates from the police?' Rory asked, sitting down on the wingback chair opposite Declan.

'Nothing new as such,' Declan struggled to keep his feelings in check. He didn't want to be discussing Esme with Rory. Flashes of the wedding video, Rory grabbing Esme's arm, haunted him.

'Lara said they were looking into the bouncers, thinking Esme might have known one of them?'

'Or she may have felt safe enough to go off with the killer. Trusted him because they had a mutual connection.'

'Right,' said Rory. He was uneasy. For all his buster and cockiness, he had never been at ease around Declan and Declan liked that. Call it respect or a simple awareness that Declan wasn't ever going to fall for his big man act. He wasn't going to be impressed by Rory's fancy car or the cut of his designer suit and they were never going to be best buddies who head down the pub for a pint while their women folk cook the dinner.

'There's talk about you and Esme. What's it all about?' Declan's voice was low.

'What? Declan, you know me. You know Esme was like a sister to me. There was nothing going on, I swear to God.'

Declan shifted his chair so that he was closer to Rory. 'If I thought for one fucking minute that there was something going on, do you think you'd be here now?'

Rory had the good sense to look uncomfortable, 'Ah Declan, come on, Jesus it's a tough time for the whole family.'

'Watch your step, lad. If I find out you had any hand in Esme's death or that you implicate Lara in any of your dirty business dealings, I'll haul you from one end of the street to the next, chair or no chair. Got it?'

Just then, Lara called out from the kitchen, 'It's ready, come on you two.'

* * *

Declan found his days punctuated by the countdown of time it took for him to see Anna. He tried to hold back, to not appear too needy. But if he went a day without seeing her, he craved her. He missed the physical contact, the warmth of her against him. Missed the insights into the case, she threw his way. Always watchful, never saying too much but still enough to let him feel involved on some level. He knew there was plenty she was keeping to herself. Nelson Brogan and the car bomb was one area of concern she had hinted at. She had responded to him telling her about that time as if she was merely enquiring about something tragic that had happened long ago. Concerned for him, and the huge impact it had had on his life. But he'd watched her and read the signals, the looking down as she phrased her questions, the slight air of contrived distractedness.

But he knew Nelson Brogan was laid up in a nursing home. Besides, the car bomb and Brogan's apparent non-disclosure was of that time. He doubted Brogan even felt his hands were sullied with the bomb. A mercury tilt device was remote from the bomber and further again from the Brogan sitting in his office reading a hit list and deciding to simply let it go unnoticed. His ilk were no longer wanted in the new PSNI.

Declan felt that old familiar tightness in his chest, and a cold shiver firing down his spine.

He'd followed Brogan once. He wasn't long out of his rehabilitation. Newly mobile with the chair and the specially adapted car, he was at a loss as to what to do with his days. Ian Devlin, his old boss, had visited him the day before to inform him of their 'concerns', as he put it. That there was likely to be some press intrusion, that rumours were circulating concerning a senior member, who had supposedly withheld information, which could have possibly helped prevent the car bomb. Devlin had spoken in carefully measured language, Declan was sure he'd rehearsed and had probably been prepped by the legal team.

Brogan wasn't named but Declan was certain if anyone had deliberately risked the life of a Catholic colleague it would be him.

The following morning, a Saturday, he found himself driving around East Belfast, the moneyed part. He knew where Brogan lived since he'd dropped him off once after a golf tournament. Brogan had been surly and ill-tempered due to too much drink and sun, but Declan had been gracious enough to offer him a lift home since it was on his way.

That Saturday morning, not long used to driving in the car converted to help with his disability, Declan followed Brogan from his house in Kingsland Park, all the way to Cushendun. He knew enough to keep a distance of at least three cars, to try to anticipate where he was going to turn off. Eventually they had come to a house in a glen, the old family home no doubt. He didn't get close enough to see him go in, instead he circled the area, looking for what, he couldn't say, like a demented two-timed lover, he sought him out. He had driven around the area, looking at all the run-down outbuildings, contrasted with the newly built bungalows with their fresh paint and neat gardens. Afterwards he did a little research, discovered that the house was registered to a family member of Nelson Brogan. That he had grown up in Cushendun. For a while it preoccupied him. Kept him busy like a strange hobby. Eventually he bored himself and let the matter die, knowing he would find no resolution in confronting Brogan.

* * *

He placed the cat on the prepared workbench, belly upward, humming to himself, a stupid song he couldn't get out of his head. Some dance beat that was on the radio all the time. He chose his instruments, a scalpel and bone shears, to begin with, from the neatly lined up selection before commencing to loosen the skin. He had given the creature time for the rigor to relax, there was little point rushing it and trying to work with a stiff animal, he had learnt early on that this was not to be advised. Mistakes were there for learning from. He bent the legs apart to relax the joints, and then cut an opening running from the forelegs down through the middle of the breastbone. He worked his fingers in under the skin and massaged the flesh away until the first leg bone was free of the skin, taking care not to break it. Then, by taking hold of each hind leg, and pulling it to release it from the skin, he was able to push the skin back and in effect turn the legs inside out, right down to the scrawny bone of the ankle joint. Just like removing a piece of clothing.

He prided himself in not mutilating his creatures, so he worked methodically, and carefully, prising the skin away from the flesh, feeling the cold tissues give way under his warm hands. He worked on, right the way down the body to the bony tail skeleton. The skin here needed to be sliced open and to be sewed back up when he was finished. With practice, he was now able to release the tail without damage to the structure. He continued, skinning up to the neck and the ears. Finally, the skin stretched away from the skull so that he could see the white membrane connecting the eye to the skull.

Chapter 40

Anna woke early. The bedroom felt like her's now. She had never been one of those women keen to create a home. Bedsits and student living would've suited her for another few years. Jon had pushed for them to get on the property ladder. To settle into the grown-up rhythm of chores and DIY. She liked this house though. It had character, a sort of homeliness that felt natural, not orchestrated out of some interior design magazine. She turned around in the bed and pulled the duvet up around herself.

Aisling Mackin was on her mind. CCTV showed Aisling, distinctive in her red coat, entering the bar at 9.48 p.m. and at no stage did she leave. This meant that she must have left via the rear doors, and to do so meant that whomever she was with had knowledge of the alarm system and the layout at the back of the building, away from the public areas. Fibres from Aisling's coat had been found caught on the latch of a door to the rear of the building. The general public was not permitted into the back rooms, which housed the staff quarters, the kitchen and the cellars. Aisling had been led from the main bar into the back office. They had footage showing Aisling talking to two different men. One of them had been identified as a gaffer on the period drama. He remained in the bar until closing time and had left with his girlfriend, who had provided him with an alibi. The second man was seen chatting to Aisling at the bar, buying her a drink. He is then seen leaving, exiting through the front door. It was possible that he returned, coming in through the back way, and had been undetected by the security cameras.

She got up and showered before heading down to the kitchen for a quick cup of coffee. There was still no sign of the cat.

She had taken to calling it Misty in her mind. She'd have to watch it, or she'd end up becoming some crazy cat lady. Still, it was nice to have him around; if it was a him.

She filled the kettle, took out a slice of bread to put in the toaster when looking out the back window, over the frost-covered lawn, something caught her eye. At first, she thought it was meat, something maybe Misty had killed and left for her as a gift. Cats did that sort of thing. Bring back their prey to the one who feeds them.

Anna opened the back door to have a better look. As she got closer, the icy grass crunching under her feet, she saw it was a slab of something. Something meaty, bigger than a bird, or even a rat. It was raw sinewy, almost like a lamb, but it was the tail that gave it away. Slick, white, mauve and salmon pink, the body lay stretched out for her to find. Her heart quickened and a wave of nausea rose up from the depths of her stomach. She heaved, spitting onto the icy ground. It was Misty, skinned and displayed, left for her to find.

She went back to the kitchen, sickened and shaky. It took a couple of goes before she could call up her contacts on the mobile.

'Thomas, you better come over to my house and take a look at something.'

* * *

Thomas was there with twenty minutes. The roads were gritted but traffic was slow.

'What's the problem, Tonto? Can't get the lid of your peanut butter jar?'

He swaggered in, all scrubbed faced, freshly shaved and smelling of lemons.

'Out there, go look. I think he's been here, the killer.' 'What?' he walked through the kitchen and out into the garden, Anna followed behind. 'It's a cat, I was feeding it. I think it's from next door. It would call by and I would leave out some bits of chicken for it.'

'Jesus.' He bent down to look at it. 'How do you know it's the same cat you were feeding?'

'Well, I don't for sure. Hard to tell when it doesn't have its fur. It hasn't been around all week, and then this turns up. I assume it's the same cat, either way it's creepy as fuck. He's sending me a message.'

'Right, we'll get it bagged and have the place checked over. You need to assess your security too. He could have come up that laneway at the back of the houses and climbed over the wall.'

'The house is secure. He's sending out a message, not threatening me as such.'

Thomas stood up.

'We don't know what that message is, so in the meantime we take precautions.' He looked at her with concern. 'The press conference, he's probably saw you on that.'

Anna nodded. 'Anyone could've followed me home from work. It isn't hard to find out who's working a case these days.' She didn't like the idea of the killer having been lurking around but she didn't need her partner thinking she couldn't handle herself either.

Thomas walked around the perimeter of the garden, looking for a gap in the hedging. 'Looks like he knows a thing or two about skinning animals. The taxidermy angle again.'

'Yeah, I was thinking the same thing.' They stared at each other. 'Are you ok?'

'Yeah, I'm fine. Not happy about this psycho running around leaving a poor defenseless cat for me to find in this state.' Her knees were still shaky but she wasn't about to let Thomas see how badly it affected her. There was something obscene about being upset over the cat when three girls had been murdered.

He put his hand on her shoulder, 'Right, let's get the ball rolling on this. Talk to neighbours, see whose cat has gone AWOL and bring the techs in to take it in for testing. Who knows what it will throw up by way of information.'

Chapter 40

This time there was a small Christmas tree standing in a bucket in Kathleen's living room. It was twinkling, draped artfully in assorted coloured lights and decorated with strands of gold tinsel. A red and gold angel topped it off. Christmas cards cluttered the mantelpiece and Anna was suddenly embarrassed that she hadn't thought to bring a gift or a card. Christmas was passing her by. She hadn't given any thought to how she would spend it and she dreaded telling her dad she had no intentions of going home. She couldn't afford to take the time off work – the case was consuming her every thought and this afternoon away to see Kathleen was as much of a break as she hoped to take.

'Let me get your coat. Was the traffic bad?' Kathleen asked busying herself around Anna. The tea tray was already set up, with mince pies on a festive holly and ivy patterned plate.

'Yes, the traffic was busy. Everyone seems to be heading out of Belfast.' Anna handed Kathleen her grey wool coat and sat down. She accepted the cup of hot tea and declined to take a mince pie. The trappings of Christmas were everywhere. She liked the idea of opting out of the festivities and drowning herself in work.

'I hope you aren't worrying about your figure, because the Maguires never get fat.'

Anna laughed and said, 'Good to know.'

'So how have you been from when I was last here? I hope I didn't upset you too much dragging up the past like this.'

'There hasn't been a day pass that I haven't thought of you, or our Jamesie. It isn't as if I put it behind me and forgot.'

'You didn't tell me how come I ended up being adopted in Wales. Did you leave Belfast after Jamesie died?'

'No, but I made sure I got you out. Word on the street was that Sean had done a bunk after turning in our Jamesie. If they knew I was carrying his child I'd have been tarred and feathered at the very least.

'Jamesie had a girl back then. Roisin, she was called. She worked in the solicitor's office with him. A trainee solicitor in her father's practice. Smart and gorgeous, tall with dark shiny hair. Our Jamesie was smitten all right. When Jamesie died, she was heartbroken, she came down to our house to pay her respects, like. Something in the way she looked at me made me sure that she knew I was pregnant. How she could tell, was beyond me – I was whippet thin, but on her way out the door she turned and said to me – right quiet like – if you need my help give me a call. She jotted down her number and was gone.

'That night I prayed to God that Roisin would help me, and in the morning I went up the Ormeau Road, found a phone box and made the call. I felt that I could trust her.

'She said she knew I'd phone, and that there were organisations across the water to help to get rid of a baby, but I told her I couldn't murder an innocent baby, that there had to be another way. I didn't want it going into one of the unwanted babies' homes either. The thought of the nuns scared the life out of me. I was convinced they would know whose baby it was and tell on me. Roisin told me to give her a few days to think it over and she would get back in touch.

A week later she met me outside the school. I felt so sick and tired by this stage that I was sure I would faint, and then everyone would know my secret. Roisin took me into a café in the town. Bought me a Paris bun and a cup of tea. She had a plan. She had an aunt who lived in Wales who worked for the social services. She said if they got the baby to her they could get it adopted. Now all we had to worry about was hiding the pregnancy.

'I knew that our Jamesie would have helped me if he could, and here in his place was this angel of mercy taking his place.'

Kathleen stopped and dragged on her electronic cigarette. 'Terrible looking these things are, but they're supposed to be better for me than the real things.'

'So where was I? Oh yes, Roisin. Well, she concocted this plan I was to tell mummy and daddy, I'd been offered a job in Portaferry for the summer, minding two children and cleaning for a good Catholic family. Our family was still in the fog of grief that I don't think they would've noticed what size I was or where I was going. I was neat enough and kept myself covered up.'

Anna stretched her legs out, 'Did they fall for the story?'

'Oh, aye they did, I finished school in June and I was on a ferry to Holyhead by 2 July. Roisin's aunt, Linda, was there to meet me at the port. She took me in and let me stay with her until it was time for you to come. And funny enough, after it was all over, I did end up moving here, to Portaferry, and my sister Maura followed me. We wanted out of Belfast, as far from the trouble as we could get without leaving Ireland.

'I'd never been out of Ireland before I had you. The green hills and valleys reminded me of Ireland but it all felt so different. The people talked all funny. I could scarcely make out what they were saying and they couldn't understand me either. But they were nice people. Kind and gentle, and I felt that the baby would be all right brought up in such a place.

'I sent letters home via Roisin, along with an envelope with my family's address written on it. She put them in a new, Belfast addressed envelope and posted them so that the postmark made them think I was still in Northern Ireland. She was clever that way. I'd have been that stupid. I'd have given the game away.

'Anyway, we didn't have long to wait for you to arrive. 22 August. The skies were full of rain; it teemed down. Expect that's why the place is so green, plenty of sunshine and rain. You came out with hardly a whimper. Me, I'd squealed enough for both of us,' she smiled at the memory.

'I didn't get to see you, not properly. They cleaned you up and all I got to see was the top of your head; dark, thick hair. They said it was better that way. Would make it easier for me.

'Last I heard, Linda said she had found a nice couple who'd been trying for a baby for years. The baby will be wanted and loved, I was told, and I held on to the thought for years.'

* * *

Anna woke with a start. She had fallen asleep on the sofa listening to the haunting melodies of Ben Howard. The music had lulled her into a shallow sleep plagued by dreams of barricades and burning buses. Kathleen's story had replayed in her mind the whole way back from Portaferry. The trauma that Kathleen must have faced, finding herself pregnant to Sean and the desperate fear of being mixed up with him and his deadly game of acting as an informer. Where was he now, she wondered? It was tempting to do some digging and see if he was in the system. Except that all such inquiries were logged and she couldn't be seen to be investigating him without a valid work reason. The thought of him becoming an informer bothered her. She couldn't understand her feeling of disgust; that he was wrong to turn on his own community. To have betrayed the people he had grown up with, just to save his own neck. But then, who was she to judge a conflict she had only ever read about.

She thought of her own teenage years in Cardiff and a girl from her school that had got pregnant at sixteen. Rosalie Morgan had sex with her steady boyfriend of four months and found herself, six weeks later, in the toilets of St David's shopping centre, peeing on a stick from a pregnancy testing kit she'd stolen from Boots. After much crying from Rosalie and gossiping among the girls at school, Rosa and her mum headed off to a private abortion clinic in Cyncoed. Within a week, Rosa was back at school, playing netball and by the end of term they had largely forgotten that it had all seemed like such a big drama.

Kathleen's experience was so different. Anna was a product of this place. She was part of the pain, the suffering, the fear, and the disquiet. For once, Anna felt like she was beginning to get a hold of what it meant to be from here.

Chapter 41

Anna unbuttoned her suit jacket and placed her hands on the table. The early morning wakeup call didn't appear to have caught Finnegan on the hop. He was clean-shaven, wearing a crisp blue shirt, beneath a dark suit. His lawyer, Paul Murphy, was at his side again.

Nailing him hadn't been easy. The problem was they were chasing after him, for the wrong crime. Digging around in the murky depths of Finnegan's dealings had thrown up a few snifters of considerable interest, and now they had enough to haul him out of his comfy bed and into the station for full on questioning.

'Mr Finnegan,' Thomas began, 'we would like to have a chat with you about some of your business associates and transactions.'

He looked to Murphy, as if he'd been taken by surprise. He probably assumed they would be questioning him about Esme and Grace again. Anna sat down, 'We can trace you to deals done to secure a portion of a private equity portfolio. Toxic loans, following the 2008 property crash; can be pretty lucrative if you are buying them at the right rate. And it appears that your mate Aidan Anderson has been receiving kickbacks for providing access to all sorts sensitive information.'

Thomas opened a manila folder of bank statements, 'You see Mr Finnegan, we need you to help us out. We aren't used to looking through this kind of financial quagmire, but even to my culchie sensibilities, transfers to overseas accounts smell kind of dodgy. But you know, really, it's not our problem. We are handing the whole shebang over to the UK's National Crime Agency.

Anna leaned back, 'I hear they've an algorithm set up for dealing with this kind of thing. Whole departments and ranks of computers designed to sniff out any financial misconduct.'

'They sure have,' Thomas said, 'aye they've the right people to shift through the paperwork, crunch the numbers and spew out the guilty parties. Not the kind of boring police work I would want to be doing, but bad guys are bad guys.'

'There's a few points of interest for us. Esme Wells. Remember her? Your sister-in-law? Yeah, well Esme's middle name was Rachel. One of the accounts, set up in the Isle of Man – nowhere exotic like the Cayman Islands or Switzerland. Bloody boring old, Isle of Man, land of Manx cats and TT racing. One of the Isle of Man accounts was set up in the name of Rachel Wells. Not exactly hard to work that one out – we could identify pretty quickly who Rachel Wells was. So, you get your wife-to-be's little sister, to sign a few chits of paper?'

'What did you tell her?' Anna asked. 'That it was an investment for her university fees? Or was she so enamored by you that she didn't even question your motives?'

Thomas took over, 'She gets a generous pay-back for being your in-between person. We've been able to draw the dots together and do you know what the overall picture looks like?'

Finnegan looked like he was about to be sick. He looked to Murphy for guidance but even Murphy looked uncertain, 'I will need to speak to my client alone.'

'All in good time, Paul, all in good time.'

Anna picked up the thread, 'I believe its five to ten years for this kind of fraud. Allowing for good behaviour you'll be hitting your forties by the time you get out.'

Finnegan looked to Murphy again. 'My client has been put under undue stress. We cannot be expected to answer these allegations without conference first.'

Anna smiled, 'Well of course you will be given every opportunity to straighten up your story but before that we want to know who your fixer is. That one person who has acted as your go between. It has to be someone with political clout. Someone with friends in high places, and low gutters. And if we have to go up the chain of command at Stormont to find him or her, you can be certain we will.'

'I have nothing further to say,' Finnegan replied.

Thomas looked to Anna, 'You have a half an hour to converse with your solicitor and then the boys from NCA are taking over.'

Chapter 42

It was late afternoon, a little before four, when Anna headed out of the station. She drove up the Lisburn Road, hoping to grab something to eat from one of the many deli shops, when she noticed she had someone tailing her. A red Mazda 3. She'd been aware of it as she turned onto Balmoral Avenue and now as she pulled into a parking space on Lancefield Road, she watched as it pulled up on the opposite side of the road.

It was the journalist, Ivan McGonigle. She recognised him from his by-line photograph. With a shock of red hair and his geek boy glasses he was easily identifiable.

She stilled the engine and got out of her car, grabbing her bag from the passenger seat as he approached her. She noted his easy way of striding across the road to her, ducking in and out of the traffic backing up from the still busy Lisburn Road. She caught a glimpse of his AC/DC T-shirt beneath his jacket.

'Can I have word DI Cole?' He flashed his press card at her, as if it would somehow make her more likely to stop for him, and grabbed her car door.

'No, I don't talk to journalists. Go through the press office like everyone else.'

Anna tried to push her car door closed, but he had placed himself neatly between her and the car, blocking her arm from the door.

'Plenty are saying the PSNI serious crime unit are out of their depth and have enlisted you from across the water for your expertise. Care to comment?'

'No, I don't.'

'Maybe you would be more interested if I ran with the story about your mother's death. Tragic really. You nursed her through her cancer, didn't you?' He spoke quietly, scanning Anna for a reaction. She didn't miss a blink.

'My mother's death is none of your business,' she hissed.

'Don't worry, I'm not running it, but I think you deserve a head's up on an even bigger story. I've been told by a reliable source that you and Declan Wells are having an affair. He's been seen leaving your house. Feel free to respond with a quote on the record, like,' he pushed his glasses back up on the bridge of his nose.

Anna felt as if he had knocked the wind right out of her. She hadn't time to react, to compose her features.

'Get the fuck away from my car, or I'll charge you with harassment.'

He stepped back, smirking, 'I'll take that as another no comment, shall I?'

Anna jumped back in her car, slammed the door shut and floored the accelerator. She sped off, thumping the steering wheel with her right hand. *Fuck, fuck, fuck.* She should have seen it coming. Every instinct of her being told her that being involved with Declan was a time bomb waiting to detonate. She'd lose her job, and destroy the entire case. Rage at herself, rage at McGonigle rippled through her body. She had no choice but to face McKay with the story herself before it broke in the paper. It was only a matter of time before the inquest into her mother's death had caught up with her. McKay would have two reasons to sack her. She almost went through a red light and a car horn lambasted her.

That little shit of a hack had no business prying into her life. Camille was gone, and no one could be sadder and more regretful about that than Anna. If she were faced with the same choices again, the outcome would be the same.

As for Declan, while she knew the risks and the sense of not being involved with him, she couldn't deny that part of her was glad it was out in the open. The fear of being found out had hung over them. She thought of all the reasons she had used to convince herself that their affair was not compromising the investigation. She doubted McKay would buy into any of them.

* * *

They had spent months going from one hospital appointment to the next. Sitting in dreary NHS waiting rooms waiting to be told what they already knew – that the cancer was back and this time there would be no remission. The options were limited -intensive chemotherapy to buy time, but spend her last weeks in pain and sickness. Initially Camille had thought she had a choice – to say no to the treatment, to bow out gracefully in the comfort of her own home and to slip away without causing too much fuss. Of course, it wasn't so straightforward. The consultant had patiently explained that sometimes the chemo was to keep the symptoms of the cancer at bay, to make the last few weeks more tolerable.

'Sometimes the chemotherapy in end stage is to help ease your passage. We will do everything possible to make you comfortable, but you have to realise that rejecting treatment isn't always the best option.'

So, they found themselves back in the cycle of IV drips, hospital stays, low blood counts and infections. Camille endured as much as she could with good grace, as was her character, but Jimmy struggled to cope, and Anna watched him turn away more than once rather than face watching her mother suffer.

* * *

Anna let herself in and threw the keys on the hall table. She unzipped her boots and padded into the living room. The move to Belfast had seemed reactive. It was a knee jerk decision. She hadn't brought over any personal items, except for one – a framed photograph of Camille taken last year. She lifted it down from the mantelpiece and looked at the face smiling out at her. The thick ash blonde hair had gone; wisps of fine baby-like hair were all that remained. She had her make up on, eyes expertly lined and a smudge of grey powder on her eyelids, and as always finished off with her favourite coral lipstick. Anna had taken the photograph in the garden at home. She could see the pearly white magnolia blossoms in the background, and knew from memory that her father was in the kitchen trying to sort out some drinks. Even such a small job as pouring a few drinks seemed to flummox him. They were all wore out with stress and worry, but there amongst it all sat Camille, looking radiant.

Within two weeks they had had the news that the cancer had spread to her thoracic spine. She was riddled with it, paralysed by it, and in such pain and suffering that her anguished cries could be heard throughout the house. Morphine was pumped in through the dreaded syringe driver, doing little more than inducing fitful sleeps, during which she whimpered and begged to be helped. Hospice nurses, always well meaning, came and went according to a pattern of shifts yet no one could help her, not really. Every time a new face would appear at the door, full of concern and goodliness, they hoped this would be the one, the one guardian angel to help them all work this out. Anna came to realise that sometimes the answer lies within. You have to do the unthinkable and live with the consequences.

Chapter 43

Anna hadn't thought about getting drunk during the day since university. Drinking was still new to her then, the buzz of a night out, the banter with friends, the talking shite until 4.00 a.m. when she'd fall asleep on Cerys' bed or in some boy's arms. She missed those days.

'So, what are you drinking?'

'Thomas!' she exclaimed, delighted to see him.

'Don't act all surprised, you called me twenty minutes ago.'

'I know, but you *came*!'

She moved over on the leather sofa to give him room. The bar was fairly empty; a couple sat close together, head's touching, over by the window, and two women perched on bar stools were studying the cocktail menu deep in debate about the merits of a Woo Woo over a French Connection.

'So, what's the occasion?' Thomas asked.

'I fucked up. Big time.'

'Ah so, we're drowning our sorrows, are we?'

'Yep, that's about the sum of it,' she knocked back the last of her glass of vodka and tonic.

'I'll get you glass of water and you can tell your uncle Thomas all about it.'

Anna screwed up her nose, 'Who made you school prefect?'

'I'm sure you'd do the same for me if I was two sheets to the wind.'

'Fine, water it is, but first, I have to pee.'

'Off you go then and don't be falling asleep on the bog. I'm not going in there to carry you out.'

She smiled at him. He was cute in that over-grown boy sort of way. Why couldn't she have fallen for him instead of Declan?

* * *

Thomas was back with the drinks on the table when Anna returned.

'Are you going to tell me what you've done that's so terrible to need us to be plastered this early in the evening?'

She took a long drink of the iced water. 'It's Declan Wells.'

'Declan Wells. What about him?'

'Well he and I …' she let the sentence trail off and saw wheels turning and then the shock register on Thomas' gormless face.

'What? You are shagging Declan Wells?' he hissed low, as if afraid that someone would hear them.

Anna nodded. She didn't intend to cry or expect to, but the tears came anyway.

'Fuck, you've went and done it now Tonto. Does McKay know?'

'Not yet, but Ivan McGonigle has got wind of it and he's threatening to run with it,' she sniffed back her tears.

'Here, blow your nose,' he gave her a crumpled hanky retrieved from his jacket pocket.

'I'm sorry, Thomas. I know McKay will say I've jeopardised the case but honest to God, I haven't. Declan's desperate to know who killed Esme and the others. He and I have been working together, profiling and well, I didn't pass on anything which would be of risk from prosecuting Rory Finnegan or anyone else.'

'Shit Anna, you can't know that for sure.'

She put her face in her hands feeling pure despair.

Thomas paused and then said, 'We need to get on top of this before it breaks. Can McGonigle prove you two have been at it?'

'I don't know. I don't think so. So, what if someone has seen him leave my house? We weren't exactly snogging on the door step.'

'We go for denial then.'

Anna was silent for a moment.

'I'm not sure that will work. I've fucked up big time. I don't want to do anything more to compromise the investigation, or myself. Maybe it's better to come clean.'

Thomas took a sip of his pint. The froth stayed on his upper lip, making Anna think of milk moustaches. 'Are you going to tell McKay?' he asked. She loved his loyalty to her, the fact that he asked if she was going to McKay rather than forcing her to.

He had every right to tell her to resign immediately. It was reassuring to know he was in her corner.

'My judgment of late has been off course. I can't trust myself to deal with this alone. I don't want to be off the case but I can't walk away from this either.'

'You won't have to,' he took her hand.

'There's a very good chance I'll be sacked. If I'm lucky, I'll be sent back to uniform and probably back to Cardiff.' She could hear her voice breaking. Thomas squeezed her hand.

'Nah, it won't come to that. McKay's all right. He'll stand by you. He'll throw a complete hissy fit first though, so be warned.'

'What about the case? We're getting somewhere I can feel it. He has slipped up with Aisling. It didn't go as planned and that's how we are going to get him. The soil sample, the car plates, the CCTV and the photo-fit – it's all falling into place. We know he's a watcher. He plans everything and waits for his moment.'

She saw a flicker of something pass over Thomas' face. 'I don't want to jump to conclusions and scare you, but had you considered that the killer has been watching Declan, and by extension you?'

'But I wouldn't fit with his type. I'm not on the shelf yet, but I'm not a young girl either.' She thought of the cat and knew that he had been watching her.

'We don't know his motivation, so we can't rule anything out, and if grease bags like McGonigle know about you and Declan, then the chances are others might know too, especially someone keeping an eye on Declan Wells.'

'So, you're saying you think Esme was picked out and targeted because of her dad?'

'We can't rule it out, not for sure. All we know is that Brogan junior has been moonlighting for the security firm, probably working under the name Luke Nead and we can't trace him. He's hiding something. Finnegan is a low life in a sharp suit, but I don't think he is our murderer.'

Anna felt icy cold. She took another drink of the water and felt sick.

'Come on now, dry your tears Tonto. We need to sober you up and go see McKay before McGonigle writes up his copy.'

* * *

He didn't always live like this; alone and bitter. There was a time when he had plans, friends and a life of expectation. By his fifth year at grammar school he had found his gang, Glenn, Vincie and Dan. They played video games in Vincie's house, his mother always welcoming, too much make up and dressed like she was eighteen, but they loved her. She'd buy them Chinese takeaway and give them a can of Harp larger each. He loved those easy moments when he could forget about home. The banter, talk of girls they couldn't get off with, finding a stash of porno mags behind the row of shops, giving each other dead arms in jest, the heady thrill of it all – it was all he lived for. They kept to themselves, not venturing into the main social life of school.

It wasn't to last, though. By the Easter of fifth year, when he should have been working for his GCSEs, his mother had become sick. Really sick.

After school, he should have gone to university, that was the plan. He would've liked to have studied history maybe or even philosophy. He liked reading about Descartes, Kant and Nietzsche. The thinkers. He wasn't stupid, far from it. But that path wasn't to be. When his mum became ill he gave up, school didn't seem so important. He stayed home to help her hide her illness, to have the dinner on the table for his Da coming home, to keep the place tidy, just the way his Da liked it. Military neatness, that served no purpose beyond an exertion of his power. The Big Man barked his orders and they both jumped.

They concealed the illness for a while. Letters from the hospital kept hidden, appointments attended when they knew he would be at work. But gradually, the weaknesses showed, the shaking hand, the limp leg. By the time she told his Da what was going on, she was past the point of no return. Those months of looking after her, cooking for her, feeding her and even on a few occasions bathing her, were precious to him. He didn't resent her or the illness, and accepted it as part of his lot. There was never any suggestion that it was his Da's place to do it all. That would never have occurred to them. It was afterwards, when she was dead and buried that he looked back and felt the resentment gather like a low wind feeding a fire. It developed in to a sour anger that kept rising and falling, breaking against him like a wave hitting the shore line. Each time it retreated, he was left with the debris, shards of broken conversations, unexplained grievances, hurts that cut so deep that they were beyond healing.

Chapter 44

There had been other bad days when she'd been called before a Super to answer for bad judgment. Yet nothing could have prepared her for McKay's apoplectic rage. Her face burned with the shame of being balled out like a child in a classroom. She had no defense, no excuses. Yet she felt totally crushed by her own stupid actions. While she didn't regret a second of being with Declan, she regretted the impact it had on the case and how she had risked everything. She felt it all rain down around her, while McKay continued to rage.

'You have called this force into question... Risked our reputation and harmed our case, should we ever get as far as the crown prosecution...' A nerve, near his temple, fluttered and pulsed, like a butterfly trapped under his skin.

'Unavoidable... evidence... protocol.' Spittle flew from his contorted mouth and landed on her cheek. She didn't dare wipe it off. It went on and on, all the while she could hear the tumbling rush of blood surge in her ears, as she tried to hold it together. She thought of her mum, Camille, and the papery soft feel of her hands, the loosening of her skin, the intricate map of violet veins running across her head, the bald, baby soft skull.

'Fucked up, big time. Come in here, to our force and cause havoc. What do you have to say for yourself?'

She snapped back into the moment.

'Nothing sir, I've nothing to offer in my defence I was wrong, totally out of line, and I'm sorry.'

'Have you considered what a good defence lawyer would do to a case like this? Have you given *any* fucking thought as to how this will look to the families of the other girls? We have let them all down!' his voice was thundering. The whole station must be listening in, she thought. She was aware of Thomas' presence shift beside her. He had kept quiet, knowing he couldn't offer anything to help her but now she could feel him getting ready to intervene.

'Sir, if I can interrupt.'

'You better not have known this was going on King,' McKay focused his savage stare on to Thomas.

'No, sir I didn't but I would like you to consider your actions before you take Cole, us, off this case.'

'You don't get to advise me on how we proceed,' McKay snapped.

'No sir, I wouldn't assume to advise you, but please hear me out.'

'You've two minutes to convince me that I shouldn't sack Cole on the spot and hand this whole fucking debacle over to HR in Wales to sort out. She's still under their jurisdiction.'

Thomas cleared his throat, 'We are getting close. I can feel it. Nead, the name we have for the rogue security guard, has been as an alias used by Robert Brogan, son of Nelson Brogan. Initially we ruled him out. He wasn't scheduled to work that night so we took him out of the equation.'

'Go on,' McKay said.

'But what if he had actually turned up as if he was supposed to be working. If the other security staff saw him they would just assume he had been on the rota. He has the perfect cover to blend in.'

Anna continued, 'He knows the venue, he has worked there before, and he has possibly met Esme at one of Finnegan's soirées. She wouldn't feel threatened by him because he's familiar.'

Thomas took over, 'If Robert Brogan is acting on some sort of grudge against Declan Wells, then this story breaking would put Cole in danger. He could see Cole as his next target.'

'What about the other two girls, how do they fit into your theory?'

'We are working on the assumption that Esme was his first. The other two girls, Grace Dowds and Aisling Mackin, have been follow up acts. He kills them to make it look like he is a serial killer out to get any young woman, but really it was Esme who was his prize kill all along.'

McKay sat his chair and sighed. 'If you're wrong King, if this has nothing to do with Brogan and you have me risking this station's reputation I swear to fuck I'll have your bollocks on a silver platter by the end of this.'

'Yes, sir, I understand.'

'And Cole, do you buy into this? Do you think Brogan is our man?'

'Yes sir, I do.'

'And there's something else, sir.' Thomas said. They told him about the cat, making the link between the dead bird found at Esme's scene of death and the robin inserted into Grace's mouth.

There was silence as McKay processed what he'd been told. 'Right, you pair of idiots go prove to me you deserve not to be flung out on your ears, get this case wrapped up.'

'Sir?'

'What now Cole?'

'I'm not off the case? I'm not sacked?'

'Not yet. If King is right, you could be at risk, if this is our man he knows where you live and he's sending you some sort of sick little love note in the form of a skinned cat, and while at this minute I feel like kicking you from here to Tipperary, I'm not about to set you loose for some psycho to get easy access to you. If you are still on the case, we can keep a close on eye on you,' he paused, 'Besides, I think you are a bloody good cop, despite your best efforts to fuck up a stellar career. If I hear of you as much as texting Declan Wells, I will not hesitate to cut you off cold. Do you understand?'

'Yes sir.'

'From here on in, it's damage control all the way. I'll speak to McGonigle's editor.'

They turned to leave the room when McKay said, 'One more thing, I've heard back from the Financial Intelligence Unit. It looks like Aidan Anderson has been implicated along with Finnegan in a deal worth £4.2m.'

Anna's eyes widened. Thomas blew out a stream of air, 'Shit boss, we've got him.'

'Apparently, a payment has been made into an offshore account linked to a private equity property portfolio. Finnegan had first bite at the cherry and paid less than £750,000 to get in on the deal.'

McKay put his hands behind his head, looking smug. 'It's been confirmed that Aidan Anderson had diverted monies to an account of which he was the sole beneficiary for get this 'professional fees,' due for his part in the handling of the deal. They won't be able to brush this under the carpet; once it goes public there will be calls for an independent inquiry. Don't go patting yourselves on the back yet, though. Go find Brogan Junior and get a solve before I put the pair of you in uniform.'

Chapter 45

Anna woke with a start. She listened, checking to see if something had woken her, but after a couple of moments she realised that she had been dreaming. Fragments of the dream came back to her. She had been standing at Camille's graveside. The soil, which was piled high to the side, to allow for the burial, had begun to move towards Anna engulfing her, and pushing her into the open mouth of the grave. Mourners were watching. No one was helping; they were merely spectators as if they had come to see this. To watch her be buried alive.

Her skin was clammy and hot and her mouth was dry. She couldn't shake the feeling that it had been full of the dry soil from the graveyard. Lying in the bed she watched the early morning light seep into the room. She checked her phone and saw that it was five thirty. It would be a long day.

* * *

Thomas gave Anna that hard stare of his. She had heard he'd been trying to get hold of her. 'What's wrong?' she asked, taking a chair next to him in the canteen.

'I can't be your go-between Anna. I delivered the message but that's it. I'm not passing love notes between the two of you like fourth year students with the hots for each other.'

'I don't expect you to. That's it. It's over.'

Finishing with Declan had been difficult. With a no-contact ban from McKay she'd been forced to ask Thomas to deliver the bad news. She knew Declan wouldn't take it well, not least because it would mean he had lost his hold in the case. But was that all she was to him? She had spent a restless night trying to work out how she felt about Declan. When she was with him everything felt so clear, so right. Then she'd go to the station, get on with work and wonder at her poor lack of judgment and her ability to mess up her life.

When the story broke, it didn't have the same bite. Obviously, McKay had some clout with the editor for McGonigle merely hinted at an affair with someone in the force connected to the case. Neither Anna nor Declan's names were mentioned. It was all innuendo and gossip. Anna breathed a sigh of relief. They had a reprieve, but she wasn't going to risk the wrath of McKay again. Declan had been warned to stay away.

'You told him about McGonigle, right?'

'Yes, I told him. I told him how you'd almost lost your entire career.'

'Well, that's it. It's over.'

'Back to work, Tonto. Let's crack this thing.'

Later that day Anna walked along the station corridor thinking how the bland, pale green walls and artificial lighting reminded her of her old place of work. Inside the building, she could be in any police station in the country, but the compound security of the outside, reminded her at every turn, that Belfast police stations needed to be semi-fortresses even in times of relative peace and political stability.

Her phone buzzed as she made her way to the incident room. It was a text from Denis in forensics, to let her know the report on the cat had been emailed to her. She hurried into her office and logged on to her computer to access the report. They had found out that the cat had been missing for five days. The owners, who lived next door to Anna had reported the cat missing to the local vet, three days before it turned up on Anna's back lawn and it had been the grey and white one she'd been calling Misty.

She hit the call button on her phone, deciding to speak to Denis directly to get a run down of what he had found.

'Denis, Anna Cole here. I got your text about the report so talk me through it,' she opened the email attachment as she spoke.

'Hi there, DI Cole, well the report tells you the wee cat had its neck broke. That's the cause of death.'

'Go on.'

'We can't categorically say it's the same assailant that left the bird at the previous crime scene, or the killer who put the robin in the second victim's mouth but all three were cleaned with the same detergent solution – borax and disinfectant, to remove all traces of the killer an also to make the animal clean to work with.'

Anna scrolled through the report notes on her screen while he spoke.

'Whoever skinned the kitty knew how to handle a small animal in that way. It takes a fair bit of skill and practice to skin a cat and keep it intact.'

'Anything else?'

'As you know the removal of the eyes in the guillemot was clean and precise, no damage to the bone sockets and whoever did this to the cat was as equally well practiced, I'd say,' Denis said.

Anna ended the call and read through the report. Denis had provided her with a list of possible tools used to skin the cat, along with information on the process: a seam would have been made in the belly, working the knife along the inside, treating its pelt like a coat to be removed.

She leaned back in her chair, going over all the information in her head and then reached for her notepad and began writing down a list of all the known associates connected to the girls. Within a minute, she had a list of names, some with question marks beside them, dates, places and queries. She stared down at her scrawled handwriting. Finnegan – dirty and sure of himself. He'd used Esme to launder money through her name. Had employed her as a waitress at his murky soirées, where he'd entertained, doling out cocaine and prostitutes, to sweeten his dodgy deals. It was likely he had a relationship with her. Lara would know about this soon enough, and Anna suspected she would have enough sense to kick him out of their home. His connections with Stephen Dowds were not suspect; it could be coincidence that they knew each other. Northern Ireland was a small pond after all, but Aidan Anderson was a different story. The hood-turned-politician was enjoying the power of his newfound politicking, and liked to feel his palm slicked. Power was his nectar. Finnegan's relationship with Anderson was one of bribes to secure the success of business deals. Having friends in the council, at such a high level, had enabled Finnegan to bypass planning regulations and to skip through red tape when it suited his business needs.

Then there was old Maude Briers. She obviously loved Robert Brogan. He was the child she never had. Should he need it, Anna was certain she would step in and given him an alibi. There was something in her manner, her defense of Robert Brogan, that made Anna think she was used to standing up for him. And Brogan himself, the offspring of a bent copper; Nelson Brogan, a bully of a man who dealt with the stresses of the job by terrorising his wife and most likely his son too.

Sometimes with a case like this one, Anna found herself drowning in detail. Stepping back and looking at bigger picture, trying to see beyond the obvious connections was useful.

Anna put her pen down and stared out of the rain-washed window. Her desk was a cluttered mess of papers. So much for logging everything into the document sharing system. Sometimes the old-school method of paper and pen was more effective for helping her process the information. She kept going back to Robert Brogan. If he was special to Maude then perhaps he was fond of her too. Sooner or later he would go back to the house in the Glens.

* * *

The graveyard was vast, row upon row of neat plots. His mother was near the manmade lake, which was really no more than a big pond.

A willow tree leaned over the still body of water with its thin curling branches reaching down to touch the surface. Her grave was marked with a simple wooden cross. It had weathered well considering. He'd have to replace it at some stage, but it would suffice for another year. There were no flowers, just a simple rectangle of grass.

When the end was approaching, he'd been in denial, thinking, hoping she'd improve. He hadn't believed she would go back to good health; she'd been declining for so long he could barely remember her well. But he thought she'd at least be well enough again to sit up unaided, sip some soup or ask him how school was going.

As she slipped away, his father became even more withdrawn and morose than normal. The fear of sparking his temper was ever present, but he no longer lashed out. Instead his darkness festered in him, emitting a sourness over everything.

Afterwards, he realised her being there was enough. He shouldn't have asked for or expected any more.

Chapter 46

Returning to the Brier woman's home wasn't planned. It was one of those restless evenings where Anna felt a sense of panic building. A feeling that they weren't doing enough, fast enough. Thomas had gone home with a plan to catch up on some much-needed sleep and she missed Declan's company. She couldn't sit around doing nothing. McKay was threatening to reduce manpower and to hand control over to someone more experienced. Thomas had been seething, but she knew they were idle threats. No one wanted to risk another victim, but McKay had to be seen to be keeping the pressure on.

The local uniforms had been instructed to keep an eye on Maude's house and to be on the lookout for Robert Brogan and a small white Ford van. Anna was approaching the laneway leading to the Brier house, debating whether she should call on the pretense of further questions, when suddenly she saw an old green Polo drive past. Even in the relative darkness there was no mistaking the grim set of Maude Brier's face behind the wheel. Hoping the woman hadn't noticed her, as she ducked down into her seat, she watched in the rear-view mirror as the car sped away. Giving Maude a few minutes to be clear from the house, Anna swerved out and made her way up the lane. The early night sky was the colour of a deep bruise, pinpricked with stars.

The outbuilding stood to the left of the main house. At first glance it was dilapidated, but there was evidence of some minor repairs. It would have been a vital part of the farm, at one time, used to house pigs or farm equipment. Now it was an almost wreck of over-grown ivy and crumbling stonework. The slate roof sagged over the side door, weighed down by the push of roof tiles dislodged over time. Corrugated iron had been used to patch it up in places where the roof tiles had been beyond repair. Someone, probably Robert Brogan, had made small improvements, but it wasn't as cared for as the main house. It did look too secure for such a run-down building. Brogan could have been using it as a store or a base to hide out in.

A tuft of grass grew straight up from the guttering and clumps of emerald green moss sat, fat and slug like, on the ridge. The windows, two small square panes were whitened out as Thomas had said. In the gloaming of the early night it was impossible to see beyond them. It wasn't a place you'd want to linger. Loneliness and a certain misery seeped out of it. Anna could imagine how isolated it would feel during the depths of a harsh winter. She couldn't help conjuring up images of charcoal silhouettes of the buildings against a threatening sky.

The wooden door looked like it had been replaced at some stage. Anna pushed against it but found it was unmoving, solid. The windows were jammed shut too. There was no point in smashing the glass and alerting a returning Maude to her obvious presence. She walked around the building and remembered seeing an old oil drum near the main house. If she could push it back to the outbuilding, with a bit of luck she could use it to climb up onto the roof and perhaps dislodge some slates and make her way through. She was relying on the roof beams to be exposed so that she could see beyond them into the room below.

The oil drum wasn't full but it would be hard going to move it with her shoulder injury still nagging. She tried rolling it across the gravel, but found it cumbersome. It took a bit of pushing and pulling before she managed to get it on its side and build up some momentum. When she had secured the drum in place at the back of the outbuilding, she looked around for a branch or a stick of some sort that she could use to push the roof tiles back.

Once she was on top of the oil drum she looked across the yard to the main house. It was still in darkness and there was no sign of Maude's car. Climbing up was difficult; she wobbled precariously and caught hold of the guttering to stop herself swaying backwards. The roof tiles were moss slickened and looked slippery. Her shoulder was still stiff and sore but she wasn't going to let it stop her getting a look inside.

She hoped old Maude wouldn't return and catch her. She didn't want to have to explain her actions to her or McKay.

Anna heaved herself across the roof and felt it shift beneath her weight. 'Shit,' she whispered to herself, trying to keep her weight evenly distributed despite the pain in her shoulder. She steadied herself and used the branch to dislodge the tiles beyond her reach. They moved easily enough, concertinaing on top of each other, until she could sense a gap big enough for her to peer through. A bat startled; 'Fuck,' she said, nearly falling backwards. It flew straight at her, causing her to jolt again and almost lose her footing. Her heart raced, making her feel light headed and dizzy. She needed to be quick, to be far away before Maude returned.

Carefully, she shimmied on up, lying low against the slates and hoping she wasn't about to fall through. With her left hand, she carefully reached for her phone from her pocket, to use as a torch and illuminate the room below the rafters.

Hanging in neat rows were animals, skinned and bloodless. She could identify a hare, long and lean, like a child slivered fresh from between its mother's legs. A bird of some sort lay on a table directly below. It was close enough for Anna to see its glassy-dead, bead of an eye. Its feathered wing spread out like a fan and was pinned to the board it lay on. Farming tools and other implements lined up against the back stonewall. She could see knives of various sizes, what looked like scalpels and a clamp of some sort, along with a frame being used to stretch a furred skin. A coppery smell of blood with an undercurrent of something chemical, made her stomach roil. She'd seen enough. Clambering back down the roof, she slipped and almost ended up falling off. Her foot found purchase on the rusty guttering and she was able to manoeuver herself down onto the oil drum.

She froze, suddenly aware of another presence.

'Looking for something, Detective?' It could only be Brogan.

She gasped as she turned and saw him and then again as his hand slammed against her face, the heal of his palm striking forcibly against her chin in one fluid upward movement. Her head was forced back and cracked against the stonewall. A quick jab of a punch to her stomach made her buckle over in pain, all air swiftly knocked out of her, rendering her powerless to fight against him. He forced her upright back against the wall, pushing his fist into her windpipe. She took in the strangely calm expression; his eyes close enough for her to see flecks of green against a blue background, his skin, clear and unlined, damp with the drizzling rain, which had been falling softly on them. His hair was cut short, almost like a crew cut, something vaguely military about it and slicked back against his head. She could see the soft skin of his neck, the hair follicles where he'd shaved uneven. Up close she could see he was young looking. Maybe about twenty-five. He had that angelic look about him, something, almost otherworldly. She thought of the photograph she had seen sitting on Maude Brier's dresser, a young boy looking out, happy and confident as if the sun shone only for him.

'You couldn't stay away, could you? Had to go sticking your nose in where it's not wanted. Think you can come over from the mainland and tell us hicks how to run our country?' His pretty boy features rearranged into a snarl.

Anna couldn't reply for he kept her locked in an upright position, one hand pressing hard against her windpipe, the other gripping her coat. She thought of her Glock lodged in her trousers and at the same moment, in one swift movement, he whisked it away from under her coat, punching her deftly in the side.

The sharp pain made her cry out in a strangled moan as he still squeezed against her throat.

The rumble of a car further up the lane, possibly Maude Briers returning, caused him to act quickly. He pulled Anna with his right hand, swung her round so that her back was pressed against his front and put the Glock to her head. She felt her legs unsteady beneath her, but before she could catch her breath, he was dragging her across the field towards a copse of trees. She could make out a dark coloured small van partially hidden by the dense foliage. He must have approached the property by another lane and rolled the van as close as he could without Anna hearing him. She felt vomit threaten to rise up from the depths of her stomach, as the pain in her side continued to spark and flare, from where he'd punched her. She could hear the car come closer; it could only be seconds away. She fought with every fibre of her body, arching against him, kicking backwards with all her strength, but before she had any chance of being heard or escaping, he used the Glock to strike her once on the left temple.

Chapter 47

Declan had little else to do other than trawl through online academic journals trying to glean any information which could bring light to the case. He was well versed in broken home and attachment theories; it wasn't a stretch to assume that the killer had come from some sort of dysfunctional background. The scope of psychoanalytic theories resting on the three major personality mechanisms: the id, ego and superego formed the basis of most criminality theories. The id containing the instinctual, unconscious desires both sexual and aggressive with which we were all born. The ego tried to achieve the desires of the id while respecting the perceived normal social conventions. Children would only develop a strong ego if they had a loving relationship with their parents. The superego contained two functions, the conscience and the ego ideal. The conscience acted to inhibit instinctual desires that violated social rules, and its formation depended on parental punishment arousing anger that children then turned against themselves. But research had moved on from Freud, there was much more to throw on to the fire.

These were all notions and theories he had written about in papers submitted to journals as part of his academic life. The practicality of working in a crime field enabled him to see these theories tested, proved and disproved. Sometimes he would be aware of the workings of the moral development in a case study. He could see clearly how a young boy brought up in a home of violence, alcohol abuse and drug abuse could go on to become an offender. Others weren't so obvious. Strangely he didn't see the killer as psychotic. Instead he appeared to be a sociopath who has gestated a particular agenda and acted upon certain fantasies, to fulfil this agenda. The fact that the murdered women were all young, suggested sexual excitement was involved but yet, he did not sexually violate them. His fulfilment came from the murder.

He was lost in thought when his phone beeped out a rattling buzz.

'Hello?'

'Is she with you?'

He couldn't place the voice.

'Who is it? Is who with me?'

'Anna. Is Anna with you?' Declan could hear the impatience, the worry in the voice.

Thomas King.

Anna's partner. The messenger sent to tell him to stay away. He'd done as he was told, for Anna's sake. He realised how their relationship would impact on her career if it got out. Part of him worried that she'd made up the press story as a ruse to end things between them but when he'd seen the thinly veiled coverage in the Belfast News he understood that she had no choice but to walk away. God, how he missed her.

'Why would she be here? I've done as she asked, and kept my distance. Why would you think she was here?' he stopped, a snake of dread coiled in his stomach.

'She's gone AWOL. She didn't turn in to work this morning and there's no sign of her at home,' Thomas sighed down the line.

'Shit, you think she's in trouble?' Declan could barely allow his mind to go there, to acknowledge that she might be in danger.

'I know Anna probably told you stuff about the case, so if you can think of anything that can help to track her down, you have to tell me. Did she tell you about any angle she was working on alone? Anything she may not have told me?'

Declan sighed, 'No. Nothing. Sure, we talked about the case, but you know more than me. Do you have any inkling who you are looking for?'

'Yeah, off the record, we think it's Brogan.' 'It can't be Nelson Brogan.'

'No, his son, Robert Brogan. Fits the profile, he was working as a security guard under a false name. He had the opportunity, if not a clear motive, to kill all the girls.'

'What can I do?' Declan asked, his T-shirt sticking to him with cold sweat.

'Think of any possible connection, where he could have taken her. Anything at all.' He could hear the desperation in Thomas' voice. A cop that cared about his partner, who would lie down and take a bullet for her.

Chapter 48

Anna woke to hear a car driving away. She found herself sitting upright, but in some sort of brace. She couldn't move her neck or head and could only see straight ahead. Screws were embedded tightly against her skull, some sort of metal clamp held her neck while her arms were pulled behind the chair and bound together with cord. She tried to wriggle her hands to see if there was any give. None, it was secure. Her ankles were bound too. Even if she had freed her hands she didn't know how she could get the brace off. The screws were boring into her temples making her head pound like the chug-chug of an oncoming train. She struggled to hold down a wave of panic. *Breathe, think, stay calm* she told herself like a mantra, thumping along with the pounding of her heartbeat. She listened; the silence was heavy, still and thick. She was alone. He hadn't blindfolded her and he hadn't gagged her mouth so she could assume he hadn't feared her calling for help and being heard.

A sliver of moonlight fell across the dirt floor, past the open mouth where the grate of a fire had once been. She could smell an earthy, mossy scent mixed with the acrid smell of her own sweat and fear. A rough wind was nipping at the roof, causing a low murmuring howl. Somewhere, far off, a gate was swinging, calling out to be oiled.

She was cold, so cold that her teeth chattered incessantly. Fear pulsed through her body making her hyper alert, hearing far off noises that belonged to the night. Her breathing was ragged, short rapid breathes. She wanted to cough and clear her throat but her chest was constricted with some sort of binding. She barely had enough room to fill her lungs and the thought of it caused her to panic. With great will she tried to calm herself down, to focus on her breathing, counting the breaths in and out; *in one out two in one out two*. It was working. She could feel her heart begin to slow, so she focused on keeping herself under control. Panic wouldn't serve her well.

Her shoulder was hurting and she desperately needed to pee. She thought of her Dad, Declan and Kathleen. She wanted to tell them things, to let them know she loved them. To feel their warmth and care. In the weeks after Camille had died she had seriously considered leaving her job. She needed to feel like herself again. To stop the guilt, the anger, the sorrow. She had wanted to run away from it all. To be independent and free of expectations. She hadn't exactly run far. Northern Ireland had seemed like a good compromise. Halfway between heaven and hell.

She thought of her mother, Camille. To watch her suffer in the final throes of death had unhinged something in Anna. She hadn't done the brave or courageous thing; she'd taken the only option open to her. How easy it had been to administer that fatal dose of morphine, to help Camille find death when life was causing so much pain. She had acted on instinct, but ever since, she had felt the ground beneath her feet was unsteady, that the axis of the world was off kilter. Somehow it all made sense that she would end up here. As if she deserved what was coming to her.

Death is but a beat away. It is waiting for all of us, she thought. Some meet their end in an untimely, brutal fashion. Others die, no less violently in the clutches of disease, fighting against invasive tumours and the good intentions of medical science. Few get to fall asleep and not wake up, slipping away peacefully. What Anna had done, felt right.

Or was it righteous?

What separated her from the likes of Robert Brogan? Did a pure motive, borne out of love, make her crime less deserving of justice? She recalled the cemetery where they had laid Camille, row upon row of granite headstones, some diminished by the battering rains and winds of the valley. Epitaphs engraved to commemorate loved ones. She had wandered around the old cemetery, nestled between the grey stone chapel, and the rectory in the bowl of the valley. The majesty of the green fields rising up behind her, emphasising her insignificance. She took it as a sign that what she had done was of no consequence beyond her tiny, insignificant life. That the world was so much bigger than her, and what did it matter to take one life if it was done in love? A life nearing its own natural end, sentenced to spend the last days in agonies of pain more suited to something from a Faustian description of the depths of hell.

One of the older headstones, a white and grey marble arched shaped stone, pock marked by the elements, carried the Welsh inscription:

hedd perffaith hedd

Peace, perfect peace

That's what Anna craved. Peace.

Anna's neck ached. Her shoulder, already damaged, felt as if it had been dislocated again. Her arms drawn behind her and tied, had reached that numb state. She couldn't move and trying to was a fruitless enterprise, which would only bring about further panic.

It was funny how she could detach herself and think fairly rationally while being in such a state of desperation. Stillness washed over her as she allowed her mind to drift beyond the stone croft, to drift back to times she didn't usually care to remember. Huge swaths of her memory had been stolen – blocked out by whatever mechanism her mind employed to enable her to function, to go on with life. She knew that they had held a wake of sorts for Camille, that many people had come to pay their respects, but she could remember none of it. The day of the funeral was gone from her too, stolen in a haze of grief.

But what she could remember, with great clarity, was that night at the end of September. The streets were washed with the early autumn rain. She noticed the tarmac road looked like it had seen an oil spill, for an iridescent shimmer caught her eye. There was a beauty in the blues and violets radiating outwards across the road in a shallow puddle catching the last rays of light before sun down. She parked in North Church Street near the Greek church of St Nicholas and made her way down the road, on towards Bute Street. She didn't want her car license plates being picked up by CCTV so she had parked a few streets away. She wore a long dark hooded coat, her tight jeans and a battered pair of old trainers. Her hair, which was too long for her liking, was bundled in a low ponytail and tucked underneath an old beany hat.

She had instructions, telling her where to go and now she stood outside the building, furtively glancing around, making sure she hadn't been seen. Anyone passing by would think the red brick, former linen factory, was condemned, ready to be flattened and make way for offices or apartments to house young professionals, but Anna knew inside she would find a squat of sorts. It was still possible to find the odd building like this one – remnants from a past before Cardiff had reinvented itself with civic pride, fancy Assembly buildings, the Wharf and Dr Who film sets.

She located the door buzzer, hidden behind a facade of old letterboxes, and as instructed, rang it twice. Within a moment the door opened. A tall skinny guy, with dreadlocks the tawny colour of a mouse, led her through the dark hallway. She could smell something cooking, reminding her of school dinners, mince, boiled carrots and potatoes. Without speaking he indicated that she should go on through to the door on the left at the end of the corridor. She could hear tinny music playing far of in the bowels of the building, something like Biffy Clyro, a jangle of guitars and a low thump, thump of a bass.

The metal door was open slightly so she cleared her throat and pushed it wider. The inner room had been an office at one time; it's ceilings high and crisscrossed with steel beams. A large flat screen television was on, showing a video of Beyoncé marching around in yellow swinging a baseball bat, with the sound turned down. A brown leather sofa sat in front of the television and on it lay a small girl-like woman, no older than Anna. She was smoking while scanning her phone.

'You found it, then,' she said, not taking her eyes of the phone, her accent suggesting a valleys upbringing, Merthyr or Abergavenny perhaps. One of those towns decimated when the pits closed, now mere satellites of Cardiff, where young people either stay and waste away into marriage, parenthood and middle age, or flee as soon as they can.

'Yeah, easy enough.' 'You parked far enough away?'

'Yes, round by Maria Street.'

'Right,' she looked up from her phone, 'I'm not to be hassled. You'll make sure I'm given a by ball?'

'I told you. I'll do my best. I can tell them you're giving me information.' 'And I've told you, I'm no snitch, so don't come looking for information afterwards,' she blew out a plume of blue coloured smoke. 'How much are you looking for?'

'I'm not sure, I don't think it would take much but I need to be certain it will be enough.'

'I've midazolam, buprenorphine, oxytocin or oxycodone. Which do you want?'

'Whichever is closest to regular morphine.' 'Best go with oxytocin. 30 mg should do it. Grind it up and spoon it in with something. She'll ride off into the sunset within half an hour, give or take.'

The woman got off the sofa and made her way over to a filing cabinet where she took out an envelope containing the pills. Anna handed over the money. Over the odds, but she wasn't going to haggle. She shoved the envelope containing the small plastic bag of pills into her deep pocket and left.

When she returned to her family home on Llandennis Avenue, the silence told her that Camille had received her seven o'clock syringe driver push. The hospice nurse, a middle-aged woman from Ponty, would return at eleven o'clock and stay with them until morning, allowing Anna and her dad to get some sleep.

She had a few hours in which to crush up the tablets, and feed them to her mother before the nurse returned. It wasn't unusual for Anna to sit with her mother in the evening, allowing her father time to mull around the house, watering his plants in the garden or take the opportunity to rest. He respected Anna's need to have time with her mother alone.

'There you are. Hard day at work?' he asked as she hung her coat up in the cloakroom.

'Oh, the usual, you know. Nothing too bad. How is she?' she nodded toward the bedroom above them.

The slump of his shoulders and the grim set of his mouth told her it had been yet another bad day. The cancer was eating Camille up. Metastases had spread to her spinal fluid and the cancer had wrapped itself around her thorax, slowly crushing her to death, one breath at a time. Anna barely recognised the woman who had brought her up. The shrunken shell of a woman was more like something dug up from a watery grave. Her skin was jaundice yellow and weeping in places, where the morphine itch had driven her to tear at her skin in distraction. Her hair, which had begun growing back in random clumps, was darker than it used to be, thicker too and made her look slightly demonic in the way it sat up like horns.

Every time Anna entered the room she had to steady her nerve, to mentally prepare herself for what lay within. The curtains were partially closed but open enough for the streetlight to illuminate the room. Camille lay on the double bed, still, apart from the deep watery guttural breathing, like a gutter burbling over with too much rainwater. She was lying on her back, her face turned to one side, away from Anna. There was a scented candle burning in a thick glass jar, pertaining to emit a smell of clean cotton. It was a sweet, cloying smell that Anna disliked but tolerated, as she knew it was her father's doing; his way of trying to cloak the strange bedfellow smell of death and medicine.

'Mum, it's me, Anna. I'm back from work.'

Her mother continued to sleep in the slumber of the morphine, enough to knock her out, but never enough to totally take away the pain. Anna was wracked at the thought of Camille suffering, but so incapacitated by the drugs, so as to not be able to cry out in her agony.

Anna positioned herself on the bed, lying down at Camille's side. She gently placed her arm around Camille's delicate frame and whispered close into her ear, 'Mum, it won't be long now. I've done what you asked. I got the stuff.' It had been early August when Camille had first mentioned her intentions, that if the pain became too much, she would need help to end it. Anna had told her to stop being ridiculous and that she was asking for the impossible, but as the weeks went on and Camille struggled to cope with the pain, Anna remembered her request. The how and the when were never discussed. Anna thought of the home life Camille had gave her, the love and care so carefully imparted. She owed her this.

Anna lay like that for a few moments, feeling the rise and fall of her mother's sunken chest against her arm, not knowing if she heard the words, or understood. A little after nine her father checked on them, bringing Anna a cup of coffee, always made exactly to her liking.

'I'll wake her up in a little while and try to give her some of that custard she likes,' Anna said setting her mug on the bedside cupboard.

Her father nodded, 'Yes she needs to keep her strength up. The custard will do her good.'

They were each performing little rituals, dancing around the inevitable.

* * *

The kitchen window looked out over the back garden, a strip of lawn bordered with shrubs. The shed light was on. Her father was out there, smoking his daily evening secret cigarette. Anna knew she had five, maybe seven minutes tops, to prepare the custard mixture. She looked out towards the shed but could only see her reflection looking back at her. Her eyes glassy, her face thinner than normal, and her hair lank over her shoulders. She'd have to get it cut before the funeral, she thought.

She poured the warmed custard into a bowl and mixed in the already crushed up drugs. It was important get the powder into the first two mouthfuls, anymore and she risked Camille being sick. She barely ate these days, surviving on custard and high protein milkshakes provided by the hospital pharmacist. Not for the first time, Anna wondered about a system trying to keep a dying woman alive. It made no sense. Helping her slip away was the best solution and while Anna knew her father would be horrified, she had no doubts that it was the only thing to do.

* * *

Camille was propped upright against the soft pillows. Her mouth gaped open ready to take the spoonful of custard proffered. Anna gave her a small amount to begin with, scraping the edge of the spoon against her bottom lip to catch the drips. She moaned as she swallowed it down, anticipating the pain of her body performing such an everyday task. A cough gargled up from her diaphragm; scaring Anna into thinking she wouldn't be able to take the full amount needed. The next spoonful went down easier and the third, given to be sure, sat in her mouth threatening to be spat back out and swallowed down at the last second, as Anna reached for a tissue to catch the mess.

Anna stood, kissed her mother's cool, clammy forehead and went down to the kitchen to wash up. She was careful. The chopping board where she had pulverized the pills had to be scraped clean and washed with hot water and bleach, along with the bowl and spoon. With luck, Camille would slip into a coma and simply forget to breathe, her body beyond fighting the effects of the drugs.

* * *

Sleep, Anna thought, she needed to sleep. Her neck ached and her shoulder once a tyrant of pain was now deadened and numb. She tried to push the memories away. She didn't want to revisit that time. To be in that bedroom in their family home in Cyncoed, to be there when her father sobbed on his knees as he realised Camille was gone from them.

Instead, she willed herself to think of their holidays in Cornwall. How they had walked along the steep hills of cobbled streets, passing cafes with painted signs advertising clotted cream teas, hand churned ice cream and pasties. Camille always trying to look for the delight in every shop window, exclaiming over the quaintness, the tremendous view over the beach, the postcard perfect rows of pastel coloured houses. Anna trudging along with that, I'm bored, attitude of pre-teens. On one such day they had come across a small art shop. Anna had stood transfixed at the window looking at the display of an easel, wooden cases holding tiny tubes of oils and acrylics in every shade imaginable and jars brimming with long handled brushes.

'Come on, we'll go in,' Camille said, seeing the wonder on Anna's face. Inside the smell of the turpentine and oils settled on Anna like a warm hug. To this day, it was her favourite scent. The shopkeeper was working at a painting of her own, a local scene so typical of what tourists would buy, a shaded cove and a bobbing red boat on the distant sea. She spent time explaining to Anna and her mother about the different types of paints, the charcoals, oil pastels and brushes. They had come away with a small wooden case of watercolours and a set of the softest sable-hair brushes, along with a fat pad of textured watercolour paper. Anna spent the remainder of that holiday experimenting with her paints, exploring the depths of colour and the shade and the light, delighting in her first attempts of capturing the essence and likeness of the landscape around her.

If it came to it, to her final moments, then that's the time Anna wanted to focus on. To remember those days spent picnicking on the cool sand, clambering over grassy dunes, paddling in rock pools and studying the paint splurged out from the tiny tubes on to a porcelain plate.

She heard a car. The headlights swept along the wall. He was back. The room fell into darkness again as the headlights dimmed and then switched off. The car door slammed shut.

The croft door screeched as he pushed against it. The wooden panels, probably swollen in the damp, making it too big for its frame, for she could sense the effort it took for him to push against it. Then footsteps, soft and even.

'Ahhh, you're awake,' his voice was a fraction too high, with a soft burr of a Belfast accent. The intonation rising towards the end of the sentence, as if he was a friend rather than foe.

He walked in front of her and she could see he was carrying a leather hold all bag. Its contents seemingly heavy for he placed it down on the floor with a thud.

'You couldn't leave it alone, could you?' he was walking around the room, she could hear his footsteps, feel his words rise and fall, as he moved. 'This wasn't your fight. You could have stayed out of it. I saw you. I watched you on the news, standing to the side, your eyes on McKay, all official and holier than thou. The good guys, seeking the bad. Well, real life isn't like that. Sometimes the good guys are the worst, and sometimes people do evil things for good reasons.'

She felt his breath close to her cheek, could smell him – antiseptic, like TCP or Dettol, over laid with a caramel sweetness. She wanted to gag. He moved away from her.

A bird squawked nearby, something tremulous and high. A fox barked in the distance, while the wind buffeted and roared against the croft walls, catching the underside of the tin roof. The outside world seemed so close, yet escape was impossible.

'That girl, Aisling, she was to be my last. I'd done what I'd set out to do. I was going to keep her as my poppet – do you know what a poppet is? A doll. Maybe you saw the one in my aunt's house, on the dresser. She loves that old thing, because she knows I restored it for her. Did every delicate stitch myself.'

Anna could feel her body trembling. She fought against it, not wanting him to see the fear he was inducing, but she could do nothing to control the quivering of her skin. It was as if being close to him, to his evilness, made her body react in a physical revolt.

'But here we are. I have you, instead of the lovely Aisling. Maybe you can be my own little doll, beautifully preserved.'

She felt him stroke her hair, as gently as a light breeze; her whole body responded in a shudder of revulsion.

'Do you want to know, how I shall make my poppet?' his fingers tips, rough and calloused, toyed at her ear.

'First, I need to skin you,' he stroked Anna's cheek. Her breathing was rapid, her heart thumping against her ribcage.

'I make an incision here and slice right across the scalp line. Just like so,' he dragged a nail slowly across her hairline. 'I'm sure you've seen autopsies; you know how the face peels away from the skull. It takes a bit of practice, but I'm experienced now. My creatures have been my training ground. Each one teaching me something new, about the art of preservation.

'Think how lucky you are to be kept for evermore. No empty cavern of damp earth for you. Aww' he said mockingly, 'Look at you, like a little bird, trembling, all of a flutter. Don't worry poppet, it will be all over soon.'

Anna quaked and felt the warm seep of urine wet between her legs.

Chapter 49

The morning light was breaking as Declan drove through the empty, rain-washed roads. A blue haze settled over the landscape in a misty gauze. He was working from memory, trying to visualise the journey he had taken many years ago, that day when he'd followed Nelson Brogan from his home in Dundonald to the old house in Cushendun. If Brogan's son was hiding out then maybe he was holed up in the stone cottage. It was a long shot but it was all he had to work with. He saw a tourist sign advertising '*the glorious glens*' and turned off the main road down a country lane. If he remembered correctly, the Brogan homestead wasn't far away. Thomas had assured him that Maude Brier's house was on their search list and that they were aware of the close relationship between Robert Brogan and the aunt. Declan couldn't sit back and wait. He had to go there for himself. He remembered how Nelson Brogan had walked across the yard of the property with that look of arrogance. When Declan told Thomas about the other out buildings he said he was aware, that they would be searching all surrounding properties.

The lane was overgrown and full of dips. Branches scraped the car as Declan drove slowly up the dirt track with his headlights off. The car lurched and revved in and out of potholes. Then, just when he thought he had taken a wrong turn, he saw the cottage standing in a clearing. He killed the engine and watched. He was sure this was the place. There was a small car parked in the driveway. The curtains were drawn over the front bedroom window.

He remembered watching Nelson Brogan amble up to the house with an air of propriety. The hulk of his shoulders and the way he carried himself made Declan think of a bear.

He really had no idea why he was there or what he intended to do. It was a need to feel that he could mark Brogan out. Watch him; maybe put a hit on him if he felt like it. All conjecture and fantasy. None of it would give him his legs back. Now he found himself in the same spot, watching for Brogan's son, terrified that he was holding Anna and that she could have already met the same fate as Esme.

What now? He thought. He couldn't sit back and do nothing. If Brogan had Anna, he'd, he'd … He'd what? What could he do about it? Feck all. He was a useless hunk of flesh. No use to anyone.

'Fuck.' Declan slammed his hand against the steering wheel. The frustration was too much. Thinking of Anna being hurt, and that this could be the bastard who killed Esme made him burn up with anger and a rage so pure and resolute that he could feel it power him onwards. Bile sloshed around in the pit of his stomach.

He could imagine that Anna had come here, that she had made her way through the dense hedging and skulked the perimeter like a cat looking for some sign of Brogan. Declan cursed his useless stumps and the bastards that had brought his disability on to him. He was a liability. No use to Esme as she lay dying in the grounds of the hotel, and now of no use to Anna.

He stilled the engine off and let the car roll quietly towards the front yard. He steered it around to the side of the stone cottage and listened. Not a sound. The night air was deathly still, almost expectantly so. Opening the car door and putting his chair in motion was more noise than Declan cared to make. The mechanism to lower his chair on to the terrain was motorised and emitted a low rumble. He cursed silently. There was only one thing for it; he'd have to crawl out. Thomas had promised him that the police were doing everything possible to track her down. He'd been warned to stay at home, to keep his phone on should she call but the night had dragged and he was going out of his mind with worry.

He used his forearms to drag his weight up towards the house. The curtains in the front bedroom window were drawn. All looked quiet. No sign of police patrols though Thomas had assured him that they had already visited Maude Briers and found nothing untoward. They were watching the property should Brogan turn up, but Declan needed to check for himself. If Brogan was holding Anna then maybe the old aunt was in on it too.

He hoisted his weight forward, slithering with little grace towards the house. An outbuilding sat to the west of the property. The rough gravel was digging into his hands and his stumps as he made his way closer to the property. How he'd get all the way over there he didn't know, but he had to try. Something in the distance caught his eye. A light flickered. Once then twice. He scuttled onwards like a soldier on a low crawl, desperate to avoid detection. There was no stealth in his movements, every action laboured and tiring. Then almost before he could respond to the awareness of someone running at him he felt a heavy weight land on top of him. He bucked his back with as much power as he could summon but there was no shifting it.

Brogan. It had to be.

He was no threat to Brogan, and could put up no defense. His hands grabbed at Declan's face, his teeth grazing across his ear and then in one swift action reached backwards and with a quick jolt rolled off, releasing him.

Gasping, Declan pressed up against the wall of the cottage, knowing he had nowhere to go, no way of escaping. Brogan smirked as he reached forward, a flash of metal glinting in the early morning sun, and with a quick jerking action, he jabbed the blade into Declan's side.

With the force of the blade, he felt as if all power was slammed out of him. He slumped backwards on the ground, the cold dampness seeping into his bones. Declan's breathe was ragged. The pain felt like little more than a quick sharp punch but the warm wetness seep out on to his fingers told him it was bad enough.

'What did he do to you Robert? What did your father do to make you feel so worthless?'

'You know nothing of my father. He was a good man. Things got to him. Just like me. He felt too deeply.'

'He knew nothing but hate and bigotry. Are you going to finish what he started? Was that your plan? To kill me?' Declan heaved himself into a sitting position, feeling the burn of pain surge through him, his back now slumped against the stone house. 'Why kill the girls, my Esme? Why do it? You could have come after me.' The anguish made his voice break, the words faltering.

Brogan looked like a lost man. 'You didn't see them, young girls out with their mates, laughing and joking around, not a care in the world. They'd flirt, give me the come on but I wasn't interested in all that.

'Esme would smile and be polite. Nice even. I met her at one of Finnegan's parties. She was working, same as me. She talked to me, asked my name. It wasn't til later that I found out you were her da. Then on the wedding day I saw you in the chair. I knew your name and put the stories together. You were the reason my father ended up the way he did. He didn't put that bomb under your car, but he was made to pay for it. He gave everything to the force. Everything. There was nothing left when he came home to us. My mother would shush me, don't bother him she'd say, let him be. But I was only a boy; I wanted my father to see me, to acknowledge me.'

'Even if it meant taking a beating?' 'Yeah, sometimes he'd use his fists, but he couldn't help it. It was the job, the pressure. We understood. Maude took care of me in ways my father and mother never could. She understood me and loved me for me.'

'Anna, where's Anna?'

'What's it matter? It's all over now.'

'No, no it's not over for Anna, tell me where she is?'

Brogan placed the knife to his own throat. Declan could see his own blood still slick and wet on the blade. 'You think you know suffering? Stuck in your wheel chair, the invalid hero? Well. I've taken your daughter and I've made your lover-girl suffer. Before long you'll want out of this place.'

'Don't do it. Tell me, where is she?' he whispered it, desperation squeezing his breath out of him.

Chapter 50

Brogan was standing above him, the blade still poised at his throat but Declan could sense a hesitation. He had to keep him talking, to find out where Anna was.

'You couldn't let it go, could you?' Declan wheezed as he breathed in. The knife wound was below his left lung and was bleeding profusely now. He pressed on the wound with his hand, trying to stem the blood loss.

'The way life was then, the bombings, the shootings, the punishment beatings, it was a way of life you wanted to hold on to.'

Brogan looked defeated. Lost. 'You don't know what is like to see someone you love waste away. You lot treated him like shit. He gave his life to the RUC, day in day out. Checking under his car, alternating our route, moving house every six months. My mother waiting up at night, desperate for him to walk in the door. Every time the phone rang thinking is it him? Is it bad news?'

'We were all living the same way. They were bad times. You didn't need to kill the girls. They had done nothing to you.' Brogan laughed, 'They did everything to me. They'd the life I should've had.'

Declan was beginning to see what was driving Brogan – the powerlessness, the struggle to prove something to his father, that need to feel control. He cleared his throat, 'Robert, your father wouldn't have wanted this. It has to end here and now. Tell me where Anna is.'

He had a far off look in his eyes, maybe thinking of his father, considering what could have been.

'You don't know my father. You don't know what it was like growing up with his expectations. His *punishments*.'

The morning light was gathering. The sky was pale pink, a hint of the new day breaking. Declan needed to keep him talking, with any luck he'd tell him where Anna was being held and that the patrol would come along and see all was not as it should be. Where the fuck was Thomas King when you needed him?

'You didn't live up to what he wanted, did you Robert? You were too soft, too much of a mummy's boy for his likening? Is that it Robert?'

'Shut up! You know nothing about me. He was always getting me to prove I was man. Once our cat caught a bird and brought it into the kitchen. A little sparrow it was. Brown with speckled markings. Not quite dead, still breathing. 'Look son,' he said. 'It's still alive. Injured but alive. The kind thing is to put it out of its misery.' He lifted it away from the cat and held it out to me. I knew before he told me what he expected me to do. Its little chest thumping so hard I could feel the patter on the palm of my hand. Its beak was a glorious yellow colour and its black, beady eyes were searching for refuge. Go on son, do what you have to do. Sometimes we have to be cruel to be kind.'

'And I did. I squeezed the life out of it, in my fist until I felt its warm guts exploding into my hand. The bones crackled like dried twigs and the blood and flesh dripped out between my fingers.

'Da laughed. 'Your mother will have something to say if you get that mess on the tiles. Let the cat have a good feed.' I opened my hand and let the feathery gore fall into the cat's dish. The bloody cat didn't want it. The fun was all in the chase for him. Too well-fed.'

He inhaled and then said quieter, 'It wasn't supposed to be like this.'

'No, but you have the power to stop it here and now. Don't make it worse. Tell me where Anna is. Let me save her, please.'

Brogan stepped forward, 'It's over,' he said lifting the knife, like he knew his time was up, that he was ready to end it all. Their eyes met and in that second Declan could see Nelson Brogan in him, the pronounced forehead, the deep-set eyes. It was him all right. The father, apparent in the son.

Then a loud crack of gunfire broke through the reverie.

'Drop your weapon and put your hands behind your head!'

The Calvary at last. Declan slumped back and let the pain of the knife wound finally catch up with him. Then the morning light caught the blade as Brogan pushed it into his own throat, blood spluttering out as he dropped to his knees. The door of the house opened and a woman ran out, her dressing gown flapping behind making her look like some sort of mythical winged creature. The aunt, he supposed. Everything felt so very far away. He was losing his grip, he needed to fight, just as he had done once before, to hold on. The woman was on her knees now, cradling Brogan's head, roaring, 'Rabbie, Rabbie, no, no. Not Rabbie.'

Declan dragged himself closer. The wound was still bleeding but nothing was spilling out of him. He'd live if he got medical attention soon. Thomas King was radioing for help, but all Declan wanted was for him to find Anna.

'Where is she?' he shouted at Maude Briers, 'If she is hurt, if she should die, and you know anything, it will be on your head.' Desperation was giving him a final shot of power to drag himself closer.

Maude lifted her head, 'I don't know, but check the old house, further up the glen. It's where my mother came from, we still own it, but it's only a shack now. Sometimes, as a boy Rabbie would go up there to lay traps and hunt animals.'

Thomas ran towards them.

'Go, go, to the glen further up the lane!' Declan panted with the exertion of shouting – 'There's an old house, check it out. She might be there. I'm ok. Just go!' he yelled at Thomas. There was nothing more he could do for Anna, but he prayed to a God he wasn't sure he believed in, that it wasn't too late. He could hear singing; it seemed far away, a hymn he thought and he listened to the words of damnation and redemption as he clung to consciousness, fearful of slipping away.

Chapter 51

Brogan survived.

The knife wound missed the carotid artery by millimetres but nicked his trachea. He almost died of air starvation, but they paramedics worked quickly. Declan thanked God when he heard. He wanted to see Brogan in court. To have him sentenced for what he'd done, to know the stench of his own sweat and piss after being locked up in a cell.

Declan's own injuries healed. Twenty-two staples along his side. More scars to add to the collection. It was touch and go as to whether or not he'd lose a kidney. Thankfully the damage was repairable.

Those moments waiting to hear if King had found Anna alive, well, they felt like an eternity. He lay there in the gravel, bleeding, pain scorching through him, watching Maude Briers sing hymns while she rocked a bleeding Brogan in her arms like an errant child.

The cop car arrived, an ambulance too, sirens blazing and then word came through. *Anna was safe.* They'd done it. He cried with the relief. Tears pouring out of him, for Esme, for the other girls – Grace and Aisling, for Anna and for himself. He wanted to stay until he'd seen Anna rescued and brought from the old house but the paramedics took over. He found himself carted off on a trolley bed, that old helpless feeling of not having the power to walk away or to run for his life. The tears and the uncontrollable shaking continued until he was in the hospital, wrapped in blankets and being rush through to surgery. The relief of counting backwards knowing oblivion was coming, giving him a respite from the agony while surgeons fought to repair the damage Brogan had inflicted on him.

* * *

When he came round that night, he could hear whispering voices, Lara, Izzy and a man's voice he couldn't quite place. He let the conversation flow around him while he contemplated what had happened, aware of bandages around his lower back, an IV stand dripping something into his veins.

The voice again. King. It was Thomas King. He shifted in the bed, tried to lift his head.

'Steady Declan, don't be moving about. We're here for you. The surgery went well.' Izzy looked tired. Her blue grey eyes still arresting, her skin clear and luminous.

He turned his head towards Thomas, 'Anna, how is she?'

'She's just fine. Doing great.'

Declan dropped his head back on the pillow. Relief surging through his every cell, recharging his will to live. He saw a look pass over Izzy's face. She knew.

Chapter 52

Anna rubbed at her neck. The bruising was fifty shades of purple. She stared at her sorry reflection in the mirror. The hospital lighting wasn't exactly helping, but she looked like hell. There was a haunted look around her eyes that no amount of make-up could hide. Time, she told herself it'll take time. She gently touched her cheekbone, where a gash had been sutured with neat precise little black stitches. The wound felt tight and itchy, a sign it was healing. It was tender to touch, still swollen and puffy. Her hair lay lank and wet around her shoulders. The shower had been intermittently hot but it had been a powerful spray and now at least she felt clean and fresh.

Thomas had promised to buy her a pair of pajamas to save her from having to shuffle around in the hospital gown. Still, they said she could go home soon, maybe even tomorrow, if everything checked out ok. She'd make sure she was the model patient, anything to get home to her own bed. Anna smiled. *Home.* Belfast had got to her. In spite of everything that had happened, she liked this godforsaken place.

She roughly towel dried her hair and decided she would go looking for Declan. He was on the next floor somewhere. Possibly ward 8C. She had made sure to listen in to Thomas' telephone conversations, trying to glean whatever information he was telling the boss. Every time she asked him stuff, he'd tell her not to worry her head. To get better and then deal with the shit storm waiting for them.

She shuffled along the corridor in disposable slippers looking for ward 8C. A man passed by carrying a helium filled balloon with 'sorry you're sick' scripted across it and a bunch of sad looking peach roses under his arm. He looked like a right gobshite as Thomas would say. The sign for ward 8C loomed up ahead. She'd barely walked twenty metres and she felt weak and light headed. Nearly there. She reached for the door and stopped just in time to catch a glimpse of Izzy and Lara through the window, sitting at the bedside. Declan was lying still, his eyes closed, hooked up to an IV stand. He looked content. A man at peace with himself, with his family around him. Of course, he would want them with him. Need them even. She was stupid to think otherwise. With immense effort, she turned and began the slow walk back to her hospital room, where she would allow herself to cry, big, heart-wrenching tears of pure self-pity.

Epilogue

The cemetery was huge. She had to go to the office and ask for coordinates of where to find the grave. A small crowd had gathered outside the crematorium, waiting for the coffin to be carried inside. Anna made her way down towards the rows and rows of graves. Some had elaborate headstones proclaiming angels watching over their loved ones, while a simple plaque placed at the foot of a tree marked other graves.

There was so much she needed to tell him; with the nuclear fallout of the press exposé on their relationship, the kidnap and her subsequent rescue, the apprehension of Brogan and the culmination of all their work, she had barely been able to consider the future. Now, she waited for his arrival, unsure of where they would go from here.

She watched as a few people mulled around the graves of their loved ones. Some tidying up patches of earth, freshly dug, removing dead flowers and replacing them with fresh bunches. Others, standing in silent prayer. The morning sun hung low in the pale blue sky.

Then she saw his Volvo car pull up and watched as he maneuvered himself out of it. The slow mechanical whirr of the traction and the unfolding of himself into the wheelchair. He looked good, tired maybe, a bit drawn round the eyes, but still the sight of him made her heart quicken. She turned to greet him as he made his way down the slope towards the grave. 'I didn't expect to see you here,' he said.

'Izzy told me I'd find you here.'

'Yeah, it's become a bit of a ritual. I like to start the day by checking on Esme's grave.'

Anna nodded. She knew there were no words of comfort to offer.

'You look good,' he smiled, his eyes taking her in.

'So, how have you been?' she asked.

'I'm healing. The stitches are out. It wasn't as bad as it looked.'

'What about you?' his voice was low and Anna thought she could hear the concern laced in it.

She paused, 'I'm doing ok.'

They both looked down at the grave. A headstone had been erected. A piece of dark grey polished granite, inscribed with Esme's name, and date of her death. Nothing ornate, no platitudes, or prayers. The soil was still freshly turned. No grass had been planted yet.

Anna thought of Camille's grave back in Cardiff. Wondered if her dad still tended to it on a regular basis. She'd have to ask him next time she called him.

'Izzy is moving out,' Declan said.

'She told me. Said I was to look after you. That you were a good man.'

'Sounds like you two had quite a talk. Do you think you'll be sticking around then?'

Anna smiled, 'For now. I've had the secondment extended. McKay has ideas of putting me in historical inquiries – outside eyes looking at old cases.'

'The past,' he said shaking his head, 'It never really goes away in this place,' he said. 'Sometimes it feels like the legacy of bloodshed is still casting shadows over the future.'

She couldn't argue with him. His daughter lay beneath the earth, a terrible reminder of how the past had ricocheted into the present.

Anna took his hand in hers, 'We have to make sure those shadows are shortened, that better days are here to stay.'

He kissed her hand, pulling her closer to him and looked lost in thought.

'What are you thinking?' Anna asked.

'That the dead want for nothing. Justice doesn't affect them. Like funerals, it's for the living. Without it I'd be left with nothing but bitterness and fury. I'm glad I don't have to live that life.'

THE END

Acknowledgements

There are many people who have been important to me while writing this book. First, writer, Louise Phillips, thank you for your support and mentoring. Your insights and generosity with your time, and editorial feedback were essential in helping me finish the book.

I am grateful to Damian Smyth and the Arts Council NI's Support for the Individual Artist Programme, which gave me both validation and a deadline.

Thanks also to Neil Henry for his policing insights.

Betsy and Fred, and all at Bloodhound, especially editor, Emma Mitchell, thank you for your professionalism and enthusiasm.

To my Scribes and Scribblers, especially Jackie, Linda, Frances, Gary, Marianne, Kate and Eibhlinn. Thank you for sharing your stories with me and helping me grow as a writer. Thanks also to Witches with Wolves especially Mary Montague and to Jane Talbot from Women Aloud.

To my PORT buddies, especially Neil, Danielle and Ginny, this book has been the reason I haven't been reviewing documents as frequently as I would like.

I won't get away with not thanking my GPk gang. You girls are so important to me, especially Roma, Katie, Joan, Andrea and Carmel.

Finally, to my family – Mum and Dad, Liam, Kate, Owen and Sarah, thank you.